THE PIRANHAS

Roberto Saviano was born in 1979 and studied philosophy at the University of Naples. *Gomorrah*, his first book, has won many awards, including the prestigious 2006 Viareggio Literary Award, and was adapted into a play, a film, and a television series.

ALSO BY ROBERTO SAVIANO

Gomorrah

ZeroZeroZero

THE PIRANHAS

ROBERTO SAVIANO

TRANSLATED FROM THE ITALIAN BY ANTONY SHUGAAR

PICADOR

First published 2018 by Farrar, Straus and Giroux, New York

First published in the UK 2018 by Picador

This edition first published 2019 by Picador
an imprint of Pan Macmillan
20 New Wharf Road, London N1 9RR
Associated companies throughout the world
www.panmacmillan.com

ISBN 978-1-5098-7923-6

Originally published in Italian 2016 as *La paranza dei
bambini* by Feltrinelli Editore, Italy

1 3 5 7 9 8 6 4 2

A CIP catalogue record for this book is available from the British Library.

Printed and bound by CPI Group (UK) Ltd, Croydon, CR0 4YY

Visit **www.picador.com** to read more about all our books
and to buy them. You will also find features, author interviews and
news of any author events, and you can sign up for e-newsletters
so that you're always first to hear about our new releases.

To the guilty dead.
To their innocence.

Where there are children, there is a golden age.

—NOVALIS

The protagonists of this book are imaginary, as are their life stories; therefore, any and all references to people or public establishments that may actually now exist or have once existed and which might be found in the text of this book can only be considered coincidental. Events mentioned in a historical or journalistic context, as well as nicknames that refer to people, trademarks, or companies, are used only to confer plausibility on the narrative, without any pejorative intent or, in any case, any prejudicial meaning for their possessor.

The same disclaimer that appears at the beginning of the movie *Hands over the City* applies to my novel: The characters and events that appear here are imaginary; what is authentic, on the other hand, is the social and environmental reality that produces them.

CONTENTS

CHARACTERS

MARAJA	Nicolas Fiorillo
BRIATO'	Fabio Capasso
TUCANO	Massimo Rea
DENTINO	Giuseppe Izzo
DRAGO'	Luigi Striano
LOLLIPOP	Vincenzo Esposito
PESCE MOSCIO	Ciro Somma
STAVODICENDO	Vincenzo Esposito
DRONE	Antonio Starita
BISCOTTINO	Eduardo Cirillo
CERINO	Agostino De Rosa

PART ONE

THE *PARANZA* COMES FROM THE SEA

The word paranza *comes from the sea.*

Those who are born on the sea know more than one sea. They are occupied by the sea, bathed, invaded, dominated by the sea. You can stay far away for the rest of your life, but you're still drenched in it. If you're born on the sea, you know there's the sea of hard work, the sea of arrivals and departures, the sea of the sewer outlet, the sea that isolates you. There's the sea of filth, the sea as an escape route, the sea as an insurmountable barrier. There's the sea by night.

At night people go out on the water to fish. Dark as ink. Curse words and not a prayer. Silence. The only noise is the engine.

Two boats set sail, small and rotting, riding so low in the water they practically sink under the weight of their fishing lamps. They veer off, one to the left, one to the right, while fishing lamps are hung off the bow to attract the fish. Lampare, they're called. Blinding spotlights, briny electricity. The violent light that punches through the water without a hint of grace and reaches the sea floor. It's frightening to glimpse the sea floor, it's like seeing the end of everything. So this is it? This jumble of rocks and sand that is covered up by this immense expanse? Is that all there is?

Paranza is a word for boats that go out to catch fish through the trickery of light. The new sun is electric, the light occupies the water, it takes possession of it, and the fish come looking for it, they put their trust in it. They put their trust in life, they lunge forward, mouths open wide, governed by instinct. And as they do, the net that surrounds them spreads open, rushing swiftly; the meshes stand watch around the perimeter of the school of fish, enveloping it.

Then the light comes to a halt, seemingly attainable by those gaping mouths, at last. Until the fish start to be jammed one against the other, each flaps its fins, searching for space. And it's as if the water had turned into a pool. They all bounce, and as they race away most of them run smack up against something, up against something that isn't soft like the sand, but which also isn't hard like rock. Something that seems penetrable, but there's no way to get through it. The fish writhe and wriggle up down up down right left and again right left, but then less and less and less, less and less.

And the light goes out. The fish are lifted, to them it's as if the sea suddenly rose, as if the seabed were rising toward the sky. It's only the nets being reeled up. Throttled by the air, their mouths open in tiny desperate circles, their collapsing gills look like open bladders. Their race toward the light is done.

THE BESHITTING

Are you looking at me?"

"Huh, who gives a shit about you?"

"Then why are you looking at me?"

"Listen, bro, you've got me mixed up with someone else! I wasn't even thinking about you."

Renatino was surrounded by other kids, they'd singled him out for a while now in the jungle of bodies, but by the time he even noticed, four of them were standing around him. The gaze is territory, homeland— looking at someone amounts to entering his home uninvited. To stare at someone is a form of invasion. Not to look away is a manifestation of power.

They were occupying the center of the piazza. A little piazza enclosed by a semicircle of apartment houses, with a single road in or out, a single café on the corner, and a palm tree that was all that could impress a whiff of the exotic upon the place. That tree jammed into a few dozen square feet of topsoil transformed the perception of the façades, the windows, and the entrances to the apartment houses, as if it had blown over from Piazza Bellini on a gust of wind.

Not one of them was a day over sixteen. They stepped closer, inhaling one another's breath. By now it had come down to a challenge. Nose to nose, ready for the head butt, hard skullbone smashing into nasal septum— if Briato' hadn't stepped in. He'd placed his body between them, a wall marking a boundary. "Why don't you shut up already? You still keep yacking! Fuck, you won't even lower your eyes."

The reason Renatino wasn't lowering his eyes was that he was ashamed to, but if there were a way to get out of that situation with a gesture of submission, he would gladly have done it. He'd have bowed his head, even gotten down on his knees. It was a bunch of them against one: the rules of honor don't count when you're about to *vattere* someone. *Vattere* in Neapolitan doesn't translate simply as "fight" or "beat up." As so often happens in the languages of the flesh, *vattere* is a verb that overflows the basin of its definition. *Ti vatte* means "beats you," but in this broader, Neapolitan sense of the word, while *ti picchia* is the narrower, standard Italian phrase. Your mamma *ti vatte*, the police *ti picchia*, your father or your grandfather *ti vatte*, your teacher at school *ti picchia*, your girlfriend *ti vatte* if you let your gaze rest too long on the eyes of some other girl.

A person *vatte* with all the force he possesses, with genuine resentment and without any rules. And most important of all, a person *vatte* with a certain ambiguous closeness. A person *vatte* someone he knows, a person *picchia* a stranger. A person *vatte* someone who is close to him in terms of territory, culture, and knowledge, someone who's a part of his life; a person *picchia* someone who has nothing to do with him.

"You're liking all the pictures of Letizia. You're adding comments everywhere I turn, and now I come down here to the piazza, and you dare to look me in the eye?" Nicolas accused him. And as he talked, he was pinning Renatino like an insect, with the black needles he had for eyes.

"First of all, I'm not even looking at you. And anyway, if Letizia posts pictures, that means I can add comments and put likes," Renatino replied.

"So you're saying I can't *vattere* you?"

"Oh, now, Nicolas, you've busted my balls enough."

Nicolas started shoving him and jerking him around: Renatino's body stumbled over the feet that stood beside him and bounced off the bodies facing Nicolas, like a billiard ball hitting the cushions on the table. Briato' pushed him against Drago', who seized him with one hand and hurled him against Tucano. Tucano pretended to smash his head into Renatino's face, but then handed him back to Nicolas. There was another plan.

"Oh, what the fuck do you think you're doing! O!!!" His voice came out like the sound of some animal, or really like the yelping of a frightened puppy. He kept emitting a single sound that came out like a plea, an invocation of salvation: "O!!!"

A flat, simple sound. A guttural, apelike, despairing "O." Calling for help amounts to signing your name to a certificate of your cowardice, but he secretly hoped that that one letter, which is after all the final letter in the Italian cry for help—*aiuto!*—would be understood as a supplication, without the ultimate humiliation of having to openly beg.

No one around them was lifting a finger, the girls went away as if a show was about to begin that they didn't want to see, that they *couldn't* see. Most of the others stayed, almost pretending that they weren't there, an audience that was actually extremely attentive but ready to swear, if questioned, that they'd had their faces turned away the whole time, toward their iPhones, and that they'd never even noticed what was going on.

Nicolas shot a quick glance around the piazzetta, then gave a hard shove that knocked Renatino to the ground. He tried to get back up, but Nicolas's foot stamping square in his chest knocked him flat to the pavement. The four of them, the whole gang, arrayed themselves around him.

Briato' set about grabbing and holding both of Renatino's legs, by the ankles. Every so often one of them would slip out of his grasp, like a big Christmas eel trying to fly through the air, but he always managed to sideslip the kick in the face that Renatino was so desperately trying to deliver. Then he strapped both of Renatino's legs together with a light chain, the kind used to fasten a bicycle to a pole.

"It's good and tight!" he said after snapping the padlock shut.

Tucano bound both of Renatino's hands together with a pair of metal handcuffs covered with red fur, something he must have found in a sex shop somewhere, and started giving him a series of kicks in the kidneys to quiet him down. Drago' held his head still with a certain delicacy, the way EMT nurses do after a car crash while putting on a neck brace.

Nicolas dropped his trousers, turned his back, and squatted over Renatino's face. He reached down rapidly and grabbed both the boy's handcuffed hands to hold them still, then started shitting in his face.

"What do you say, 'o Drago', do you think this piece of shit"—he used the classical Neapolitan epithet *omm' 'e mmerda*—"is ready to eat some shit?"

"I think he is."

"Okay, here it comes . . . *buon appetito.*"

Renatino was twisting and shouting, trying to get free, but when he saw the brown mass emerging he suddenly stopped moving and shut himself up tight as he could. He clamped his lips, wrinkled his nose, contracted his face, hardening in hopes of turning it into a mask. Drago' held the head firmly in place and only released it after the first piece of shit flopped onto Renatino's face. The only reason he let go, though, was fear of getting some on his hands. The head started moving again, as if the boy had gone crazy, right and left, doing all he could to toss off the piece of shit, which had lodged between his nose and upper lip. Renatino managed to knock it off and went back to howling his *O!* of desperation.

"*Guagliu'*, here comes the second piece of shit . . . hold him still."

"Fuck, Nicolas, you really must have eaten a big meal . . ."

Drago' went back to holding Renatino's head, still gingerly, with the caution of a nurse.

"You bastards! O!!! O!!! You bastards!!!"

He shouted helplessly, and then fell silent the instant he saw the second piece exiting from Nicolas's anus. A hairy dark eye that, with a pair of spasms, chopped the excremental snake into two rounded pieces.

"*Ua'*, you almost got some on me, Nico'."

"Drago', do you want some shit tiramisù all for yourself?"

The second piece dropped onto his eyes. Then Renatino felt Drago' release him, both hands letting go at the same time, so he started whipping his head around hysterically, till he started to retch, on the verge of vomiting. Then Nicolas reached down for the hem of Renatino's T-shirt and wiped his ass, carefully, without haste.

They left him there.

"Renati', you need to thank my mother, you know why? Because she feeds me right. If I ate the stuff that *zoccola di mammeta*—that slut mother of yours—cooks, then I'd have crapped a faceful of diarrhea on you, a shower of shit."

Laughter. Laughter that burned up all the oxygen in their mouths, that choked them. More or less like Lampwick's braying in *Pinocchio*. The most nondescript kind of ostentatious laughter. The laughter of children, coarse, mocking, overdone, meant to meet with approval. They took the chains off Renatino's ankles and unlocked his handcuffs: "You can keep them, consider it a gift."

Renatino sat up, clutching at the fuzzy handcuffs. The others left the piazzetta, shouting and revving their motor scooters. Like gleaming bee-tles, they accelerated for no reason, clutching at the brake levers to avoid slamming into one another. They vanished in an instant. Nicolas alone kept his two black needles pointed straight at Renatino right up till the very last. The wind tousled his blond hair, which one day, sooner or later—he'd decided—he was going to shave to the scalp. Then the motor scooter he was riding on as a passenger took him far from the piazzetta. Then they were just black silhouettes.

THE NEW MAHARAJA

Forcella is the material of History. The material of centuries of flesh. Living matter.

It is there, in the folds of those narrow lanes, the *vicoli*, which carve it like a weatherbeaten face, that you find the meaning of that name. *Forcella*. Fork in the road. A departure and a parting of the ways. An unknown factor that always lets you know where you start out from but never where you'll arrive, or even whether you will. A street that's a symbol. Of death and resurrection. It greets you with an immense portrait of San Gennaro painted on a wall, watching you arrive from the façade of a building, and with his all-understanding eyes, it reminds you that it's never too late to get back on your feet, that destruction, like lava, can be stopped.

Forcella is a history of new departures, new beginnings. Of new cities atop old ones, and new cities becoming old. Of teeming, noisy cities, built of tufa stone and slabs of volcanic piperno rock. Stone that built every wall, laid out every street, changed everything, even the people who've worked with these materials all their lives. Actually, in fact, who've farmed them. Because people talk about farming piperno, as if it were a row of vines to water. Types of rock that are running out, because farming a type of rock means consuming it. In Forcella even the rocks are alive, even the rocks breathe.

The apartment buildings are attached to other apartment buildings, balconies really do kiss each other in Forcella. And passionately so. Even when a street runs between them. And it isn't the clotheslines that hold them together, it's the voices that clasp hands, that call out to each other to say that what runs beneath is not asphalt but a river, crisscrossed by invisible bridges.

Every time Nicolas went past the Cippus of Forcella, he felt the same burst of joy. He remembered the time, two years ago, though it seemed like centuries, when they'd gone to steal the Christmas tree in the Galleria Umberto I and they'd brought it straight there, complete with all its glittering globes, which were actually no longer glittering because now there was no electricity to make them glitter. That's how he'd first caught Letizia's attention, as she left her apartment house on the morning of the day before Christmas Eve, turning the corner, she'd glimpsed the tip of the tree, like in one of those fairy tales where you plant a seed the night before and, when the sun rises, hey presto! a tree has sprung up and now stretches up to the sky. That day she'd kissed him.

He'd gone to get the tree late at night, with the whole group. They'd all left their homes the minute their parents had gone to sleep, and the ten of them, sweating over the impossible task, had hoisted it onto their puny shoulders, doing their best to make no noise, cursing softly under their breath. Then they'd strapped the tree onto their motor scooters: Nicolas and Briato' with Stavodicendo and Dentino in front, and the rest of them bringing up the rear, holding the trunk high. There'd been a tremendous downpour and it hadn't been easy to navigate the mud puddles on their scooters, to say nothing of the veritable rivers of rainwater spewing forth from the sewers. They might have had motor scooters, but they weren't old enough to drive them, legally. Still, they were *nati imparati*, born knowing how, as they liked to say, and they managed to maneuver the bikes better than much older boys. Making their way across that pond of rainwater hadn't been easy, though. They'd halted repeatedly to catch their breath and adjust the straps, but in the end they'd succeeded. They'd erected the tree inside the Forcella quarter, they'd brought it to where they lived, among their people. Where it ought to be. In the afternoon the police Falchi squad had come to take the tree back, but by then it didn't much matter. Mission accomplished.

Nicolas sailed past the Cipp' a Furcella—a cippus, or short column, dedicated to St. Anthony, emblematic of the quarter—with a smile on his face and parked outside Letizia's building. He wanted to pick her up and take her to the club. But she'd already seen the posts on Facebook: the photographs of Renatino beshitted, the tweets of Nicolas's friends announcing his humiliation. Letizia knew Renatino and she knew he was sweet on her. The only sin he'd committed was to put some "likes" on several of her pictures after she'd accepted his friend request, which was unforgivable in Nicolas's eyes.

Nicolas had pulled up outside her apartment building, he hadn't bothered to ring her buzzer. The intercom is something only mailmen, traffic cops, detectives, ambulance drivers, firemen, and people not from the quarter bother using. When you need to alert your girlfriend to your presence, or your mother, your father, a friend, your neighbor, anyone who by rights considers themselves part of your life, you just shout: everything's wide open, as public as can be, everyone hears everything, and if they don't it's not a good sign, it means something must have happened. From downstairs Nicolas was yelling at the top of his lungs: "Leti'! Letizia!" Letizia's bedroom window didn't overlook the street, it faced onto a sort of lightless air shaft. The window overlooking the street that Nicolas was looking up at illuminated a spacious landing, a space shared by a number of apartments. The people climbing the apartment house stairs heard him yelling and knocked on Letizia's door, without bothering to wait for her to come and answer. They'd knock and continue on their way; it was a code: "Someone's calling you." If Letizia answered the door and there was no one there, she knew someone had been calling her from the street below. But that day, Nicolas called her with such a powerful voice that she heard him all the way back in her bedroom. She finally stuck her face out the window and bawled in annoyance: "Just get out of here. I'm not going anywhere with you."

"Come on, get moving, come down."

"No, I'm not coming down."

That's the way it works in the city. Everyone knows you're fighting. They can't help but know. Every insult, every raised voice, every high note resonates off the stones of the alleys and lanes, the *vicoli* of Naples, long accustomed to the sounds of lovers skirmishing.

"What did Renatino ever do to you?"

Nicolas asked, in a mixture of disbelief and pride: "You've already heard the news?"

Deep down, all he cared about was that his girlfriend knew. The exploits of a warrior are passed by word of mouth, they become news, then legends. He looked up at Letizia in the window and knew that his deed continued to resonate, ricocheting from flaking plaster to aluminum window frames, rain gutters, roof terraces, and then up, up, up among the TV antennas and satellite dishes. And it was while he was looking up at her, as she leaned on the windowsill, with her hair even curlier after her shower, that he got a text from Agostino. An urgent, sibylline text.

That put an end to the quarrel. Letizia watched as he climbed back on his scooter and took off, tires screeching. A minotaur: half man and half wheels. To drive, in Naples, is to seize all rights of way, yield to no one, ignore traffic barriers, one-way signs, pedestrian malls. Nicolas was on his way to join the others at the New Maharaja, the club in Posillipo. A majestic, imposing club with a vast terrace overlooking the bay. The club could have thrived as a business on that terrace alone, renting it out for weddings, first communions, and parties. Since he was a child, Nicolas had been drawn to that white building that stood in the center of a jutting rock promontory in Posillipo. What Nicolas liked about the Maharaja was its brashness. There it stood, clamped to the waterfront rocks like an impregnable fortress, every inch of it white, the door frames and window frames, the doors themselves, even the shutters. It looked out over the sea with the majesty of a Greek temple, with its immaculate columns that seemed to rise directly out of the water, buttressing on their shoulders that very same terrace, where Nicolas imagined the men he wanted to become one day strolling comfortably.

Nicolas had grown up going past the place, gazing at the ranks of cars, motorcycles, and scooters parked out front, admiring the women, the men, the fine clothing and displays of wealth, swearing that one day he'd set foot in there, whatever the cost. That was his ambition, a dream of his that had infected his friends, who at a certain point had decided to dub him with a variant as his nickname: "'o Maraja." To be able to walk in, head held high, not as waiters, not as a favor someone could indulge them in, as if to say, "Go on, take a look around, but then get the hell out of here": no, he and the others wanted to be customers, ideally they wanted to be highly esteemed guests. How many years would it take, Nicolas wondered, before he'd be able to spend the evening and the night there? What would he have to give to get in?

Time is still time when you can imagine, and maybe imagine that if you save for ten years, and you win a civil service exam, and with some luck, and putting all you have into it, maybe . . . But Nicolas's father earned a high school phys ed teacher's salary and his mother owned a small business, a pressing shop. The paths cut by people of his blood would require an unacceptably long time to get him into the New Maharaja. No. Nicolas needed to do it now. At age fifteen.

And it had all been simple. Just as the important decisions you can't turn back from are always the simplest ones. That's the paradox of every generation: the reversible decisions are the ones you think through, consider carefully, weigh judiciously. The irreversible ones are made on the spur of the moment, prompted by an instinctive impulse, accepted without resistance. Nicolas did what all the others his age did: afternoons on his motor scooter in front of the school, selfies, an obsession with sneakers— to him they had always been proof you were a man with both feet planted firmly on the ground, and without those shoes he wouldn't even have felt like a human being. Then, one day a few months ago, in late September, Agostino had talked to Copacabana, an important man in the Striano family of Forcella.

Copacabana had approached Agostino because he was a relative: Agostino's father was his *fratocucino*, that is, his first cousin.

Agostino had hurried over to see his friends as soon as school got out. He'd arrived with a bright-red face, more or less the same vivid color as his hair. From a distance it appeared that, from the neck up, he was on fire, and it was no accident that they called him Cerino—Matchstick.

Panting, he reported everything he'd been told, word for word. He'd never forget that moment as long as he lived.

"Wait, do you even understand who he is?"

Actually, they'd only ever heard his name mentioned in passing.

"Co-pa-ca-ba-na!" he'd uttered, emphasizing each syllable. "The district underboss of the Striano family. He says he needs a hand, he's looking for *guaglioni*. And he says he pays well."

No one had gotten especially excited to hear this. Neither Nicolas nor the other members of the group recognized in this criminal the hero that he'd been for the street kids of an earlier time. They didn't care how the money was made, the important thing was to make lots of it and show it off, the important thing was to have cars, suits, watches, to be lusted after by women and envied by men.

Only Agostino knew a little more about the history of Copacabana, a name the man had earned by purchasing a hotel on the beaches of the New World. A Brazilian wife, Brazilian children, Brazilian drugs. What really elevated him to greatness was the impression and the conviction that he was able to get practically anyone to come and stay in his hotel, from Maradona to George Clooney, from Lady Gaga to Drake, and he posted pictures of himself with them on Facebook. He could exploit the beauty of the things he owned to tempt anyone to come there. That had made him the most prominent and visible of all the members of the Striano clan, a family in dire straits. Copacabana didn't even need to look them in the face in order to make up his mind who could work for him. For almost three years now, following the arrest of Don Feliciano Striano, Nobile, he had been the only boss in Forcella.

He'd emerged from the trial of the Striano family in pretty good shape. Most of the charges against the organization concerned a period of time when Copacabana had been in Brazil, so he'd been able to beat the charges of Mafia conspiracy, which constituted the biggest risk for him and others like him. That was the criminal trial. Next came the appeals court, which in Italy could be pursued by the prosecution. And that meant that Copacabana was up to his neck in it and the water was rising, so he had to get started again, find new, young kids to drum up business for him, show the world he'd taken the worst they could throw at him. His boys, his *paranza*, the Capelloni, were good soldiers but unpredictable. That's the way it works when you rise too far, too fast, or at least when you think you've made it to the top. White, the underboss, pretty much kept them in line, but he was constantly snorting. The *paranza* of the Capelloni only knew how to shoot, they had no idea how to establish a market, open a piazza. For that new beginning, he needed more malleable raw material. But who? And how much were they going to cost him? How much was he going to need to keep on hand? Nobody ever sweats the details on business and the money you need to invest, but when it comes to your own personal money, that's quite another matter. If Copacabana had sold just a portion of the hotel he owned in South America, he could have kept fifty men on a regular salary, but that was his own money. To invest in business, he needed clan money, and it was in short supply. Forcella was in the crosshairs; prosecutors, TV talk shows, and even politicians were focusing on the quarter. Not a good sign. Copacabana had to rebuild from scratch: there was no one left to carry on the business in Forcella. The organization had imploded.

And so he'd gone to see Agostino: he'd tossed a small brick of hashish under his nose, just like that, first thing. Agostino was off school and Copacabana asked him: "A little brick, this size, how fast can you sling it?" *'Nu mattoncino accussì, in quanto te lo levi? Levarsi il fumo*—slinging hash—was the first step on the road to becoming a drug dealer, even though the apprenticeship to earning that title was a long one; slinging hash meant selling it to friends, family, anyone you knew. There was a skinny, skinny margin of profit, but there was practically no risk to speak of.

Agostino had ventured: "I dunno, a month."

"A month? You'll polish this off in a week."

Agostino was barely old enough to drive a motor scooter, but that was what interested Copacabana. "Bring me all your friends who're interested in doing a little work. All your friends from Forcella, the ones who hang outside the club in Posillipo. They've been standing there with their dicks in their hands long enough, right?"

And that's how it had all begun. Copacabana would arrange to meet them in an apartment house at the edge of Forcella, but he was never there himself. Instead, there was always a man who was quick with words but very slow on the uptake; they all called him Alvaro because he looked like Alvaro Vitali, the actor. He was about fifty, but he looked a lot older. Practically illiterate, he'd spent more years behind bars than on the street: prison at a very young age back in the day of Cutolo and the Nuova Famiglia, prison during the gang wars between the cartels of Sanità and Forcella, between the Mocerinos and the Strianos. He was responsible for stashing weapons, he'd been a *specchiettista*, the one who fingers the intended victim. He lived with his mother in a *basso*, an airless ground-floor apartment, his career had never gone anywhere, they paid him a pittance and tossed him the occasional Slavic prostitute to bring home, forcing his mother to go over to the neighbors' house till he was done. But he was a guy Copacabana trusted. He was reliable when it came to taking care of business: he'd drive Copacabana places, he'd hand off the bricks of hash on his behalf to Agostino and the other kids.

Alvaro had shown him where they were supposed to stand. The apartment where they kept the hash was on the top floor. They needed to go down to the atrium. It wasn't like in Scampia, where there were gates and barriers, none of that. Copacabana wanted a freer dope market, less fortified.

Their assignment was simple. They'd show up on the spot a short time before the real activity began, so they could use their own knives to cut the hash up into various chunks. Alvaro joined them to chop up a few chunklets and big pieces. Ten-euro chunks, fifteen-euro chunks, fifty-euro chunks. Then they'd wrap up the hash in the usual aluminum foil and keep the pieces ready; they'd sort the grass into baggies. The customers would ride into the atrium of the apartment house on their motor scooters or else come on foot, hand over the cash, and turn to go. The mechanism was reliable because the quarter could rely on lookouts paid by Copacabana, and a vast number of people who would hang out on the street, ready to sound the alarm if they spotted cops, carabinieri, or financial police, whether in plainclothes or full regalia.

They'd do their dealing after school, but sometimes they didn't even bother showing up at school, since they were getting paid a percentage of what they sold. It was the fifty or a hundred euros a week that made all the difference. And that money went to just one place: Foot Locker. They took that store by storm. They'd troop in, arrayed in compact formation, as if they were ready to knock the place off and then, once they were through the front door, they'd scatter. They'd grab ten, fifteen T-shirts at a time. Tucano would put the T-shirts on one over the other. Just Do It. Adidas. Nike. One symbol would vanish only to be replaced by others in a split second. Nicolas bought three pairs of Air Jordans at the same time. High-tops, white, black, red, all he cared about was if Michael was on them, slam-dunking one-handed. Briato', too, had gone crazy for basketball shoes; he wanted them green, with neon soles, but the minute he picked them up Lollipop had checked him, saying: "Green? What are you, a faggot?" and Briato' had put them down immediately and hurried over to paw through the baseball jackets. Yankees and Red Sox. Five per team.

And so all the kids who hung out in front of the New Maharaja had started slinging hashish. Dentino had done his best to stay out of it, but that had lasted only a couple of months, then he'd started peddling hash at the construction site where he worked. Lollipop was slinging hash at the gym. Briato', too, had started working for Copacabana, he'd do any-thing Nicolas asked him to. The market wasn't gigantic the way it had been in the eighties and nineties: Secondigliano had absorbed the whole market, then the business had flowed away from Naples proper, to Melito. But now it was migrating to the historic city center.

Every week, Alvaro called around and gave them their pay: the more you sold, the more you earned. They always managed to skim a little extra off the top with some sly maneuvers outside the regular dealing, break-ing off some smaller chunks or ripping off some rich and particularly dim-witted friend. But never in Forcella. There the price was the price and the quantity was preset. Nicolas didn't do a lot of regular shifts because he sold at parties as well as to his father's gym students, but he'd started really bringing in money only when the students had started protesting and had occupied his school, the Arts High School. He'd started dealing hash to everyone. In the classrooms where there were no teachers, in the gym, in the hallways, on the stairs, in the bathrooms. Everywhere. The prices rose as they spent more nights in the school. Only now he was get-ting dragged into political discussions, too. One time he'd gotten into a fistfight because, during a collective session, he'd said: "If you ask me, Mussolini was an impressive guy, because guys who know how to command respect are impressive. I like Che Guevara, too."

"You'd better not even dare utter Che Guevara's name," said one of the guys with long hair and an unbuttoned shirt. They'd chest-bumped, shoved each other, but Nicolas didn't give a damn about the jerk from Via dei Mille, they didn't even go to the same school. What did that guy know about respect and being impressive? If you're from Via dei Mille, you've assumed everyone respects you from the day you're born. If you're from lower Naples, you have to go out and fight for respect. The comrade might talk about moral categories, but to Nicolas, who'd just seen a few pictures of Mussolini and a few old film clips on TV, the words *moral category* had no real meaning, and so he'd slammed a head butt into the guy's nose, as if to say: here, let me explain it to you this way, you jackoff, you don't know what you're talking about. Just and unjust, good and bad. They're all the same. On his Facebook wall Nicolas had lined them up: the Duce shouting out a window, the king of the Gauls bowing down to Caesar, Muhammad Ali barking at his adversary flat on his back. The strong and the weak. That's the only real distinction. And Nicolas knew which side he was on.

It was there, in that very private narcotics market of his, that he'd first met Pesce Moscio. While they were smoking big bomber joints, there was a kid who happened to know the magic word:

"Oh, but I saw you out front of the New Maharaja!"

"Okay, so what do you know about it?" Nicolas had replied.

"I hang out there, too," then he'd added: "Listen here, listen to this music." And he'd initiated Nicolas, who up till then had only ever listened to Italian pop music, into the toughest American hip-hop, the vicious kind, the kind that vomits out an incomprehensible gush of words, every here and there jutting out a "fuck" just to keep things in order.

Nicolas really liked that guy, he was shameless but he treated him with respect. And so, after the end of the occupation, when Pesce Moscio had also started slinging hash at his own school, despite the fact that he wasn't from Forcella, every once in a while they'd let him work in the apartment house.

It was inevitable that sooner or later they would be caught. Right before Christmas there was a sweep. It was Agostino's shift. Nicolas was just arriving to relieve him and he hadn't noticed anything. The lookout had been caught off guard. The narcotics cops had pretended to stop a car to inspect it and then they'd come down on them just as they were trying to get rid of the hash.

They'd called Nicolas's father, who showed up at police headquarters and just stood there, contemplating the sight of his son with a blank expression that gradually turned into a glare of rage. Nicolas had kept his eyes on the floor for a good long while. Then, when he finally made up his mind to look up, he'd done so without a shred of humility, and his father had smacked him twice, once a straight-armed slap and the other the back of his hand, both powerful blows, longtime tennis player that he was. Nicolas hadn't uttered a single syllable, only a pair of tears had welled up in his eyes, the product of the physical pain, not from any sorrow or grief.

Only then had his mother come in like a fury. She'd appeared, taking up the entire doorway, arms thrown wide, hands on the door frame as if she were trying to hold up the building. Her husband had stepped aside to leave the scene to her. And she'd taken it. She'd crept slowly closer to Nicolas, with the gait of a ferocious beast. When she was finally right in front of him, as if she were about to embrace him, she'd whispered in his ear: "What a disgrace, what *scuorno*." And she'd continued: "What company have you been keeping, what company?" Her husband had heard without understanding, and Nicolas had lurched violently away from her, so that his father had lunged at him again, crushing him against the wall: "Now just look at him. 'O *spacciatore*—the drug dealer. How the fuck can this be?!"

"Drug dealer, my ass," his mother had said, pulling her husband aside. "Oh, the shame."

"So what do you think," Nicolas had blurted out, "that my closet turned into a Foot Locker display case just by accident? By working at a gas station on Saturdays and Sundays?"

"Nice asshole you are. And now you're going to do some jail time," his mother had said.

"What jail time?"

And she'd hauled off and slapped him, with less force than his father, but sharper, more resounding.

"Shut up, enough's enough. You're not going out again, you only go out under strict supervision," she'd said, and, to her husband: "Drug dealer, no way, you got it? No way, no way on earth. Let's get this taken care of and go home."

"Curse all the saints, to hell with them," his father had limited himself to muttering. "And I even have to pay the lawyer!"

Nicolas had gone home, escorted by his parents as if they were a couple of carabinieri. His father stared straight ahead, looking out for those who would be greeting them: Letizia and his younger son, Christian. Let them see the disgraced wretch, let them look him right in the face. The mother, on the other hand, stayed by Nicolas's side, her eyes downcast.

The minute he spotted his brother, Christian had switched off the TV set and leaped to his feet, covering the distance between the sofa and the door in three long steps, reaching out to shake hands the way he'd seen in the movies—hand, arm, and then shoulder to shoulder, like *duje brò*, a couple of brothers. But his father had glared daggers at him, jutting his chin. Nicolas had forced himself to keep from laughing in front of his younger brother, who idolized him, and told himself that later that night, in their bedroom, he'd have plenty to sate his kid brother's curiosity. They'd talk through the night, and then Nicolas would run his hands through Christian's hair, the way he always did before telling him good night.

Letizia, too, would have liked to embrace him, just so she could ask him: "But what was it? Why?" She knew Nicolas was slinging hash, and that necklace he'd given her for her birthday had certainly cost him something, but she didn't think things had gotten so serious so fast, even if things weren't really so bad after all.

She spent the following afternoon applying Nivea cream to his lips and cheeks. "That'll make the swelling go down," she told him. These were the kindnesses that had started to weld them together. He yearned to eat her alive, he'd tell her so: "I feel just like the vampire in *Twilight!*" but her virginity was just too important. He accepted that all the decisions had to be up to her, and so they'd gorge themselves on kisses, oblique petting strategies, hours listening to music with one earbud apiece.

They sent them all home from police headquarters as persons under investigation, free on their own recognizance, even Agostino, who, caught red-handed in the middle of his shift, was probably in the worst shape legally. For days they spent their time trying to remember what they had written in the chat rooms to one another, because their cell phones had all been confiscated. In the end, the decision was an easy one: Alvaro would take the fall. Copacabana put together an anonymous tip, and the carabinieri found the whole drug supply in his *basso*. He even took responsibility for having given the hash to the kids. When Copacabana had informed him that he was going back to prison, he replied: "No! Again? What the fuck." Not another word after that. In exchange, he'd get a regular payment, a pittance, a thousand euros. And before he turned himself in at the front gate of Poggioreale prison, a Romanian girl. But, he'd asked, he wanted to marry her. And Copacabana had replied, very simply: "Let's see what we can do."

In the meantime, they'd gotten their hands on new smartphones for just a few euros, clearly stolen, just to start keeping the group together again. They'd resolved not to write anything about what had happened in the chat they'd just restarted, especially not a thought that had occurred to them all, but that only Stavodicendo had been able to put into words: "*Guagliu'*, sooner or later, Nisida Reform School is waiting for us. Maybe that's where we were bound to wind up."

At least once, each of them had imagined the trip toward the juvenile detention center aboard the police paddy wagon. Rumbling across the jetty that connects the little island to the mainland. In you went, and a year later, out you came, transformed. Ready now. A man.

For some, it was something you had to do, to the extent that they were happy to let themselves get caught on some misdemeanor. After all, once you were back out, there'd be plenty of time.

When all was said and done, though, the kids had held up their end, they'd kept their lips sealed, and apparently nothing had emerged from their chat that could be used as evidence. And so Nicolas and Agostino had finally been invited by Copacabana to come into the New Maharaja.

But Nicolas wanted a little something more, he wanted to be introduced to the district underboss. Agostino had worked up the nerve to ask Copacabana in person. "Sure, of course, I want to meet my kids," he'd replied. So Nicolas and Agostino had entered the New Maharaja accompanied by him in person: Copacabana.

Nicolas was meeting him for the first time. He'd expected him to be old, instead he was a man just a little over forty. In the car, on the way to the club, Copacabana told them how happy he was with the work they were doing. He treated them like his messenger boys, but still, with a certain courtesy. Nicolas and Agostino weren't bothered by it, their attention was fully absorbed by the evening in store for them.

"What's it like? What's it like in there?" they asked.

"It's a club," he answered, but they knew exactly what it was like. YouTube had instructed them, displaying events and concerts. By asking "What's it like?" those two kids were asking what it was like to be in there, have a private, reserved room, what it was like to be in the world of the New Maharaja. What it was like to belong to that world.

Copacabana ushered them in through a private entrance and led them to his reserved room. They'd spiffed up and dressed to the nines, they'd announced to parents and friends where they were going, as if they'd been summoned to an audience before the most illustrious court. To a certain extent, it was true, even the Naples of rich young jerks, the trendy little snot noses, really did socialize there. The place could have been a symphony of kitsch, a panegyric to the worst possible taste. Instead it wasn't. It managed to strike an elegant balance between the finest Campanian coastal tradition of pastel-hued majolica and an almost playful reference to the Far East: that name Maharaja, the New Maharaja, came from an enormous canvas at the center of the club, brought all the way from India, where it had been painted by an Englishman who had later come to Naples. The mustache, the curve of the eyes, the beard, the silks, the comfy sofa, a shield upon which appeared an assortment of gemstones and a moon facing north. Nicolas's life had begun there, in the fascination of the enormous painting of the Maharaja.

For the rest of the evening, Nicolas and Agostino feasted their eyes on the people in the club, with champagne corks popping, one after the other, as background. Everyone who was anyone was here. This was the place where businessmen, sports stars, notaries, lawyers, and judges all found a table where they could sit down and get to know one another, crystal glasses to clink in toasts. A place that immediately took you light-years away from the local tavern, the typical Neapolitan restaurant, the place where they'd serve you an *impepata di cozze* and a family-style pizza, the places your friends know about, the places you'd take your wife. Instead, this was a place where you could meet anyone without owing anyone an explanation, because it was like bumping into them on the piazza. It was the most natural thing in the world to meet new people at the New Maharaja.

In the meantime, Copacabana talked and talked, and Nicolas kept stretching in his head a clear image, which added to the shapes of the food and the well-dressed guests the music of a word. *Lazarat.* The name of a village and its exotic allure.

Albanian grass had become the newest driving force. In point of fact, Copacabana had two lines of business: the legal one in Rio and the illegal one in Tirana. "One of these days, you ought to take me there," Agostino said to him, as he leaned forward to grab his umpteenth glass of wine. "It's the biggest plantation there is on earth, *guagliu'*. Grass everywhere," Copacabana replied, referring to Lazarat. It had become the platform for the largest possible harvests of marijuana. Copacabana told him how he'd managed to finagle major purchases, but it was never clear exactly how he transported them from Albania to Italy, just like that, without difficulty: the sea lanes and air routes from Albania were by no means secure. The shipments of grass moved through Montenegro, Croatia, and Slovenia, and managed to slip into Friuli. In his telling of it, it was all very confusing. Agostino, stunned by the dazzling world that swirled all around him, heard those stories and yet didn't hear them, while Nicolas would never have willingly stopped listening.

Every shipment was stacks and stacks of cash, and when that cash became a river in spate, there was no longer any way of hiding it. A few weeks after their night out at the New Maharaja, the investigation of the Antimafia Squad began, all the newspapers had headlined it: they'd arrested one of Copacabana's mules and now a warrant had been issued. He had no alternative but to go on the run. He vanished, perhaps to Albania, or else he'd managed to make it to Brazil. No sign of him for months. The Forcella market had run through its supply.

Agostino had tried to understand but, with Copacabana who knows where, and Alvaro in prison, it proved impossible.

"But 'o White's *paranza* is struggling . . . *Adda murì mammà*, if the shit doesn't come in," Lollipop had commented. May his mother die, was his phrase in dialect.

For Nicolas and his guys, where to go to get the dope, and how much of it, what type to sell, what shifts to work had become a problem. The city's drug markets were split up among the families. It was like a map, redrawn with new names, and each name marked a conquest.

"So now what are we going to do?" Nicolas had asked. They were in the back room, a no-man's-land created out of the junction of bar, tobacco shop, mini video arcade, and betting parlor. Everyone was welcome. Those with their noses in the air, cursing as they watched a horse gallop too slowly, those perched on stools with their noses stuck in demitasses of espresso, those who were busy flushing their salaries down the drain on the slot machines. And then there were Nicolas and his friends, as well as the Capelloni. White had just shot up, he was clearly wrecked on cocaine, which he no longer ingested through his nostrils but, with increasing frequency, through his veins. He was playing foosball all by himself, taking on two of his men, Chicchirichì and Selvaggio. He'd leap with agility from one handle to another, twisting the rods like a *tarantolato*, someone in the proverbial frenzy caused by a tarantula bite. Extremely talkative, but antennae picking up everything, every word that might chance to reach his ears. And he'd picked up on that utterance of Nicolas's: "So now what are we going to do?"

"*Vulite faticà, criatu'? Eh!*" he'd said, rolling a joint the whole time. "So you want to work, kid? Okay! You can work now, but as substitutes. I'll send you out, and you can work on some other market that needs you . . ."

They'd accepted unwillingly, but they really had no other option. After Copacabana was shuffled off the stage, the Forcella market was out of business for good.

They'd started working for anyone who had a hole to fill. Arrested Moroccan dealers, pushers with a fever, unreliable *guaglioni* dismissed from the crew. They worked for the Mocerino clan of Sanità, the Pesacane family in Cavone, sometimes they even went as far as Torre Annunziata to lend a hand to the Vitiellos. The locations where they peddled had turned into a nomadic wandering. Sometimes it was Piazza Bellini, other times the main station. People would reach out to them at the last minute, their cell-phone numbers known to all the Camorra scum of the region. Nicolas had gotten tired, little by little he'd stopped pushing the extra hash and was spending more time at home. All the kids who were older than them were making money even if they really weren't much good at their work, people who'd been caught red-handed, people who shuttled in and out of Poggioreale: White offered third-rate working conditions.

Still, the weather vane of fortune had started to veer.

That, at least, was the meaning of the text Agostino had sent Nicolas while he, outside Letizia's apartment house, was doing his best to convince her that Renatino's humiliation had been nothing more than an act of love.

"*Guagliu'*, Copacabana is back in Naples," said Agostino as soon as Nicolas halted his scooter next to his and Briato's. They were idling there, motors running, at the last turn in the road before the New Maharaja. The club could just be glimpsed from that location, and when it was closed it looked even more imposing.

"And he's an asshole for coming back, because they'll take him down for sure," said Briato'.

"No, no, the reason Copacabana came back is something super-important."

"So we can start selling hash and grass!" said Briato', and he glanced at Agostino with a smile. The first one of the day.

"Yeah, ri-i-i-ight! Get serious . . . I swear to you, he's back to organize 'o Micione's wedding, he's going to get married to Viola Striano, *guagliu'*!"

"Are you for real?" said Nicolas.

"Yes," and he added lest there be any lingering doubt: "*Adda murì mammà.*"

"Which means that now the guys from San Giovanni are in charge here, at our house . . ."

"So what does that matter?" Agostino replied. "Copacabana is here and he wants to see us."

"Where?"

"Here, I already told you, and right now . . ." he said, pointing at the club. "The others will be here any minute."

The time to change their lives was now. Nicolas knew it, he could sense that the opportunity would arrive. And now here it was. You go, you answer the call. You have to be strong with the strong. He actually had no idea what was going to happen, but he could use his imagination.

BAD THOUGHTS

Copacabana was parked in front of the club in a Fiat Fiorino packed full of cleaning supplies. He got out as soon as he was told the kids had arrived. He pinched their cheeks as he said hello, as if greeting toddlers, and they made no objection. This was a man who could step them up big-time, even though he looked skinny and pale, with long hair and patchy whiskers. His eyes were red and bloodshot. Life on the run must have been pretty tough. "Here they are, all my children . . . all right then, kids, come with me, you're here to look pretty . . . I'll take care of everything else."

Copacabana gave Oscar a big hug. Oscar was the guy in charge at the New Maharaja. His father's father had bought the place fifty years ago. He was a fat man who loved monogrammed, tailor-made shirts, though he always wore them one size too small, which meant you saw the buttons in the buttonholes struggling and squirming to hold things together. Oscar returned the hug shyly, practically holding Copacabana at arm's length with some discomfort, lest their hug paint him as the wrong sort of person.

"I'm about to do you a great honor, *Oscarino mio* . . ."

"I'm all ears . . ."

"Diego Faella and Viola Striano are going to celebrate their wedding here . . . in your place . . ." And he spread his arms wide to take in the whole club, as if it belonged to him.

At the mere sound of those two surnames uttered in the same breath, Oscar's face went beet red.

"Copacabana, I love you like a brother, but . . ."

"That's not the answer I was expecting . . ."

"I'm a friend to one and all, you know that, but as the majority shareholder in this club . . . our policies are to steer clear of . . ."

"Of?"

"Of difficult situations."

"Still, you're happy to take money that comes from difficult situations, aren't you?"

"We take money from everyone, but this kind of a wedding . . ." He didn't bother to finish the phrase, there was no need.

"But why would you avoid the honor of doing something like this?" asked Copacabana. "Do you have any idea of how many weddings you'd book because of this one?"

"Then they'll put micro recording devices on us."

"What micro recording devices are you talking about? Leaving aside the fact that the waiters aren't yours, I have my own *guaglioni* who'll be doing it . . ."

Agostino, Nicolas, Pesce Moscio, Briato', Lollipop, Dentino, and the others hardly expected that they'd have to work as waiters, they didn't know how, they'd never done such a thing. But if that's what Copacabana had decided, that's how it would go.

"Ah, Oscar, I don't know if it's clear to you that these people are ready to give you a deposit, tomorrow morning, of two hundred thousand euros . . . for this wedding, for this lovely party . . ."

"Copacabana . . . you see, I'd gladly give up all this money, but really, for us . . ."

Copacabana gestured with the back of his hand as if waving away the air from in front of his face. There was nothing left for him to do. "We're finished here." Angry and offended, he left the room. The kids tagged after him like hungry pups chasing after their mother.

Nicolas and the others were positive it was just a tactical retreat, that Copacabana was going to come back, even more pissed off, with his eyes redder than before, to smash Oscar's face in, or else with a pistol hidden somewhere on his person, which he'd pull out and use to kneecap Oscar. No such luck, though. He got back into the Fiat Fiorino. He leaned out the window and said: "You'll hear from me. We're going to hold this wedding in Sorrento: we can only have our own *guaglioni* as waiters, we can't go through any agencies, or they'll just go ahead and send over the financial police."

Copacabana headed off to Sorrento, where he put together the wedding between the two royal families. "*Ua*', they're throwing a megagalactic wedding on the Coast, but when we get married, sweets, it'll be even better!!!" Nicolas wrote to Letizia; but she still had it in for him on account of what happened with Renatino and answered him only after an hour, with a "So what makes you think I'll marry you?" Nicolas didn't think it, he knew it. That ceremony in Sorrento kindled his dreams, pushing him to write back with a string of messages, each of them full of increasingly sumptuous details, overflowing with promise. They'd taken each other for love, the two of them, love and nothing more, and now he needed to take all the rest, starting with his admission into the world that mattered—by way of the tradesman's entrance—a world he was determined to become part of, even though it was a world on which the sun was setting.

Feliciano Striano was in prison. His brother was in prison. His daughter had decided to marry Diego Faella, aka Micione. The Faellas of San Giovanni a Teduccio were formidably powerful in the fields of shakedowns, cement, votes, and the distribution of foodstuffs. They controlled an enormous market. The duty-free shops in airports in Eastern Europe belonged to them. Diego Faella was extremely strict: everyone had to pay, even the newsstands, the strolling vendors, everyone had to pay into the coffers of the clan, everyone according to their earnings—and that final qualification made him feel magnanimous. Even lovable. Feliciano Striano's daughter, Viola, had managed to live far away from Naples for many years, she'd gone to university and taken a degree in fashion design. Viola wasn't her real name, she just used it because she couldn't stand the name Addolorata, inherited from her grandmother, or even the more tolerable version, Dolores, which had already been appropriated by a small army of female cousins. So she'd chosen her name all by herself. When she was barely older than a child she'd gone to her mother and proclaimed her new name: Viola. She'd returned to the city after her mother decided to separate from her father. Don Feliciano had already found a new wife, but Viola's mother had refused to give him the divorce he'd asked for—*commare* she was and *commare* she remained—so Viola had chosen to go and stay with her and give her support in the early days of the separation. Her mother had never moved out of the family home in Forcella, so Don Feliciano had just moved next door. The family is sacred, but for Viola it was even more so; to her it was the DNA you carry inside you, and you can't exactly claw the blood out of your veins, can you? That's what you were born with, and that's what you'll die with. But then Don Feliciano had become a *pentito*, a state's witness, or a rat, and Viola had decided to divorce him as her parent. The name of Addolorata Striano had immediately been added to the family protection program. The carabinieri had headed out immediately to pick her up at home in a bulletproof car, in civilian clothes, to take her as far away from Forcella as possible. And that was where the theatrics unfolded: Viola had gone out onto the balcony to do her screaming, spitting, and inveighing against her would-be bodyguards. "Get out of here! You godless bastards. Sellouts! My father is dead to me, no, wait, he was never born, he never was my father! Go on, beat it!" And so she'd refused to go into the protection program, she'd refused to turn state's witness, and she'd rejected her father and uncles. She'd remained shut up at home for a long time, designing dresses, purses, and necklaces, while out on the balcony all manner of insults landed: bags full of dogshit, dead birds, pigeon entrails. And then there were the Molotov cocktails that set fire to the curtains, graffiti on the walls of various apartment houses, the downstairs intercom charred by a fire. No one believed what she had to say for herself, and yet she persisted. Until the day that Micione came into her life. By marrying Viola, Diego Faella had freed her at one fell swoop of all the accusations that had pinned her in that cage. And most of all, by taking the family blood that remained intact, Diego Faella had taken Forcella.

People said that Micione had courted her at some length. Viola had a shapely body, her father's eyes—a dazzling blue—a prominent nose that she'd wondered all her life whether to keep or get fixed, deciding eventually that her nose was actually her trademark. Viola was one of those women who know everything that's going on around them, for whom the most important rule is to pretend not to be aware of it. The two of them getting married meant a merger between two fundamental families. It seemed like an arranged marriage, like the ones engineered among the nobility: after all, they were the crème de la crème of Camorra aristocracy, and they struck many of the same poses as the dynasties covered in the popular magazines. Perhaps Viola was sacrificing herself; Micione seemed head over heels. Many observers were convinced that the winning move in his courtship had been when he managed to get her appointed chief designer for a company under the control of the Faella clan that manufactured luxury handbags. But talk is cheap, and for Viola their marriage had to be a triumph of True Love. If she'd chosen her own name for herself, then she could certainly make up her mind about what her future would look like.

As Copacabana had promised, the call came a few days later. Nicolas told his mother: "I'm going to work as a waiter at a wedding. For real, I'm doing it."

His mother scrutinized him from beneath his soft wave of messy blond hair. She was searching that phrase and her son's face for what she knew and what she didn't know, what might be true and what wasn't. The door to Nicolas's bedroom was open and she went so far as to search the walls for signs, taking in with that glance an old backpack lying carelessly on the floor, a pile of T-shirts at the foot of the bed. She tried to overlay the reported news ("I'm going to work as a waiter") upon the barriers that her son had never once stopped constructing after his parents had been summoned to police headquarters. She knew that the fact that he hadn't wound up at Nisida Reform School that time had nothing to do with his being innocent. She knew all about the things that Nicolas got up to, and whatever she hadn't heard about, she was easily able to imagine; unlike her husband, who saw a future, and a good one, for his son, and who therefore worried endlessly only about his bad manners. His mother, on the other hand, had eyes that could drill through human flesh. She pushed back her suspicions and hugged him close. "Good boy, Nicolas!" He let her do it, and she laid her head on his shoulder. She was letting herself go in a way she'd never done before. She closed her eyes and sniffed sharply, to get a whiff of the son she'd been so afraid was lost, but who now came home with an announcement that almost tasted of normality. It was enough to stir her hopes that this might be a new beginning. Nicolas returned the gesture as per script, but without hugging her tight, just laying his hands on her back. Let's just hope she doesn't start crying, he thought, mistaking love for weakness.

They untangled and Nicolas's mother refused to let him go back into his room, behind closed doors. They studied each other in silence, waiting for some new move. To Nicolas that embrace was just the kind of hug a mother gives a son when a son is obedient, when a son does something, anything, as long as it's better than nothing. She assumed that he'd just tossed her a bone, that out of some strange form of generosity he'd chosen to reward her with a smidgen of normality. What normality?! That kid has thoughts in his mind that scare me. What does he think, I can't see those thoughts? One crowding in after the other, nasty, vicious, as if he were out to avenge some wrong done him—*comme se avess' 'a vendicà 'nu tuorto*. And no one had done him wrong. What wrong could he claim? She couldn't share these thoughts with her husband. No, not him. Nicolas was able to guess—in the vastness that always opens out in the face of a mother—at that steady inspection, that rough and ready rummaging mixture of knowledge and suspicion. "*Mammà*, who'd have ever thought it? I'm going to be a waiter." And he mimed a plate, balanced neatly between wrist and forearm. He made her smile; after all, she deserved it. "How on earth did I make you blond?" she blurted out, steering her inner murmurings to some new subject. "How did I make you so handsome?"

"You made a fine waiter, Mamma." And he turned his back on her, but with the sensation that her gaze went on, as in fact it did.

Filomena, or Mena, as she was known, Nicolas's mother, had taken over a cleaners' and pressers' shop on Via Toledo, up toward Piazza Dante, between the Basilica dello Spirito Santo and Via Forno Vecchio.

It used to be a dry cleaner's, owned by a little old couple who'd handed over the management of the place and charged her a very low rent. She'd hung out a new light blue sign, and on it she'd had the English words *Blue Sky* painted, and underneath, in Italian, "Everything clean as a clear sky," and she'd started her business with a couple of Romanian women, and then a married Peruvian couple, the man tiny, a first-class presser, a diminutive person who never spoke, and the woman broad and beaming, saying nothing about her husband and his silence but *"Escucha mucho."* Mena had done some Neapolitan dressmaking in her youth, she knew how to sew by hand and machine, and therefore the services offered by Blue Sky also included small alterations, the kind of work usually done "by Indians," as people said, but then again, you couldn't just turn over the market to Indians, Sinhalese, and Chinese. The shop was a hole in the wall, crowded with machines and shelves to store dresses, suits, and linen, with a small door in the back opening out onto a dark courtyard. The door was always open; in the summer to get a breeze, in the winter to catch a breath. Sometimes, though, Mena would stand out in front of the shop, her hands akimbo on her shapely hips, her raven-black hair brushed a little too hastily, and watch the passing traffic, the people going by, she'd start to recognize the customers ("Signo', your husband's jacket came out a jewel, a gem") and they'd start to recognize her. You see how many unmarried men there are, she said to herself, here in Naples, just like up north, and they're bound to bring in their clothes to be washed, pressed, and stitched up. Quietly, unobtrusively, they come in, they drop off, they pick up, they turn to go. Mena studied the world of that neighborhood she didn't know, where in fact she was an outsider, Mena from Forcella, but the owners had introduced her properly, because there's not a profession where someone doesn't vouch for someone else. And she'd been vouched for. She couldn't say how long things would go on that way, but in the meantime she was happy to bring home a little extra money, because a high school gym teacher can't really support a family, and her husband was a *uomo cecato,* so to speak, a blind man who couldn't see these problems, couldn't see what his children needed—he just couldn't see. She had to take care of things herself, and protect that man, whom she still loved deeply. When she was in the shop, the steam iron gasping, she lost herself gazing at the pictures of her sons that she'd hung up between a calendar and a cork board with a cascade of receipts pinned to it. Christian at age three. Nicolas at age eight, and then another one now, with his blond mop of hair: who'd have ever thought that he was her son? You had to see him next to his father and then it became a little clearer. She darkened as she stirred at the thought of all that young beauty, darkened a little because to some extent she sensed, she could hear; she wondered—curious, eager to know, and she even devised ways of finding out, certainly not through the school, because there was nothing to be learned there, and not from Letizia, either, but rather from those young thugs Nicolas was friends with and was so careful to keep at a safe distance from his home, but not careful enough to keep her from catching a whiff of it, an idea of it, and not a very nice idea, either. He was comfortable with them. He'd put on that face that didn't scare her, but that might make someone say, someday, *"Chill'è 'nu guaglione con la faccia buona e i pensieri cattivi."* Sure, a young man with a sweet face and evil thoughts. And who kept bad company. Where did they come up with all the vicious knowledge they had? Once you have that kind of knowledge, there's no way of getting rid of it. She was reminded of a proverb of sorts that was familiar to her from her childhood: *"A chi pazzèa c' 'o ciuccio, non mancano i calci."* If you play with the donkey, there's no shortage of kicks. But who was *'o ciuccio,* who was the donkey in question? She could just picture her boy Nicolas spending his time with the donkey of the proverb, and it wouldn't take much to peel him away. *'O ciuccio* is afraid. But maybe, and as she thought these things she turned to straighten a silk dress that had been left on the table, just maybe it was me who first put the evil thought in his head. She ran her hand through her thick, mutinous head of hair and studied *Escucha mucho* as he ran the iron over a white shirt. "Take care there, that's a Fusaro shirt, you know." There was no need to say it, but she said it all the same. And she was reminded of a Sunday afternoon, many years ago. Back then she'd had a *malo sentire*—a bad feeling—that only now she was able to tie to the bad thoughts, the donkey, and the day at police headquarters. All four of them had been down by the water, not far from Villa Pignatelli. She was pushing Christian's stroller. It was hot out. The sun was setting fire to metal roller blinds and rummaging amid palm trees and bushes, as if trying to slaughter all surviving shade.

Nicolas was trotting along at a quick pace, and his father was barely able to keep up with him. Then, all of a sudden, a brutal silence, a sharp blade of silence, and the sounds that followed it. Someone walks into an establishment, maybe a restaurant. First you hear one gunshot, then another. The people on the sidewalks freeze, some of them scatter and vanish. And even the traffic down along the waterfront seems to fall silent. The sound of tables being overturned. Glasses smashing. Those are the sounds they hear and Mena hands the stroller to her husband and grabs Nicolas by the scruff of his neck. She feels a sort of effort as she holds him. No one abandons their post, it's like that game, freeze tag, when if you're touched you have to stand rooted to the ground like a statue. Then out of the club's front door comes a skinny, skinny guy, his tie loosened, his sunglasses stuck to his forehead. He looks around, and what he sees is space, and a street that a short distance ahead turns at a right angle. He seems to have no hesitation, he lunges forward and covers those few yards, veering to the right and then, spotting a parked car, he lies flat on the ground and, making a series of small but extremely quick movements, slides under the car. The man with the gun comes out into the sunshine, takes a step, and then stops, too, just as all the others are motionless around him. Then, though, he notices a man on the opposite sidewalk looking at him and gesturing, pointing at that car, around the corner, not far away. A tiny, barely noticeable gesture that's underscored by all the motionlessness that surrounds it. The man doesn't hurry off in search of the guy who slithered under the car. He even takes a moment, a short pause. He strokes his weapon, he squats down easily, he lowers the pistol to street level, parallel to the asphalt, his cheek pressed against the car door, like a doctor listening to a patient's heartbeat. And that's when he fires. Twice, then a third time. And he goes on shooting, constantly moving the gun barrel in a new direction with each shot. Mena can feel Nicolas tugging forward. When the man who fired has made his escape, Nicolas twists out of Mena's grip and runs straight toward the parked sedan. "I see blood, I see blood," he cries loudly, pointing to a rivulet running out from under the car, and at that point he kneels down and observes what the others cannot see. Mena runs forward to yank him away, hauling him by his striped T-shirt. "There's no blood," his father says, "that's just jam." Nicolas ignores him, he wants to see the dead body. His mother manages to drag him away, with some effort. She can sense that her family is suddenly becoming the true protagonist of that scene. The blood, with the assistance of the slight slope of the street, is now streaming in rivulets. Mena only manages to haul the little boy to a safe distance, yanking him, shoving him, but without managing to rid him of that bold, fearless curiosity, that game.

Every so often, that afternoon comes to mind, and her son comes to mind, at the age of the photograph she has hanging on the wall of her shop. Something claws at her stomach when it does, a vise, a pair of pliers. *Ch'aggio fatto?* What have I done, she asks herself, going back to the iron with an impetuous fury, and it strikes her that that implement, that shop, that work of washing, arranging, grooming also has something to do with her duties as a mother. Nicolas has no fear, she tells herself, and she's afraid to admit it. But that's the way matters stand: she can see it. That face, kissed all over by youth, full of sky, forget about *blue sky*, that face refuses to let itself be overshadowed by bad thoughts, it tucks them under the skin and goes on emanating light. For some time now she's been thinking of taking him to the shop with her, after school. But what shop, but what school? She's tempted to smile. The idea of Nicolas taking the Peruvian's place and pressing a gleaming white shirt sleeve. She decides that maybe he's better off where he is. But where is he? And to keep from letting herself be infected by the shiver that's starting to crawl across her flesh, she goes back to the shop's front door, and she feels beautiful there, with the eyes of the world on her.

THE WEDDING

The day before the wedding they all had to show up to attend a lightning course in catering. Copacabana had chosen a maître d' who'd presided over dozens of weddings like this one; people even said that he'd been at Asinara Prison when Cutolo got married, that it was he who'd cut the wedding cake. Bullshit, obviously, but he was a trusted individual. When Nicolas and the others arrived at the restaurant, riding a herd of sputtering motor scooters, the maître d' was waiting for them at the tradesman's entrance. He was of an indeterminate age, somewhere between fifty and seventy, cadaverous, with jaundiced, jutting cheekbones. He stood there, stock-still, in a Dolce & Gabbana suit: slim tie, black trousers and jacket, gleaming shoes, dazzling white shirt. It all fit him to a T, Lord only knows, but on him it somehow seemed wasted.

They parked their motor scooters, continuing to do the same thing they'd done while riding: namely, shouting and telling one another to fuck off. Copacabana had told them that the maître d' would meet them, and that he'd be able to tell them all they needed to know, how to move, which dishes to bring, what timing to follow, proper behavior. In other words, he'd be the commanding general of this gang of improvised waiters. A gang that was missing Biscottino, who was still too young to be credible as a waiter, and Drago', who was a cousin of the bride, and therefore an invited guest. The maître d' had received a list of their names in advance and had supplied them with uniforms.

The man in Dolce & Gabbana cleared his throat—a shrill sound, incongruous, which made everyone turn around—and then pointed a bony finger at the tradesman's entrance and disappeared inside. Tucano was about to say something, but Nicolas smacked him on the back of the neck and followed the man. In single file, and without a word, the others went in as well, and found themselves in the kitchen.

The newlyweds-to-be wanted elegance and austerity. Everyone was to be wearing outfits by D&G—Viola's favorite designers. The maître d', in a shrill, thin voice that did nothing to help pin down his exact age, handed out the uniforms, still in their garment bags, and ordered them into the storage area to change into them. When they came back, he had them line up against the immaculate stainless-steel wall that housed the burners and then pulled out the list of names.

"Ciro Somma."

Pesce Moscio stepped forward. He'd fastened the suit trousers the way he'd fasten his usual oversized rapper baggies: low on the waist so you could see the elastic waistband of his Gucci underpants. Pesce Moscio loved to wobble in his clothes, so that the folds and drapery would hide those extra pounds, but the maître d' quickly made it clear to him with the same pointing finger as earlier that this wasn't right, that he needed to pull up his billowing Zouave britches.

"Vincenzo Esposito." Possibly one of the most common names in Naples.

Lollipop and Stavodicendo both said, "Present," and each raised his hand. They'd been classmates ever since elementary school, and every time attendance was taken the same little skit played out.

"The one with the Swiss cheese face," said the maître d'. Stavodicendo blushed, inflaming even more the acne that devastated his cheeks. "You're fine, but stand up straight. You'll be in charge of getting the plates off the table, that way the guests won't have to look you in the face."

These kids certainly weren't used to being treated this way; still, Nicolas drummed it into them that the day had to come off smoothly. At all costs.

And that meant they were also going to have to put up with this jerk-off of a maître d'.

Lollipop smiled behind his little soul patch of a beard; despite his age, fourteen, he had the whiskers of a grown man. He'd designed a narrow line of beard that ran from his sideburns down to his chin, then along the lower lip, and back up the other side to complete the circuit. The shirt fit him to perfection, thanks to the hours he spent defining his abs in the gym, and the trousers concealed the skinny little legs which he neglected, focusing on the upper part of his body, including the gull-wing eyebrows.

"You, beanpole," said the maître d', pointing at Briato'. "You'll be in charge of the cake, it's going to be seven layers, and I need someone tall enough to reach the top." Briato' really couldn't get that tie to hang straight over the curve of his belly, but his black hair swept back with all that gel—well, that was stupendous.

"Agostino De Rosa."

Cerino didn't look right at all. He'd bleached his hair—when Nicolas laid eyes on him, he'd lost his temper: *stava 'na chiavica*, he thought to himself in dialect, he looked like shit—and his shirt collar wasn't enough to cover the tattoo he had on his chest: a fiery red sun whose rays extended all the way up to his Adam's apple. The maître d' grabbed him by the collar and yanked it upward a couple of times, but there was no concealing those rays. If it had been up to him, the maître d' would have sent him packing with a swift kick in the ass, this wasn't how you turned up, but Copacabana had warned him to take it easy, and so he went directly to the last names on the list. He called them en masse, he wanted to get an idea of how they'd move in the presence of crystal and porcelain.

"Nicolas Fiorillo, Giuseppe Izzo, Antonio Starita, Massimo Rea."

A ragged platoon broke away from the group. The maître d' walked over to the two shortest members—Dentino and Drone—who wore their suits as if they were pajamas (they'd rolled up the sleeves and the pant legs to keep them from dragging on the floor) and gave them each two dishes, one for each hand. Then he turned to Tucano, refrained from saying a word because by now time was running short, and handed him a silver serving tray. He'd arranged a handful of champagne flutes on the tray, and now the crystal glasses were tinkling against one another. He spent a little more time studying Nicolas, and concluded that those broad shoulders, lithe physique, and solid, powerful legs could tolerate a different array of weights. He asked him to hold out his arms—the suit adhered to him like a second skin—and arranged two plates on the right and two more on the left, one on each forearm and one on each palm. Then he asked all four of them to take a turn around the island that divided the kitchen into two equal parts. Dentino and Drone performed the circuit at something approaching a dead run, and the maître d' upbraided them. Their stride needed to be fluid, composed, they weren't at McDonald's, for Christ's sake. Tucano did well, in the end just one of the flutes tipped over onto its side, but without taking the other glasses with it as it fell. Nicolas completed the round, as wobbly as if he were walking a tightrope. But in the end, he too managed to come through unscathed. The maître d' lifted his cadaverous hand to his chin and scratched it, then he said, in a resigned tone of voice: "Again."

Nicolas set the plates down on the island and strode over to the maître d', who had to lift up onto his tiptoes to meet his glare. "Are we done now, *vicchiarie'*?" he asked, calling him "little old man" in Neapolitan.

The maître d' didn't turn a hair, and just rose a little higher on the tips of his toes. Then he dropped down, with both heels flat on the floor. "You're ready" was all he said.

Copacabana knew he was running a risk, since he was a fugitive from the law, by taking part in such a prominently visible wedding, with so many guests: the rumor of his return would spread in next to no time, even though at this kind of a wedding the guests were all invited to leave their cell phones at the front table, and to use them only in the "phone room."

While Nicolas tried on his uniform and practiced serving the various dishes, he sidled over to Copacabana, who was supervising the whole operation. He was all cleaned up. Now his hair wasn't flying in all directions, maybe he'd even gotten a dye job. His gaze was a little more focused, but his eyes still showed that same reddish patina.

"Copacaba', don't you think it's dangerous . . . in front of all these people? Letting everyone see you, I mean."

"Even more dangerous not to let them see me, to stay hidden. Do you know what that means?"

"*Adda murì fràtemo.* May my brother die. That you're a fugitive, but they already know that."

"No, no, Nicolino . . . if you're at a wedding and you see an empty chair at a table, what do you do?"

"I let someone sit in it."

"Exactly, *'o zi*'! Bravo. Which means that if my chair at this wedding is empty, then the guys from San Giovanni a Teduccio will have one of their people sit in it. So you tell me, what's more dangerous, showing up at a wedding or hiding while you wait for them to come take your place?"

"You let yourself be seen to tell the Faellas, *sto ccà.* I'm here. This is my territory. I haven't gone anywhere."

"*Bra', staje imparanno.* Good boy, you're learning. I'll come with my wife and my children, they need to see me."

"I still think it's dangerous . . ."

"This place is full of eyes, *'e guagliune miei* are on the lookout . . . but I'm happy to see that you worry about your uncle Copacabana, that must mean I'm paying you enough . . ."

So began the beginning of the lavish party in the palace in Sorrento. Nicolas could see it all before his eyes, it was up to them to play their part as waiters, to be good actors, they'd all be performing against that brightly lit backdrop. They needed to plunge in headfirst. Get a glimpse of the world. Off they went, chop chop, in single file. There was something magical. And an expectation, a sense of expectation, that all his fellow *paranzini* wore on their faces, just as he did.

The celebration that followed the ceremony was lavish, and Copacabana boasted that he hadn't overlooked a single detail in organizing the event. He liked to say that if it was only "too much"—*troppo* was the word he used—then it wasn't enough. It had to go beyond *troppo*, because *abbondanza* is the twin sister of the good. Doves? By the dozen. Every course served at the banquet was to be greeted with a spectacular flight of liberated doves. Musical entertainment? The finest *neomelodico* musicians of the province of Naples, and for nightfall he'd arranged for a samba crew with twenty dancers. Furnishings? The hall had to be full. And Copacabana always tried to utter this word, *pieno*, as close as possible to *troppo*. *"Tutto pieno, tutto troppo!"* All full, all too much! Statues, chandeliers, candelabra, plants, dishes, paintings, tables. Flowers everywhere, even in the bathrooms, and they all needed to be in hues of purple, in homage to the bride. And balloons, which were to be dropped from the ceiling after every burst of doves that flew into the air. And extravaganzas of Sicilian *cassatina*, cakes, five first courses, five entrées, a cornucopia of foodstuffs. And last of all, a tapestry, forty feet long, that he'd found who knows where, covering a section of wall with an allegorical scene of Good Government. Copacabana had decided to place it behind the newlywed couple as a mark of their auspicious beginnings.

There were a great many tables, and Nicolas was just heading out to serve. Everything was under control. There was the table where White was sitting, with Orso Ted, Chicchirichì, and all the *guaglioni* of Copacabana's *paranza* who were running the street markets and learning how to run the stadium. There were lots of them and they were always higher than hell. They weren't much older than Nicolas and his gang. There was the table where Drago' and his family were sitting. Given that he was a cousin of the bride, he was sprawled in his chair, enjoying the spectacle of his friends all busy serving tables. His jacket was askew, as was his boxer's nose, and the knot on his tie hung loose as he rejected every dish, sending back one after another, with critiques befitting a five-star chef.

Then there was the reunion with Alvaro, who'd been given a special prison furlough to take part in the wedding. A marginal guest, who hadn't even been given a seat at the table. He was outside with the others, playing cards on the hoods of the parked cars. Nicolas would bring him the various dishes, and all he'd say was: "Bravo, bravo!"

The wedding followed its rhythms. Slow and fast. Then faster still, then very, very slow, like molasses, sticky and adhesive.

"Now here comes the elevator of sensuality," Briato' whispered to Nicolas, as he was stepping out of the kitchen with an armful of dishes.

"You're sex disguised as a woman," Drone whispered as well, into Nicolas's other ear. Maraja lengthened his gait and walked into the dining room. If he'd remained there, he'd have dropped several platefuls of *pennette al salmone* with lumpfish caviar.

They had a long evening still ahead of them. There was another singer to be heard from, and then the samba dancers were scheduled to make their entrance. A group of guests, standing on their chairs, were shouting the title of the *neomelodico* singer's most popular song while waiting for him to take the stage. From behind a curtain, which like so many other items at that wedding was in a shade of purple, burst Alvaro, instead of the *neomelodico*. He was moving at a run, his comb-over flopping to one side. He made straight for Copacabana's table: "The cops! Get out, get out!" and then he vanished, heading straight back where he'd come from, hitting one of the guests who was standing on his chair and knocking him flat to the floor. The comic effect died away quickly. Twenty or so plainclothes police officers burst into the room from four different entrances, to block all escape routes. Something must have gone astray in the surveillance system, perhaps Copacabana had overlooked one of the security cameras, or else the carabinieri had received a tip and had come over the roofs, eluding the eyes of the lookouts. Alvaro must have noticed them between one hand of cards and the next. While the carabinieri were passing between the tables and the murmuring of the guests rose over the silence that had fallen the minute the officers burst into the room, Copacabana slid over to the podium, and with a glance signaled to the drummer to move away from his instrument so he could take his seat. He sat there, drumsticks in hand, watching the policemen as they arrested a couple who belonged to the Faella clan. Arms were jerked, voices raised shrilly, threats uttered. The usual script, with the usual finale: handcuffs. The couple had a small baby, and they entrusted the boy to none other than Copacabana's wife: a kiss on the forehead to the newborn and they were gone. They put the baby in the woman's arms without a word. Micione, who had been sitting until that moment with his arms crossed, suddenly leaped to his feet and said: "A hand for the inspector, he wants to wind up in the newspapers, which is why he's come to interrupt my wedding." They all started clapping, even the married couple with their arms locked with the carabinieri made one last effort at jerking away from their grip so they could clap their hands. They went straight to their targets, the carabinieri did, they didn't even ask for identification. Then they grabbed another couple of people who had violated the terms of their house arrest to take part in the wedding. In the meantime, Copacabana was starting to convince himself that maybe they hadn't come for him, that there were much more appetizing fish than him to fry at that wedding. He set down his drumsticks and allowed himself to catch his breath.

"Sarnataro, Pasquale, what are you doing, freelancing as a drummer these days?" The inspector was making his way through the guests, and he gestured to two of his men to approach the stage; it wasn't even necessary to give them any further instructions.

While he was lying there immobilized on the floor, with a carabiniere's knees in the middle of his back, Copacabana turned to Diego Faella and said: "'O Micio', don't you worry. By the time your baby's ready to be baptized, I'll be back."

The boys had stood frozen to the spot, watching the scene, their trays still shaking in their hands out of fear. "You see? I told you it was a dumb move to appear in public like this," Nicolas told Agostino. The police sweep was over but the party continued. The show must go on, the bride demanded it. This was her day, and those arrests weren't going to be enough to ruin it. And so Nicolas and the others resumed their duties, as if nothing had happened. Finally the last singer came on, followed by the dancers. But at midnight it was all over. The atmosphere was spoiled, and anyway the newlyweds had to get up early. An airplane to Brazil awaited them: Copacabana had even taken care of their honeymoon, they would be staying in his hotel.

The young waiters went to change clothes in the kitchen. It was time to get out of these duds and get their pay. They'd sweated for it. Nicolas, in particular, was disenchanted. Pomp and circumstanace, no doubt. Wretched excess, for sure. Power. Lots and lots of power. But he'd been expecting silver serving trays piled high with cocaine, and instead he'd had to look on as burlap sacks picked up in some antique shop somewhere were passed around, requesting donations from the wedding guests for the families of men serving time. Those sacks clanked and rustled, Nicolas could hear them whenever he walked past, and he personally was tempted to just grab them and run. Instead, that evening they pocketed not a single penny—no salary and no tips. They left carrying only the bombonières full of favors—in this case, the bombonière was an enormous stuffed blowfish, complete with spikes. The reason for choosing blowfish as a gift bag was a mystery to one and all. Still, Nicolas decided to take it home as proof that he'd done the evening's work, to allay his father's mistrust—unlike his mother, Nicolas's father hadn't believed him when he'd said he was going to be working as a waiter.

After all, it was still early. Nicolas, Dentino, and Briato' joined up in the back room, which really never closed, not even at Christmas. There was the whole array of the Capelloni, White, Carlito's Way, Chicchirichì, Orso Ted, and Selvaggio. Alvaro was there, too, and no one had seen him since the roundup. He wanted to say so long to everyone before going back to prison.

"Alva', did you come back to give us our salary?" asked Nicolas. With Copacabana in Poggioreale, things had become complicated for them, but Nicolas wanted his money. They were being paid a hundred euros apiece for twelve hours of work. If they'd been selling hash, they would have earned ten times as much.

"What are you doing, an honest day's work? An asshole's day's work?" asked White. He was still high out of his skull, and he was clinging to the foosball table.

"*Overo è*," Dentino said. "True enough."

"Anyone who works is an asshole."

"Ah, because we don't work from dawn to dusk?" Briato' broke in.

"We're always out on the streets, on our motor scooters. But what we do isn't work," said Nicolas. "Work is for assholes, and for slaves. And in three hours of work we make what my father earned in a month."

"Well, that's not really true," said White.

"But it will be," Nicolas promised. He was really talking to himself, and in fact no one paid any attention to him, in part because their attention was now focused entirely on White, who was lining up a tidy grid of lines of coke on the side of the foosball table.

"You want a snort, *guagliu'*?" asked White.

Nicolas and his friends were gazing in enchantment at the powder. This certainly wasn't the first time they'd seen it, but it was the first time they'd seen it so openly available. They just needed to take a step, lower their heads, and snort it up.

"*Grazie, brò*," said Briato'. He knew what he needed to do, and so did the others. They stood in line, each waiting his turn, and took part in the banquet.

"Come on, Alva', you have some, too," said White.

"No, no, no, no, what is this filth? Plus, I need to get back."

"Don't worry about it, we'll give you a ride; come on, it's late."

White had his black SUV parked outside. It looked like he'd brought it straight over from the dealership. Nicolas, Dentino, and Briato' had been invited to join the crew, and they accepted gladly. Their exhaustion had been completely swept away by that first snort of coke. They felt euphoric, ready for anything.

White kept an arm around Alvaro's shoulders. "So you like this car?" and Alvaro replied, "Yes, sure!" and he got in front. The boys crowded in the back.

The SUV was sailing along smoothly. White drove with precision, impeccably even though he was loaded, or maybe precisely because he was loaded. The road that led to Poggioreale wound through the lights that reminded Nicolas of novaed stars that he'd once seen in his science textbook. Then it happened.

The car as it slams on its brakes and then swerves at the last minute and plows down a dirt road. Then another jerking halt, even more decisive, and the car slams to a stop. The three of them sitting in the back have to throw up their arms to protect themselves, to keep from banging against the seat backs. When the recoil whips their bodies back, they all glimpse in a flash White's arm stretching out, a pistol that appeared out of nowhere gripped in his fist, his index finger squeezing twice. Boom boom. Alvaro's head looks like a balloon popping: a shard of cranium sticks to the car window, another scrap on the windshield, and the body flops over as if the soul had just fled.

"Oh, but why?" asked Nicolas. In his voice, more than alarm, the urgent need to know. Dentino and Briato' sat there, hands still clapped over their ears, eyes staring straight at the same gooey mass splattered onto the steering wheel, but Nicolas was already capable of reacting. *He* still had his brain, anyway, and it was working overtime. He wanted to understand the reason for Alvaro's execution, what transgression had led to his death, and what it meant that White had brought them along for the ride, whether this was more of a test, an honor, or a warning.

"*Ll'aggio fatto pecché me l'ha 'itto Copacabana.*" He did it because Copacabana had told him to.

Now the lights had changed color, they'd taken on a purplish tinge, similar to the theme of the wedding. White ought to have brought along the Capelloni to give him a hand with the passenger, but instead that was their job now. Because they were *guaglioni*, minors with no criminal records, nobodies?

"But when did he tell you?"

"He said: Give my regards to Pierino, the one who sang best tonight. When he was arrested, that's when he told me."

"But when did he tell you?" Nicolas asked again. All that had reached him of White's response had been the sound of it, not the meaning.

"*Quando l'hanno arrestato, te l'aggio ritto. Damme 'na mane, ja', levammo sta schifezza 'a ccà.*" His response came brusquely. When Copacabana was arrested, like I told you. Now help me get this filth cleaned up. The blood that had soaked the car roof dripped onto the now-empty seat. Both Dentino and Briato' kept their hands up even after the SUV took off with a jerk and retraced the route to the club, until they were finally in the back room again. White had driven just as confidently as a short while before, and the kids paid no attention to his ranting, his assurances that Alvaro would be given a proper funeral, they weren't just going to dump his corpse somewhere, and how they were going to have to get reorganized now that Copacabana had been taken in. Everything needed to be thought through, adjusted, and White kept talking. He talked and talked and talked. He never stopped, not even when he slammed on the brakes for a stop sign and Alvaro's corpse, in the trunk, rolled forward and the impact made a *thud* that drowned out his words for a fraction of a second.

When they got to the back room they parted ways without a word, each climbing onto his own motor scooter and heading home. Nicolas sailed along on his Beverly at a cruising speed that allowed him to let his thoughts roam more freely than usual. He kept the motor scooter in the center of the road with one hand on the handlebars, while with the other hand he toked on a joint that White had offered him before he, too, vanished into the night. What was going to happen now? Would they go on dealing? For whom? The smell of the sea wafted into the streets and, for a moment, Nicolas even thought about forgetting it all and just going to take a swim somewhere. But then the blinking yellow traffic lights brought him back to his Beverly and he revved the engine to get through an empty intersection. Alvaro counted for nothing, he'd met an ugly fate, but after all, his destiny had been predetermined; Copacabana, though, had been caught like an ordinary *guaglione*, and hadn't even bothered to react, simply hiding behind a drum set. Lots of talk, lots of words. Albania, Brazil, bucketsful of money, fabulous wedding celebrations, and then he'd wound up just like any other loser, like any old ordinary *mariuolo*. No, Nicolas wasn't going to end up like that. Better die trying. Wasn't it Pesce Moscio who'd had that phrase of 50 Cent's tattooed on his forearm, *Get Rich or Die Tryin'*?

Nicolas revved his scooter again, and this time the fumes of the exhaust covered over the smell of the sea. He took a nice deep breath and decided that the first thing he needed to do was get hold of a pistol.

THE CHINESE PISTOL

esce Moscio had immediately offered to go pay Copacabana a visit in prison. There were too many questions to be asked and lots of answers to be obtained. What was going to happen now? Who was going to occupy the now-vacant throne of Forcella? Nicolas felt like when he was a little boy and he'd gone to jump off the rocks into the waves off Lido Mappatella. He knew that once he was in free fall, he'd no longer be afraid, but still—just before jumping—his legs always shook. And in fact, his legs were now trembling, but not out of fear. He was excited. He was about to plunge into the life he'd always dreamed of, but first he needed to hear it directly from Copacabana.

When Pesce Moscio came back from the prison, the guys all gathered in the back room. Nicolas immediately cut off all description of the visiting room, the wooden counter, and the low pane of glass that barely separated convict and visitor. "I could even smell Copacabana's breath. Like a sewer." What he wanted to hear was the words, his exact words.

"'O Pesce, what did he tell you?"

"I already told you, Maraja. We need to be patient. We're all his children. We don't need to worry."

"And so what did he tell you?" Nicolas insisted. He was pacing the half-empty back room. There was only a little old man who'd fallen asleep at a slot machine, and the bartender who was somewhere back in the kitchen.

Pesce Moscio turned his hat around with the bill in the back, as if it were the visor that was somehow keeping Nicolas from understanding.

"Maraja, how am I supposed to tell you? That guy was sitting there looking back at me. Don't worry, stay cool. He said that, *adda murì mammà*, he'd take care of Alvaro's funeral, that he'd been a good man. Then he stood up and told me that we have the keys to Forcella in the palms of our hands, some bullshit like that."

Nicolas's legs were no longer shaking.

Nicolas and Tucano found themselves all alone at Alvaro's funeral. Besides the two of them, there was an old lady, who they learned was Alvaro's mother, and a woman in a miniskirt, with the body of a twenty-year-old and, screwed onto the top of it, a face that bore the marks of all the johns she'd seen and serviced. Because there was no doubt about it, she was one of the Romanian whores that Copacabana used to send Alvaro, and from what they could tell, she was one of the fondest, given the fact that she was standing there next to his casket with a handkerchief in her hand.

"Giovan Battista, Giovan Battista," the mother kept saying, and now she was leaning on the other woman, who might well have been a whore, but at least she'd had some genuine feeling for her unlucky son.

"Giovan Battista?" asked Tucano. "For real, what an absurd name, and what a shitty way to die."

" 'O White is a piece of shit," said Nicolas. And for a second he tried to put together the image of Alvaro's shattered brain with the last farewell of that woman with fine firm legs.

He was sorry about Alvaro, though he wasn't exactly sure why. He didn't even know if what he was experiencing was sorrow. That poor wretch had always taken them seriously, and that had to count for something. They didn't even wait for the ceremony to be over; they just left the church, with other things already on their minds.

"How much money have you got on you?" asked Nicolas.

"Not much. But I've got three hundred euros or so at home."

"Good, I got four hundred today myself. Let's go buy a handgun."

"Where are we going to buy this handgun?"

They'd come to a halt on the steps of the church, because that seemed like an important question to resolve; they looked each other in the eye. Nicolas wasn't thinking of any particular pistol, he'd just done a little research on the Internet. What he needed was a gat to pull out when the time was right.

"Someone told me the Chinese sell plenty of old pistols," he said.

"But excuse me, the Capelloni have more guns than they need, why don't we try to get some from them?"

"No, we can't. They're System people, they'd get word to Copacabana in prison immediately. In no time he'd know everything, and he'd never give us the authorization, because it's not our time yet. But the Chinese don't talk to the System."

"But who ever told them whether it's time or not time? They took their time, and we need to take ours."

To Nicolas's mind, it was a bullshit question to start with. The kind of question only someone who will never be in command would even think of asking. Time, as Nicolas understood it, presented itself in only two forms, and there was no middle ground between them. He always kept in mind an old story from the quarter, one of those stories that treads the fine line of truth, but is never called into question except to add details that reinforce the story's moral. There was this kid, a guy with super-long feet. Two guys had come up to him and asked the time of day.

"It's four thirty," he'd replied.

"What time is it?" they'd asked him again, and he'd repeated the same answer as before.

"Is it your time to command?" they'd asked at last, before shooting him dead in the middle of the street. A story that made no sense, except to Nicolas, who'd immediately absorbed the lesson. Time. The instantaneous time of a claim to power, and the time smeared behind bars to let it grow. Now it was his turn to figure out how best to use his time, and that wasn't the moment to lay claim to a power he hadn't yet gathered.

Without a word, Nicolas headed for his Beverly and Tucano followed along, climbing on behind him, well aware he'd said too much. They went by Nicolas's house to get the money, then they shot over to China-town, to Gianturco. A ghost quarter, that's what Gianturco looks like, abandoned industrial sheds, a few little factories still chugging along, and warehouses for Chinese merchandise, adding red to a landscape that would otherwise smack only of grayness and anger etched on shattered walls and rusty roller blinds. Gianturco—which in Italian smacks of the east, of the color yellow, of fields of grain—is actually only the surname of a cabi-net minister, Emanuele Gianturco, a minister in the newly united Italy, who championed civil rights as a guarantee of justice. A jurist long since deprived of his given name, who now stands for streets lined with aban-doned warehouses, who now reeks of chemical refineries. It was once an industrial quarter, when there was still industry here. But this is how Nicolas had always seen it. He'd been here a few times as a child, when he still played on the soccer team of the Church of the Madonna del Salvatore. He'd started at age six with Briato', one of them striker, the other goalie. But then it happened that during a game in the Under-12 championship among the parish churches, the referee had favored the Church of the Sacred Heart's team, on which the sons of four city councilmen played. There'd been a penalty kick and Briato' had managed to block it, but the referee had called for a retake because Nicolas had crossed the line be-fore the whistle. It was true, he had, but being such a stickler over a parish church soccer match, after all, maybe they could have turned a blind eye, after all, they were just kids, after all, it was just a soccer match. At the second penalty kick, Briato' had blocked the ball again, but this time, too, Nicolas had set foot across the line before the whistle, and the referee had called for the penalty kick to be repeated a third time. The third time, all eyes were on Nicolas, who didn't move a muscle on this round. But the ball went into the net.

Briato's father, the engineer Giacomo Capasso, with an impassive face and a slow stride, walked onto the field. With the most absolute calm he put his hand in his pocket, pulled out a switchblade knife, and gutted the soccer ball. With flat, undramatic gestures, with no visible sign of nervous-ness, he folded the blade shut, put the knife away in his pocket, and sud-denly came face-to-face, nose-to-nose, with the referee, who was cursing, red-faced. Despite the fact that Capasso was shorter, he still dominated the situation. He spoke curtly and imperatively to the referee: *"Tu si' 'n omm' 'e mmerd'*—you're a piece of shit—and that's all anyone can say about you." The torn ball on the ground was a green light for a general incursion onto the field, a full-fledged invasion with the full array of parents and children shouting in rage, with, here and there, a tear or two.

Nicolas and Fabio were taken by the hand by the engineer and led off the field. Nicolas felt safe, clinging to the hand that had held the knife minutes ago. He felt important, clutching that man's hand.

Nicolas's father, on the other hand, was tense, disgusted to have witnessed that scene in a crowd of children, on a little parish-church soccer field. But there was nothing he could say to the father of Fabio Briato'. He led his son over to the side of field, and that was that. When they got home, all he said to his wife was: "This boy's not playing soccer anymore." Nicolas went to bed without eating dinner: not because he was upset about quitting the team, as his parents mistakenly believed, but for the shame—*lo scuorno*—to have had the misfortune of a father who was unable to command respect, a man who counted for less than nothing.

That marked the end of Briato's and Nicolas's soccer careers, as in the most classic story of friends and kindred spirits; they'd lost all desire to train. They went on kicking a soccer ball around, but without discipline, on the streets.

Nicolas and Tucano parked the Beverly in front of a Chinese department store stuffed with merchandise.

The walls seemed to be on the verge of exploding with all the items packed inside. Shelves stacked high with lightbulbs, home power tools, stationery and school supplies, unmatched suits, children's games, firecrackers, packets of tea and sun-faded boxes of cookies, and coffeemakers, diapers, picture frames, even an array of motor scooters—you could even buy the parts off them. Impossible to find any rationale for the way those objects had been arranged, save for a rigorous space-saving principle.

"Sti cinesi che hanno cumbinato, tutta Napoli s'hanno pigliato, poco

ci manca e pure 'o pesone l'amm' 'a pavà!" As he was singing Pino d'Amato's song, Tucano rang the call bell that announced a new customer.

"Eh, still, that's the truth," said Nicolas, "sooner or later we really are going to have to pay rent to the Chinese to be able to live here."

"But how do you know that they sell weapons in this shop?" They wandered up and down the aisles, past young Chinese men who were trying to squeeze hangers onto a rack that was already full to overflowing, or else climbing up on teetering ladders to stack up the umpteenth ream of paper.

"I was on a chat, and they told me that this is the place to come."

"No kidding?"

"Yeah, they sell lots of things here. We're supposed to talk to Han."

"If you ask me, these guys make more money than we do," said Tucano.

"No doubt about it. People buy more lightbulbs than they do chunks of hash."

"I'd only ever buy hash, forget about lightbulbs."

"That's because you're a drug addict," Nicolas replied with a laugh and squeezed Tucano's shoulder. Then he spoke to a shop clerk: "Excuse me, is Han here?"

"Che vulite?" the shop clerk replied in perfect Neapolitan. What do you want? The two of them stood staring at the Chinese shop clerk and failed to notice that the anthill they'd walked into had frozen to a halt. Even the shop clerk standing poised on the ladder looked down on them, with a notebook in one hand.

"Che vulite?" the first Chinese clerk insisted, and Nicolas was about to repeat the question when a middle-aged woman whom they'd barely noticed behind the cash registers started screeching at them.

"Out, get out, go away, get out!" She hadn't even bothered to get up from the perch where she had to sit all day taking in cash. From that distance, Nicolas and Tucano saw only a fat woman with teased-out hair and a flower-print shirt waving her arms at them to get back out the door they'd come in through.

"Eh, signora, what's the matter?" Nicolas tried to understand, but the woman just went on shrieking, "Get out, both of you!" and the clerks who had at first seemed to be scattered throughout the big store were now encircling them.

"These fucking Chinese," Tucano commented, dragging Nicolas along behind him. "So you see it was a bullshit mistake to get information in a chat room . . .

"These fucking Chinese. *Adda murì mammà*, when we're in charge, we'll kick them out of here," said his friend. "We'll kick all them out of here. There are more Chinese than ants," and as a form of moral redemption, he swung his hand at a good-luck cat that sat on a fake antique side table next to the entrance. The cat flew into the air and landed on the price scanner of one of the cash registers, cracking it, but the furious woman paid no attention, and kept on shouting in her loop of insults.

As they got on the Beverly, Tucano kept saying: "I knew it had to be bullshit," and they drove off in the direction of Via Galileo Ferraris. Away from Chinatown. They'd accomplished nothing.

A short distance farther along, a motorcycle pulled up behind the scooter. The scooter sped up, and the motorbike revved its engine too, speeding up and staying close. Now they were really moving, determined to reach the stretch of road that empties out onto Piazza Garibaldi, where they could get lost in traffic. Swerving, darting between buses and cars, Vespas, pedestrians. Tucano kept craning his neck to check on the progress of whomever it might be that was following them, trying to gauge their intentions. The other guy was Chinese, impossible to say his age, a face he didn't recognize, but he didn't seem pissed off. At a certain point, he started beeping his horn and waving his arms, gesturing for them to pull over. They'd turned down Corso Arnaldo Lucci and come to a halt just before the Central Station, which was the boundary between Naples's Chinatown and the casbah. Nicolas slammed the brakes on and the motorbike stopped right next to them. Both of them turned their eyes to the Chinese man's delicate hands, but he gave no sign of pulling out a knife, or anything worse. Instead he reached over to shake hands and introduce himself: "I'm Han."

"Ah, so you're Han? Then why the fuck did *mammeta* kick us out of the store?" Tucano snapped.

"She's not my mother.'

"Ah, well, if she's not your mother she sure does look like it."

"What are you looking for?" Han asked, jutting his chin out a little.

"You know what we're looking for . . ."

"Then you need to come with me. Are you going to follow me or not?"

"Where are you taking us?"

"To a garage."

"Sure." They nodded and followed him. They were going back the way they'd come, but retracing your route in Naples can cost you hours in traffic.

The Chinese never dreamed of going all the way around the piazza; instead, the motor scooters took advantage of the gap for pedestrians between the concrete posts, and emerged in front of the Hotel Terminus. From there, back onto Via Galileo Ferraris and another left turn onto Via Gianturco.

Nicolas and Tucano realized they were going around in circles when they made their umpteenth left turn onto Via Brin. They'd left bright colors and commotion behind them. Via Brin looked like a ghost street. There were signs announcing warehouses for rent everywhere, and Han stopped outside one of these. He tilted his head, gesturing for them to follow him inside—better get the two motorbikes inside. Once they turned through the main gate, they found themselves in a courtyard lined with warehouses, some of them abandoned and tumbledown, others packed to the rafters with bric-a-brac and junk of all kinds. They followed Han into a garage that seemed no different from any of the others, except that it was neat as a pin. In particular, there were toys, copies of famous brands, more or less barefaced counterfeits. Shelves upon colorful shelves lined with all manner of wonderful products. Just a few years ago a place like this would have driven them out of their minds with delight.

"So we finally discovered that Santa Claus's elves are Chinese."

Han laughed aloud. He was identical to all the other sales clerks in the shop, perhaps he'd been one of the crew who surrounded them in the shop; maybe he'd laughed with gusto in the faces of those two when they were trying to find him.

"How much can you afford?"

They had more than they admitted, but they started out low: "Two hundred euros."

"For two hundred euros I wouldn't have even started my motorbike, I don't have anything for that much."

"Then I guess we'd better go," said Tucano, ready to turn around and head out the exit.

"But if you guys can dig a little deeper, then I can offer you . . ."

He pushed aside boxes full of plastic machine guns, dolls, and plastic buckets and pails for the beach, and pulled out two pistols. "This is a Francotte, it's a revolver." He handed the one he'd identified to Nicolas.

"*Mamma mia*, it weighs a *cuofano*," he exclaimed, astonished at how heavy it was.

And it was heavy. It was an ancient revolver, an 8mm; the only attractive thing about it was the handle, smooth, wooden, heavily worn, like a stone that had been polished by time underwater. All the rest of it— barrel, trigger, cylinder—was a leaden gray, dotted with stains that wouldn't go away no matter how you buffed it, and it had that army surplus feel to it, or even worse, the feel of a gun used to shoot old Westerns, the kind that jam in two shots out of every three. But Nicolas didn't care. He rubbed the handle and then started squeezing the barrel, while Han and Tucano continued bickering.

"This one works, eh, they brought it to me from Belgium. It's a Belgian revolver. I can let you have it for a thousand euros . . ." Han was saying.

"Oh, to me it looks like a Colt," said Tucano.

"Eh, it's a *fratocucino* of the Colt."

"Does this thing shoot?"

"Yes, but it only has three bullets."

"I want to try it, otherwise I'm not buying it. And you've got to let me have it for six hundred."

"No, but really, this gun, if I sell it to a collector, I'll make five thousand euros. *T' 'o giuro*," Han swore in dialect.

Tucano tried out a few threats: "Sure you will, but then the collector, if you don't sell it to him, it's not like he's going to come around and burn down your warehouse, or have you arrested, or set fire to your shop."

Han kept his cool and turned to Nicolas to say: "Did you bring your sheepdog with you? Does he have to keep barking at me?"

Whereupon Tucano bared his teeth: "Keep it up and you'll see if we're all bark and no bite. Do you think we're not hooked up with the System?"

"Then they'll come for you."

"Who are they going to come for?!"

With every exchange they drew a little closer, until Nicolas put an end to the discussion with a flat: "Oh, Tuca'."

"No, seriously, now you've pissed me off, now get out of here, or else I'll have to use this pistol on the two of you," said Han. Now he had the knife by the handle, so to speak, but Nicolas had no interest in going any further, and dictated his conditions: "Oh, *cine'*, take it easy. We only want one, but it has to fire."

"Go on, give it a try," and Han put it in his hand. Nicolas couldn't even get the drum to swing out so he could load it. He tried a second time, but it was no good: "How the fuck is this thing supposed to work?" and he handed it to Han, showing his disappointment.

Han took back the gun and fired off a shot, nonchalantly, without even bracing his arm. Nicolas and Tucano leaped into the air the way you do when you hear an unexpected detonation, and it's not your conscious mind that's reacting, only your nerves. They both felt ashamed of that uncontrolled reaction.

The bullet had taken the head clean off a doll on a high shelf, leaving the pink torso motionless. Han just prayed they wouldn't ask him to make the same shot again.

"What are we going to do," asked Tucano, "with this hunk of junk?"

"For now this is the best we've got. Take it or leave it."

"We'll take it," Nicolas concluded. "Still, since it's a piece of crap, you can give it to us for five hundred euros, not a penny more."

Nicolas took the pistol home. He carried it jammed into his shorts, barrel pointed downward, scalding hot.

He walked, loose-limbed, down the hallway lined with white and green tiles. His father was waiting for him in the dining room. "We're eating dinner. Your mother will get home later."

"*Vabbuo'*," Nicolas acknowledged sullenly.

"Since when do you say *vabbuo*'! What kind of way is that to talk?"

"It's how I talk."

"You write better than you talk."

His father, wearing a plaid shirt, was sitting at the head of the table. From there he observed his son's gait as if he were the offspring of strangers. The dining room wasn't big, but it was clean, decent, almost in good taste: simple furniture, the set of good crystal glasses on display behind glass, a piece of Deruta pottery, an artifact from a trip to Umbria, which was usually used to serve fruit, tablecloths with fish patterns, and faded kilim carpets on the floor. They'd only overdone it with the standing lamps and ceiling lamps, but that was an old controversy: a compromise between the past (chandeliers) and the present (floor lamps). Mena wanted lots of light in that apartment; he would gladly have done without. There were plenty of books in the hallway and on a set of shelves in the living room.

"Call your brother and come sit down to dinner."

Nicolas did nothing more than raise his voice and call loudly, without moving: "Christian!"

His father had an outburst of anger, but Nicolas paid him no mind. He lowered the volume of his voice ever so slightly, and called his brother's name again. And this time his brother appeared, in shorts and a loose white shirt, and with a big, grateful smile lighting up his face. He went over and sat down immediately, dragging his chair across the floor.

"Hey, Christian, you know your mother doesn't want you to drag your chair. Pick that chair up."

He lifted up the chair even though he was fully seated on it, and did it with both eyes fixed on his elder brother, who was standing there motionless as a statue.

"Would you care to take a seat, Signor Vabbuò," snapped the father, and lifted the lid off the pan that he'd carried to the table. "I cooked you *pasta e spinaci*."

"Pasta with spinach? Where are we? Nisida Reform School?" Nicolas retorted.

"What do you know about what people eat at Nisida?"

"I know."

"He knows," his little brother repeated.

"And you keep your mouth shut," said his father as he dished out the food, and to the other boy: "Sit down, do me a favor." And Nicolas sat down in front of the plate of pasta and spinach with the pistol he'd bought from the Chinese guy stuck down the back of his underwear.

"What did you do today?" he asked.

"Nothing," said Nicolas.

"Who'd you see?"

"Nobody."

His father sat there with a forkful of pasta halfway to his mouth: "What's all this nothing? And who are all these nobodies?" He said it with a glance at Christian as if he was trying to coax him over to his side. But as he spoke, he remembered that he'd left the meat on the stove, and he stood up and vanished into the galley kitchen. And from there, he could be heard, still talking: "Nobody. *Chillo esce cu nisciuno.* This boy goes out with nobody. This boy does nothing, you get that? Nothing. And I work like a slave for all this nothing." He came out into the dining room with a serving tray full of steaks to repeat that last phrase: "I've worked like a slave for all this nothing."

Nicolas shrugged his shoulders and sketched patterns on the table-cloth with the tines of his fork.

"Go on: eat," said the father, because he'd noticed that the younger boy had cleaned his plate while the older one still hadn't touched a bite.

"So what did you do? Did you go to school? Wasn't there anyone else at school? Did they test you on history?" He was reeling off questions and the boy was sitting there like someone who didn't understand the language, with an expression of courteous indifference.

"Yeah, so eat something," the father went on, and Christian said: "Nico' is great."

"Great how? Great for what? You just need to shut up, and you, eat something," he said, speaking to Nicolas. "You do understand that you need to eat? You come home, you sit down at the table, and you eat."

"If I eat, then I'll get sleepy and I won't be able to study anymore," said Nicolas.

His father, angrily, regained his composure. "So are you going to study later?"

Nicolas knew where to strike his blow. At school he'd caught the attention of various of his teachers, especially on his compositions, because when a topic fired him up, there was no one who could outshine him. De Marino, his literature teacher, had told his father the first time they'd met at parent-teacher night: "Your son is talented, he has a very specific way of viewing the world and expressing those views. How to put this . . ." and he'd smiled. "Well, he knows how to shape the noise of the world and find the right words to describe it." Words that the boy's father had stitched into his chest and nurtured like a hen on a brood of eggs, repeating it to himself like a mantra every time something about Nicolas's behavior rubbed him the wrong way or discouraged him. And he was ready to let himself be reassured whenever he saw his son raptly reading, studying, doing his research online.

"No, I'm not going to study. Why would I bother to study?" and his eyes swept the room as if to pile up new certainties about the flimsiness of those walls, the bric-a-brac, to say nothing of the picture of his father in a tracksuit with the team of kids who, ten or so years earlier, had won some volleyball tournament, damned if he could remember which one. Volleyball? What is that, even? He ought to write an essay about these miserable championship tournaments for idiotic kids, that's what he ought to do. Describe the miserable excuses for parents, the pimply players. He was reminded of the hard-on he had in his pants, and touched himself.

"Why are you touching yourself? What are you touching?" The crease that appeared at the center of his father's brow always meant he was playing the role of the head of household. "Eat, don't you understand you need to eat?"

"No, I'm not hungry tonight," Nicolas said, and turned a blank expression on his father, without a glimmer of openness, far worse than a rebellious insult. What do I have to do? he could read in his father's eyes. You're worthless, Teach, his son shot back with quiet indifference.

"You ought to study, you're really good. When the time comes, I'll pay for a serious school, you can earn a master's. You can go to England, go to America. I've heard there are lots of kids who do it. Yes, I know what's going on out there. And when they come back, everyone wants to hire them. I'll get a line of credit to pay for it . . ." And though he'd pushed his plate away, he started picking at his food to keep from seeming pathetic, he filled his mouth and threw himself at his adolescent son's feet, though when Nicolas heard the words "a serious school," he felt like snickering. He didn't, though, not out of respect, by any means, but because for the first time he found himself adding up the numbers and lost himself in fanciful imaginings of how, if he wanted to, he'd be able to pay for that school, that serious school, out of his own pocket, he'd have paid cash, the way a real boss does, cash on the barrelhead, none of those miserable monthly installments that everybody else pays, a monthly installment on the car, a monthly installment on the motor scooter, a monthly install-ment on the TV. Then his little brother swam into his field of vision and he finally let a smile come to his lips.

"Papà, I have to finish school. This school, here," he said. "Even if it doesn't count for a thing."

"Nico', you need to cut it out with these nothings, these nobodies. We're here for you . . ." He wanted to conclude triumphantly with a neat phrase, to come off as an understanding father.

Dinner was over. His father cleared away the things he needed to and carried them into the kitchen, straightened up by himself, and, to keep from being left all alone in that domestic setting, did his best to restart the conversation.

Christian had eaten in silence, his eyes on his plate: he couldn't wait to be alone with his brother in their bedroom. Nicolas had shot him a wink a couple of times with the smile of someone who knows what they're talking about; it was clear that he had something to tell him. A smile that their father had noticed and that had rekindled his anger: "Who the fuck do you think you are, Nicolas? All you've done is cause trouble. You've brought shame on this family, you've brought *scuorno*. You were held back for a year. Where does all this arrogance come from? You're just an over-blown ass. God Almighty gave you talent, and you're squandering it, *comme a 'nu strunzo!*" He took advantage of his wife's absence to let loose with a hearty Neapolitan insult, calling his son a fool and a shit.

"I know this song already, Pa'.

"Then why don't you see if you can learn it by heart? Then you might not be quite so arrogant."

"What am I supposed to do?" he replied, and yet his father almost seemed to have guessed something. However skillful Nicolas might be at feigning, camouflaging, and concealing, still he brought home the signs of his change of fortune. An important event is a rope that knots itself around you and binds you tighter with every move you make, it rubs and tears at you, and in the end it leaves marks on your flesh that are visible to everybody. And Nicolas was dragging behind him, knotted around his waist, a rope that led all the way back to the garage run by the Chinese in Gianturco. Back to his first pistol.

There's no place where it's easier to pretend nothing's happened than in the domestic setting. And Nicolas was pretending nothing had happened.

When his father felt like he'd taught him the lesson he needed to, Nicolas darted away to his bedroom, followed by Christian.

"I'll bet you've pulled off some slick move," Christian said with a smile, clearly eager to know more. Nicolas meant to savor his power, letting his brother dangle a little longer, and he fooled around with his cell phone for a good solid minute, until their mother stuck her face in the door, having just come home. As if they were dropping on their feet from exhaustion, both boys hopped into bed, with the TV turned off and a hasty "Ciao, Ma'" their only response to her timid attempt to strike up a conversation. The silence that greeted every one of her questions made it clear she wouldn't be hearing anything more.

As soon as the door was shut again, Christian jumped onto his brother's bed: "Come on, tell me everything."

"Lookie here!" he replied, and pulled out the old Belgian gat.

"Beautiful!" said Christian, grabbing it out of his hands.

"Hey, careful! It's loaded!"

They handed it back and forth several times, caressing the weapon.

"Open it up, why don't you!" Christian begged him. Nicolas flipped open the cylinder of the revolver and Christian spun it. He looked like a little boy with his first cowboy six-shooter.

"So what are you going to do with this now?"

"Start working."

"Meaning?"

"We'll have some fun . . ."

"Can I come with you when you do?"

"Well, we'll see. But listen, don't say a word to a soul."

"Seriously, are you joking?" Then he threw his arms around Nicolas the way he always did when he was begging for a present: "Can I hold on to it tonight? I'll keep it under my pillow."

"No, not tonight," said Nicolas, tucking the pistol away in his bed. "Tonight I'm keeping it under my pillow."

"Tomorrow I get it, though!"

"All right, tomorrow you get it!"

The game of war.

BALLOONS

Nicolas had a single thought in his mind: how to clear up the situation with Letizia. No matter how often he called her, she wouldn't answer. Not on the phone, not from the window: this was the first time she'd acted like this, ignoring him when he was giving her the soft soap, begging her forgiveness, swearing his undying love. If she would only just yell at him, the way she had at the beginning, the way she always did when they were fighting, if she would only insult him, but instead nothing; she wouldn't even give him that. And it seemed to him that, if she wasn't beside him, his days were empty. Without her messages on WhatsApp, without her sweetness, he felt bereft. He missed the touch of Letizia's fingers. The caresses a workingman deserved.

It was time to come up with a good idea, and for starters he went over to see Cecilia, Letizia's best friend.

"Leave me alone" was her first reaction when she saw him. "*Lassame perdere, so' fatti vostri.*" Leave me alone, it's your problem.

"No, come on, Ceci'. You just need to do me a favor."

"I don't do favors."

"No, seriously, just a small favor," and he forced her to listen to him by blocking the front entrance. "You need to make sure Letizia leaves her vehicle, her motor scooter, in front of your apartment building, because there's something I need to do. At her house she keeps it in the garage, so I can't get to it." He could easily get to it, of course, but it probably wasn't a very good idea to break into Letizia's family's garage.

"No, forget about it. Just drop it, Nico'," and she crossed her arms.

"Ask me for something, ask for whatever you want, and I'll do it, if you do me this favor."

"No . . . Letizia really, that is . . . you overdid it with Renatino, what you did was disgusting, it really was filthy."

"What does that have to do with anything! When you really love a person, I mean a lot, but really, really a lot, then no one else can even think of getting near that person."

"Sure, but not like that," said Cecilia.

"Tell me what you want, but do me this favor."

Cecilia seemed resolute, unapproachable and unbribeable in her refusal. In reality, though, she was just evaluating his offer.

"Two tickets for the concert."

"Okay."

"Don't you even want to know which one?"

"It doesn't matter, any one you name, I have lots of friends who are scalpers."

"Okay, then I want to see Benji and Fede."

"Who the fuck are they?"

"Ua', you don't know Benji and Fede?"

"No, not really, I don't give a damn. The tickets are yours. So when are you going to do this thing for me?"

"Tomorrow night she's coming over to my place."

"Perfect. Send me a text, write something like 'all set,' and I'll understand."

He spent the whole day trying to find someone who could get him the most expensive balloons available, he asked everyone.

Maraja

Guagliù, balloons, but not the kind you can
find at the market. Nice ones, guagliù, and on
every balloon it has to say I love you.

Dentino

Nicolas, where the fuck do we find them?

Maraja

Ah, help me out here.

The next day they drove all the way out to Caivano, where Drone had
learned from an Internet search that there was a party store that had supplies for major events, theme parties, and even for some movies and music
videos. They bought two hundred euros' worth of balloons and a portable
tank so they'd be able to inflate them with helium.

When he got Cecilia's text, they were already positioned downstairs
in the street, and they flexed their biceps getting bags and bags of balloons
blown up. One and two and three and ten. He—Nicolas—Pesce Moscio,
Dentino, and Briato' were blowing them up and knotting them with a red
ribbon and tying them to his motor scooter. When the scooter was festooned with balloons tugging toward the sky, it was only apparently an-
chored to the ground by its kickstand, with both wheels lifted an inch or
so off the pavement.

He texted Cecilia, "Tell her to come down," and then they hid behind
a moving van parked on the other side of the street.

"I need to go downstairs for a minute, Leti'," said Cecilia, gathering
the hair that hung down her back all the way to her bottom with a
scrunchie and getting up out of her chair.

"But why?"

"I have to go out for a second. *Aggi'a fà 'nu servizio.* I need to run an
errand."

"Right now? You never said anything about that. *Ja', stammocénn'a
casa,*" Letizia said, sliding into dialect as she begged to stay home, half-

sprawled on her girlfriend's bed, her eyes overbrimming with laziness. She made no movement except swinging her legs, first one then the other, and it seemed as if that cadenced movement concentrated all her life-force.

She'd been this way for days on end, so, even if Cecilia was a little jealous of their love story, she couldn't stand having her friend in that state any longer, and by now she just hoped that things between Letizia and Nicolas could get back on track. "No, no, I just have to go out for a second. It's super-urgent, seriously. Come on, it'll do you good, we'll get some fresh air, come on."

It took Cecilia a few minutes, but in the end she talked Letizia into it. As soon as they walked out onto the street, Letizia saw the extravaganza of balloons and, in an instant, she understood. Suddenly there was Nicolas in front of her, as if he'd appeared by way of some magic trick, and at last she spoke to him: "*Ua'*, you're a bastard," she said through her laughter.

Nicolas went over to her: "My love, let's raise this kickstand and fly away together."

"Nico', I don't know," said Letizia. "You've really pulled some dumb pranks."

"It's true, my love, I make mistakes, and lots of them, I make mistakes all the time. But I'm doing it for you."

"Eh, for me, that's just an excuse, you're violent by nature."

"I'm violent, I'm a disgusting mess. You can accuse me of anything you want. The only reason I do it is, when I think of you it's like there's a fire inside me. But instead of burning me up, the higher the flames, the stronger they make me. There's nothing I can do about it. If a guy looks at you, *'o volesse punì*, I've got to beat him up, it's stronger than me. It's as if he were taking part of you away from me."

"That's ridiculous, you're just too jealous," she said, holding out with her words, but stroking his cheeks with her hands.

"I'll try to change. I swear to you. *T' 'o giuro.* Everything I do, I do it with the dream of marrying you someday. By your side, I want to be the best man you ever met, really and truly the best." He took advantage of her gesture to grab both her hands, turn them palm down, and kiss them.

"But the best man doesn't behave like this," she retorted, starting to pout and doing her best to get her hands out of his.

Nicolas held her hands to his heart for a moment, then gently let them go. "If I did wrong, I only did wrong trying to protect you."

Letizia had Nicolas's eyes on her, but also Pesce Moscio's, and Dentino's, and Briato's, and Cecilia's, and the eyes of all the people in the quarter: she gave up all resistance and threw her arms around him, to a burst of applause.

"Good for them, they made up," said Pesce Moscio. Whereupon Dentino took a deep breath of the helium for the balloons and started talking in that weird querulous voice, and all the others followed suit. And those ridiculous voices seemed much more appropriate than the serious, important voices they were trying to assume.

Then Nicolas pushed his way through the balloons on the motor scooter, lifted Letizia up and set her down practically in his lap, took the scooter off the kickstand, and said: "Okay, now let's fly, *ja'*, let's fly."

"I don't need any balloons to fly," Letizia said, embracing him. "All I need is you."

At that point Nicolas pulled out a pocket knife and slowly started cutting the ribbons holding the balloons. Yellow, pink, red, and blue: one after another they rose into the sky, filling it with bright colors, while Letizia watched them go, her eyes finally cheerful and full of wonder.

"Wait, wait! Will you give them to us?" A bunch of kids six or seven years old came over to Nicolas, attracted by all those beautiful balloons unlike anything they'd ever seen.

The children had addressed him respectfully, using the semiformal *voi*, and he liked that.

"*Adda murì fràtemo*, for real."

And he started cutting the ribbons and tying them to the wrists of the children. Letizia watched him with admiration and Nicolas exaggerated the caresses he was giving the children, looking around for all the kids he could find to give balloons.

ARMED ROBBERIES

Nicolas showed up in front of the New Maharaja, where he ran into Agostino.

"It's no good, Nico', they won't let us in, *nun ce fanno trasì*."

Next to him, Dentino was nodding sadly; for a moment he'd touched the sky with one finger, but now they'd kicked him back onto the miserable earth. Lollipop, instead, freshly emerged from the gym, his hair wet from the shower, seemed excited.

"What? The bastards!"

"That's right, he says that without Copacabana around, he's not sure we'll pay. And anyway, they've already given away Copacabana's private dining room."

"Fuck, they didn't waste any time! The minute he's arrested, he's already been replaced," said Nicolas. He looked around, as if to find a service entrance, any door he could use to get back in.

Agostino came over: "Maraja, what are we going to do? They're smearing shit on our faces. The others are all working and we can't . . . We're always just substitutes. We're always just filling in, and the others are full professors."

It was time to figure out how to reorganize. And that was up to Nicolas, he was the boss.

"We need to pull an armed robbery," he said flatly.

It wasn't a suggestion, it was a statement of fact. The tone was that of a final decision. Lollipop opened both eyes wide.

"An armed robbery?" said Agostino.

"That's right, an armed robbery."

"With what, with our dicks in our hands?" asked Dentino, who had been stirred out of his torpor by Nicolas's startling call for armed robbery.

"I've got a gun," said Nicolas, and he displayed the old Belgian firearm. When he saw it, Agostino burst out laughing. "What is that old piece of junk?"

"Madonna, yeah, what is it! 'O Western! Now you've turned into a cowboy!" added Dentino, piling on.

"This is what we've got and this is what we'll work with. Let's get our full-face helmets and go."

Nicolas was standing there with both hands in his pockets. Waiting. Because this was a test, too. Who was going to pull back?

"What, do you have a full-face helmet? I don't," said Agostino. He was bullshitting, he had a full-face helmet and it was brand new, too, but he was seizing on any excuse to stall for time, to figure out if Nicolas was just talking or really meant it.

"I've got one," said Dentino.

"So do I," confirmed Lollipop.

"Cerino, you wear a scarf, one of your Mamma's shawls . . ." said Nicolas.

"We need a baseball bat. Let's go take out a supermarket," Dentino proposed.

"So we're just going like that? Without knowing a thing, without scoping out the situation in advance?" asked Agostino. Now the scale was tipping toward armed robbery.

"*Ua'*, scoping out the situation? What are you talking about? What is this, *Point Break*? We'll go, we'll be inside five minutes, tops, we steal the day's take, and we skedaddle. After all, this is closing time, right now. Then we'll leave there and take out a couple of cigarette shops, over by the station."

Nicolas arranged for the three of them to meet outside his house an hour later. Motor scooters and helmets, that was the assignment, and he'd bring the baseball bat. A few years earlier, he'd developed a passionate interest in baseball and he'd started collecting baseball caps. He didn't know a thing about the rules of the game, and one time he'd actually watched a game on the Internet but he got sick of it right away. Still, his fascination with that intensely American world had never loosened its grip on him. And so when he got a chance he'd stolen a baseball bat that they'd forgotten to put a price sticker on at Mondo Convenienza, the discount store. He'd never used it, but he liked it, he found it aggressive, brutal in its simplicity, exactly like the one that Al Capone used in *The Untouchables*.

He already knew who to hand it to, and when Agostino saw the bat being offered to him, he didn't blink an eye, he'd known this was coming. He'd expressed too many doubts.

Agostino was riding along behind Lollipop on his motor scooter. For the occasion Lollipop was wearing a Shark full-face helmet, though who knew where he'd found it? Nicolas, on the other hand, had Dentino riding behind him, and they both wore helmets that had long ago lost their original color, now replaced by dents and scratches.

They revved off in the direction of the supermarket. They'd chosen an old CRAI market, a safe distance from Forcella, so that if things went wrong they wouldn't wreck their reputations too badly. The market was about to close for the day, so there was a private security company's squad car parked out front.

"*Ua'*, those bastards!" said Nicolas. He stroked the well-worn butt of his gun; he'd discovered that it helped him to relax. He really hadn't expected this. An error, one he wouldn't make again.

"Hey, I told you we needed to stake it out, asshole! Let's go straight over to the cigarette shop, come on," said Agostino, reveling in his little moral victory, and he slapped Lollipop's shoulder, and the other guy instantly twisted the throttle on the motor scooter and waved his arm in the air to show he knew where to go. The destination was a tobacco shop, just like any of a million others all over Italy. A couple of plate-glass windows festooned with scratch-and-win tickets and letter-format sheets of paper that verified that, yes indeed, right in that shop just the other week, someone had won twenty thousand euros, and more than twice that sum last year, as if good luck had chosen that location to let loose with its full array of opportunities. Out front, not even one of the usual beggars hoping for a pittance. The sidewalk was deserted. The time was right. They parked their scooters, angled in the direction of the escape route they'd instinctively decided was the best bet: a heavily trafficked intersection that ran under an overpass. They'd be able to zigzag through the other scooters and lose themselves among the cars.

Nicolas practically didn't bother to wait for the others to hop off their scooters; he strode in, pistol leveled: "Hey, you bastard, put the money in here." The tobacconist, a short man dressed in a filthy undershirt, was arranging the packs of cigarettes on the shelf behind the counter and all he heard was a muffled voice from under the helmet. He hadn't understood a word Nicolas had said, but the tone of voice alone was enough to make him turn around with his hands up in the air. He was a man well past retirement age, and must have lived through this situation countless times before. Nicolas leaned over the counter and pressed his pistol against the man's temple.

"*Muóvete, miett' 'e sorde, miett' 'e sorde,*" Nicolas said roughly in dialect, telling him to hurry up and put the money in the plastic bag that he tossed to him. He'd stolen it from his mother after emptying out the doctor's prescriptions she kept in it.

"Take it easy, take it easy, take it easy," said the tobacconist, "take it easy, everything's okay." He knew that the right way to act was midway between cooperation and firm determination. Too passive and they'd think you were making fools of them. Too aggressive and they'd decide this was going to be your last day on earth. Either one would lead to the same outcome: a bullet in the brain.

Nicolas leaned even farther forward, until the barrel of his gun was pressed against the tobacconist's forehead. The man lowered his arms and grabbed the bag. Just then, Agostino came in with the baseball bat, held high over his shoulder, ready to knock one out of the park.

"*Allora a chi aggi' 'a scassà 'a capa!*" So whose head do I need to bust open in here?!

Dentino came in, too. He'd brought the backpack he wore to school, and now he was grabbing candy, chewing gum, pens, everything he could find, while Nicolas kept his eye on the tobacconist as he filled the bag, crumpling up ten- and twenty-euro notes.

"*Guagliu', facite ampress'!*" Lollipop yelled in from outside, urging them to hurry it up. He was the youngest of the four and he'd been assigned to stand watch as a lookout. Nicolas swung his pistol in the air, urging the tobacconist to get moving. The man grabbed everything that was left in the register, and then put his hands back up in the air.

"You forgot to grab the scratch-and-wins," said Nicolas.

Once again, the tobacconist lowered his arms, but this time instead of obeying Nicolas's order, he used them to point at the bag and convey the idea that the money that he'd put in it was really enough. They were free to go.

"Give me all your scratch-and-wins, you cocksucker, give me all the scratch-and-wins!" Nicolas bellowed. Agostino and Dentino stared at him in silence. When they heard Lollipop shout, they'd already rushed toward the door and couldn't understand why Nicolas was wasting time on the scratch-and-win tickets. That plastig bag bulging with money seemed like plenty enough to them. But not to Nicolas. As far as he was concerned, the tobacconist's attitude was an insult, and so he grabbed the bag out of the man's hand and slammed him in the head with his gun, knocking him flat to the floor. Then he turned to the other two and said: "Go."

"*Ua'*, you're totally crazy, Nico'!" Agostino shouted to him as they zipped off through the traffic in pairs.

"And now, *guagliu'*, let's take out a café," Nicolas replied. The café looked like a carbon copy of the cigarette shop. Two grimy plate-glass windows, though these were covered with ads for the ice-cream cones that were popular a decade ago: a nondescript little establishment, always visited by the same customers. The place was ready to close for the night, the metal roller blind halfway down. This time, too, Nicolas was the first one in. He'd tucked the bag of cash from the cigarette shop robbery under his seat and had grabbed a plastic bag from an empty trash can on the street. The barista and the two waiters were putting the chairs up on the tables and practically didn't notice that Nicolas and Dentino—who had convinced Agostino to let him carry the baseball bat—had both entered the place.

"*Ràtece tutt'e sorde, ràtece tutt'e sorde, mettite tutt'e sorde ccà dinto,*" Nicolas howled, repeating the order in cutting dialect to give up the cash, stuff it into the bag, and he threw the plastic trash bag at the feet of the waiters. This time he hadn't drawn his pistol because the adrenaline was pumping in his veins and the final image of the tobacconist slumped on the floor had confirmed his belief that nothing could go wrong this time. But the younger of the two waiters, a kid with an acne-pitted face who might have been a couple of years older than Nicolas, gave a mocking kick to the plastic sack and sent it under one of the little café tables. Nicolas reached his hand around behind his back—if these guys wanted to wind up filled with holes, that would be fine with him—but that baseball bat was burning a hole in Dentino's hands. He started with the espresso cups lined up and ready for the next morning's breakfast crowd. He hauled off and smashed them at a single blow, making shards fly in all directions, even at Nicolas, who instinctively yanked his hand back and reached up to cover his face, even though he was wearing the helmet. Then it was the turn of the bottles of hard liquor. Dark brown spurted out of a bottle of Jägermeister and hit the young waiter who'd kicked the plastic bag, right in the middle of his forehead.

"*Mo' scasso la cassa, ma, adda murì mammà, la seconda è 'na capa,*" Dentino snarled in dialect, promising to smash open the cash register, and after that, someone's head. He pointed the baseball bat first at one waiter, then at the other, as if trying to make up his mind which cranium he'd crack in half first. Nicolas decided he'd have it out with Dentino later. This wasn't the time for it, though, so to emphasize their point, he finally managed to snatch out the handgun.

The pockmarked waiter fell to his knees and grabbed the bag, while his partner hurried over to the cash register and pushed the button that unlocked it. It must have been a good day, because Nicolas saw plenty of fifty-euro notes. In the meantime, Agostino, attracted by all the commotion, had wormed his way into the café, and started stuffing bottles of whisky and vodka, the ones that had been spared Dentino's fury, into another backpack.

"*Guagliu', state qua da 'nu minuto e miezo, 'n'ata vota. Ma che spac-cimm' 'e lentezza!*" Lollipop shouted through the door, reminding the three kids again that they'd been in the shop for a good minute and a half, and denouncing them as disgusting snails. In the blink of an eye, they had all scooted out the door and were back on their bikes, lost again in the flow of traffic. It had all been so easy, so fast, like a first-class jolt of coke. Only Nicolas had his mind on other things, and while he used his right hand to jerk the handlebar to veer around a Fiat Punto that had decided to jam on its brakes for no good reason, with his left hand he was writing a text to Letizia: "Good night, Little Panther." *Buonanotte Panterina.*

When he woke up, his eyes still blurry with sleep and in his ears the sounds of the day before, the first thing Nicolas did was check his phone. Letizia had replied the way he'd hoped, and she'd even sent him a series of little hearts.

By the time he got to school it was already ten o'clock, and seeing that he was already late he figured another half hour would make no difference. He holed up in the restroom and smoked a joint. In third period, if he was remembering right, he had De Marino. The only teacher he could stand. Or at least the only one he wasn't indifferent to. He didn't give a shit about the things he talked about, but he had to acknowledge the guy's determination. He refused to resign himself to going unheard and he really tried to dig in deep with the kids in his classroom. Nicolas respected that about him, even if he knew that Valerio De Marino was never going to save anyone.

The bell rang. The sound of doors swinging open and footsteps in the hall. The restroom where he'd holed up would soon be taken by storm, so Nicolas tossed the rest of the joint into the toilet and went to sit at his desk. Signor De Marino came in, eyeing the class, but not the way the other teachers did, who thought of the teacher's dais as another place on an assembly line. For them, the quicker the shift ends, the sooner you get to go home.

He waited for them all to come in and then picked up a book, which he held rolled up in one hand as if it were something of little or no worth. He was sitting at his desk on the raised podum and drumming on his knee with that book.

Nicolas was staring at him, indifferent to the fact that De Marino was staring back at him.

"So, Fiorillo, it would be pointless for me to test you today, eh?"

"Really pointless, Teach. I've got a headache that's killing me."

"But at least you know what we're studying, don't you?"

"Of course I do."

"Mmm. All right, I won't ask you this question: At least tell me what we're studying. I'll ask you a nicer question, because you'll be willing to answer a nice question, and you'll run away from a tough one. Am I right?"

"Whatever you think best," said Nicolas, and he shrugged his shoulders.

"What do you like most about the things we've been discussing in class lately?"

Nicolas actually did know what they'd been talking about.

"I like Machiavelli."

"Why is that?

"*Pecché te 'mpara a cummannà.*" Because he teaches you how to take charge.

PARANZINA

Nicolas had to find some other way of bringing in cash now that, after Copacabana's arrest, the outdoor drug markets were out of commission. He took a good look around, trying to figure out where to start over. Copacabana knew that what money needed above all was to get out and work, that there was no time to waste. Don Feliciano had turned state's witness, and now he was coughing up everything. The appointment of a replacement for district underboss, now that Viola Striano was married to Micione, was in fact his responsibility. Strictly speaking, Micione ought to be talking to Copacabana about it. But he wasn't.

In prison, Copacabana wasn't getting any messages. The bosses were silent and so were their wives. What was going on? He wasn't interested in shakedowns. There were two ways to go: either you started doing shakedowns or you opened up the street markets again and started peddling hash and coke. Either the shops weren't kicking back their share and were holding on to the markets or else the shops were paying and they didn't want any other business competing with them. That was his belief.

Nicolas, Agostino, and Briato' were planning to pull off their first shakedown with that old Belgian hunk of junk, after the robberies.

"We're doing it!" said Briato'. "Nicolas, *adda murì mammà*, we're actually doing it!"

They were in the back room, gambling away the spare change from the armed robbery at video poker, and making plans meanwhile. Dentino and Biscottino preferred just to listen, for the moment.

"The strolling vendors . . . All the strolling vendors that are working the Rettifilo—Corso Umberto Uno—have to pay us," Briato' continued.. "We'll stick a gun barrel in the mouths of every last one of these fucking Moroccans and negroes, and we'll make them give us ten or fifteen euros a day."

"What are we going to do?" asked Agostino.

"And then, at the stadium, we can be sure we'll find everyone who was paying Copacabana," said Nicolas.

"No, if you ask me, Copacabana wasn't getting paid at the stadium."

"Then we'll rip off the parking attendants after the game," said Briato'.

"Sure," said Nicolas, "but, *guagliu'*, if we don't pool our money, if we don't do things together, then we're still jobless employees working for someone! Can we get this straight or not?!"

"That's fine with me. For now, we work, and then we'll see," said Agostino, and he dropped two euros into the video poker machine; then, as he pushed the start button, he added: "That's what Copacabana said."

"What do you mean, what did he say? Did he talk to you?" Nicolas blurted out.

"No, it's not like he spoke to me . . . But his wife, the Brazilian, did say that, until 'o Micione makes up his mind with him, nothing's happening, and so we have to live for ourselves, which means he can't say anything to us, we're just putting together our monthly payday."

"Oh, right, so now it's 'o Micione," said Dentino, "just ask him . . . He's never given a flying fuck, o' Micione decides for himself and that's that! If Don Feliciano was still in charge this wouldn't have happened. How can it be we still don't know who's the boss in Naples?" He slammed his hand against the side of his car, which in the meantime, while they were chatting, had guzzled down thirty euros in just a matter of minutes, and he sat down on a plastic chair nearby.

"That piece of shit Don Feliciano abandoned us," said Nicolas. "The less we mention his name, the better off we are."

"He wasn't always a piece of shit," Dentino put in.

"Forget about it," said Agostino, who leaned both of his elbows on the table to roll a joint in silence, and then they passed the joint around in silence. The odor of marijuana was still the best there was; it immediately put them in a state of grace. Dentino exhaled the smoke through the hole in his shattered incisors, that's the way he always smoked and there had been times when he'd succeeded in picking up chicks with that little trick. When the joint came around to Biscottino, he inhaled greedily, then, as he handed it to Agostino, he took the floor: "If you ask me, 'o Maraja has a point. We need to work together . . . It's no good for each of us to strike out on his own."

What was tormenting Agostino was that forming a *paranza* meant both striking out in favor of someone and striking out against someone else. Instead, working day by day for just yourself meant at the very most getting someone angry and then asking their pardon, giving them a piece of what you were earning or, at the very worst, taking a beating, a *mazzia-tone*. Starting to work together, to get organized, also meant having a boss, and Agostino knew that wouldn't be him. He also knew that in that case he'd have to consult with his father's *fratocucino* about what to do, and that his fate was either to become a loyal follower or a turncoat, an *infame*, and he found neither of these alternatives particularly appealing.

As if to reinforce his statement, Biscottino pulled a large wad of cash out of his pocket. It was all crumpled together like candy wrappers.

"How the fuck are you carrying all that cash?" asked Dentino, eyes big as plates.

Biscottino shut him down: "*A wise guy don't carry his money in a wallet*. Have you forgotten about Lefty?"

"*Ua', scassate i ciessi*. Out of sight. Biscottino made you look like a fool," said Nicolas, smacking Dentino on the back of the neck.

"But Lefty kept his cash all neat and clean in a money clip. The way you've got them, though, they're disgusting. Look at them—*tutti ammap-pociati*. All crumpled up."

"*Guagliu'*," said Nicolas, "who remembers what Lefty called a dollar?"

"Lettuce," said Agostino, stubbing out the roach of the joint on the bottom of the table.

"Exactly," Nicolas confirmed, and got straight to the point: "And just how did you make all this lettuce, Biscottino?"

"With my two friends Oreste and Rinuccio."

"And who the fuck are they?" he asked, wary and alert now, because every new name was a potential enemy.

"Oreste!" he said again, raising his voice just a little, as if he were talking to a centenarian who was hard of hearing.

"You mean Oreste Teletabbi?" He got his nickname from the Teletubbies.

"Yes!"

"But he's eight years old! So you're saying that you, Teletabbi, and . . . ?"

"And Rinuccio!"

"Do you mean Rinuccio, the brother of Carlito's Way from the Capelloni?! Rinuccio Pisciazziello?"

"Exactly, he's the one!" he exclaimed, as if to say: "Eh, you finally caught on!"

"Well? How did you make the money?" Nicolas stared at him with those dark eyes of his kindling into flame, midway between incredulous and interested. How had those snotnoses managed to put together all that cash? However they explained it, Biscottino had the money, and he must have got it from somewhere.

"Oh oh," said Dentino, "they fought the children's war."

"We hit all the bouncy castles where the kids hang out."

He said it in utter seriousness, his chin jutting high in pride. The others all burst out laughing.

"Bouncy castles for kids? What the fuck are those? Playground toys? Merry-go-rounds?"

"No, all the parks and playgrounds and all the bouncy castles at the malls!"

"So what're you saying, what the fuck do you do?"

"You want to come watch? Today we're hitting Piazza Cavour."

Nicolas nodded, he was the only one who'd taken him seriously: "I'll come with you now."

Briato' zipped after Nicolas's scooter, while the others cupped their hands over their mouths and shouted from the side of the street: "Tell us all about this bank job when you find out, and especially what Pisciazziello does to help!" Biscottino got on his Rockrider mountain bike and, hearing them still laughing with gusto, turned around and stuck his tongue out.

He pedaled all the way to Piazza Cavour, stopping only when he got to *'a funtana d'e paparelle*, the fountain of the ducks as it was traditionally known, where the Triton was still spotted with sky-blue paint from S.S.C. Napoli's first national championship. Back then his father had been more or less his age now, and he'd often told him how, after that victory, the city had celebrated for days and nights on end, and that he'd seen them with his own eyes painting the bronze statue of the Triton. He liked the fact that some trace of that celebration had come down to him, still intact, and every time he went by Piazza Cavour he got a lump in his throat, and he felt closer to his father there than at the grave he visited on Sundays with his mother.

He rose up to a standing position on the pedals to bolster his four foot five inches of height, and started turning his head left and right like a blackbird looking for a mate. He saw where Nicolas and Briato' had taken up their positions, at the entrance to the park, and then he saw Pisciazziello and Oreste Teletabbi arrive. They were a couple years younger than him, maybe just one year younger, actually. They had the faces of children who already knew everything, they talked about sex and guns: no grownup, since the day they were born, had judged any truth, fact, or behavior unsuitable for their ears. In Naples there are no paths to growing up: you're born straight into reality, into the thick of it, you don't get a chance to discover it a little at a time.

They weren't alone, Pisciazziello and Teletabbi. Each of them had two other kids on their bike, standing behind them, and behind them straggled a crowd of little kids. Unmistakably, these were Gypsies. Nicolas and Briato' dismounted from their motor scooters and stood gazing at the scene in amusement, arms folded across their chests. The *paranzina*, the mini-*paranza*, approached the playground equipment, the merry-go-rounds and swings, and started making a tremendous amount of noise: they were taking the littlest kids off the rides and the seesaws, shoving other kids so they fell on their faces, frightening them and making them cry. The mothers and the babysitters shouted at them in incensed outrage: *"Che siete venuti a fà?! Via!"* and *"Uh maronna, ma che vulite cumbinà?"* What are you trying to do? Get out of here! and Madonna, what do you think you're up to? As they exclaimed and called out, they hurried to console the little ones and take them by the hands, hustling them away.

In a few minutes, the whole playground turned into a melee of confusion and shouting, a mess it was impossible to untangle and picture clearly. Then Biscottino, putting on a respectful face that ill became him, broke in to restore the peace: "Signo', Signo', don't worry, I'll get rid of them, I'll get rid of them for you, ladies!" and he turned and started shouting at the Gypsies: "Get out, get out of here! *Zingari 'e mmerda! Jatevénne!"* Calling them a bunch of fucked-up Gypsies in dialect, he told them to clear out.

He and Teletabbi started shooing them out. They'd go a certain distance, but then come back, over and over. That was when Biscottino started saying: "Signo', if you give me five euros, I'll get rid of them for the whole day, and you won't see them again!"

That was the toll they needed to pay if they wanted to enjoy the playground undisturbed; the women figured it out fast, and so some of them handed them five euros, others just gave them three . . . Each gave according to what she had . . . and that was fine with them.

Once they'd gathered the money, the *paranzina* said goodbye and the playground went back to its usual routine, like before they arrived.

Biscottino headed over toward Nicolas and Briato' and introduced them to Pisciazziello and Teletabbi. Pisciazziello said to Nicolas: "I know you, I've seen you with my brother!"

"Give him my regards. How's Carlito's Way?"

"Out of his mind."

"Good, that means he's happy."

"But he's the best," said Biscottino, referring to his friend. "Working together we pull a ridiculous con."

"Like how?" asked Briato'. After what they'd seen, he was no longer surprised at what those little snotnoses would come up with next.

"Basically, once the Gypsies get out of here, he shows up and snatches two or three purses. You see, the grandmothers leave them on the benches . . . And I chase him down and get back their handbags for them. The ladies are so grateful they give ten euros, sometimes twenty. The grandmothers are always loaded."

Nicolas bent over and squatted down to look them right in the eyes and, putting a hand on Biscottino's shoulder and the other on Pisciazziello's, squeezing slightly, he said: "How much do you pay these little Gypsies, these *rometielli?*"

"No, I don't pay them a cent . . . I buy them a fried pizza, a croquette or two. For instance, now they're working for free because I gave them my sister's bicycle, she doesn't ride it anymore anyway."

So these little feral puppies had found their own way of making money with their inventive shakedowns, establishing an alliance with the Gypsies. He was going to have to find someone higher up he could make an alliance with, that was fundamental if he wanted to start a *paranza* of his own. But who? Don Feliciano Striano had turned state's witness, Copacabana was hanging tough, but still, he was in Poggioreale prison, and Micione was the outsider devouring the heart of Naples.

SOLDERING IRON

They were in the back room, as usual, when at a certain point, with his smartphone in hand, Tucano said: "*Guagliu'*, look at this. Look at this item on Twitter."

No one looked up, only Lollipop commented: "Those assholes who do fantasy soccer leagues."

"It's got nothing to do with fantasy soccer. They've completely cleared out the New Maharaja. Every stick of furniture. There's an article here."

Nicolas immediately said: "Send me the link."

His eyes darted from one page to the next, and with his thumb he ran over photographs, statements. They'd broken in at night and taken everything that wasn't nailed down. Everything. Dishes, utensils, computers, candelabra, chairs. A truck had come and hauled off everything on the place's weekly closing day. The alarms had been deactivated.

"Fuck," said Nicolas. "And now I'm curious to see who it was. And especially what that shithead Oscar does now, if he just gives up."

He immediately called Oscar, but there was no answer. So he sent him a text: "It's me, Nicolas, answer." Nothing. He texted him again: "It's me, Nicolas, answer, super-urgent." Nothing. He called Stavodicendo: "Hey, did you see what happened at the New Maharaja?"

"No, what happened?"

"They cleaned the place out!"

"What are you talking about?"

"That means they left nothing! We've got to figure out who it was."

"Why? What are you now, a private detective?"

"Stavodicendo, if we can figure out who it was, the private back room is ours for good, no one will take it away again . . ."

"If they stole everything in the place, then maybe it'll shut down."

"Impossible. With that terrace over Posillipo, no one can shut them down. Come on home!"

Stavodicendo arrived an hour later.

"What the fuck did you do?" Nicolas greeted him. In that hour, he'd thought of everything, including pulling out the Francotte and holding it on him for a while, to see how long it took him to start shitting his pants. But then Stavodicendo made him change his mind: "I went and talked to my father."

Stavodicendo's father had been a fence for years, and now that he was out of prison, he was working as a waiter in a restaurant at Borgo Marinari.

"My dad told me that we need to go . . ." and as he sat down on the bed, he paused dramatically.

"Where?!"

"Eh, I was just saying, to see the Gypsies."

"To see the Gypsies?"

"Eh, I was just saying exactly that! We need to go see the Gypsies."

"Well?"

"My dad said that he was pretty sure that it was either the Gypsies or else someone trying to make money off the insurance. Which would mean that Oscar and them did it themselves."

"That would seem strange," Nicolas said quickly. "They've got plenty of money."

Stavodicendo had clasped his hands behind his head and shut his eyes. When he opened them again, Nicolas was aiming the gun at him, but he didn't so much as blink. The confidence he lacked in speaking and the obsessive use of words that had earned him his nickname was more than made up for by the cold composure he maintained in the face of the most dangerous situations.

"Ah, so you brought a gat, too," he said in a raucous voice.

"Exactly," Nicolas replied, and tucked the pistol down the back of his pants. "Let's go pay a call on the Gypsies."

They hopped onto Nicolas's Beverly and pushed past Gianturco. They headed straight for the Gypsy camp. A favela that, before it reached your eyes, wafted right up your nostrils, with its stench of unwashed clothing, sunbaked corrugated sheet metal, filthy children wallowing in the mud. Waiting to meet them, in front of the trailers, were just women and children. All around them a horde of little kids chased after them, shrieking, playing with a half-inflated ball. As soon as he got off his scooter, Nicolas immediately turned aggressive and started shouting into their faces: "Who's in charge here? Do you have a fucking leader or not?" Among the many strategies that could be adopted, that of the dog that barks first and loudest struck him as the most effective.

"What do you want, who are you looking for?" a woman replied; she was broad in the beam and stood up from the plastic chair she'd been sitting in, and took a few wobbly steps toward him.

"I want to talk to your leader, your husband, whoever the fuck is in charge here. Who is it who goes and does your stealing for you? Who cleans out villas? Who is it that robbed the New Maharaja? *L'aggi' 'a sapé!* I need to know!"

"Get the hell out of here!" A young kid showed up and started shoving him. Where had he materialized from? In response Nicolas simply kneed the kid in the gut, knocking him to the ground, in front of the women, who came running awkwardly, tripping over their overlong skirts. The woman who looked to be the youngest, her ash-blond hair pulled back under a scarf, spoke to Stavodicendo: "What are you two here for? What do you want?" There wasn't so much as a gram of fear in her voice, only surprise and annoyance.

In the meantime, the other women were yanking at Nicolas, pulling him here and there by the hem of his T-shirt; he seemed fought over much more than under attack. He tried to brace himself to regain his balance, but then another woman would come along and tug him toward her.

If Nicolas hadn't drawn his gun and aimed it at the demented swarm, the dance could have gone on indefinitely. And then it all happened at once: he found a biceps wrapped around his neck, crushing his throat from behind. He couldn't catch his breath, and it felt as if his Adam's apple was in his mouth. While his vision was growing blurry, he saw Stavodicendo take off at a run toward the motor scooter.

The Gypsies didn't seem to notice, or more likely they didn't care; they'd captured the one they were interested in. They dragged Nicolas into a shack and tied him to a wooden chair with metal legs they must have stolen from a school or a medical clinic, then they started slapping and punching him, asking him obsessively what he was looking for and why he'd come: "Now we're going to kill you."

"Did you want to shoot at our children?"

Nicolas felt himself infected by fear, and the thought disgusted him, because he certainly had no reason to be afraid of Gypsies. He kept on saying: "You're thieves, you're thieves!" He seemed completely stunned. And the more he repeated it, the more punches and slaps he took.

In the meantime, Stavodicendo was going to get the one person capable of helping, the only one with blue blood: Drago'. He was a Striano and the Gypsies couldn't even live in the camp without the approval of the families. But Drago's cell phone wasn't picking up; after he called for the third time without getting an answer, Stavodicendo raced to Forcella.

When Stavodicendo finally found him, he was in the back room playing pool. Stavodicendo went in without a word to anyone and rushed over to Drago', who was bent over the table.

"Drago', we've got to get going, come on, come on, come on!"

"What's going on?" asked Drago', who'd figured out this was a serious matter and had put down his pool cue.

"Nicolas, the Gypsies took him!"

"Right, right, sure, they kidnapped him," he said, laughing.

"No, they really got him, get moving, come on!"

Drago' didn't say another word, left the unfinished game, and followed him out. On the motor scooter Stavodicendo shouted out an explanation of how they'd wound up there.

"But did he really fuck up like that?"

"He says that they were Gypsies but, like I was just saying, I really don't know who those people are."

Meanwhile, the man who must have been the boss came into the shack where Nicolas was being held prisoner. He moved as if everything in that space belonged to him. Not human beings, not even animals. Just things. And of course, things that were his property. He wore an Adidas tracksuit that seemed to have just come from the store. It was a couple of sizes too big, and so the Gypsy had rolled the sleeves back a couple of times and the pants dragged on the ground. He was clearly worried about the invasion and greedily chewed on a toothpick. He spoke only a halting Italian; he must have just arrived in the country.

"Who the fuck are you?"

"Nicolas, from Tribunali."

"Who do you belong to?"

"To myself."

"You belong to yourself? They told me that you were sticking your gun in the kids' faces. Around here you're going to die, you know that?"

"You can't kill me."

"Why not? Do you think we're afraid that your mother might come around here looking for the last few scraps of you?" The Gypsy was avoiding Nicolas's eyes, and he walked along staring at the tips of his shoes. Adidas. Gleaming and new. "Around here you're going to die," he said again.

"No, instead around here *you* earn the right to go on living," said Nicolas, and he rotated his head to bring them all into it. Then he went on, addressing the leader of the group: "You earn the right to go on living because when I become the head boss, I won't come here to kill you and all the rest of you Gypsies one by one. That means you can't hurt me, because if you do, you'll all die." The backhanded smack that hit him square on his right cheekbone blurred his vision, then Nicolas blinked his eyes a couple of times and the man in the tracksuit swam back into sight.

"Ah, so you're going to become a boss . . ."

Another backhanded smack, this time delivered without the same conviction. The cheek was already red, the capillaries were lacerated, but there was no bleeding yet, just a hint on the teeth, on account of the lips slamming against them. They were curious to know who was behind him, and that's what they were worried about. He heard a chorus of children's voices outside, and a man stuck his head into the shack: "Your friend is back."

Then he heard Stavodicendo's voice: "Nicolas, Nicolas, where are you?"

"Ah, look, your little girlfriend came back," said the leader, and hit him again. In the meantime, Drago' and Stavodicendo had been surrounded by the usual group of woman and little kids. Entering that Gypsy camp was like stamping on an anthill: people came running by the dozen the way ants climb up your foot, your ankle, your calf to defend their nest.

"I'm Luigi Striano," Drago' shouted. "You know my father."

Silence fell over the shack and the circle of bodies that was tightening around the two young men fell back, too.

"My father is Nunzio Striano, 'o Viceré, brother of Feliciano Striano, 'o Nobile, my grandfather is Luigi Striano, 'o Sovrano, and I have his same name."

At the words 'o Viceré, the Viceroy, the head of the Gypsies froze in place, rolled up the sleeves of his tracksuit as if to make himself presentable, and walked out of the shack. As he walked up, there formed a path through the people who had surrounded Drago' and Stavodicendo, the way the stalks of wheat move aside with every step through a field.

"You're the son of 'o Viceré?"

"Sì, è pàtemo." Yes, he confirmed, that's my father.

"I'm Mojo," he said, extending his hand. "What the fuck are these people doing? What the fuck are you doing here? We got no word from 'o Viceré, what's going on?"

"Let me talk to Nicolas."

When they found him, he was smiling brashly. Now things were turned around, and he could afford to work up a mouthful of spit and blood, which he used to soil the Gypsy's fucking spotless tracksuit. The gob of spit landed with great precision on the black Trefoil logo, and Mojo lunged forward. But Drago' blocked him with the flat of his hand, reminding him of where he'd come from and to where he, Mojo, would be sent back.

"Untie him, and fast," said Drago'.

Mojo tilted his head and Nicolas was freed. Drago' was tempted to ask Nicolas what the fuck he was doing there, but Mojo would then have understood that they weren't there at Viceré's behest at all, so he went on with the masquerade: "Nicolas, explain to Mojo exactly why you're here!"

"Because you stole, you stole from the New Maharaja."

"We haven't stolen anything."

"Yes, it was you, and now you have to give it all back."

Mojo put his hand around his neck: "But we didn't steal a fucking thing!"

"Easy, easy," and Stavodicendo separated them.

Nicolas looked at him: "Well, the New Maharaja in Posillipo was picked clean, and only you could have done it, they used trucks."

"We didn't do a fucking thing."

Drago' improvised: "My father thinks it was you, though, all the families in the System think so."

Mojo raised both arms in surrender and then invited them to follow him: "Come and see, come take a look at the vans!" There were three white Fiat Fiorino vans, without logos on the side, identical and well cared for. Unsuspectable. Ready to go.

Mojo opened the van doors and, while he did his best to clean the spit off his tracksuit with the back of his hand, he said: "Look, look at what's here." In the dim light, they could make out boxes containing washing machines, refrigerators, television sets, even a complete set of kitchen appliances. There were lawn mowers, hedge trimmers, electric saws, a glittering array of tools for an avid gardener, as if Naples were a city suited for someone with a green thumb. All things that had nothing to do with the New Maharaja.

"Eh, you're no fool," said Nicolas, "you got rid of the stuff from the New Maharaja right away, maybe it's already safe in Roma land."

"We haven't stolen a fucking thing, and if we had I'd be naming a price right now. I wouldn't give anything back free of charge."

"My father would have made you give it back free of charge," said Drago'.

"Even your father has to bargain with Mojo."

Mojo had shown that he didn't pull bullshit moves, and now he could afford to sit on his high horse with those three kids.

"What's your name . . . Mocio Vileda," he said mocking him by calling him the name of a popular mop, "my father would have come here, burned down the whole camp, and sold off whatever he wanted, you understand that or not?"

"Why does 'o Viceré want to burn?" Mojo looked worried and the boys loved it.

"No, I'm saying that if you stole without authorization . . . you've done it other times . . ."

"Mojo isn't authorized, Mojo steals, and if the families of the System want something, they come here and they take it."

Mojo was respectful, even now that they had realized he was working in other areas. Those vans were packed full of stuff he'd sell at street markets on the outskirts of town. Those Gypsies weren't even burgling apartments. The bulk of their livelihood came from armed robberies and especially arson: they ran a whole illegal ring in rags, rubber, copper. Keeping up with their normal line of work was already a challenge, they didn't have time to pick clean a club like the New Maharaja.

"All right, I'll tell my father you didn't do it. And you certainly aren't going to go telling my father stories, are you?"

"No, no, Mojo doesn't lie," said Mojo. He nodded his head toward one of his men, who came over with Nicolas's Francotte. Mojo tossed it to him, and it landed in the mud in front of the Beverly's front wheel.

"Now go."

"But why are you fixated on this idea of catching whoever it was who cleaned out the New Maharaja?" asked Drago'. They'd stopped at a *kebabbaro*, a kebab shop, because everything they'd been doing had whetted their appetite, and then Nicolas had asked for a chunk of ice to put on his lip. He hoped Letizia wouldn't notice.

"It's the only way to get a private dining room for good," he said. He was chewing on one side, the side that hadn't been beaten up as bad, and even if it hurt him, he'd refused to do without his kebab.

"Earlier, I was just telling you that my dad says maybe they did it themselves, to defraud the insurance company . . ." said Stavodicendo.

"If that's the way it is, then there's nothing we can do about it," said Drago'. He'd ordered a super-greasy hot dog, dripping with oil. He was sick and tired of Arab food; his mother told him that they put rotten meat in those things. "Still," Drago' continued, "I couldn't care less about who pulled off that caper, all we get is a private dining room, and nothing more? Why the fuck are we doing this?"

"Like fuck, that's all we get," Nicolas replied. "What we get is a private dining room forever, not just for one night. Spend time in the club and get to know everyone. We show our faces."

"And for that we're supposed to do this favor for Oscar, we got to get all his stuff back? It must be a million euros' worth of stuff, and we're handing it to him on a silver platter? They stole all kinds of things, did you read about it in the paper? The doors and the handles, even the window frames . . ."

"You're out of your mind, Drago'. If we have the private dining room, then no one can tell us whether or not we can go in, we don't have to come up with excuses anymore or try to find someone who can get us in the door. We just walk in, simple as can be, forget about working as waiters. All of Naples will see that we're in there, everyone. City commissioners, soccer players, singers, and all the bosses of the System. It sets us up to join them, can't you get that through your head?"

"*Ma, nun me ne fotte proprio di stà llà tutt' 'e ssere . . .*" he said. I don't give a fuck about spending all my evenings there.

"Not all our evenings, just when we want to."

"Sure, okay, but it's still not worth it . . ."

"Spending our time in the palace next to the ones who are in charge is always worth it, I want to walk with kings, I'm sick of hanging out with people who don't count for a fucking thing."

The days that followed were empty ones. No one had said anything more about the story of the Gypsy, but everyone was just waiting for a disturbance to reexhume it. And it was none other than Viceré who rekindled the fire.

Drago's mother had called her son in because he needed to go visit his father, at the prison in L'Aquila. For the past year he'd been talking to him through bulletproof glass and an intercom. Nunzio, Viceré, was serving time under the 41 bis regime.

The 41 bis regime is a sarcophagus. Everything is controlled, observed, monitored. A security camera is trained on you always, morning, noon, and night. You can't choose to watch a program on TV nor can you ask for a newspaper or a book. Everything goes through censorship. Everything is filtered. Or at least it should be. Family members can visit only once a month, and the visits take place through a slab of bulletproof glass. Under that transparent partition, reinforced concrete. Over that transparent partition, reinforced concrete. An intercom you can talk through. Nothing else.

Drago' took a long, silent journey, interrupted only by the steady stream of texts he was receiving. They were from Nicolas, who wanted to know if he'd arrived, if he'd talked to his father, if all of this had anything to do with their situation. He sensed that they were at a tipping point, he just didn't know what kind.

Drago' found his father with a grim expression on his face, and he understood.

"All right, then, Gigino, how are you?" In spite of his anger, his voice betrayed affection, and the man laid a hand on the bulletproof glass that separated them.

Drago' laid his hand against his father's. From the other side of the glass, no warmth reached him. "I'm good, Pa'," he said.

"So what's this I hear about you going to Romania, you don't say a thing to your mother and your father, you just decide on your own?"

"No, Pa', it's not that I particularly want to go to Romania myself."

Even though he'd had no instructor in the art, he knew how to speak in code, and when he didn't understand, he was capable of finding a way of requesting information. He went on, getting closer to the intercom, to make sure that his words were as clearly understandable as possible: "It's

not that I particularly want to go to Romania myself, it's that Nicolas wants
to go at all costs, he says it's a new experience."

"But if you do this, if you start going to Romania, you're leaving your
mother all alone, and you're making me worry," and with his eyes he
would have liked to break that glass and slap his son silly.

"Well, this thing about going to Romania together, he told me while
we were in Posillipo, we were in a club that was empty, everyone had left,
and Nicolas said that everyone's going to Romania because it's more fun
and that's why the restaurants and clubs here are empty. So he told me I
should go, too, because in Romania, all alone, it can be scary. He says
they'll kidnap you," and he paused on that point.

His father began speaking immediately: "The fact that the club is
empty has nothing to do with Romania, nothing at all. And after all, what
the fuck do you care if the clubs are empty? What the fuck do you care if
Nicolas goes to Romania? Eh? What the fuck do you care?"

Drago' would have liked to reply that he really didn't give much of a
fuck about it at all, that it was really something Nicolas was into, that he'd
kept him close, indifferent to the fact that he was blood of the blood of a
pentito, someone who had turned state's witness. He understood his mo-
tivations, certainly, and he understood just as well that for an aspiring
boss, approval was a fundamental factor. But Drago' thought of himself
as a soldier, sure, a soldier of noble blood, and the way Nicolas struggled
to get permanent access to the private dining room struck him as pretty
much a waste of time. He was looking through the dictionary for words
in code to convey that thought process to his father when Viceré decided
to put an end to the conversation.

"Tell your friend that he doesn't understand a thing about tourism or
customers, that it isn't true that they've stopped going out to the restaurants because they want to go party in Romania, they've stopped coming
to the restaurants and clubs because they just don't want to go there anymore. It's gotten too expensive."

"They don't want to go there anymore? It's gotten too expensive?"
asked Drago'. But Viceré, instead of answering the question, rapped his
knuckles on the glass, as if slapping him in the face. And Drago' would

have been glad to take that slap in the face. Instead, though, he didn't even have time to say goodbye before his father had turned his back on him.

"So 'o Viceré is basically buried in a tomb?" asked Stavodicendo as soon as Drago' returned from the prison in L'Aquila.

"That's right."

"And he can't see anyone at all?"

"Only his family, once a month."

"And, I was just saying, what about the exercise hour?"

"Eh, one hour a day. He does it with one person, or with another. Three or four people at the very most."

"And do they talk?"

"They talk, sure, but they're all shitting their pants because they're convinced the guards are planting micro recording devices on them. So Papà has become a talking crossword puzzle. You can never figure out what he's trying to tell you," and he repeated his father's words.

"They don't want to go there anymore? It's gotten too expensive?" Nicolas repeated.

And right behind him, Stavodicendo followed suit: "They don't want to go there anymore? It's gotten too expensive?"

Stavodicendo felt guilty. It had been his father who'd given him bad advice and now it was up to the son to untangle the mess. He offered to give his father a ride on his motor scooter to Borgo Marinari, and as they were zipping along Via Caracciolo, he said: "*Ué*, Pa', you sure made me look like shit."

"How so?" shouted his father to make himself heard above the noise.

"It wasn't the Gypsies, even 'o Viceré says so."

"Fuck, so for real you dragged 'o Viceré into this. What does he know about it? He's in prison."

"He told Drago' that the Roma have nothing to do with it, and then he added some phrase like 'the tourism isn't involved, either.'"

"Tourism?"

"I was just saying . . . 'O Viceré said that it has nothing to do with it, that there are no tourists in the restaurants, but not because everyone's going to Romania, but because they don't want to go there anymore, because it's gotten too expensive. And Drago' just didn't understand it at all . . . The New Maharaja has never paid for protection."

The father burst out laughing and almost knocked his son off the bike.

"Papà, I was just saying, what's it got to do with anyting?"

"It has everything to do with it, actually . . . Don't you know that the real shakedown is the protection from private security?"

"Private security?"

"Clearly, they asked for more money and the club wouldn't give it to them, so that's the private security that doesn't work any longer."

Stavodicendo accelerated, passing cars two at a time, then he cut off a delivery van, which had to slam on its brakes, and swerved off down a narrow alley. He dropped his father off outside his restaurant and revved away. Seconds later, he screeched swerving to a halt, kicking up a cloud of smoke and fumigating with the stench of burnt rubber a couple of tourists sitting at outside tables. He turned back to look at his father: "Thanks," he said, "I've got to go now," and he screeched out of there once again.

Stavodicendo texted his father's interpretation to Nicolas, and they immediately talked it over with Drago'. No doubt about it, now Viceré's message was clear. They needed to talk about it with Oscar, but he kept ignoring their calls and messages, so Nicolas went and stood outside his house. It was almost midnight. Oscar lived in an apartment house just a short walk from the New Maharaja because, as he put it, his whole life was right there. From the third floor, which was where Oscar had his apartment, light filtered out through the half-closed shutters. Nicolas leaned on the buzzer, determined not to let up until the front door clicked open. Nothing. No answer. Not even a "Fuck you, get out of here." So he put both hands together over his mouth and started shouting through that jury-rigged megaphone. "It wasn't Copacabana, it wasn't the Gypsies, it was the Puma Agency, the private security outfit, the Puma Agency . . ." Suddenly the shutters flew open and a woman in a nightgown appeared briefly, shouting down to him to shut up, and then vanished back into the light. Nicolas decided to give her ten seconds' time—one, two, three . . . —and then he'd start leaning on the buzzer again. He'd reached nine when the front door emitted a metallic click.

Oscar, in pajamas, was sitting in his armchair, in a daze. A spumante bottle that he'd probably brought home from the club lay on its side, unnoticed, on the carpet in front of him. Nicolas tried to get him to think, but he was fixated, he kept mumbling that it was probably Copacabana who'd had the club ransacked and emptied out because he'd said no about the wedding.

"It wasn't him, he really couldn't give a damn," Nicolas told him, speaking slowly, calmly, the way you'd talk to a child. "He wants all the friends he can get, if he'd wanted to he would have burned your club to the ground, he wouldn't just have stolen your things."

Nicolas looked over at the TV cabinet and noticed a bottle standing on top of it, identical to the one that the master of the house had guzzled. It wasn't chilled, who knows how long it had been standing there, but Nicolas grabbed it anyway, popped the cork, and filled the glass that Oscar still held in one hand. And he said what he'd wanted to say ever since his first phone call to Oscar: "If I can track down everything, you have to give me three things: the private dining room at my disposal, whenever the fuck I want it; fifty percent discount on anything I eat or drink in the club, for me and for all my friends; third, tell the Puma Agency to get fucked and I'll protect you instead."

"You?" For a second, Oscar seemed to regain a modicum of control and awareness, tossed back the spumante, and started to get up, but then fell back awkwardly into the armchair. He threw the glass at Nicolas but aimed the throw badly, missing him and hitting the 40-inch TV mounted on the wall. "I don't want anything to do with the Camorra, I've never paid for protection, and the last people I'd pay are you snotnose kids, *muccusielli* is what you are. Now do me a favor and clear out!"

His wife had reappeared in the meantime, fully dressed and hair neatly brushed as if she were expecting guests, and she, too, started shouting that this was the home of respectable people and that she would call the carabinieri. Bullshit, you will, Nicolas thought to himself, but this wasn't the moment to force the situation and he wasn't going to get anything else out of Oscar. The man had finally managed to get up out of his chair and now he was sniveling as he stared at the crack in the TV screen.

It didn't take Nicolas long to figure out exactly what this Puma Agency really was, everyone seemed to know about it: it was an old private security agency founded sometime in the 1990s, with money from the Nuova Famiglia, the New Family. Then the original founder had died. The man was a friend of Lorenzo Nuvoletta, one of the most powerful Camorra bosses in the nineties, and now the place was being run by his son, who happened to enjoy the protection of none other than our old friend Copacabana.

"'O White, did you see all the shit that went down at the New Maharaja?" Nicolas asked the chief of the Capelloni.

White was resting up after a game of pool. He was swirling a demitasse cup full of opium, just to uphold his reputation for consuming drugs that most people couldn't afford. He found it repulsive to get high on the kinds of drugs others used.

"Oh, yeah, fucked-up situation over there."

"Do you know who people say did it?"

"Who?"

"Copacabana."

"Bullshit," said White with a grimace. A shudder ran through him that came close to making him overturn his cup. Then he lifted the opium to his lips and the trembling stopped immediately. "If Copacabana wanted something, he'd just plant a bomb in the place, you think we give a shit about Posillipo? In fact, we actually like the place . . . And after all, what do you care about it? If someone hired you to learn more, though, I need to know so I can tell 'o Micione."

"Nobody subcontracted me to do anything. It chaps my ass, though, to hear people put the blame on us when we had nothing to do with it . . ." Nicolas tossed out. He'd developed a taste for bluffing, for pushing other people into a corner.

"So you're a vigilante," said Chicchirichì. He'd taken White's place in the pool game, and he was speaking to Nicolas with his back turned, as he lined up a cushion shot. "We? Who's we? I'm not in business with you and you're sure not in business with me."

"None of us from Forcella had anything to do with it."

"Of course not, this has got to be those Gypsies . . ." White did his best to minimize it. Now he was bluffing, too, because for a theft this big, people could even come looking for the Capelloni.

"It had nothing to do with the Gypsies, trust me," said Nicolas.

White looked him over from head to foot and took a couple of sips from his cup of opium. He pulled out an iPhone and for a minute typed in something that Nicolas could only guess at from behind the phone case, which sported a Jolly Roger. Maybe this time he'd gone too far, maybe now White was calling some of his men. Or maybe he was just chatting with his girlfriend and enjoyed keeping Nicolas standing there, twisting in the wind. When he was done tapping on his phone screen, White looked up and started staring at Nicolas again, this time right in the eyes, and lowered his gaze only when his iPhone emitted a beep that meant someone had answered. One of his men? No, impossible, why reach out to others when, right behind Nicolas, Chicchirichì and the rest stood ready to pounce at a twitch of their master's finger? His girlfriend? But did he even have a girlfriend, anyway? White read rapidly, set down the cup, and said: "So let's do this. You want to get yourself a place at the New Maharaja. That's fine."

"No wait . . ."

"Shut your mouth. If you get what I think you will, then I'm going to have to arrange for protection at the New Maharaja. At the very most, you can earn a salary, based on a percentage."

Nicolas knew that he had no option other than to say: "I don't want to take a salary from anyone." Behind Nicolas's back, the pool game had come to a halt. Not a good sign. White had leaped to his feet and grabbed the pool cue that Chicchirichì was extending in his direction. This wasn't the moment to look weak.

"I don't want to take a salary from anyone," Nicolas said again.

"Hey, asshole," said White, "enough is enough." Nicolas clenched his abdominals, bracing for a blow to his stomach from the pool cue. It was going to hurt, but if he was lucky he wouldn't slam to the floor with the wind knocked out of him and he'd have a second or two to throw a punch at someone, maybe even at White himself. In his mind, he was already underneath a human mountain of kicking feet and cursing, with his arms struggling to limit the damage to, alternately, head and testicles. Instead, though, White dropped the pool cue on the floor and got comfortable in his chair again. He had another tremor that he shook off, grinding his teeth. And then he started telling him the story. The day of the burglary, security in Posillipo had been handled by two cops who bought coke from a market that was under their protection. He'd had confirmation of this fact from Pinuccio Selvaggio, who actually supplied that very same market, and he'd added that those two Rambos with their ridiculous mustard-yellow shirts were well-known customers of his. Therefore, White had immediately looked into what had happened at the New Maharaja. But unlike Nicolas, he hadn't told anyone about what he'd learned.

For two days, Nicolas didn't emerge from his bedroom and spoke not a word to his brother. He answered Letizia's calls with short, simple texts: "Sorry, sweets, I'm not feeling good, I'll call you soon." He only accepted the food that his mother left outside his door. She tried to knock on the door, get his attention, she was worried, she said, but Nicolas got rid of her, claiming, when he talked to her, too, that he wasn't feeling well, nothing serious, he'd be over it soon, she had no reason to be afraid, but most of all she just needed to stop knocking on his door because that noise was splitting his skull. His mother left him alone, she assumed that son of hers had pulled another one of his tricks, and she just hoped that this time he hadn't really fucked up big-time, even though of course she didn't talk that way, and then it seemed odd to her that he couldn't handle the sound of her knuckles rapping on his door, since he was constantly listening to music that sounded like it came straight from the devil's grotto.

"We got guns, we got guns. Motherfuckers better, better, better run."

Nicolas had taken only a second to track down the song and mark it as one of his favorites on YouTube, setting it to loop. White sang that verse, and that verse alone, continuously, under his breath, occasionally bursting into a full-voiced baritone that clashed pretty vividly with his persona as an opium fiend, sometimes just whispering it into the ear of the first person to come within reach. He was singing it, too, when he saw Nicolas again outside Pinuccio Selvaggio's apartment house. He'd made an appointment to meet there to arrange the New Maharaja situation. Chicchirichì was there, too, and, four floors up, in a one-bedroom with a large kitchen in an apartment house just outside of Posillipo—a place that had had its last paint job sometime in the seventies, if even then—Pinuccio was expecting them. He'd lured in the two security guards with the excuse that he had a new shipment of good shit, Mariposa network, Bolivian, world's finest. Nicolas knew that he was supposed to wait with White and Chicchirichì in the toilet with the door closed, and that at Pinuccio's signal—"This shit is better than a woman, it's pure fucking sex"—he was supposed to leap out the door, grab the rope knotted into a noose that White had given him in the elevator, slip it around the guy's neck, and yank it tight. Tight enough to blur his vision and then stop when White asked a question. Demanding an answer.

And that's what had happened. Except that the two security guards didn't want to admit that they'd pulled off the job, and in fact, now they were threatening them, telling them they were retired financial police and they were going to make them pay for this. At this point, White got fed up, he'd lost his temper but he was still singing that same verse under his breath.

"*We got guns, we got guns. Motherfuckers better, better, better run.*"

He'd told them that he just needed five minutes, he had to go downstairs, there was a hardware store on the corner. He needed to buy some things. Exactly five minutes later, he was back, as promised. He'd bought a soldering iron and some motor scooter engine oil. Nicolas and Chicchirichì looked like a couple of dog owners out at the park; they had the two security guards on leashes as if they were bulldogs, and when White told the two of them to choose one, tie him up, get his pants down, and stick a rolled-up washcloth in his mouth, they did as instructed without blinking an eye. White unscrewed the cap on the motor oil, poured the liquid down the asshole of the chosen victim, and then jammed in the red-hot soldering iron.

"We got guns, we got guns. Motherfuckers better, better, better run."

White sat down in an armchair, crossed his legs, and for a moment mused as to whether he should snort the Mariposa.

Later, lying in bed back home, Nicolas could still smell the stench of burnt flesh. Of burnt anus. Shit, blood, and roast chicken. The other guard, who had witnessed the scene, had collapsed immediately and made a full confession: yes, they'd done it, they'd recruited Albanian thugs to help them. Now that Copacabana was in prison, they figured they'd increase the cost of their protection service to that club and all the other clubs they were protecting. Anyone who refused to pay, they'd just empty the place of everything that was in it, and the New Maharaja hadn't paid up.

"We got guns, we got guns. Motherfuckers better, better, better run."

White had said: "The truth that doesn't come out of the mouth always comes out the asshole," and then he'd ordered the officer to take them to the warehouse where they'd hidden the stuff. They'd left the one with the burnt asshole there to cool down a little bit.

Nicolas wanted his private dining room. In fact, he demanded it as his by right. He pulled out his smartphone and filmed it all. Chairs, candelabra, carpets, computers. Even the enormous canvas with the Indian guy, the Maharaja. Even the safe, which they'd extracted with picks and crowbars. Then he sent the video to Oscar, who, Nicolas imagined, probably watched it in the same armchair he'd last seen him in. He'd given in and accepted all of Nicolas's conditions. Oscar would hurry over to the carabinieri: "I just received an anonymous phone call. The loot is here. It was the people from the Puma Agency, because I refused to pay them for protection." He'd become an antiracket hero who'd had the courage to go to the cops and in the meantime he'd start paying White for protection: a thousand euros for every event and a thousand euros per weekend. After all, it could have gone worse.

Nicolas? Nicolas didn't want a percentage of the racket that White had imposed on Oscar. Better to take nothing than to be on someone's payroll. He'd obtained total access to the club for himself and his friends. The New Maharaja was his now.

When he decided to emerge from the bedroom, it was to tell the whole story to Christian. He took him out into the street, where the only witnesses were the flaking walls. He wanted to serve as a model for him, teach him all the things that he'd had to learn for himself.

"*Ua'*, so for real now we have full access to the New Maharaja?" asked Christian.

"Exactly! Whenever we want."

"*Ua'*, Nico', I can't believe it. Can I keep the gun under my pillow tonight?"

"All right," his older brother conceded, running his hand over Christian's crew cut.

THE PRINCE

At the Arts High School, in the only workshop, they held an optional course on multimedia studies, focused on audiovisual tecnology. It was very popular. "Hey, Teach, let's make a music video!" was the most popular request. A group of kids played music, they'd even performed in a few local clubs, they already had a dozen pieces they could record, and they were looking for a producer. On Via Tasso you could rent out rehearsal rooms, and you could record, too. They'd brought in a flash stick with two songs on it and the teacher, who didn't have an actual degree in any of this but who had attended courses at the Italian National Film School in Rome and now offered his services to local productions and to the art institute, was more worried about the equipment, which belonged to him, than he was about the quality of his students' songs. Uocchio Fino is what they'd dubbed Ettore Jannaccone. Of all the credits he could boast, one outshone them all: he was on the production crew of the classic Italian soap opera *Un posto al sole* . . . He taught lessons in production theory and only occasionally let his students get their hands on his "sensitive digitals"—as he called the video cameras that he brought back and forth from his home, urging the principal in the meantime to make an investment in school equipment. "We're in Naples, everyone has creative flair," he loved to say. And De Marino had come up with an idea. Record his students reading extracts from works of literature. Jannaccone set aside certain times in the morning hours, chose the set, and established the sequence of passages to be read. Fifteen kids, fifteen passages, no more than ten minutes apiece.

"What are you doing, Fiorillo?" De Marino asked Nicolas, catching him off guard as he was putting his cell phone in his pocket, waiting to file into the classroom.

"Huh, Teach, what do you mean what am I doing?"

"What are you going to read in front of the video camera?"

Nicolas walked over to a desk, grabbed a female classmate's anthology, read through the table of contents, and jabbed his finger down onto a page.

"Chapter Seventeen of *The Prince*."

"Very good, Fiorillo. Now read it through carefully and then you can describe in front of the video camera what you just read."

With Fiorillo he was willing to run the risk. All the others did nothing but read mechanically. He wanted to see how Fiorillo would react. Fiorillo appeared and disappeared. The girls shot him sugar-sweet longing gazes. His male classmates avoided him, or actually, he made damn sure they did. What was there inside this *guaglione*?

Nicolas took a glance at the book, another glance at his teacher, and a third at his classmate who was twisting her finger in her hair.

"What do you think? I'm afraid? Sure I'll do it."

De Marino saw him vanish with a book to the far end of the big courtyard where Jannaccone was surrounded by curious boys and girls. "*Ué, Professo'*," someone was yelling in his direction, "are you going to let us shoot an episode of *Un posto al sole*?"

And another student pretended to yank down his trousers: "An ass in the sun?" And everyone laughed.

Nicolas had holed up in a corner, his blond head bowed over the pages. At last, he said he was ready. Uocchio Fino focused the lens on his face and, for the first time that morning, he had the sensation that he was filming someone who punched through the screen. He kept that sensation to himself, but he worked a little harder this time to frame his shot properly. Nicolas sat perfectly motionless, there was no kidding around with his classmates, and, most of all, he didn't hold the book in his hands. Jannaccone asked no questions about why this *guaglione* was working from memory, he was just satisfied that he could concentrate his vision on that face, glad he didn't have to tell him every three seconds not to laugh and to hold the book down low, outside the frame. When he decided the moment was right, he said: "You can begin."

Later that morning De Marino screened the footage. He got a copy of the reading and then shut himself up, all alone, in the visual arts workshop where there was a room with audiovisual equipment. Nicolas's face appeared on the screen. His eyes were gazing straight into the camera, and to tell the truth, seeing him like that, framed by the camera lens, Fiorillo was all eyes. Now, he does have a fine eye, he thought. Like his name, Uocchio Fino. That young man knows how to see. Nicolas had taken up the challenge and now he was recounting the beginning of Chapter Seventeen of *The Prince* the way he wanted: "Someone who's going to be prince shouldn't care whether the people fear him and say he spreads fear. Someone who's going to be prince doesn't give a damn about being loved, because if you're loved those who love you do so only as long as things are going well but, the minute things go sideways, they'll fuck you first thing. It's better to have a reputation as a master of cruelty than of mercy." He seemed to concentrate at that moment; he sought a sort of consensus around him with his eyes, or perhaps not, maybe he'd just forgotten what he meant to say. He ran a finger over his chin, slowly. De Marino was tempted to rewind so he could watch that gesture again—hovering somewhere between timidity and arrogance. Then he came out with a phrase, more in dialect than proper Italian: "*Nun s'adda fà professione 'e pietà.*" There is no benefit to professing pity. Where had he come up with that expression? "Professing pity."

He went on, clearly and intensely enunciating the words: "Love is a tie that breaks, fear will never abandon you."

Nicolas took another pause and turned, offering Uocchio Fino his silhouette for further examination. In silhouette, the arrogance dissolved, he had delicate features, the face of a boy. "If the Prince has an army, that army must constantly remind everyone that he is a terrible, terrifying man, because otherwise you can't hold an army together, if you don't know how to make yourself feared. And great achievements come from the fear you instill, from the way you communicate that fear, because that is the appearance the Prince makes, and everyone sees that appearance and recognizes it and your reputation will spread far and wide."

On "far and wide" he dropped his eyes for the first time, and remained like that for a moment, as if to announce that he was done.

"How'd it turn out, Teach? Shall we upload it to YouTube now?" His voice caught De Marino by surprise. Fiorillo had remained behind, he'd wanted to see.

"Good job, Fiorillo, you scared me."

"I learned it from Machiavelli, Teach. Politics works better with fear."

"Calm down, Fiorillo. Don't get worked up."

Nicolas was leaning one shoulder against the wall, at the far end of the room. He pulled a couple of folded and refolded pages out of the rear pocket of his blue jeans.

"Teach, Machiavelli is Machiavelli, this is Fiorillo. You want to give it a read?"

De Marino didn't get up from the console, he just reached out his hand, as if to say: "Bring it here."

"I'll read it. Is that your paper?"

"It is what it is."

Nicolas handed it over and then turned on his heel. He raised his right hand, waving goodbye to his teacher, without turning around again.

De Marino went back to the screen, ran it back a few seconds, and watched Fiorillo as he said: "Everyone sees how you look and recognizes it and your reputation will spread far and wide." He smiled, turned it off, and started reading the paper. This is what Fiorillo had written, or something very close to it.

PART TWO

THE FUCKERS AND THE FUCKED

There are the fuckers and the fucked, and nothing more. They exist everywhere, and they always have. The fuckers try to gain advantage from any situation, whether it's a dinner someone else pays for, a free ride, a woman to take away from someone else, a competition to win. The fucked always get the worst of any situation.

The fucked don't always seem like it, frequently they pretend to be fuckers, just as it is only natural that the opposite should exist as well, that is, that many of those who seem to be fucked are actually extremely violent fuckers: they pass themselves off as fucked in order to raise themselves to the rank of fuckers with a greater degree of unpredictability. To seem beaten or use tears and lamentations is a typical fucker strategy.

Let it be clear, there is no reference here to sex: however you're born onto this earth, man or woman, you're still divided into one of these two categories. And for that matter, the division of society into classes has nothing to do with it, either. That's bullshit. What I'm talking about are categories of the spirit. You're born a fucker, or you're born fucked. And if you're fucked, you can be born into any walk of life, into a mansion or a stable, and you'll still find those who take away what you most care about, you'll find the obstacle that keeps you back in your work and your career, you won't be able to harness within yourself the resources to achieve your dreams. Only the crumbs will be left to you. The fucker may be born in a barracks or in an alpine hut, on the outskirts of town or in the center of the capital, but everywhere he turns he will find resources and fair winds, all the cazzimma, or the cruel strong-mindedness, and ambiguity necessary to obtain what he wants. The fucker achieves what he desires, while the fucked allows it to slip through his fingers, he loses it, he lets them take it away from him. The fucker might not even have as much power as the fucked, maybe the fucked has inherited factories and stock, but fucked he remains unless he manages to climb beyond the extra advantage offered him by good luck and laws that favor him. The fucker, on the other hand, knows how to reach beyond misfortune and can figure out how to use laws or pay to sidestep them, or even ignore them entirely.

"From the hour of their birth, some are marked out for subjection, others for rule; and there are many kinds both of rulers and subjects." That's what good old Aristotle has to say. In other words, to put it concisely, you're born either fucked or a fucker. The latter knows how to steal and deceive, and the former knows how to be stolen from and deceived.

Look inside yourself. Look deep inside yourself, but if you're not ashamed, you're not looking deep enough.

And then ask yourself if you're fucked or a fucker.

COURTROOM

One of Micione's men had wound up in court, the charge was that he'd murdered Don Vittorio Grimaldi's son, Gabriele. This was certainly true, and Don Vittorio, aka the Archangel, had even seen his son die before his eyes.

It had all happened so quickly in that country, Montenegro, where father and son had decided to take their business. And so they went there together. There was an old iron waterwheel, badly rusted, all that remained of a tumbledown mill. The stream kept it turning, and the Archangel saw the man clearly, saw his face, saw his eyes, saw his hands as they shoved Gabriele against the blades of the waterwheel that the flowing waters of the stream had chipped until they were jagged and sharp. Don Vittorio saw it happen from the window of their villa, which wasn't far away, and he ran down in desperate haste. He tried to stop the waterwheel with his own hands, but he was unsuccessful. He saw his son's body smash into the water again and again until he was helped by the domestic staff. It took them a long time to untangle Gabriele's corpse from those blades. And yet, throughout the entire trial, Don Vittorio defended Micione's hired killer. He refused to bring evidence, he refused to provide any information. Gabriele Grimaldi's killer was Tigrotto, the right-hand man of Diego

Faella, Micione. That's how Micione wanted to conquer Montenegro and, more important, take over San Giovanni a Teduccio and from there enjoy unhindered access to Naples. He was present in the courtroom during the trial, and the prosecuting magistrate asked whether he recognized him. Don Vittorio said no. The prosecuting magistrate insisted, hoping to bring the trial to a conclusion: "Are you certain?" He addressed Don Vittorio as *voi*, avoiding the more formal *lei*, in an attempt to bring both sides together. And Don Vittorio said no. "Do you recognize Francesco Onorato, 'o Tigrott'?"

"Never seen him, don't even know who he is." Don Vittorio knew that those hands were stained with the blood of his son and many of his fellow clan members. Nothing. Diego Faella's thanks weren't exceptional. In the heart of the state's power, we're all men of honor. The silence of Don Vittorio Grimaldi was viewed as the normal behavior of a man of honor. The concession that Micione offered was life, or rather, survival. He put a halt to the gang war against the Grimaldis, he allowed him to go on dealing, confining him to a reservation in Ponticelli. A handful of streets, the only place where he'd be allowed to sell and exist. The boundless resources that the Grimaldis had once had—heroin, cocaine, cement, garbage, shops, and supermarkets—had now dwindled to a few square kilometers, and scanty profits. Tigrotto was acquitted and Don Vittorio was returned to house arrest.

It was an enormous success, the lawyers exchanged hugs, a few people in the front row applauded. Nicolas, Pesce Moscio, Drago', Briato', Tucano, and Agostino watched that trial from start to finish, and you could almost say they grew up together at it. When they'd started going to watch, they only had a few stray hairs on their faces, and now some of them had beards worthy of an ISIS militiaman. They continued to enter the courtroom by showing the same fake IDs they'd first displayed two years earlier, during the very first hearings. Because you could enter the courtroom to watch the trial, no question, but only if you were an adult. Getting hold of those fake IDs had been child's play. The city specialized in the production of fake IDs for jihadists, so there surely would have been no obstacles for local youngsters, *guaglioncelli*, who wanted to get into a courtroom. Briato' had taken care of it. He'd taken the photographs and identified the right counterfeiter. A hundred euros apiece, and there they were, three or four years older. Stavodicendo and Biscottino objected to having been left out, but in the end they were forced to give in: they couldn't have fooled anyone with those baby faces of theirs.

The first time they assembled outside the court complex, looking up at those three glass-and-steel towers, they were surprised to feel a sort of sneaking attraction. They all felt as if they'd wandered into an American TV series; instead they were in front of the criminal court buildings, the same structures that the bosses they were going in now to see in the flesh had arranged to burn, systematically, while they were still under construction. The allure of glass and steel and height and power had deflated the minute they'd walked in the front entrance. Here everything was plastic, wall-to-wall carpeting, and echoing voices. They'd climbed the stairs, daring one another to see who could reach the top first, yanking on one another's T-shirts and making noise; then once they were inside the courtroom, they'd been greeted by that slogan—The Law Is Equal for All—at the sight of which Nicolas had had to stifle a laugh. As if no one knew the truth (*mannaggia il patriarca*, he swore to himself), that the world was divided into just two categories, the fucked and the fuckers. That's the only law that counts. And every time they went to watch that trial, unfailingly, as they went in, a crooked smile showed on their faces.

Inside the courtroom, they'd spent hours sitting quietly, something they'd never done before in their short lives. At school, at home, even in clubs, there was always too much to see and try out for them to waste time sitting still. Their legs danced in impatience, always forcing their bodies to go somewhere else, and from there to yet some other place. But the trial was all of life itself, laying itself out before their eyes and revealing its secrets to them. There was so much to learn. Every single gesture, every word, every glance offered a lesson, a teaching. Impossible to look away, impossible to lose your focus. They looked like a group of well-behaved children attending Mass on Sunday, their fingers intertwined, hands resting on their legs, eyes wide open, attentive, heads ready to swivel quickly in the direction of the important words, no nodding, no nervous movements, even cigarettes could wait.

The courtroom was divvied up in two perfect halves. In the front were the actors, farther back was the audience. And between them, six-foot-high steel bars. The voices came across slightly distorted by the echoing acoustics, but the meaning of the phrases was never lost. The kids had carved out a single space for all of them, in the next-to-last row, over beside the wall. It wasn't the best location; at the theater these would have been the cheap seats, but they could still see everything: the untroubled gaze of Don Vittorio beneath a silvery head of hair that in this light looked like a mirror, the defendant's back—he was broader across than he was tall, but with a pair of yellow feline eyes that put the fear in you—the backs of the lawyers, the backs of the people who had managed to snag a front-row seat. They were Chinese shadow puppets, at first only shapeless blurs, but then the light shifts in intensity and the eyes of the audience adjust, sharpen, and then everything makes sense, right down to the finest details. And not far away, perhaps just a couple of rows up, the members of several *paranzas*, whom you could recognize by a snippet of some tattooed phrase sticking out of the collar of their shirt or a scar that their shaven skull brazenly displayed.

In the front row, just a few short steps from the bars, sat the *paranza* of the Capelloni. They'd never made an issue of age and often showed up en masse. Unlike Nicolas and the others, the Capelloni didn't seem to thirst for every word, every silence, and you'd often see them stroll along the rows of chairs, stop for a moment to place their hands on the bars, indifferent to the objections of those who were behind them, and then go back to their seats. White was the only one who never stood up, perhaps because he worried that his drunken-cowboy gait might attract the attention of the carabinieri. At other times, you might chance to see the Barbudos from Sanità. They sat down wherever they could find a spot. They'd sit there, deep in conversation, stroking their Bin Laden beards, and every so often go out for a cigarette. But there was no tension, no wary studying of one another. All eyes were on the stage.

"*Ua',*" said Maraja in a very low voice. He'd leaned his head back only as far as needed, speaking out of the corner of his mouth because he couldn't bring himself to turn his gaze away. "If we had half the balls of Don Vittorio, not even fucking God could stop us."

"That guy is protecting the guy who shed his own son's blood . . ." whispered Dentino.

"All the more reason," Maraja reiterated, *"adda murì mammà* if he hasn't got a pair of balls on him. As long as he can stay true, he'd be willing to keep the one who crushed his son's body from going behind bars."

"I don't think I could maintain all this loyalty. That is, either I kill you or if I'm in prison I rat you out and make sure you get life without parole, *omm' 'e mmerda,*" said Pesce Moscio. Piece of shit.

"E questo è da infami," Maraja replied, and then repeating the same words, "This is infamous, a turncoat's play. It's easy to preserve your honor when you have to defend your own money, your own shit, your own blood. It's precisely when it would be easy to mouth off and sing like a canary to everyone who'll listen that, instead, if you keep your mouth shut, then that means you're number one, that you're the best. That you've busted everyone else's ass. That they can all just suck your dick because you're head and shoulders above, because you know how to defend the System. Even when they've murdered your son. *Hai capì, Pescioli'?"* Understand, Little Fish?

"He's preserving it in front of someone who murdered his son, and he doesn't say a thing," Pesce Moscio went on.

"Pesce Mo'," Dentino commented, "you'd already be singing if you were there . . . you've got a career as an informant."

"No, *strunzo,* I'd have already sliced him open."

"So listen to Jack the Ripper," Tucano concluded.

They were talking like a couple of Texas hold 'em players, never looking each other in the eye. They tossed out phrases onto the green felt, showing what they had in their minds, and after a while someone, like Tucano had done, would sweep the table and deal out another hand.

No one could imagine, though, just what it was that Nicolas was hoping for deep within. Maraja liked Don Vittorio, but it was Micione who, having married Viola, the daughter of Don Feliciano, had the blood in their quarter. Rotten blood, but still, the blood of kings. The blood of their quarter was hereditary, as the rules of ownership require. Don Feliciano had always told his men: "The quarter has to remain in the hands of those who were born there and live there." And Copacabana, who had been a faithful envoy of the Strianos, had grabbed for Forcella with both hands, immediately after the arrest of the head of the family. It had in fact been the arrest of the boss, almost three years earlier, that had led to the trial.

The entire quarter had been surrounded. They'd been on his trail for days on end, and the *catturandi* squad, the equivalent of the U.S. Marshals, couldn't believe it: Don Feliciano had come back to Naples and was out on the street, dressed in a tracksuit, in contrast with the sartorial distinction he usually flaunted in public. He hadn't tried to hide, he was spending his time on the run from the law right in his own home quarter, just like everyone, but without lurking behind fake walls, under double floors, down wells, in hidey-holes. They had burst out of the alley, the *vicolo*, and they'd called his name: "Feliciano Striano, sir, please put your hands up." He'd stopped, and that "Sir, please put your hands up" seemed to have calmed him down. It was an arrest, not an ambush. He'd shot a chilling glance at his lazy bodyguard, who seemed determined to heat things up by firing his gun; the bodyguard changed his mind and immediately turned to run, eager to escape handcuffs himself. Don Feliciano allowed himself to be cuffed. "Go on, go ahead," he'd told them. And while they were wrapping his wrists in case-hardened steel, the carabinieri, without even noticing it, suddenly found themselves surrounded by crowds of kids and ladies. Feliciano smiled. "Don't worry, all of you, stop worrying," he said, calming the nerves of the people who were leaning out the windows and doors and starting to shout: *"Ue', maronna mia!"* The children were wrapping their arms around the carabinieri's legs and biting their thighs. The mothers were keening: "Let him be, leave him be . . ." A crowd poured forth into the streets, the apartment buildings seemed like so many bottles overturned, gushing people and more people and still more people out into the *vicoli*.

Don Feliciano was laughing: the Casalesi bosses, the bosses of Secondigliano, Palermo, and Reggio Calabria, would surely have been caught deep underground in caves, behind fake wall partitions, in subterranean labyrinths. He, the true king of Naples, was being arrested out on the street, in view of one and all. The one thing that Don Feliciano regretted was that he wasn't well dressed; it's clear that the carabinieri who usually gave him confidential tips had sold him out, or else they'd been unable to get word to him of the impending arrest. All he would have needed was half an hour: not to make his escape, but to select the right Eddy Monetti suit, shirt, and Marinella tie. All the times he'd been arrested, he'd always been caught impeccably dressed. And he dressed impeccably because, as he always liked to say, it can always happen, someone might shoot you or arrest you without advance warning, and you can't let them catch you looking shabby. Everyone would be disappointed, everyone would say: "So Don Feliciano Striano, is that all he was?" And now they were going to see him, and maybe they'd say: "Is this all he was, after all?" This was his one misgiving, he knew all the rest and what little he didn't know he could imagine. The crowd pressed in, jeering, around the carabinieri squad cars. The sirens didn't intimidate anyone. Nor did the regulation sidearms. Even if they'd wanted to, under absolutely no circumstances could they have opened fire. "In those apartment buildings, there are more weapons than forks and knives" was the only thing that their commanding officer had told them, urging them to keep cool. The force at play was disproportionate and the advantage was distinctly on the side of the people in the apartment buildings. Camera crews showed up from the national news broadcasts. A couple of helicopters were buzzing overhead. The people in the streets of the quarter were waiting for a sign, any sign at all, to distract the carabinieri, who were anything but ready to face up to a mass insurrection. The arrest had been authorized in a moment of calm and quiet, the streets were deserted, it was the middle of the night. Where had those children come from? Had those people simply been catapulted directly from their beds out into the streets? Among all the faces that looked on with worried veneration, the way you look at a father as he's being carried off for no good reason, Copacabana stepped forward. Feliciano Striano smiled at him and Copacabana gave him a kiss on the lips, the utmost symbol of loyalty. Mouth shut. No one speaks. Seal of silence.

"*Basta ammuina*" was Don Feliciano's phrase. "Enough uproar." Copacabana passed it along, and it spread like a domino that eventually knocked down all the others. In the blink of an eye, they were all gone, everyone stopped their yelling. They hurried away to keep company with Don Feliciano's wife and daughter, as if in a sort of wake, conveying their condolences. That had been Don Feliciano Nobile's decision. It was the last act of strength of a clan decimated by the war against the Sanità quarter, against the Mocerino clan, with whom the Strianos had at first tried to ally themselves, until they were both forced to kill each other off in reciprocal slaughter. Don Feliciano Nobile's final winning strategy had been to show himself, prove to his men and his quarter that he hadn't been forced into hiding—which would naturally mean turning himself into an easy target, and therefore dying. That it would come to an end seemed inevitable after his lengthy reign, inherited from his father, Luigi Striano o' Sovrano, and he knew that well. In the days still available to him, though, appearing publicly like this meant giving the Striano clan the image of still being fearless, free, and at home in their quarter. Which mattered.

Then that last kiss, given to Copacabana, was betrayed by none other than Don Feliciano. Over the course of the following few months the Apocalypse befell them, unexpected, violent, and unimaginable. Don Feliciano had made up his mind to talk, and his betrayal—his *pentimento*, or repentance—brought down far more structures than any earthquake. It's not a metaphor, it's exactly what happened. He redesigned the entire map of the System. Whole buildings emptied out because of waves of arrests or else witness-protection programs that transported Don Feliciano's family members to safe zones. It was far more ghastly than any feud. It heaped shame on every man and woman in the clan, the same shame that comes over you when you realize that everyone knows about your husband's or your wife's betrayal. And you feel watched, mocked. They'd felt Don Feliciano's blue eyes, his level gaze on them every minute for years now. Those eyes were both a threat and a protection. No one could come into Forcella to do as they pleased, no one could disobey any of the System's rules. And the System's rules had been dictated and were enforced by the Strianos. Those eyes were safety and fear. And Don Feliciano had decided to close those eyes.

As was the case with his arrest, it was night when the quarter learned he had turned state's witness. There was a blitz of helicopters and even an armor-plated bus filled with hundreds of arrestees. Don Feliciano informed, reporting the paid killers, the gang members, the extortionists, the dope-peddling bases. He informed on his own family, and the whole family spilled the beans in a daisy chain. They all started betraying one another, providing information, talking about bribes, public works contracts, checking accounts. Commissioners, deputy ministers, bank directors, and businessmen: they all started singing like canaries on one another. Don Feliciano talked, and talked, and talked some more, while the whole quarter rose up with a single question: "Why?"

For months to follow, this interrogative adverb could mean only one thing: "Why did Don Feliciano turn state's witness?" There was no need to complete the sentence, all you had to say was "Why?" and everyone understood. In cafés and bars, at the dinner table on Sundays, at the soccer stadium. "Why?" just meant: "Why did Don Feliciano do it?" There were weighty catalogs of answers, but the truth was simple, even obvious: Don Feliciano had turned state's witness because he would rather kill Forcella than turn over ownership of it to anyone else. Because he hadn't had the fortitude to put a noose around his own neck, he chose to put the noose around everybody else's. He tried to make people think he'd found his conscience, but how do you wipe your conscience clean of guilt for hundreds of deaths? Bullshit. There'd been no repentance, he didn't regret a single thing. He was talking just as a way to go on killing. Before he'd done it with guns, now he was doing it with his words.

Drago's father, Nunzio Striano Viceré, had taken the convictions and the sentences: Feliciano had informed on him for every sort of traffic, every misdeed, every crime that he'd committed, but Viceré had refused to talk. All the other brothers had turned state's witness, but Viceré would not. He continued to do his time behind bars, and with his silence he protected a few apartments and his son. He didn't want Luigi to wind up like Don Feliciano's daughter, who until she married Micione had been reviled and ostracized by everyone. "*Pentita*," they called her.

No one was so naïve as to be unable to glimpse, hovering behind Tigrotto in the defendant's box, the looming shade of Micione, as if he were actually present in the courtroom in flesh and blood. In the meantime, Don Vittorio persisted in remaining silent in the face of the prosecuting magistrate's onslaught: "Your son, as we've been able to demonstrate, has been identified, by various informants working with law enforcement, as an enemy of the Faellas, with whom you not only share your quarter but also a history as allies. In that case, do you have any knowledge that the Faellas might have wished the death of your son?"

"My son, as good and kind as he was with everyone, could hardly have stirred in anyone the desire to kill him, at least that's my belief. Impossible to imagine. Especially in someone from our own quarter and who would therefore have known his deep and abiding love for Ponticelli, its children, and all the people he'd always loved, and who turned out in throngs for his funeral."

It was a back-and-forth in a technically proper Italian, doing its best to keep at bay the words in dialect that were seething up from under, but which then and there would have compromised that sunny calm.

In the meantime, Tigrotto's arrogance didn't seem to unsettle Don Vittorio at all; he was even quite willing to lock eyes with him. Tigrotto tried to dismiss it all with a sort of grimace of disgust.

"I knew Gabriele Grimaldi, but only to say hello. I knew he was never around in Ponticelli, and anyway, I never spent time at Conocal. I've never spent time out on the streets." Tigrotto used those words to report Micione's words. He wanted to emphasize the difference in their origins, different blood, different interests, born in a villa, not out on the streets. In the silent interplay of references, those words meant: Micione isn't a narco, he doesn't live on drug dealing alone, he lives on cement and politics and business, and far from the street. Don Vittorio could do nothing but let him go on saying these things. Could only show himself to be submissive.

Nicolas understood the dynamic of the game, in all its nuances. He understood that behind it all there was always this thing with blood, affiliation, what's clean and what's dirty. There was no theory to hold together these concepts as old as mankind itself. Dirty and clean. Who decides what's dirty? Who decides what's clean? It's blood, it's always blood. It's clean and it can never enter into contact with dirty blood, the blood of other people. Nicolas had grown up with these things, all his friends had grown up with them, but he wanted to have the courage to declare that that system was old. And it needed to be abolished. The enemy of your enemy is your friend, aside from any issues of blood and relationships. If in order to become what he wanted to become he was going to have to learn to love what they had taught him to hate, well, he was certainly willing to do that. And to hell with blood. Camorra 2.0.

HUMAN SHIELD

The *guaglioni* of Don Vittorio Grimaldi were obliged to read the names of the streets of the Conocal district every day, because they couldn't leave that place, that section of Ponticelli. Leaving meant running the risk of being shot by Micione's men; all the Faellas had them in their crosshairs. And so they stayed inside, within the perimeter of those streets that form a rectangle missing a corner, up top, on the right. When they read articles in the papers that other people wrote about them, they grew furious, because of the pontificating about urban decline, about the apartment buildings that were all alike, about the lack of a future. No matter what they might say, though, those rabbit-warren apartments were there, and, arranged in a hypocritical geometry, were meant to define a living space that was actually a confinement. Like a prison cell. But those *guaglioni* had no interest in winding up like Scampia and becoming a symbol. They weren't blind, they had eyes to see that there, where they lived, everything looked like it was third-hand, even fourth-hand. Tattered curtains, baked by the sun, charred garbage, walls spitting threats. Still, this was their quarter and their whole world, and so probably best to accept it and like it, even if that meant denying the facts that were right in front of them. It was a matter of identity, of belonging.

Identity is a landing on a staircase. Identity is a street and the streets become the only space where you can possibly live. A single café, just two mini-markets, the rooms of old dry-goods stores that are starting to sell all their inventory. Pawnshops and junkyards transformed into warehouses full of toilet paper and laundry soap because there is no supermarket in the quarter, or it's too far to be accessible to the elderly, or those on motor scooters, or those who just can't leave their quarter. That's what was happening to the Grimaldis. There, though, they could continue to sell drugs. The customers who made it to Conocal were hoping to buy hash, cocaine, and balls of crack at a deep, deep discount. But Don Vittorio had insisted they not drop the price too sharply. It would have been a negative sign, a mark of death. Which meant their customers would stop going there, and they couldn't venture out looking for customers.

Not everyone, however, played by the rules. Aucelluzzo was skilled at racing along on his scooter, actually rocketing along, faster than the bullets that might easily take him down, quicker than the eyes that might identify him and pin him down, secretive and furtive in his peddling. Visible to the buyer, invisible to the lookouts. Aucelluzzo therefore had no fear of setting foot outside Conocal. All the same, in spite of the fact that he took courage and eliminated his fears by sucking confidence from the X-Men that occupied so much of his body in the form of tattoos, he was destined to die young. Copacabana, in his cell, allowed no one from outside, and especially no one connected to the Grimaldis, to deal in his territory. He'd have overlooked any other family, in exchange for a percentage, but not them. They had set themselves against Forcella, they'd waged war: they smuggled heroin, cocaine, and grass from the West, while the Grimaldis imported the same products from the East.

Copacabana wanted to take the East away from the Grimaldis, and he was succeeding. And so three streets in Naples were a fair trade for the capital of Montenegro, a patch of the Balkans, an entire Albanian plantation. Aucelluzzo sensed this, but he didn't really know it. And he went on racing around on his scooter, with those long, skinny legs that were concealed behind the cowling, so that when you saw him coming, it looked as if the torso and all the rest of him just sprouted directly from the saddle. He always posed aerodynamically, even when there was no need, even when he was riding an ancient Vespa assembled out of spare parts from his father's Vespa: he leaned so far forward that his face touched the odometer and he splayed his elbows wide, so wide that more than once they'd hit side mirrors. His nose was birdlike as well, pointed and downward curving, like a sparrow hawk's.

White's men—Carlito's Way, Chicchirichì, and Selvaggio—took off after him the minute they glimpsed from a distance those two outsplayed elbows. Aucelluzzo spotted them out of the corner of his eye, revved his engine, and zipped on his Vespa into the infinite wall of slow-moving traffic. "Next time, we'll leave your name on the asphalt," they shouted after him, but Aucelluzzo had vanished, and even if he had heard them it wouldn't have made a bit of difference to him and he would have come back all the same. Up in Forcella he actually engaged in open defiance, and would freely pass by the back room.

"The hungrier a bird is," said Copacabana when they reported these facts to him in prison, "the less afraid it is when you stamp your feet or clap your hands." He used the dialect term *aucielli*, a clear reference to Aucelluzzo. "You know what I mean, 'o White, how when you clap your hands and these flying rats won't even budge? And why won't they? Because they're hungry. And they don't give a damn about escaping, even if you've made up your mind to kill them, because they're bound to die anyway and they know it. Either of hunger or because you shoot them. We don't shoot them, and the pigeons cover us with shit. That's how things go with the Grimaldis."

Aucelluzzo brought hordes of kids with him. He'd stake them out for an hour or two. Every so often he'd even bring old guys who could no longer justify a salary. Like Alfredo Scala 40, who'd strewn the pavement with dead bodies, and who'd even been district underboss for a certain period. He'd earned a hundred million lire a week, back when they still had the lira: about a hundred thousand euros. What with lawyers' fees and general squandering, now he hung out near the markets to rob customers, downgraded to a common dealer, or even a lookout. You started young, in the System. And if you didn't die right away, your career collapsed eventually anyway.

It was too much. The cancer that was Aucelluzzo was already starting to metastasize, so the Capelloni set off on a mission to rub him out: White decided to see to it in person. Aucelluzzo was on his Vespa as usual, he'd dared to set up shop on Piazza Calenda, his back against a scaffolding. Before the gunshots, he heard the metallic sound of White's bullets hitting the tubing of the modular scaffolding. White was holding his pistol the way he'd seen guys do in gangsta rap movies—horizontally. Bang. Bang. Bang. Three times, at random, because lately he'd been doing lots of morphine, the same kind that he'd been selling so successfully via the pushers who reported to him, and therefore to Copacabana. With the money he'd purchased an apartment for La Koala, his sister. But morphine and precision never go hand in hand, and so once again Aucelluzzo was saving his pinfeathers from death.

If Nicolas, that day, hadn't been passing by—he and Dentino had plunged into a sudden crisis of ravenous hunger and they were riding down Via Annunziata trying to decide where to go—if he hadn't recognized those metallic bangs, if he hadn't made a sharp turn, fishtailing and slamming a foot down onto the pavement to keep from sprawling across the asphalt, to correct the trajectory that threatened to take him out into Piazzetta Forcella, that is, in the opposite direction, well, if he hadn't done all these things, then he wouldn't have witnessed the scene and perhaps he'd never have had his idea, which he immediately put into practice, while on Dentino's face the sign of the cross appeared.

A human shield. Nicolas threw himself between Aucelluzzo and White, who had now leveled his pistol and had shut one eye to take his aim. He got in the middle. White stopped. Aucelluzzo froze in place. Dentino grabbed his T-shirt and shouted: "Maraja, what the fuck are you doing?!" Nicolas spoke to White, who was still standing there, aiming his gun, one eye closed, as if he were waiting for Nicolas to get out of the way so he could start shooting again.

"'O White," said Nicolas, revving closer to him on his motor scooter while Aucelluzzo finally screeched off, "we're just killing more people and doing nothing to get rid of the cops and the checkpoints. You're out of your mind. Next thing you know, you'll kill an old man, a lady, a child. Aucelluzzo got away, we'll pick him up. Leave it to me." He said it all in a single breath. White lowered his gun, but said nothing. There were two possibilities, Nicolas considered. Either he raises the pistol again and it all ends here. Or else . . . White half closed his mouth and flashed a smile of chipped, nicotine-yellowed teeth, then he jammed the pistol down his pants and roared off. Nicolas heaved a sigh of relief, and even Dentino felt it, from where he was sitting, pressed against his back.

Aucelluzzo vanished, but they knew he wouldn't be able to stay out of sight forever.

"But why did you do it?" Briato' asked him. "Aucelluzzo is against Micione, he's against Copacabana, and that means he's against us."

They were in the back room, and it was just them. The Capelloni, Nicolas decided, must be in prison reporting to Copacabana. So much the better.

"Don't worry, we aren't on 'o Micione's side, we aren't with Copacabana. We're with us," Nicolas replied.

"I still don't understand exactly what this 'us' is," Dentino said. "So far, I belong to whoever gives me money."

"Okay," said Maraja, "but if the money you gave to this one, to another, and to a third guy—what if we put it all together? And then, if the money makes us a group, don't you like that outcome?"

"But we're already a group!"

"Sure, a group of fools."

"You're obsessed. He wants to start a *paranza* whatever the cost," said Dentino.

Nicolas was visibly scratching his balls, as if to say that dreams should never be spoken aloud. And that word, *paranza*, was a word he tried to pronounce as seldom as possible.

"I want to take Aucelluzzo down myself," said Maraja, "so if you see him, no one else gets to do it."

They'd been discussing what Nicolas had done for a good solid hour. They were telling him he'd been a lunatic, a true madman. What if White had unleashed a firefight? And what if, as Nicolas himself was saying, old men and little children got caught in the crossfire? Plain crazy. Maraja listened. Because what he was receiving from the others was a genuine investiture. What Briato' and the rest of the group were calling madness, Maraja considered to be instinct, and Maraja commanded by instinct, it was a natural gift of sorts, more or less like skillfully handling a soccer ball without ever having set foot on a pitch, or else knowing how to add and subtract when you're just a kid who's never received lessons from a teacher. He felt infused with a sort of spirit of command, and he liked it when the others acknowledged the fact.

Aucelluzzo was an insignificant little kid, but he was the front door to Conocal, and, once they got in there, they could get to Don Vittorio, and from there . . . Nicolas grabbed his balls again, a classic gesture to ward off bad luck, invoke good.

"But now that you saved his life," Briato' said, "he's not enough of a fool that he'll just wait around to be found."

"Of course he will," said Maraja, "when he runs out of feed, he's going to have to come looking for more."

"But they'll shoot him here," said Briato'.

"Sure, but it won't be easy. Here he'll have to come via Sanità, Forcella, the station, 'o Rettifilo, San Domenico. He'll take a look around, and the minute things look dicey, hc'll take off."

"Do you think he's packing?" asked Dentino.

"For real? I don't think so. And if he is, all he's carrying is the same as what we've got, a beat-up old gat and some knives."

In the days that followed, Nicolas mapped out the territory, shuttling back and forth, back and forth. By now it was an obsession with him. Letizia, too, had noticed that he constantly had something else on his mind, but then, Nicolas always had something churning in his head, and so she didn't get too worried. In the end, Aucelluzzo reappeared. He started from a considerable distance, not directly with the areas controlled by Copacabana's men. By now he was selling to blacks and little kids, and at prices that were so low that maybe his own men would soon kill him. He worked the Ponte della Maddalena, he worked the train station a little, too. And that, in fact, was where Nicolas caught up with him, on Piazza Garibaldi, in a torrential downpour, the kind that blurs your vision, but he had no doubts, it was really him. That black sweatshirt with the picture of Tupac Shakur on it? Aucelluzzo never took it off, not even when it was ninety degrees out. He had his hood pulled over his head and he was deep in conversation with some other guy Nicolas had never seen before. Maraja killed the engine on his motor scooter and tiptoed closer, pushing off the balls of his feet. He had no clearly worked-out strategy, he just hoped to catch him off guard and then improvise then and there, but a deafening clap of thunder made everyone look up, even Aucelluzzo, and then he saw Nicolas, drenched, his jeans clinging to his thighs.

Aucelluzzo grabbed the Vespa that he'd leaned against the balustrade and he was already gone, swallowed by the rain. He raced off, taking the curve *a recchia 'n terra*, as the saying went, "one ear to the ground," whizzing off as if there were no traffic, as if that traffic weren't being made even crazier by the cloudburst. He took Corso Umberto. The cars were a compact, unbudging mass, horns quarreling with other horns, windshield wipers fanning on the highest speed, sloshing water left and right. This is a tropical rainstorm, thought Nicolas, this is the rain out of the Battle of Helm's Deep, and he felt like an Uruk-hai, his jacket pulled tight around him like some impenetrable suit of armor. The people on the sidewalks were glued to the walls in the hope that the balconies above might protect them from the downpour. Aucelluzzo kicked up waves in each and every puddle, and when he spotted an opening between two cars he'd slide through it, running a hand over his face like a towel, and then revving faster and faster, ever faster. Nicolas was having trouble keeping up with him, and he shouted: "I don't want to hurt you, I just want to talk," but Aucelluzzo kept hitting the gas, his elbows thrown wider and wider, until they grazed the rearview mirrors, and anyway, with all that noise, so loud it sounded as if they were in the midst of a war, there was no way he could hear Nicolas. It went on like that for a good long while. Aucelluzzo veered suddenly, went the wrong way up one-way streets, arcing through perfect curves without ever touching his brakes. He drove the Vespa as if he were swerving through a minefield, but instead of sidestepping the mines he was driving right over them, on purpose.

In a *vicolo* that Nicolas didn't recognize because by this time he was driving blind, just trying desperately to keep his eyes on the fugitive's brake light, Aucelluzzo rode into a puddle that was at least a foot and a half deep. His wheels vanished, almost entirely submerged, and Nicolas immediately anticipated that now the dealer had fucked up good and his engine was about to stall. Instead, though, Aucelluzzo just revved the motor and the Vespa responded, kicking bucketfuls of filthy water into the air behind it. Nicolas was lurching forward, slowing down whenever he sensed that his rear tire was failing to stick to the pavement, and more than once he actually slammed into the bumper of the car ahead of him. He cursed, he threatened anyone who asked him to pull over and display his identification. He navigated around the sinkholes and potholes that open up every time the city floods. By now he could no longer even feel his hands, which had merged with the handlebars of the Beverly. He had to make sure he didn't lose his grip on the throttle or lose his line of sight on the Vespa, which was roaring along in what seemed to be its natural element. It was even zipping along on the deserted sidewalks because now the tropical downpour, if anything, had gotten even worse, intensifying and even starting to hail and sleet. Aucelluzzo took the sleet on his hoodie and just kept going. Nicolas continued to curse, but he couldn't give up, because when would he ever lay hands on him again?

The hail stopped all at once, as if someone high above had stuck a cork in it, but the street was a white expanse, it looked like snow. The Vespa left grooves that Nicolas followed with extreme precision to avoid skidding and hitting the pavement, but then the landscape altered again because the rain had slackened and people were pouring back out into the street. Aucelluzzo was still riding along. If he could create confusion by taking advantage of the blackish ooze created by the pooling rain, he'd do it. So Nicolas had to slalom between furious people who weren't fast enough to take it out properly on that devil who was fleeing for his life, just quick enough to lash out at the guy who was chasing him.

But the smell of brakes and the white-hot muffler were starting to ring alarm bells that he was going to have to pay attention to. By the time the burning smell reached Maraja, a gap had finally opened up in the clouds, but he didn't notice because he'd decided to put an end to that pursuit. Aucelluzzo must have been tired, too, and he didn't notice that Nicolas had vanished from his side mirrors. The dope dealer from Conocal was squeezing every last bit of power out of his Vespa as he passed in front of the University of Naples Federico II. Then it dawned on him that Nicolas had gone the other way around, just as he emerged from Vico Sant'Aniello a Caponapoli. For a moment, Aucelluzzo regretted not having brought a weapon, but then he surrendered. When he saw that Nicolas continued to keep both hands on the handlebars of his scooter, he started to hope: he knew that if Nicolas had been packing a pistol, he'd already have fired, at the very least.

Maraja didn't try get to the point by assembling an argument filled with insinuations and unstated subjects. He went straight to the point: "Aucellu', I need to talk to Don Vittorio L'Arcangelo."

Aucelluzzo was uneasy hearing that name uttered in the middle of the street and in front of him. He turned red in the face: out of shame, not anger.

"I need to talk with L'Arcangelo," Nicolas went on. All around them, foreign tourists armed with umbrellas and K-Way jackets were heading to the National Archaeological Museum, completely indifferent to the two of them as they stood talking in the middle of the street. "You need to tell him loud and clear that: first, if you're still alive you owe that to me; second, by now you're all just dying under the rule of 'o Micione. They're gnawing at your faces. That your *guaglioni* aren't worth a shit, they just sit and stare at their PlayStations, all the time, twenty-four seven. No one's working anymore."

"But I never see Don Vittorio."

"Sure, but you're the one who brings flowers to his son's grave, and if he chose you for that errand, it means he trusts you, he knows you."

"But I never see him," said Aucelluzzo, "I don't get in touch with him, I'm out on the street."

"Then find a way to see him. Right now, you know, I could easily slice you open, shoot you in the face. Text somebody to come up behind you and put you down. You're alive because I decide to let you live."

"What is it you want to talk to him about?" Aucelluzzo managed to get out the words. His cheeks were no longer red, but his eyes were downcast. Humiliated.

"Don't you worry about that. Tell him that there's a *guaglione* from the Forcella System who wants to speak with him. That ought to be plenty enough."

"What are you talking about, plenty enough!"

"Make it do, make it plenty. Aucellu', if you can't get me this meeting, wherever you are, you might as well stay there: I'll come and track you down. But if you can do this for me, I'll tell 'o White that you're kicking in a percentage. That you're giving us half of what you sell, but you don't have to give me anything. I'll cover for you. You decide. Either you do what I tell you to do and you stay alive and you eat regularly, or else you do what *you're* saying and you'll die sooner of hunger, because I'll make sure you can't work here anymore, and then you'll come to a miserable end. You decide and let me know."

Aucelluzzo turned his Vespa around in the opposite direction and roared off without so much as a goodbye, without saying yes, without giving him his phone number. He went back to Ponticelli, he went back to the hut made of cement and tar that he and his family had been condemned to live in. A cell open to the sky, some people called it. Guantánamo, others had nicknamed it. And inmate number one lived a peaceful life in solitary confinement because barring the way to anyone who wasn't entirely welcome was Cicognone, cook, assistant, and lady-in-waiting to Don Vittorio L'Arcangelo.

EVERYTHING'S TAKEN CARE OF

Everyone knew where L'Arcangelo lived, but no one knew how to get to him. Cicognone sorted through the various requests, cooked Don Vittorio's favorite dish—a simple pasta with tomato sauce, sprinkled with chili peppers and basil—and kept him apprised of news and rumors, in real time. His nickname had been the invention of none other than Don Vittorio himself, twenty years back or so, when Cicognone was just a teenager incapable of controlling a body that had shot up too fast and straight toward the sky. He bumped his head against ceiling lamps and knocked against cabinets, he seemed like a stork in a cage. An animal, a bird, it had occurred to Don Vittorio, who'd entirely forgotten the idea of freedom inside that off-kilter body.

Cicognone was draining Don Vittorio's pasta when he got a text from Aucelluzzo. "Cicogno', we've got to meet now, it's urgent!!!!!!!!" This was the fifth text of the morning, and with each new text that ballbuster Aucelluzzo added another exclamation mark. Cicognone didn't let the text knock him off task. He emptied the pasta from the colander into the bowl and slid the parboiled tomato over it, without tossing. Then he carried the bowl wafting its delicious aroma to Don Vittorio, who thanked him, barely pursing his lips. That was the signal that Cicognone could withdraw. Only then did he write a text in response to Aucelluzzo. He'd meet him down-stairs, he'd bestow this privilege upon him—he actually wrote those words—if he then agreed to stop pestering him.

Aucelluzzo showed up on time and had the wit not to brake screeching to a halt right there, downstairs from Don Vittorio's apartment. That would have been enough to attract notice and ruin his chances.

"Cicogno', you know what happened on Piazza Calenda, don't you?" he began without even dismounting from his Vespa. His eyes were downcast, because that tall, skinny man had always intimidated him. He reminded him of undertakers in the movies, the kind that are already measuring you with their eyes for a casket before you're even dead.

"Eh, that the Capelloni were about to skin you alive," Cicognone replied. Everyone knew that, and Cicognone knew it better than anybody else.

"Yes and, *adda murì mammà*, Nicolas saved my life, that kid from Forcella."

"I know it, but if we have to give him something, we're going to have to look around, because we're dying of hunger here."

"No, no, he asked me something."

"Which is?"

"Which is that he asked if he could talk to Don Vittorio."

"Which is to say, he wants to talk with Don Vittorio? That's not even thinkable. That is, Don Vittorio won't even talk with people who are doing everything they can to get in touch, and you think he's going to talk to this little *muccusiello*?" He paused, and then upbraided his interlocutor. "Aucellu', have you completely lost your mind? What the fuck, you call me urgently for this bullshit?" He came close to spitting in his face, in fact he would gladly have spit once for each of the seven exclamation marks he'd used in his latest text. Instead he ignored him, turned on his heel—just like a gravedigger—and, bowing his head, walked back into the apartment house's atrium.

Aucelluzzo needed to come up with something fast. But he'd always been a man of action, like Wolverine—he'd had the superhero's claws tattooed on his forearms, the blades that protruded from each of Wolverine's knuckles on both hands—the kind of guy who dodges bullets: he'd never put too much reliance on his intelligence. He buzzed around on his Vespa, riding back and forth, up and down the streets of Ponticelli, his head empty no matter how hard he might try to fill it up with increasingly fanciful plans of action. Then he thought back to what Nicolas had done the day before yesterday: he'd thrown himself into the fray, he'd thrown the whole deck of cards into the air; in other words, he'd unleashed chaos to take advantage of the reactions he prompted in others. Aucelluzzo decided to kick up a ruckus.

His first stop was the florist's. He asked the owner to give him some advice, and he left the shop with a bundle of pink and white stalks of orchids, but he couldn't help himself and cadged a little angel to hang on it for good measure. Then he revved his motor scooter, zooming straight out to Poggioreale Cemetery—"In Poggioreale you die in life, at Poggioreale you die in death," L'Arcangelo liked to say, referring to the fact that there was both a cemetery and a prison at Poggioreale—clamping the flowers tight between his legs, but not so tight that he ruined them, and then he bent over the grave of Gabriele Grimaldi. He discarded the bouquet of chrysanthemums that someone had recently deposited there, and did his best to give some shape to his orchids. He snapped a couple of photographs with his smartphone, taking them from different angles, then he hopped back on his Vespa and headed home. He posted the picture of Gabriele's grave on a fan forum for S.S.C. Napoli. And he waited.

The comments came flocking, and he replied: "Honor to a great soccer fan." And then he waited. Until a comment came in that was exactly what he'd been waiting for. "Honor to who? To a turncoat bastard who never did a bit of good to anyone in the quarter! Who colluded with Gypsies from Eastern Europe. Who lived half the time with his ass nice and warm in Montenegro. No honor. Honor to whoever got rid of him." There he was. Svizzerino85.

There could only be one Svizzerino85. A fan of S.S. San Giovanni, born in Switzerland, whose family had moved to Naples. And in fact, the name Svizzerino—little Swiss boy—was quite apt, especially when he went around wearing a Kubilay Türkyilmaz T-shirt (even though he rooted for S.S.C. Napoli), claiming that the Swiss footballer of Turkish descent had given it to him in person. Everyone mocked him, but still he wore it proudly, even though it hung practically down to his knees. Aucelluzzo took a screenshot of the page and sent it to Cicognone with a text: "This is the shit they heap on Gabriele. Let me take care of it." Cicognone wasn't sure whether to show it to Don Vittorio. In the end he decided to bide his time: he wanted to see what the little jerk was capable of doing.

And so that Sunday Aucelluzzo went to the stadium. Everyone was going to be there, as usual, and he certainly wasn't going to have to go into the bleachers to know it. By now he didn't even really need to think about the upcoming moves, he'd entrusted himself entirely to the forces of chaos—as one of his beloved superheroes might have put it, while he just used the simpler Neapolitan term for uproar and disarray: *burdello*. He'd brought two of his men, Manuele Bust' 'e Latte and Alfredo Scala 40, along with him, and he'd instructed them in what to do with a few terse phrases. He needed to have it out with Svizzerino, but he couldn't face off with him in the stands, that would be too risky, and what if the cops showed up? The restroom was the right place, and that's where they would wait for the end of the first half, when everyone went to take a quick piss. At that point Bust' 'e Latte and Scala 40 were assigned to blockade the restroom, cross a couple of push brooms in front of the doors. Out of order. Toilets closed to the public. No pissing today. The revolt would be automatic, and in the mayhem that ensued, Aucelluzzo hoped to identify Svizzerino's freckled face. Bust' 'e Latte and Scala 40 were perfect for that little assignment. Bust' 'e Latte was a first-class idiot who didn't know enough to be afraid of anything, not even a furious mob of soccer fans with their bladders bursting, while Scala 40, who'd done twenty-three years behind bars, was a man you could respect. He'd been sentenced for murder, but everyone knew that he'd killed at least ten men. Popular legend, moreover, kicked out numbers like a bingo caller: thirty murders, fifty murders . . . As far as the justice system was concerned, he'd only committed one. As for the other charges, based on accusations lodged by state's witnesses and confidential informants, he'd always been acquitted.

It was the mystery of the rumors that gave him that aura, even though he didn't have a penny to his name and was on the brink of utter poverty.

Aucelluzzo was sitting on a toilet seat putting two-euro coins on each knuckle, then wrapping his hands tight with the same gauze strips boxers use. And then finishing off with three rounds of tape. In the distance he could hear Bust' 'e Latte and Scala 40 doing their best to block the doors, and even farther off—muffled but still easily distinguishable to someone like him who sang them out full throated—the soccer chants. "It's for you, it's for you, that I'm singing for you." "In my mind I have an ideal, and in my heart, Napoli." "We're still here, we'll never stop." He sang them under his breath, Aucelluzzo did, and in the meantime he pressed down on the knuckles of each hand to make the tape stick good and hard. He sang the chants for forty-five minutes plus stoppage time, and then the referee's double whistle sent everyone to the showers. He heard those two whistles very distinctly. Had he dreamed them? He looked up for the first time since he'd come in and heard the crowd stomping down the tiers. They were on their way. Now the trouble was about to begin. And trouble it most certainly was. Cursing, shoving, brawling that was put to a halt instantly. Aucelluzzo looked out at the throng of people that first had been flowing like a river, and then had turned into a teeming clot. And he, head down, and flanked on either side by his men, walked into it. It was as if he were groping through the dark, taking shoulders and fists, but he kept going until the blue and the red of Svizzerino's T-shirt were just a few yards away. That's when Aucelluzzo charged like a bull. He was cursing as he yelled: "Piece of shit, how dare you, what were you thinking when you slung shit on Gabriele's memory!" Svizzerino took the first two punches without blinking an eye. He was small, though he could take some punishment, but it was only when the third round of punches hit him that he realized that his post on the fan forum was what this was about, and then he fought back with a head butt that smashed into Aucelluzzo's eyebrow.

Aucelluzzo kept swinging, throwing punches with enthusiasm but no tactical direction, sort of at random, and if it hadn't been for his buddies he probably would have gotten the worst of it. But it was Scala 40 wading into the fray who made the real difference. He knocked down three guys with backhanded smacks, and when he came face-to-face with Svizzerino, whose nose was completely plastered to one side, shifted onto his left cheekbone, he bellowed into his face with such fury that the other man froze to the spot. And the way it goes in any brawl that goes on for too long—when even people that have nothing to do with it start plunging in and the violence degenerates into a general melee—you see the signs that soon everything is going to flicker and die out. A few yards of reinforced concrete higher up, the referee whistled for play to resume and the cluster of people turned into a river, but now flowing in the opposite direction. Standing in the now-empty space in front of the toilet were Aucelluzzo, his two buddies, and a wide-eyed vendor with his tray hanging around his neck, piled high with bags of potato chips and soft drinks. The only thought that Aucelluzzo was able to formulate was: "Are fifteen minutes already up?"

Scala 40 dragged Aucelluzzo and Bust' 'e Latte outside, loaded them into a car, and took them straight over to Conocal, after which he vanished. They looked like two kids who'd gotten into a fight at school, only to be grabbed by the ears and marched straight to their parents for a scolding. Bust' 'e Latte had taken a boot to the face that had busted his lip, and Aucelluzzo could feel his face throbbing. He tried his best to open his right eye, but it remained glued shut. He'd really fucked up, violated the rules. He'd acted without authorization and now he was going to be punished. His plan had worked. He'd worked his way to where he'd wanted to get, and now he was going to have to play his last cards skillfully.

Cicognone, alerted by Scala 40, was waiting for them in the same location where he'd spoken to Aucelluzzo earlier. He wasn't wearing the angry expression, or swinging the leather belt that you'd see in the hands of a father or older brother outraged by a brawl. Instead, he was waving a loaded pistol, and he leveled it at their faces. "*Ma che cazzo stai cumbinanno? Che stai facenno? Stai facenno cose che non si' autorizzato,*" he blurted out in dialect. "What the fuck are you doing? What are you up to? The things you're doing aren't authorized." Aucelluzzo was swaying as he stared down the barrel of that revolver. This was the delicate part.

"*Ma che cazzo stai cumbinanno?*" Cicognone kept saying, and with every repetition of the same question, his voice kept getting louder. That *auciello*—that dirty bird—really had busted his balls for the last time. And Cicognone kept asking the same question, kept swinging the handgun back and forth, from Aucelluzzo to Bust' 'e Latte, and he failed to hear the metallic clacking that came from a few yards overhead. Don Vittorio had come out onto the balcony and now he was rapping loudly with his wedding ring on the railing. Cicognone continued asking: "*Che stai facenno?*" but now the other two, instead of looking at him or the pistol barrel, kept their eyes peeled upward. Don Vittorio was forced to add a loud "Oh! Oh!" before Cicognone realized. As he recognized the timbre of L'Arcangelo's voice, he holstered his pistol and went back inside, muttering a "Neither of you move" to the two men, out of the side of his mouth. But that was the last thing on either of their minds, as they stood there with their noses in the air like the shepherd children glimpsing the Madonna at Fatima.

A short while later, it was Don Vittorio in person who came downstairs. Strictly speaking, he shouldn't have done it: he was in violation of his house arrest, and if they caught him, they'd throw him back in prison in the blink of an eye. Especially considering how much work it had been to secure house arrest. But he wanted to come downstairs, so he did, just waiting long enough for Cicognone to warn the lookouts to make sure there was no law enforcement in the area.

"*La Cicogna e l'Aucelluzzo,*" said L'Arcangelo. The Stork and the Dirty Bird, "we've got more wings in here than at Capodichino Airport."

Aucelluzzo didn't feel like laughing, but a smile came to his lips anyway. "I heard you defended Gabriele, I heard someone had insulted him on the Internet." He grabbed him by the shoulder and took him down under the apartment house's staircase. There was a low, sheet-metal door, which L'Arcangelo opened with the keys that he was carrying in his pocket. He screwed a hose onto a faucet, took Aucelluzzo's hands, and put them under the water, washing away the blood. He held Aucelluzzo's right hand in his, while his left hand held the hose. He cleaned the bloodied palm using only his thumb, delicately. First the right hand, then the left, even though the left hand hadn't been wrapped in bandages and therefore the knuckles were more swollen but less torn up. "Didn't you have a knuckleduster?" Aucelluzzo didn't understand what he was referring to. But anything that seemed to resemble an answer "no" embarrassed him, just as this scene was embarrassing him. He and L'Arcangelo in almost complete darkness, in that space so tight and narrow that he could smell the man's aftershave. L'Arcangelo asked again: "Didn't you have a knuckleduster? You know, a knuckleduster, the, what do you call it? A pair of knucks. Brass knuckles."

Aucelluzzo shook his head and told him the story: "No, I put euro coins on my knuckles and then bandaged up."

"Ah, right, of course, because these days they'll search you. With a knuckleduster, when I was your age, I shattered plenty of cheeks." He paused and turned off the faucet. He dried the back of his hand on his trousers and then went on: "I thank you for having defended Gabriele. The insults from those shitheads, I can always imagine, keep him from resting in peace. But you should have asked me first. That way I would have told you, you could just have left him dead on the ground, no fooling around. If you leave him alive, you just give him a chance to hurt you. Someone you beat senseless is just someone you're giving a second chance. Maybe you love this guy."

"No, absolutely the opposite."

"Then why didn't you kill him? Why didn't you come to me?"

"Because 'o Cicognone won't let anyone talk to you."

"Here in this quarter, you're all children of mine."

This was the moment. He'd pulled all that insanity to get here, where he was now, face-to-face with Don Vittorio. Now or never.

"Eh, Don Vitto', I have a favor to ask you."

The boss sat in silence, as if inviting him to speak.

"May I ask you?"

"I'm waiting."

"Nicolas, who's a guy in the Forcella System, the *guaglione* who practically saved my life when the guy from the *paranza* of the Capelloni was shooting at me, asked if he could talk to you about something urgent, but he wouldn't tell me what."

"Tell him to come," said L'Arcangelo, "tell him that I'll send him a new face, a contact who'll explain what he needs to do. In a couple of days, I'll send him a new face, in Piazza Bellini."

Aucelluzzo, incredulous, thanked L'Arcangelo: "*Grazie*, Don Vittorio," and bowed down his head, to his knees, sketching out a sort of bow. Don Vittorio took his cheeks between his fingers, the way any good grandfather would have done, and they went back out into the light. Cicognone was waiting for them with both hands behind his back, but it was clear that he was pissed off. Bust' 'e Latte, on the other hand, was looking around in utter confusion. How the hell did I wind up here? he was wondering.

"Take care of yourself, *guagliu*'," said L'Arcangelo, and then headed for the front door, but after a couple of short steps, he turned around: "Aucellu', fifty percent."

"That is to say? Don Vitto', I don't understand you . . ." Aucelluzzo already had one foot in the parking lot, and he was telling himself that once he got out of that situation, he'd rush home and OD on X-Men for a week.

"Fifty percent."

"Don Vitto', forgive me, but I keep not understanding you . . ."

"What did I tell you before? Here, you're all children of mine, and no child of mine gives a damn about his own life. It's not like, just because someone was enough of an ass to save your life, that you give him whatever he wants."

Aucelluzzo squinted his good eye, as if he wanted to see in L'Arcangelo's words the point of what he was driving at.

"Sure he gave you approval to sell in his zone. Sure you can sell our shit there. Fifty percent of everything you earn, you pay it here," and he patted his trousers pocket twice, "the other thirty percent you pay to the market boss. Whatever's left over you can keep for yourself. What he promised you was too important, in fact so important that you actually provoked the insult to Gabriele. Take revenge and restore my honor, that's the way you do it, Aucellu'."

All this mess and now Aucelluzzo was left empty-handed. Before this new agreement, he was allowed to keep whatever he sold outside of the authorized streets for himself, as long as he gave thirty percent to the Conocal market boss. But now he was going to have to pay a tax directly to Don Vittorio. Aucelluzzo bowed his head, crushed, and lifted it again only when he saw Cicognone's long shadow coming toward him: "You pay it to me, every two months, and if I figure out that you're scraping a little off the top, I'll really get pissed off. I keep all the bricks carefully counted. If you take something off the top, I'll slice off your balls."

"At this point, it would have been better if I'd just let 'o White kill me directly," Aucelluzzo muttered as he got onto his Vespa.

Cicognone looked at him the way you'd look at someone who has no hope of learning a thing from even the finest teachers: "Listen, Don Vittorio just saved your life, *pisciazza*." Once again, Aucelluzzo failed to understand. "*Strunzo*, if you started earning money under the authorization of the people in Forcella, then you would have been taking in money, and there were only two alternatives: either the *guaglioni* here in Conocal were going to rub you out so they could go and sell in the city center, or else they'd start looking for other ways of going to sell in the center. That would mean no one would be selling around here anymore, and then I'd have to kill you myself." And he left him there in the parking lot, with a swollen eye that looked even more badly bruised in his pale face.

It was the end of a hard day. Before starting his scooter back up, Aucelluzzo pulled out his cell phone. He found calls from his mother, and just as many calls from his market boss, Totore, who knew he'd been to the stadium and had then wound up at L'Arcangelo's place. So Totore wanted to understand whether Aucelluzzo had broken some basic rule, and most of all, whether he himself was going to have to pay the consequences for whatever Aucelluzzo had done.

"Everything's taken care of," he wrote to his mother.

"Everything's taken care of," he wrote to Totore.

"Everything's taken care of," he wrote to Maraja.

Everything's taken care of: a universal expression. The very picture of everything going in accordance with established order. Everything was taken care of for his mother, who wanted to know why he hadn't sent her word after the soccer match. Everything was taken care of for his market boss: he wasn't going to have to pay anything, in fact, if anything, he was going to earn more now. Everything was taken care of for the aspiring *paranza* capo who wanted to obtain the protection of an old boss who was no longer a player in the game.

"Everything's taken care of." That's the way things were supposed to work.

LAIR

Drago' took them to the apartment on Via dei Carbonari. It stood on the fourth floor of a tumbledown apartment house, where the same last names had lived for centuries now. Fruit vendor the ancestor, fruit vendor the current occupant. Smugglers the ancestors, armed robbers the current occupants. There were no new tenants, except for the occasional African dope dealer who was allowed to live with the family.

There Drago' had an apartment at his disposal: "This place, *guagliu'*, is one thing the cops didn't take. It's still part of the Striano family, the good part. My grandfather used to own it, 'o Sovrano, and he would give it to the people who worked with him, on a temporary basis."

In fact, in the place you could clearly see the influence of the old families: it was furnished like an apartment from the eighties, and from that time forward it had gradually just emptied out. Become forgotten. Or better yet, been preserved. As if practically forty years ago someone had spread a slipcover over the furniture to protect it from the passage of time and had only just removed it.

Everything was lower and shorter in that apartment. The tables, the sofas, the television set. It seemed like the residence of people who just a few decades ago barely reached an average height of five and a half feet. For the boys, everything was shin height, and they had immediately converted that strange glass food cart that stood right in front of the brown leather sofa into a foot rest. An immense lamp with a flower-pattern shade stood between two armchairs, brown like the sofa. And then there were shelves, a vast profusion of shelves, loaded with things that none of them had ever seen. There were even VHS cassettes with white labels, upon which someone had hastily written the year of an international soccer match. But the most delightful object in the place was the television set. It stood atop another table that was pushed back against a wall papered in blue and white stripes. It looked like a cube and must have weighed at least a hundred pounds. The screen bulged out in a curve and reflected the faded images of the room. Dentino approached it cautiously as if it were a dangerous animal, and leaning in from what seemed like a safe distance, he pushed what looked to be the ON button; it snapped back with the sound of a spring finally released after a century of inactivity.

"Nothing's happening," said Nicolas. But then a faint red light appeared, contradicting his statement. "In the old days, members of the family would hide out here," Drago' continued. "Every so often Feliciano 'o Nobile would come here to screw some woman or other. *Chest'è casa 'e nisciuno.*" No man's home. No-man's-land.

"Fine," said Nicolas, "I like 'no-man's-land.' It's going to become our lair."

That word made people smile.

"Lair?" asked Agostino. "What's a lair?"

"Our lair, where we hole up, where we meet, where we play, where we split up everything we take."

"Well, then, the first thing we need is an Xbox," Agostino said.

Nicolas went on: "This is going to be everyone's home, so there are going to have to be some rules. The first is that we don't bring females in here."

"*Uààà.*" Stavodicendo immediately expressed his disappointment. "I wasn't expecting that, Maraja!"

"If we bring women here it'll turn into a bordello, a mess. Just us, and no one else. Not even our friends. Just us and that's all. Also," he added, "not a word to a soul about this place. This place exists for us and no one else."

"The first rule about Fight Club is: you do not talk about Fight Club," said Briato'.

"Right!" said Lollipop.

"Sure, but still people will see us come in and out, Maraja," said Drago'.

"It's one thing for people to see us, it's another thing if we tell them."

It was called Via dei Carbonari. It's still called Via dei Carbonari: it's still there, in Forcella. The name was well suited to this group of kids who knew nothing about the historical Carbonari and yet who resembled them, without their noble intentions, but still with the same willingness to sacrifice, the blind abnegation that led them to ignore the world and its signals, to listen only to their own will as an objective demonstration of the justness of their actions.

"This is the lair, *guagliu'*. We need to come here, here we smoke, here we play, here we spend our time. Drago' is in agreement. Copacabana knows nothing. This belongs to us."

Nicolas knew that everything needed to start from an apartment, a place where they could meet and talk without interference. It was a way of uniting them. That's exactly what he said: "*A ccà s'adda partì.*" This is where we start from.

Biscottino was the only one who hadn't yet spoken, as he stared at the tips of his brand-new gleaming white Adidas. He seemed determined at all costs to find a spot on them somewhere.

"Biscotti', aren't you happy?" Maraja asked.

Biscottino finally looked up. "Can I talk to you for a minute, Nico'?"

Nico', not *Maraja*, and the head turned back down to look at the Adidas.

The others didn't even notice that the two of them had moved into the bedroom. They were too busy exploring the time machine.

Right away, Biscottino said: "Nico', are you sure that it's a good thing to operate out of the apartment of a turncoat?"

Maraja came close enough for the other to smell his breath, and he placed both his shoes atop the toes of Biscottino's shoes. "A turncoat is a turncoat, not someone who has the blood of a turncoat in their veins. *Capito?* And after all, it wasn't Drago's father who talked. Now, let's go back to the other room. Everything's okay." He took his shoes off Biscottino's shoes and then said it again: "*'A ccà s'adda partì.*"

Only he and Drago' had the keys. And when the others wanted to get in touch with them, they'd send a text: "Are you at home?" The lair was the beginning of everything, according to Nicolas, a home for all of them, every little kid's dream. A place to take the money from their monthly earnings, a place to hide it in the nooks and crannies, in envelopes, among the old newspapers. To be able to hide the money there, count it, and especially pile it up. Maraja knew this exactly: that everything would get started only once the money was all piled up together, when they were truly united, when the place they started out from in their business really was held in common. That's how you create a family. That's how you achieved his dream: the *paranza*.

ADDA MURÌ MAMMÀ

We need to build a *paranza* that's all ours. *Nun amm' 'a appartené a nisciuno, sulo a nuje.* We won't belong to anyone, just to us. We've got to report to no one but ourselves."

Everyone looked at Nicolas in silence. They were waiting to learn how they'd be able to break free without resources, without a fucking penny to their name. They had no power, and their facial features—the features of children—only seemed to confirm it, to dispel any doubt on the matter.

People called them children and children is what they actually were. And just like anyone who hasn't begun to live, they were afraid of nothing, they considered old people to be dead already, buried already, history already. The only weapon they possessed was the feral nature man-cubs still preserved. Small animals that act on instinct. They bare their teeth and snarl, and that's enough to make those they encounter shit their pants in fear.

They needed to become ferocious, that's the only way that those who struck fear and respect into them would ever deign to give them consideration. Children, yes, but children with a pair of balls on them. Create disarray and reign over that disarray: disorder and chaos for a kingdom without geographic coordinates.

"They think we're just kids, but we've got this . . . and we also have this."

And with his right hand, Nicolas pulled out the pistol he had tucked down his pants. He hooked his forefinger into the trigger guard and spun the weapon as if it were light as a feather, while with his left hand he pointed to his junk, his dick, his balls. We have weapons and we have balls, that was the concept.

"Nicolas . . ." Agostino interrupted him, someone had to do it, and Nicolas expected it. He was waiting for it like the kiss that would identify Christ to the legionaries. He needed someone to take the doubt and the guilt of thinking: a scapegoat, so that it would become clear that there was no alternative, that you couldn't decide whether to be inside or outside. The *paranza* had to breathe in unison, and the respiration that needed to serve as the metronome for everybody else's need for oxygen was his.

". . . Nico', but it's never happened like this, that we could just create a *paranza*, all alone, right away, like this. *Adda murì mammà*, Nico', we need to ask permission. Now of all times, when people think there's no one left in Forcella, if we know how to act with the Capelloni, then we can work for them. Each of us will get a salary and maybe, in a while, we'll even get a market all our own. A piazza."

"Ceri', it's people like you I don't want, and people like you need to get out, right now . . ."

"Nico', maybe I didn't make myself clear, I'm just saying that . . ."

"*Aggio capito buono, Ceri', staje parlanno malamente.*" He told him he knew exactly what he was saying, and that he was wrong when he said it.

Nicolas leaned close, snorted through his nose, and spat in his face. Agostino wasn't a shrinking violet and he tried to lash back, but as he was pulling his head back to butt Nicolas in the bridge of the nose, Nicolas dodged aside, too quick for him. They stared each other in the eye. And then it was over, the drama was done. At that point, Nicolas continued.

"Agosti', I don't want people who are afraid, fear shouldn't even come into your mind. If you're starting to have doubts, then you're no good to me anymore."

Agostino knew he'd expressed what everyone else feared, he wasn't alone in worrying that they needed to reach out to the old bosses, and that spit in the face came as a warning more than a humiliation. A warning to them all.

"Now get the hell out of here, you're not in the *paranza* anymore."

"You're nothing but a handful of *stounzi*," said Agostino, red in the face.

Dentino broke in and tried to placate him.

"Austi', get out of here, you're going to get hurt . . ."

Agostino had never betrayed but, like all Judases, he was a useful tool to accelerate the realization: before leaving the room he, blithely unaware, gave Nicolas exactly what he needed to solidify the *paranza*.

"*E vuje vulesseve fà 'a paranza cu tre curtielle e doje scacciacani?*" What do you think, you're going to start a *paranza* with three knives and two starter pistols?

"With these three knives we'll slit you open like a fish!" Nicolas exploded.

Agostino raised his middle finger and waved it in the faces of those whom he had considered, just moments ago, to be blood of his blood, flesh of his flesh. Nicolas hated to let him go that way: you don't just discard someone like that, not if you know their every day, their every *fratecucino*, their every uncle. Agostino had been with him at the stadium, all the time, both at the San Paolo and for away games. You need to keep a *bro'* close, but this is how things had gone, and expelling him was useful. He needed a sponge to soak up all the group's fears. As soon as Agostino had slammed the door behind him, Nicolas went on.

"Brothers, '*o cacasotto*—the pants-shitter—has a point . . . We can't start a *paranza* with three kitchen knives and a couple of starter pistols."

And the same guys who just a second ago had been ready to fight with the few knives and rusty old gats that were all they had, because Nicolas had said so, all confirmed their disappointment once they were authorized to doubt: they dreamed of gleaming arsenals and they were forced to handle toys that they hid under their beds.

"I have the solution," said Nicolas, "and they're either going to kill me or else I'll come home with an arsenal. And if that happens, *qua adda cagnà tutte cose*—then everything around here is going to change: with weapons come rules, *perché adda murì fràtemo, senza regole simmo sulo piscitiell' 'e vrachetta.*" Because on my brother's life, without rules we're nothing but *piscitiell' 'e vrachetta.*

"We have our rules, Nico', we're all brothers."

"Brothers without an oath are nothing. And oaths are taken on things that count. You've seen that movie *Il Camorrista*, what do you call it, *The Professor*, haven't you? That scene where 'o Professore administers the oath in prison. *Veritavéllo, sta 'ncoppa a YouTube*—watch it, you'll find it on YouTube. We need to be like that, a single thing. We need to be baptized with irons and chains. We need to become sentinels of *omertà*. It's a great movie, *guagliu', veritavéllo.* The bread that if you betray will become lead, and the wine that becomes poison. And then we need to draw blood, *amm' 'a ammiscà 'e sanghe nuoste*—we need to mingle our bloods, and be afraid of nothing."

While he was talking about values and oaths, Nicolas had just one thing in mind, something that made him uneasy and made his gut feel all emptied out.

The following afternoon was a hot one and there was a game at the stadium, the Italian national team was playing. Letizia had asked him if they could watch the game together, but Nicolas had refused, he was rooting against the national team, too few players from S.S.C. Napoli, too many from Juventus F.C., so he and his buddies felt only contempt for the national team and any games it might play. They had something else to do, and it was urgent. There were six of them on three scooters. Dentino was driving his scooter, the other two scooters were zipping along a few yards ahead. From the Salita Moiariello, it was a road that ran downhill all the way. Narrow, winding alleyways, the *vicoli.* "The manger scene," people who live there call it.

If you go that way, it's quicker, and by taking Piazza Bellini, on and off the sidewalk, you avoid lots of traffic and wrong-way streets. It only takes a second.

His contact with L'Arcangelo was in Piazza Bellini, and Nicolas needed to hurry. It's true, he felt like God Almighty, but he needed this contact. And these aren't people who'll wait around if you're late. Ten minutes and he had to be there.

The three scooters covered the last stretch of Via Foria, before you arrive at the museum, riding along the wide, well-lit sidewalks, zigzagging with their horns blaring. This time they could easily have just taken the street, because there wasn't a living soul in sight and the few who hadn't made arrangements to go to the stadium were sitting staring at one of the screens that you could find at every street corner in Naples. From time to time, if they could hear cheers in the air, they'd stop their scooters and ask the score. Italy was leading. Nicolas swore under his breath.

They turned into Via Costantinopoli, riding against traffic. They rode onto the sidewalks, which here were narrow and dark, though here there were more people. Young people, for the most part university students, and the occasional tourist. They, too, were going to Piazza Bellini, to Port'Alba, to Piazza Dante—though in less of a hurry—where there were plenty of bars and cafés with televisions set out on the street. The three scooters were going too fast, and they didn't notice two strollers parked on the sidewalk, next to a group of adults sitting at tables outside a bar.

The first scooter didn't even try to brake, the stroller's nearest handle harpooned the scooter's side mirror and the stroller started skating along fast until it broke loose and fell on its side, as if it were sliding across a sheet of ice. It stopped only when it slammed into the wall: the impact made a dull thud. A sound of blood, white flesh, and diapers. Newly sprouted, unkempt hair. A sound of lullabies and sleepless nights. After a moment the child could be heard sobbing and the mother screaming. The child wasn't hurt, just frightened. The father, instead, was turned to stone, motionless. He stood, staring at the kids who had in the meantime parked their scooters and were walking off unhurriedly. They hadn't stopped. Nor had they fled in panic. No. They'd parked their motor scooters and were walking off, as if everything that had happened was simply part of everyday life in that territory, which belonged to them and no one else. Crushing all underfoot, body-slamming, running. Fast, arrogant, rude, and violent. That's the way it is, and there's no other way for it to be. Still, Nicolas felt his heart pumping blood feverishly. His attitude didn't

spring from arrogant opportunism, from *cazzimma*, but from cold calcu-
lation: the accident couldn't be allowed to modify their itinerary. There
were two police cars—one on either side of Via Costantinopoli—parked
exactly where the kids had parked. The policemen, four in all, were listening to the game on the radio and hadn't noticed a thing. They were
only a few yards from the accident, but those shouts hadn't torn them
away from their cars. What must they have thought? Shouting goes on all
the time in Naples, anyone and everyone shouts in Naples. Or else: best
to steer clear, there are only a few of us here and we have no authority.

Nicolas said nothing, and while he looked around for his contact he
was thinking that they'd come close to making a serious mistake, that they
should have given that stroller a kick instead of dragging it along beside
them for thirty feet. Everything in Naples belonged to them, and they
needed their sidewalks, that was something people needed to understand.

There he was, his contact with Don Vittorio Grimaldi, hat on his head
and joint in his mouth. He walked over slowly, and neither took off the
hat nor spat out the joint: he treated Nicolas like the little kid that he
was and not like the boss he dreamed of being.

"L'Arcangelo has decided that you can go and pray. But in order to
enter the chapel, you need to follow the instructions carefully."

Instructions in code that Nicolas knew how to decipher. The boss
would receive him at home, but that he shouldn't even dream of coming
in by the main entrance because he, Don Vittorio, was under house arrest and wasn't allowed to see anyone. You might not be able to see the
carabinieri surveillance cameras but they were there, somewhere, buried
in the cement. But those weren't what Nicolas needed to be afraid of. The
thing to fear were the eyes of the Faellas. The contact on Piazza Bellini
had made it clear that L'Arcangelo wanted Nicolas to be aware of the risk.
If the Faellas saw him, he'd become a Grimaldi. And he'd get a brutal
beating in the bargain. Period.

The truth, though, was otherwise: Nicolas and his group were so many
dickheads and the Grimaldis didn't want them to be the reason that the
suspicions of the investigators and their rivals focused on L'Arcangelo,
who already had more trouble than he could handle.

Nicolas pulled up to Don Vittorio's apartment on his scooter; after all, he wasn't as notorious as he would have liked to be, and in Conocal, far from home, none of the *guaglioni* of the System knew his face. They might recognize his name, but his face could pass unnoticed. At the sight of him, they might just assume he was there to buy hash, and in fact he pulled his motor scooter over next to some other kids and they immediately did as he'd hoped: "How much money do you have?"

"A hundred euros."

"Fuck, great. Gimme the cash."

A few minutes later the hash was under his ass, tucked beneath the seat of the scooter. He drove around the block and parked. He fastened an ostentatious padlock on the scooter, and then strolled slowly toward L'Arcangelo's apartment building. His movements were clear and determined. No hands in pockets, his head was itching, he was sweating, but he forgot about that. You've never seen a soul scratch his head at a momentous juncture. He rang the buzzer to the apartment downstairs from Don Vittorio's, as instructed. He heard a voice answer. He uttered his name, he carefully enunciated every syllable.

"Professoressa, it's Nicolas Fiorillo, can you open up?"

"Is it open now?"

"No!"

It was open, but he'd needed to stall for time.

"Push hard and it'll open up."

"Yeah, yeah. Now it's open."

CAPODIMONTE

Rita Cicatello was an old retired high school teacher who gave private lessons at prices that some might describe as popular. All the students of teachers she was friends with came to her for lessons. If they came to her and her husband for tutoring, they passed their exams; otherwise the debts came due, and then they had to go to her for tutoring anyway, but in the summer.

Nicolas climbed to the landing outside the high school teacher's apartment. He walked in calmly, like an ordinary student reluctant to subject himself to the umpteenth form of scholastic torture; actually, though, he just wanted to be certain that the security camera that the carabinieri had planted there caught every detail. He believed that, like a human eye, it might blink for a second, and so all his actions needed to be slow, in order to ensure they were captured fully. The carabinieri surveillance tapes, which would be made available to the Faellas as well, needed to see this: Nicolas Fiorillo going in to see Professoressa Cicatello. And nothing more.

The lady opened the door. She wore an apron that protected her from splattering oil and sauce. In the little apartment there were lots of kids, male and female, ten or so in all, sitting at the same round dining table, their textbooks lying open, their eyes glued to their iPhones. They liked their teacher, Professoressa Cicatello, because she wasn't like the other ones, who confiscated their cell phones before starting the lesson, forcing them to invent fanciful excuses—my grandfather is having an operation, he's in the OR right now, if I don't answer in ten minutes my mother is going to call the police—so they could hold on to them, because maybe they'd receive a message on WhatsApp or a "like" on Facebook. The teacher let them keep the phones and didn't even bother to teach the lesson herself, she kept those kids in her apartment learning from a tablet—a gift from her son for last Christmas—that was hooked up to a small speaker from which her voice issued, talking about Manzoni, the Risorgimento, Dante. It all depended on what the kids needed to study; Professoressa Cicatello, in her spare time, prerecorded the lessons and then limited herself to shouting from time to time: "Enough is enough with these cell phones, pay attention to the lesson." In the meantime, she cooked, tidied up the apartment, and made lengthy phone calls from an old landline. She came back to check the homework on Italian and geography, while her husband corrected the mathematics homework.

Nicolas went in, mumbled a general salutation to one and all; the kids there for tutoring didn't even bother to look up. He pulled open a glass door and went through. The kids often saw people come in and leave, and usually those people, after a hasty hello, vanished behind the kitchen door. The life that went on behind that door was unknown to them and, since the bathroom was on the opposite side of the apartment from the kitchen, all they knew about the Professoressa's apartment were the room with the tablet and the bathroom. They asked no questions about anything else, there was no reward for curiosity.

Her husband was also there, in the room with the tablet, always sitting in front of a television set, always with a blanket over his knees. Even in summer. The kids would go over to him where he sat in the armchair to turn in their math homework. He'd correct the homework with a red pen he kept in the breast pocket of his shirt, dismissively punishing their ignorance. He muttered something in Nicolas's direction that was meant to sound like a "*buongiorno.*"

At the far end of the kitchen there was a ladder. The Professoressa said nothing but pointed straight up. A small, amateurish-looking masonry structure formed an opening that connected the floor below to the floor above. And so, very simply, those who couldn't go to see Don Vittorio through the front door of his apartment would call on the Professoressa. When he'd reached the last rung, Nicolas knocked a couple of times on the bottom of the trapdoor. It was none other than he, Don Vittorio, who leaned over when he heard the knocking, allowing a gurgle of strain to issue from his mouth, a sound that came straight from his spinal cord. Nicolas was deeply moved, he'd only ever seen Don Vittorio in court before. From up close, though, the Don didn't strike him as quite as impressive as he'd expected. He was older, he seemed weaker to him now. Don Vittorio ushered him in and, with the same gurgle of back pain, lowered the trapdoor back into place. He didn't shake hands with him, but showed him the way.

"Come in, come in . . ." was all he said as he walked into the dining room, where there stood an enormous ebony table that in an absurd geometric effect managed to lose all its dark elegance and turn into an ostentatious and tasteless monolith. Don Vittorio sat down to the right of the chair that marked the head of the table. The apartment was full of little vitrines containing ceramics of all sorts. Capodimonte porcelains must have been Don Vittorio's wife's consuming passion, though there was no other trace of her in the place. The lady with the dog, the hunter, the *zampognaro*, or bagpipe player—evergreen classics all. Nicolas's eyes darted from one wall to another, he wanted to memorize everything; he wanted to see how L'Arcangelo lived, but what he saw he didn't much like. He couldn't say exactly why it made him uneasy, but this certainly didn't strike him as the home of a boss. There was something about it that didn't add up: his mission to this little fortress couldn't possibly be so banal, so obvious, so facile. A flat-screen television set surrounded by a wood-colored frame and two people wearing S.S.C. Napoli gym shorts: that's all there seemed to be in the apartment. The two didn't greet Nicolas, and instead waited for a nod from Don Vittorio, who, once he was comfortably ensconced, forefinger and middle finger joined as if to flick away horseflies, gestured to them in an unequivocal signal to leave, to *jaté-vénne.* The two of them went to the kitchen and before long the sound emerged of a comedian's croaking voice—no doubt there was another television set in there—followed by laughter.

"Get undressed."

Now he recognized the voice of a man accustomed to giving orders.

"Get undressed? What do you mean?"

Nicolas accompanied the question with an expression of disbelief. He hadn't expected this request. Hundreds of times he had imagined how this meeting would go and none of those times had he ever considered the possibility that he might have to undress.

"Strip down, *guaglio'*, who the fuck knows you. Who says you aren't packing a tape recorder, a bug, whatever the hell . . ."

"Don Vitto', *adda murì mammà*, how dare you think I would . . ."

He had used the wrong verb. Don Vittorio raised his voice so he could be heard from the kitchen, to drown out the comedian's voice and the canned laughter. A boss is a boss when there is no limit to what he'll dare to do.

"We're done here."

The two guys wearing S.S.C. Napoli gym shorts didn't even get a chance to come back into the room before Nicolas was already prying the shoes off his feet.

"No, no, it's all right, I'll get undressed. I'm doing it now."

He took off his shoes, then his pants, then his T-shirt, until he was standing there in his underwear.

"Everything, *guaglio'*, because you could even have a microphone stuck up your ass."

Nicolas knew that this had nothing to do with microphones. In L'Arcangelo's presence, he was supposed to feel like nothing so much as a naked worm, that was the price you paid for the appointment. He performed a pirouette, as if amused, he showed that he had no microphones or micro video cameras but that he did possess a sense of irony, a spirit that bosses lose, necessarily. Don Vittorio gestured for him to sit down, and without a word, Nicolas pointed to himself, as if to request confirmation that he could sit down like that, naked, on immaculate white chairs. The boss nodded.

"That way we'll see if you know how to wipe your ass. If you leave skid marks of shit, it means you're too young, you don't know how to use a bidet and Mammà is still wiping you."

They were sitting facing each other. Don Vittorio had intentionally avoided sitting at the head of the table, to avoid the symbolism: if he'd let him sit at his right hand, the kid might make all kind of assumptions. Better to sit face-to-face, one on one, like in a police interrogation. And he intentionally also offered him nothing to drink or eat: you don't share food at the table with a stranger, nor do you offer coffee to a guest you're sizing up.

"So you're 'o Maraja?"

"Nicolas Fiorillo . . ."

"Exactly, 'o Maraja . . . it's important what people call you. Your monicker is more important than your real name, did you know that? Do you know the story of Bardellino?"

"No."

"Bardellino, a real *guappo*. He's the one who molded a bunch of gangs of *bufalari*, cowherds, into a serious organization in Casal di Principe."

Nicolas was listening the way a devout Catholic listens to Mass.

"Bardellino had a nickname that was given him when he was just a kid, and he carried it with him even when he was a grown-up. They called him Pucchiacchiello."

Nicolas started laughing, Don Vittorio nodded his head, widening his eyes, as if confirming that the story he was telling was true, not a legend. Something that had been recorded in the transcripts of the life that matters.

"In order to get the stench of the stables and the earth off him, in order to get the grime off his fingernails, every time that Bardellino went down into town, he'd wash, he'd put on scent, he'd dress up fancy. Every day like it was Sunday. Brilliantine on his head . . . his hair glistening and wet."

"And where did this nickname come from?"

"Back then, the town was full of farmhands and sharecroppers. To see 'nu guagliunciello, a young man like him, all fancied up, started to seem normal: Pucchiacchiello, like the pussy—*la pucchiacca*—of a beautiful woman. All clean and sweet smelling, like a pussy."

"I got it, '*nu fighetto,*" he said, using a comparable term in Italian.

"The fact remains that this name wasn't a name for someone who can command. If you want to command, you have to have a name that commands. It can be ugly, it can mean nothing, but it can't be foolish."

"But you don't decide your own nickname."

"Exactly. And in fact, when he became a boss, Bardellino insisted that he only wanted to be called Don Antonio, anyone who dared to call him Pucchiacchiello was in a world of trouble. No one could call him that to his face, but still he remained always and only Pucchiacchiello."

"Still, he was a great boss, wasn't he? So that means, *adda murì mammà*, that your name doesn't really matter all that much."

"You're wrong about that, he spent the rest of his life trying to get rid of it . . ."

"So what ever became of Don Pucchiacchiello?" he asked with a smile, and then saw that Don Vittorio didn't like that smile.

"He disappeared. There are those who say that he started a new life, got plastic surgery on his face, pretended to be dead and enjoyed himself behind the backs of those who wanted him dead or behind bars. I only saw him once, when I was a kid, he was the only man of the System who *sembrava 'nu re*—who seemed like a king. There was no one like him. *Nisciuno comm'a lui.*"

"Good job, Pucchiacchiello," Nicolas commented, as if he were speaking of a peer.

"You were lucky, they nailed your monicker perfectly."

"The reason they call me that is because I spend all my time at the New Maharaja, a club up in Posillipo. That's my headquarters, and they make the best cocktails in Naples."

"Your headquarters, is it? Eh, bravo." Don Vittorio stifled a smile. "It's a good name, do you know what it means?"

"I looked it up on the Internet, it means 'king' in Indian."

"It's a name for kings, but look out, or you could wind up like the song."

"What song?"

Don Vittorio, with a broad smile, started to sing it, letting loose with his melodious voice. In falsetto:

"Pasqualino Marajà
non lavora e non fa niente:
fra i misteri dell'Oriente
fa il nababbo fra gli indù.
Ulla! Ulla! Ulla! La!
Pasqualino Marajà
ha insegnato a far la pizza,
tutta l'India ne va pazza."

Pasqualino Marajà
he doesn't work and he doesn't lift a finger:
among the mysteries of the East
he plays the nabob among the Hindus.
Ulla! Ulla! Ulla! La!
Pasqualino Marajà
taught them how to make pizza,
all of India is going crazy over it.

He stopped singing, now he was laughing, openmouthed, rudely. Laughter that ended in a hacking cough. Nicolas was annoyed. He saw this display as a form of mockery, to test his nerves.

"Don't make that face, it's a nice song. I always used to sing it when I was a *guaglione* myself. And after all, I can just see you wearing a turban, making pizzas up on the hill of Posillipo."

Nicolas's eyebrows were cocked, his brow furrowed, the self-deprecating irony of a few minutes ago had given way to rage, a rage he couldn't conceal.

"Don Vitto', do I have to sit here with my dick sticking out?" was all he said.

Don Vittorio, still sitting in the same chair, in the same position, pretended he hadn't heard a thing.

"Aside from bullshit and fuckups, looking like a fool is the thing that anyone who wants to be a boss should fear most."

"So far, *adda murì mammà*, no one's ever slapped shit in my face yet."

"The first thing that makes you look like a fool is that you're trying to start a *paranza* and you don't have any weapons."

"So far, with everything I had to my name, I've done more than any of your *guaglioni* are doing, and I'm speaking respectfully, Don Vitto', I know I'm nothing in comparison with you."

"Well, it's a good thing you're speaking respectfully, because my *guaglioni*, if they wanted to, right this second, could come in here and do to you what the fishmonger does when he cleans a fish."

"Let me insist on the point, Don Vitto', your *guaglioni* aren't up to your level. They're hunkered down here and they can do nothing. The Faellas have taken you prisoner, *adda murì mammà*, they want to make you ask permission just to breathe. With you under house arrest and the mayhem going on out there, *simme nuje a cummannà*, we're in charge, with or without weapons. Resign yourself: Jesus Christ, the Madonna, and San Gennaro have all left L'Arcangelo alone in the world."

That little kid was just describing reality and Don Vittorio let him talk; he didn't like the way he kept bringing the saints into it, and even more, he disliked that interjection, he found it odious, *adda murì mammà* . . . may my mother die. An oath, a guarantee for anything. A price for the lie uttered? *Adda murì mammà.* He repeated it with every sentence he spoke. Don Vittorio wanted to tell him to stop, but then he lowered his gaze because the young boy's body made him smile, almost melted his heart, and he decided that the reason he repeated that phrase was to ward off the danger of the utmost catastrophe that an unfledged bird—a bird that has not yet left the nest—fears more than any other. For his part, Nicolas saw the boss gaze down at the table, for the first time lowering his gaze, he thought, and he actually believed it represented a reversal of their roles, for the first time he felt powerful and strong in his nudity. He was young and fresh and smooth, and he was facing old, bowed flesh.

"L'Arcangelo, that's what they call you in the street, in prison, in court, and even on the Internet. It's a good name, it's a name that can command. Who gave it to you?"

"My father was named Gabriele, like the Archangel Gabriel, may the Lord rest his soul. I was Vittorio who belonged to Gabriele, so that's what they called me."

"And this Archangel"—Nicolas continued hammering away at the walls between him and the boss—"with his wings tied, sits helpless in a quarter where he once commanded, a quarter that no longer belongs to him, and his men don't know how to do anything but play with their PlayStation consoles. The wings of this Archangel ought to be spread wide, and instead they're closed like the wings of a goldfinch in a cage."

"That's the way it is: there's a time to fly, and a time to sit locked up in a cage. For that matter, better a cage like this one than a cage under the forty-one bis regime."

Nicolas stood up and started walking around him. He walked slowly. L'Arcangelo didn't move; that's what he always did when he wanted to give the impression that he had eyes in the back of his head. If someone is behind you and your eyes start following him, that means you're afraid. And whether you keep your eyes on him or not, if the knife is going to plunge into you, it will no matter what you do. If you don't look, though, if you don't turn around, you show no fear and you turn your murderer into an infamous coward who's stabbed you in the back.

"Don Vittorio L'Arcangelo, you don't have men anymore, but you do have weapons. What good are all the guns that you keep stored away in your warehouses? I have men, but the arsenal that you possess? I can only dream of it. If you wanted, you could arm an army, fight a real war."

L'Arcangelo didn't expect this request, he hadn't guessed that the child he'd allowed to come upstairs to his home would ever venture such a daring move. He'd expected to be asked for his blessing to operate on his territory. And yet, even if it did point to a lack of respect, L'Arcangelo wasn't bothered by it. In fact, he liked this way of operating. It scared him. And he hadn't felt fear in a long time, too long. In order to command, to be a boss, you need to be afraid, every day of your life, at every moment. To conquer the fear, to figure out whether you're still capable. Whether your fear will let you live or whether, instead, it simply poisons everything. If you can't feel fear, then it means that you're worthless now, that no one's interested in killing you, approaching you, taking what belongs to you, which after all you, in your turn, took from someone else.

"You and I have nothing in common. You don't belong to me, you're not in my System, you've never done me a favor of any kind. If only for the disrespectful request you've just made, I ought to kick you out and leave your blood on the floor of the Professoressa's apartment downstairs."

"I'm not afraid of you, Don Vitto'. If I'd just taken your weapons directly, that would have been a different matter and you would have been right to do that."

L'Arcangelo was seated and Nicolas, standing, was now face-to-face with him, hands clenched into fists and knuckles resting on the table.

"I'm old, aren't I?" said L'Arcangelo with a razor-sharp smile.

"I don't know what to say."

"Answer me, Maraja, am I old?"

"Whatever you say. Yes, if I'm supposed to say yes."

"Am I old or not?"

"Yes, you're old."

"And am I ugly?"

"Now what does that have to do with anything?"

"I must be old and ugly and I must scare you badly, too. If that wasn't the case, right now, you wouldn't be hiding your naked legs under the table, to keep me from seeing them. You're trembling, *guaglio'*. But tell me something: If I give you the weapons, what do I get out of it?"

Nicolas was ready for that question, and he almost became emotional as he repeated the phrase that he had practiced on his way there, riding his motor scooter. He hadn't expected he'd have to utter it naked, with his legs still shaking, but he said it all the same.

"What you get out of it is that you continue to exist. What you get out of it is that the most powerful *paranza* in Naples is your friend."

"*Assiettete.*" L'Arcangelo ordered him to sit back down in dialect. And then, putting on the most serious of all his masks: "I can't. It would be like putting *'na pucchiacca* in the hands of little kids. You don't know how to shoot, you don't know how to clean a weapon, you'd get yourselves hurt. You don't even know how to reload a machine gun."

Nicolas's heart, throbbing with anxiety, urged him to lash back, but instead he remained calm: "Give them to us and we'll show you what we know how to do. We'll remove the marks of the slaps to your face, the slaps delivered to you by those who consider you to be a limping invalid. The best friend you could hope to have is your enemy's enemy. And what we want most is to expel the Faellas from the center of Naples. Our house is our house. If we kick them out of the center of Naples, then you can certainly kick them out of San Giovanni and take back all of Ponticelli, and the bars, and where you used to be in charge, where you used to command."

The way things stood currently was no longer acceptable to L'Arcangelo: a new order needed to be established, and if he could no longer be in charge, at least this way he'd create general havoc. He'd give them the weapons, the guns that had been sitting unused for years. They were a strength, but a strength that isn't exercised only makes the muscles atrophy. L'Arcangelo decided to bet on this *paranza* of *piscitielli*—little fish. If he could no longer command, he could still force the ones ruling over the area to come to him and sue for peace. He was tired of having to say thank you for scraps, and that army of children was the only way he'd get a chance to see daylight before the coming eternal darkness.

"I'll give you what you need, but you aren't my ambassadors. Any bullshit you pull with my weapons can't bear my name on them. You pay your own debts, you'll lick the blood off your own wounds. But whatever I ask you, whenever I ask you, you must do without argument."

"You're old, ugly, and wise, too, Don Vitto'."

"All right, Maraja, the same way you came, now you can leave. One of my men will let you know where you can go pick them up."

Don Vittorio extended his hand, Nicolas grabbed it and tried to kiss it, but L'Arcangelo yanked it away in disgust: "What the fuck are you doing?"

"I was kissing your hand out of respect . . ."

"*Guaglio'*, you've lost your mind, you and all the movies you watch."

L'Arcangelo stood up, bracing both hands on the table: his bones were heavy and house arrest had made him put on weight.

"Now get dressed again, and hurry it up, because soon the carabinieri are going to be coming around to check on things."

Nicolas put on his underpants, his jeans, and his shoes as quickly as he could.

"Ah, Don Vitto', one more thing . . ."

Don Vittorio turned around wearily.

"In the place where I'll have to go to get the . . . no?"

There were no listening devices, and Nicolas had already uttered that word, but now that he was almost there, he was a little bit afraid.

"Well?" said L'Arcangelo.

"You need to do me a favor and post some guards that I can get out of the way."

"We'll have two Gypsies with guns in their hands, but shoot into the air, because I need my Gypsies."

"But then they'll shoot back at us."

"If you shoot into the air, Gypsies will always run away . . . Fuck, I have to teach you everything."

"But if they run away, what do you have them there for in the first place?"

"They'll tell us there's a problem, and that's when we show up."

"*Adda murì mammà*, Don Vitto', don't you worry, I'll do as you instructed."

The boys accompanied Nicolas to the trapdoor, but he'd already set his feet on the first rung when he heard Don Vittorio: "Oh!" he stopped Nicolas. "Bring a statuette to the Professoressa for her trouble. She's crazy about Capodimonte porcelain figurines."

"Don Vitto', are you serious?"

"Sure, get *'o zampognaro*, the bagpipe player, it's a classic and it will always make you look good."

RITE

Nicolas had gone to the hardware store with a whole bunch of keys, but actually there was only one key he was interested in. A multilever-lock key, the classic kind, long and heavy, used to open an armored, reinforced door. This key went to an old but very strong lock, capable of withstanding for many years the assaults of improvised marauders. He was going to the keysmith to ask for copies: "You need to give me ten, no, twelve, no, make that fifteen."

"For real?" asked the hardware store owner: "And what do you need to do with this army of keys?"

"If they get lost . . ."

"You really have a problem with your memory, if you lose all these sets of keys."

"Better safe than sorry, no?"

"Well, if you say so. All right, so that's . . ."

"No, no, make me the keys and then I'll pay you . . . or don't you trust me?"

That last phrase had been uttered with such menace that the hardware store owner had given in; the alternative would have been to copy the keys and give them to him free of charge.

Maraja opened WhatsApp and wrote to each of them, giving them an appointment.

Maraja
Guagliù, meeting confirmed at the lair.

Lair. Not *house.* Not *apartment.* Not some other random word that anyone else would have used to mislead in case their conversations were being monitored. Nicolas wrote the word and spoke it with that old-fashioned echo it carried, "lair," almost as if to heighten the conspiratorial, lurking, criminal connotation, and thereby ward off the danger of the place turning into nothing but a convenient hangout where they could smoke joints and bang away at the video-game console. He always tried to use a criminal vocabulary, even when he was alone, it was something he forced himself to do. A lesson he had taught himself, a sort of version of the "Start living the life you want now" that was touted by every American self-help book, and that Nicolas had figured out without reading it anywhere. If only someone was monitoring and overheard it! He secretly hoped so: that would be better than the lowest foothold in whatever Camorristic organization at its last gasp. All around him, Nicolas saw nothing but territories to be conquered, possibilities to be grasped. He'd figured it out immediately and he didn't want to stop growing, he didn't give a damn about waiting in line, respecting the hierarchy. He'd spent ten days rewatching *Il Camorrista*: he was ready.

Then the morning had finally come. Nicolas went to the hardware store, got the keys and a candle, and paid what he owed, soothing the shopkeeper's concerns. He savored the fear he could sense in people whenever he went into a place of business, always worried they were about to be robbed or subjected to some abuse or shakedown. He stopped by the deli and purchased bread and wine. Then he went to the lair and began his preparations: he turned out all the lights, then he took a section of candle, lit it, and set it on the table, letting it stand in a puddle of its own wax that he'd melted onto a candleholder until it hardened, fixing it in place. He pulled the baguette out of the paper bag and broke it into sections with his hands. He put on a sweatshirt and pulled the hoodie over his head.

Showing up in dribs and drabs, two, three, then four *guaglioni* arrived. Nicolas opened the door for each of them: Pesce Moscio, Dentino, Drago', who came in without knocking—he already had the keys to the lair— then Drone, Stavodicendo, Tucano, Biscottino, Briato', and Lollipop.

"What's all this darkness?" asked Stavodicendo.

"Let's have a little silence," said Nicolas, trying to create some atmosphere.

"You look like Arno in *Assassin's Creed*," Drone told him. Nicolas wasted little time confirming that he had in fact taken his inspiration from that character. Then he sat down at the table and bowed his head.

"*Aho, scassi proprio i cessi*," said Biscottino. "You are too damned cool."

Nicolas ignored him and went on: "I baptize this place just as our three elders did. If they baptized with irons and chains, I baptize it with irons and chains." Then he paused and turned his eyes up to the ceiling. "I turn my eyes to the sky and I see the North Star." And he lifted his chin, uncovering his face. He'd started to grow a beard, the first thick beard that his age allowed him. "And this club is baptized! With words of *omertà* our society is formed."

He asked the first of them to step forward. No one budged. One of them stared at the tips of his shoes, another concealed a smile of embarrassment in the presence of that all-too-familiar scene they'd viewed so many times on YouTube, a third stood teetering on tiptoes. At last, one figure broke away from the crowd: Dentino.

Nicolas asked him: "What are you in search of?"

And he said: "Of my qualification as a young man of honor."

"How much does a *picciotto* weigh?" Nicolas asked.

"As much as a feather scattered by the wind!" replied Dentino. He knew all the lines by heart, and he trotted them out with perfect timing, and with the right intonation.

"And what does a *picciotto* represent?"

"A sentinel of *omertà* who turns and turns again, and that which he sees and earns, he brings back to the society."

Then Nicolas picked up a piece of bread and handed it to him: "If you betray, this bread will become lead." Dentino put it in his mouth, chewing slowly, softening it with his saliva. Nicolas poured some wine into a plastic cup, handed it to him, and said: "And this wine will become poison. If before I knew you as a young man of honor, from this moment on I recognize you as a *picciotto* belonging to this corps of the society."

Lying open in front of him was also the Bible that he'd taken from his mother's dresser drawer. Then he pulled out his switchblade knife. The powerful springloaded blade with the black bone handle had been his favorite weapon up until that moment. He released the safety, pushed the button, and snapped open the blade. Dentino cried: "No! No, no, not the knife!"

"We must all put in our blood," said Nicolas, grabbing Dentino's hand in his own. "Give me your arm." He made a small cut precisely on the wrist, a small cut that was certainly much shorter and shallower than the one that Ben Gazzara makes in the movie. He squeezed out a beading drop of blood, just enough. After which, at the same place on his arm, Nicolas cut himself in turn. "Our blood is mingled, not the blood that comes from the same mother." They took each other's forearm and pressed them together, to mingle their blood.

Dentino rejoined the group and Briato' took a step forward. He practically had tears in his eyes. This was a genuine first communion, confirmation, and wedding all at once.

He presented himself to Nicolas, who asked him the same questions: "Tell me, *guaglio'*, what are you in search of?"

Briato' had his mouth hanging open, but no words came out, whereupon Nicolas tried to help him out, like a high school teacher trying to rescue his student: "Of . . . of my . . ."

"Life as a young man of honor!"

"No, for fuck's sake! Of my qualification as a young man of honor."

"Of my qualification as a young man of honor!"

"How much does a *picciotto* weigh?" Nicolas asked him.

"As much as the wind . . ."

Someone suggested from the back, in a low voice: "As much as a feather scattered by the wind."

"And what does a *picciotto* represent?"

"A soldier of *omertà* . . ."

From the back of the room someone corrected him: "Sentinel!"

Briato' pretended not to notice and went on: "Who brings money to the society."

Nicolas repeated the phrase for him: "No, you're supposed to say that what he sees and hears and earns, he brings back to the society!"

Whereupon Briato' blurted out: "*Adda murì mammà*, if you'd told me yesterday, I would have watched the movie again. Who the fuck can remember it, with all the words."

"*Ua*', for real," Stavodicendo commented, "*adda murì mammà*, I knew every word by heart."

Nicolas tried to restore a little seriousness to the atmosphere. He handed him the bread: "If you betray, this bread will become lead. And this wine will become poison."

Baptism after baptism the cut became shallower, because Nicolas's wrist was starting to hurt. Last of all came Tucano's turn, and he said: "Listen, though, Nico', we're supposed to mingle our blood. There's no bleeding here, you barely scratched me."

And so Nicolas took his arm and cut again. Tucano wanted to carry that scratch with him, see it over and over again for the days to come: "If before I knew you as a young man of honor, from this moment on I recognize you as a *picciotto* belonging to the corps of the society." Tucano couldn't resist the temptation, and after the exchange of blood and the rubbing of forearms he pulled Nicolas close to him and kissed him full on the lips. "*Ricchio*'!" said Nicolas, calling him a faggot, and with that last line the rite was complete.

Now in the apartment all the young *guaglioni* had become blood brothers. A blood brother is something you never turn back from. Your fate is bound up with the rules. You live or you die according to your ability to abide by those rules. The Camorra has always made a sharp contrast between blood brothers and brothers of sin, that is, the brother that your mother gives you by sinning with your father, as opposed to the brother that you choose, the brother who has nothing to do with biology, that does not come to you from a womb, from a sperm cell. The brother that is born in blood.

"Let's just hope you all don't have AIDS, 'cause we've all mixed our blood," said Nicolas. Now that the ceremony was finished, he was hanging out with all the others, like in a family.

"Eh, that's Ciro, who screws sick girls in the ass!" said Biscottino.

"Oh, go fuck yourself," Pesce Moscio replied in a thunderous voice.

"At the very most," said Dentino, "he screws fat girls, but only with a floppy fish!"

Dentino was telling an old story: the story that had baptized Ciro Somma for all time as Pesce Moscio—Floppy Fish. It dated back to the days when they'd occupied the Arts High School, when a picture of one of his girlfriends, naked and really big, had made the circuit of every smartphone in the school. He really liked that girl a lot, but he'd let himself be dissuaded by the idiotic insults of his classmates, and so he started defending himself by admitting, yes, it was true, he'd had sex with her. But not real, proper sex, instead it had been with his dick kind of hanging at half mast, like a floppy fish.

"It's unbelievable," said Stavodicendo, who was palpating his body all over as if he'd just stepped out of a miraculous fountain, "I feel like a new man, but really and truly."

Tucano fell into line: "True, so do I."

"It's a good thing you're new men," said Dentino, "because whoever you were before, you were both just a filthy mess . . . Maybe this one will be an improvement!"

For decades now these rituals had been abandoned in Forcella. Actually, Forcella had always been particularly resistant to the rites of criminal affiliation because it was opposed to Raffaele Cutolo, who had first introduced them to Naples in the eighties. Don Feliciano Nobile had once been invited to join Cosa Nostra—many Neapolitans formed alliances with the Sicilians and underwent the rite of *pungitura*, literally, pricking, allowing the tip of your forefinger to be pricked with a needle, so that the blood dripped on a picture of the Madonna, and then you burned the holy card in your hand. The Palermitans had explained the rite to him, and they'd told him that he would have to be *pungiuto*, or pricked, and his response was still remembered to that day: "I'll prick you all in the ass. I don't need any of this bullshit, it's good for Sicilian and Calabrian sheepherders. Under Mount Vesuvius, a man's word is all you need."

And yet the *paranza* only felt like a real *paranza* after the ritual: united, one single body. Nicolas had seen clearly. "Now we're a *paranza*, really and truly a *paranza*. Do you realize that?"

"Absolutely great-t-t-t-t!" The cheering started with Drago'. They all shouted in Nicolas's direction: *"Si' 'o ras, si' 'o ras!"* They all repeated the words—"You're the ras, you're the ras"—not in chorus, but almost one by one, as if they wanted to pay tribute to him individually, and that if they all merged their voices together, they would lose power. *'O ras* . . . had become the most important compliment that could be paid, from Forcella to the Spanish Quarter. Who can say out of what recesses of memory an Ethiopian honorary title, second only to the supreme title of Negus, had become a term of honor for young men who didn't even know Ethiopia existed. *'O ras* came from Amharic, but it had become Neapolitan. Titles and monickers that, in this city, preserved stratified sediment that dated back to the days of Ottoman piracy, an era that had left such a marked heritage in the language and on the facial features of that city.

Nicolas restored silence by clapping his hands sharply. The new members fell silent and only then did they notice that Nicolas had a bag between his legs. He picked it up and tossed it onto the table. The impact produced a sound of metal, and for a moment the whole *paranza* imagined that the bag contained weapons and bullets. If only that's what it had been, was their thought, once they realized that it was just a bag of keys.

"These are the keys to the lair. Every one of us can come in and leave whenever they like. Whoever belongs to the *paranza* has to have his own set of keys: the keys to the *paranza*. But you can only leave the *paranza*, *adda murì mammà*, feetfirst, the only way out is in a coffin."

"For real. *Adda murì mammà*," said Pesce Moscio, "but if I want to work at Copacabana's hotel, can I go? Even if I'm in the *paranza*?"

"You can do whatever the fuck you want, but you're still part of the *paranza*. You can't leave the *paranza*, whether you're working in Brazil or in Germany, but even there you can come in handy for the interests of the *paranza*."

"Great, that's the way I like it!" said Stavodicendo.

"Tutt' 'e sorde s'hann'a purtà ccà." He outlined the basic principle: all the money comes to the *paranza*. "We divvy up in equal parts. No side

deals, no skimming off the top. Every penny: armed robberies, the dope we deal, every one of us gets a monthly take and then the money for any special mission!"

"Mission! Mission! Mission!"

"And now that we're a *paranza*, do you know what's left to do?"

"Get the weapons we don't have, 'o Maraja," ventured Dentino.

"That's exactly right. I promised you guns, and guns are what we're going to get."

"*Mo' però dobbiamo avere la benedizione d' 'a Maronna*," said Tucano. "Now we need the Madonna's blessing. How much money do we all have?"

At the name of the Madonna, some kicked in five euros, some kicked in ten, Nicolas put in twenty. Tucano gathered up all the cash.

"*Amm' 'a accattà 'nu cero.* We've got to get a candle. A big one. And we'll consecrate it to the Madonna."

"Good," said Dentino.

Nicolas was indifferent to this detail. They all left the lair together and headed for the store that sold devotional candles.

"Here we are. In the priests' shop."

All ten of them went in. The shopkeeper grew uneasy at the sight of his shop filling up so suddenly. And he was astonished when they pointed to the biggest candles. They selected an enormous one, more than three feet tall. They put their money down on the counter, all crumpled up. It took the shopkeeper a few minutes to count the money, but by then they'd already left. Without waiting for the receipt or the small amount of change due to them.

They went into the Church of Santa Maria Egiziaca in Forcella. Nearly all of them had been baptized there or else in Naples Cathedral. They crossed themselves. Their feet grew lighter as they walked down the nave; they weren't wearing leather shoes that might echo, but Air Jordans. When they were standing in front of the immense painting of the titular St. Mary of Egypt, they crossed themselves again. There wasn't room enough to squeeze in that enormous candle, and so Pesce Moscio took his lighter and started melting the base of it.

"What are you doing?" said Dentino.

"Oh, nothing, we'll just stick it here on the floor. There's nowhere else to put it," said Pesce Moscio, and suited action to words.

While Pesce Moscio was making sure the candle was solidly fixed to the floor, Tucano opened his knife and started carving their name down the side, like a carpenter inlaying a piece of wood.

He wrote PARANZA in big letters.

"It looks like you've written *PaPanza*," said Biscottino.

"Like fuck it does," Tucano replied, taking a slap on the back of the head from Dentino.

"In front of the Madonna, you talk like that?!"

Tucano glanced up at the big painting of the Madonna and said, "Forgive me," then he bore down harder with the knife blade on the leg of the capital R. And then he read it out aloud: "PARANZA." And the word *paranza* echoed down the length of the nave.

A *paranza* that comes from the sea but now belongs to the land. A *paranza* that descends from the city's quarters that look out over the Bay of Naples, marching in formation, filling the streets.

Now it was their turn to go do some fishing.

ZOO

Maraja was ecstatic. He'd obtained exactly what he wanted: Don Vittorio in person had recognized that he had the makings of a *paranza* boss, but more important, he'd given him access to the gang's arsenal. He was bouncing up and down on the motor scooter as if some enormous energy were building up inside him, like a tightly coiled spring, as he zipped along rapidly back to the center of town, and with a smile stamped on his face. He sent a text to the chat on WhatsApp:

> **Maraja**
> Guagliù, we did it: we got our wings!

Lollipop
Adda murì mammà!

Drago'
He' scassat i ciesse!

Biscottino
Fantastic

Tucano
You're better than a can of Red Bull!

He was so electrified and anxious he would never have been able to go to see Letizia or to the lair, much less return home, so he decided to end that day by getting another tattoo. He already had one on his right forearm with his initials and Letizia's intertwined with a thorny rose, while on his chest, pride of place was enjoyed by a script rendition of his name, "Maraja," surrounded by curlicues, flourishes, and a hand grenade. Now he already had a clear idea of exactly what design he wanted inked on him, and where.

He stopped at Totò Ronaldinho's tattoo shop and barged in the way he usually did, even though the proprietor was working on another customer: "*Ua'*, Totò! You need to give me a pair of wings!"

"What?"

"You need to give me a pair of wings, a pair of wings back here," and he pointed to his back, waving his hand in broad gestures to indicate that he wanted his whole back covered by the tattoo.

"What kind of wings?"

"Archangel wings."

"Angel wings?"

"No, not angel wings: archangel wings."

Nicolas knew the difference clearly, because his art history textbook overflowed and abounded with Annunciations and altarpieces depicting archangels with broad flaming wings, and during the class trip to Florence a few months ago, he'd even seen them in real life, those cheerful wings that, however, even put the fear of God into dragons.

Nicolas wrote on WhatsApp: "*Guagliò*, I'm getting a pair of wings inked on my back. Come on down." Then he turned the cell phone to show Totò a picture of a fourteenth-century painting of St. Michael with black-and-scarlet wings and told him he had to do them "exactly like that."

"But it'll take me three days to do them," Totò objected. He was used to working off the patterns and drawings in his catalogs.

"It'll take you one. We'll start work today, and then you're going to have to do the same for all my pals. But you'll give us a good price."

"Sure, Maraja, whatever you say."

They spent the next few days going in and out of the tattoo parlor, and the tattoo artist carved into the skin on their backs, etching the flesh, with a light, attentive touch. Because to a certain extent Totò had actually taken a passionate interest in this work, work that required a minimum amount of creativity. Along with the passion, he'd also become curious, and wanted to know: "What do these wings mean to you?" He'd ask that question as he forced the ink into the skin over the shoulder blades. "Why are you and all your buddies getting them?"

Nicolas didn't mind the question, symbols were fundamental, but it was just as important that everyone be able to decipher them, those symbols needed to be as clear as the frescoes on the walls of the churches, where the instant you saw a saint with keys, you knew it was St. Peter. That tattoo needed to be every bit as immediate for all of them, the members of the *paranza*, and everyone else, outside of it. "It's like taking someone else's powers: it's as if we'd captured an archangel, which is sort like saying the boss of the angels, cut its throat, and taken its wings. It's not the kind of thing that just happens along, it's something we sweated for, that we fought hard for and won, and now it's as if we were Archangel from the X-Men, got it? It's sort of like . . . something we achieved, got it?"

"Ah, like a scalp," said Totò.

"What's a scalp?" asked Dentino.

"You know, like what the Indians do . . . they take a knife and peel the hair and the scalp off their enemies' heads."

"That's right," Nicolas confirmed, "exactly."

"Then who did you cut the wings off?" asked Totò.

"Heh heh heh," laughed Nicolas. "Ronaldi', now you're asking too many questions."

"Oh, hell, what do I know?"

"That is, it's as if to say . . . that you can learn from someone how to play soccer, how to swim fast, no? It's like taking private lessons for a foreign language, right? You learn. Well, same way, someone taught us to have wings. And now we're flying, and no one's going to stop us now."

For three days the whole paranza had pairs of flaming wings on their backs, but still not one of them had taken flight even once: they were waiting for the signal from Don Vittorio Grimaldi, and the wait was stretching out. They had no idea of how or where they'd be able to get in touch with him. Maraja was acting as if everything was going exactly the way it was supposed to go, but deep inside he was starting to seethe, and in order to brace himself he kept thinking about that meeting in the boss's home: the man had given him his word, he couldn't doubt what was coming.

In the end it was simpler than they'd expected. Aucelluzzo got in touch with Nicolas directly, he approached him on his motor scooter, no phone calls, no visits to the lair. "Guagliu', L'Arcangelo's gift to you is at the zoo."

"The zoo?"

"The zoo. That's right. South side. Go in, there's a penguin cage."

"Hold on," said Nicolas. They were talking while riding their scooters. "Pull over for a second."

"No, why are you stopping? Keep riding." Aucelluzzo was shitting his pants in fear of Micione's men because he was in forbidden territory, property of the Faellas. "Download the map of the zoo from the Internet. Anyway, the penguin section is empty. Under the trapdoor, you'll find the bags. All the gats are in the bags."

"Are the Gypsies still there?"

"Yes."

"They're not going to shoot at us, are they?"

"No, they're not going to shoot at you. You shoot in the air and they'll turn and run."

"Okay."

"Take care." After pulling away, Aucelluzzo turned around to shout back at him: "When you're done, post on Facebook, that way I'll know."

Nicolas accelerated and caught up with his boys in the apartment on

Via dei Carbonari, to organize the group that was going to go and retrieve the weapons. There was the one pistol, the one Nicolas had bought, and then they had a couple of knives between them. Dentino suggested: "I could go and see if they'll sell me a pistol at La Duchesca, or else there's the hunting-and-fishing store, we could just rob them . . ."

"Sure, let's rob a gun store, that way they'll riddle us with lead."

"Okay, forget it."

"So let's get a gat from the Chinese guy where Nicolas got the first one."

"Mm-hmm. Another piece-of-shit pistol? No way in hell. We need to head out tonight and grab the gang's arsenal. L'Arcangelo is giving us all his weapons. It's serious stuff, not this other bullshit."

"All right, then, let's do that. Let's go to the zoo."

"The zoo?" asked Dentino.

Nicolas nodded. "It's all set. We'll go in, just five of us: me, Briato', Dentino, Stavodicendo, and Pesce Moscio. Outside: Tucano and Lollipop. Stavodicendo will go ahead to scout, to see if there's any activity we don't like, and he'll call Pesce Moscio, who'll keep an eye on the cell phone. Drago' waits in the lair, because we're going to need to hide the weapons . . ."

None of them had been at the zoo since they were four years old, and at the very most what they remembered of the place was tossing peanuts to the monkeys. There was a long enclosure wall, and they saw that the main entrance consisted of a gate that didn't look too imposing. They'd assumed they were going to have to take some side entrance to go in, but instead it was super-easy to climb over the front way. The first to go was Stavodicendo, then, on his signal, the other four. They were in such a hurry to get to the swag that they went right past the signposts for the various animals without noticing. The weapons were right there within reach, they could practically smell them, instead of the whiff of guano from all the birds that ruffled their feathers as they went by. They sounded like ghosts. The guys were all excited, without a hint of fear. But also without the slightest idea of where they were heading.

They were forced to stop halfway up the lake that stretched out on their right. "Where the fuck are these penguins?"

They pulled out their iPhones and studied the map on the zoo's website: "It's a good thing I told you to memorize the way," Nicolas blurted out, even though he had no more idea of where they were than any of the others.

"Fuck, it's totally dark here." Briato' had brought a flashlight; the others trailed behind him, using their cell phones to light up the ground in front of their feet. When they came to the end of the lake they were staring into the maw of the lion's cage. The lion seemed to be fast asleep and was clearly getting along in years, but he was still the king of the beasts, and they all stopped for a moment to gaze at him. "*Ua'*, he's big, though, isn't he, I thought they were about the size of a Great Dane," said Dentino. The others nodded. "He looks like a mob boss behind bars: but even from in there, he's the one who commands." They'd managed to get distracted like a crowd of children, and they'd made a wrong turn into the section of the zebras and the camels.

"We've got this wrong. What do camels have to do with penguins? Let me look at the map again," said Stavodicendo.

"Can't you see that's a dromedary? You're always walking around with that pack of cigarettes in your hand and you can't even remember what a camel looks like!" Briato' mocked him.

"Eh, I was just saying, a dromedary, what the fuck."

"Oh, *guagliu'*, we're not taking an elementary school field trip," said Nicolas, starting to get impatient. "Let's get moving."

They took a right, leaving the big birdhouse on their left, and headed straight, passing the reptile house without uttering another word.

"Wait, is that the polar bear?! Then we must be getting close . . ." At last they found the right section of the zoo. "*Ua'*, it really smells like shit. Why do these penguins stink so bad? Aren't they always in the water? Then they ought to be clean."

"What's that got to do with anything?" asked Nicolas. "They stink because they're fat."

"How do you know? What are you now, a veterinarian?" Briato' ribbed him.

"No, but before coming here I watched a whole documentary about penguins on YouTube. I wanted to know if they were likely to attack us or who knows what else. But where is the damned manhole?" They couldn't see it.

They found themselves face-to-face with the plate-glass wall that separated the part where the penguins live by day from the area where they sleep at night, hidden from the public. Behind the glass was a diorama of Tierra del Fuego, the place the penguins originally came from. They realized that the manhole was right under the birds, behind the backdrop of the diorama where the penguins were perched, surrounded by shit and some scattered food. They stuck the flashlight into a loophole and spotted two metal covers, clearly the access points for two manholes: "What the fuck, L'Arcangelo didn't tell me a thing. *Adda murì mammà*. He just said in the manhole where the penguins are, not actually *underneath* the penguins."

"And how the fuck are we supposed to get inside there?"

"Wait, weren't there supposed to be some Gypsies here?" Briato' pointed out.

"I don't see anybody here. How the fuck would I know?"

They started kicking at the little access door; the noise of their feet on the metal scared the penguins, and they immediately got worked up in that drunken way of theirs, you'd think they'd just downed ten *chupito* shots in a row.

"Maraja, shoot at the lock, that way we'll get in faster!"

"What are you, stupid?! I've got three shots in this gun. Get to kicking!" he concluded, delivering one powerful kick as a demonstration. And with one kick after another, by the tenth powerful blow not only did the metal door swing open, but a piece of the wall enclosing the penguins' space came with it. By now the penguins were terrorized, and they were emitting cries that made it all too clear that, whatever else you might think, they really were birds. What's more, flightless though they might be, they still had big, sharp beaks on them.

With their flashlight trained on the animals, they were almost scared to go in. "Are they aggressive?" asked Dentino. "I mean, they're not going to peck at us or bite our dicks off, are they?"

"No, don't worry about that, Denti', they know they wouldn't find a thing to eat with you."

"Joke all you like, Maraja, but these are actually violent animals."

Nicolas finally made up his mind to go in, and the increasingly frightened penguins began moving around chaotically, flapping their atrophied wings. Now and then one of them would stick its head through the breach in the wall, perhaps looking out at freedom. "Let's just let them run away, that way they can get the fuck out from underfoot." Stavodicendo and Dentino started shoving them to get them to leave the space, the way you do with chickens when you're trying to get your hands on one. That was when they saw the two Gypsies, who had gone off to get something to eat, returning with their hands full of pizza and beer. "What the fuck do you think you're doing?! Who are you?" they shouted, getting the penguins even more upset, while in the near distance a few seals started emitting a ridiculous series of honk-honks.

Nicolas did as L'Arcangelo had told him to do. He grabbed his pistol and fired his first shot into the air.

But the Gypsies instead just started shooting right at him and the rest of the *paranza*. "Hey, these guys are shooting at us!" As they were taking to their heels in search of shelter, Nicolas unloaded the last two shots remaining in his handgun at the Gypsies: on the second shot they tore out of there, silent as cats.

"Are they gone?" They stood there for a minute listening, silent, Nicolas with his Francotte aimed uselessly out into the darkness, as if his ammunitionless pistol would reload with a click like in a video game.

Once it was clear that the Gypsies weren't going to be coming back around, they resumed breathing normally. Pesce Moscio grabbed the pizzas they'd dropped and tossed them to the penguins. "Do those poor beasts eat pizza, you think?"

"What the fuck, Maraja! Didn't you say that if you fired in the air the Gypsies would take to their heels?!"

In the meantime, they managed to get the manholes open. Briato' offered to go down, while their cell phones were going crazy with beeps and signals as Tucano and Lollipop kept asking from outside what was going on, if they needed them to come in. Dentino replied: "What do you think, if someone's shooting at us do we have time to answer a message on WhatsApp whether you need to come in or not?"

Nicolas slapped him on the back: "Instead of wasting time texting on your cell phone, come on in here!"

"*Ua', guagliu'*. Look what the fuck is in here!" Briato's voice floated up to them, and inside was the biggest arsenal any of them had ever laid eyes on.

Actually, they could only guess at it; they could see rifle barrels protruding from trash bags. Briato' and Nicolas, who'd brought duffel bags, started stuffing them full, putting in everything within reach. "*Facimm'ampress'*. Hurry up. Here, take this fucking bag."

"*Uànema*, how the fuck much does it weigh!" Pesce Moscio said to Stavodicendo, holding the bag up from below.

They left the penguin area, with the penguins behind them wandering off into the zoo itself, and then walked past the big cats' cage again, hauling the heavy bags full of weapons, slung on straps around their shoulders.

"*Ua'!*" Lollipop exclaimed; he had just joined them, leaving Tucano alone out front to keep a lookout. He had an idea: "*Sparammo 'o lione.* Let's shoot the lion. Then we'll take it and get it stuffed and we can put it in the lair."

"For real?" asked Dentino: "And who's going to stuff it for you?"

"I don't know. We'll look it up on the Internet."

"*Ja', ja'*, Maraja. Let me shoot it."

"What do you want to shoot, fuck off, get out of here."

Lollipop unzipped the bag, grabbed the first thing that felt like a gun, and went over to the lion's cage. Or actually, behind the lion's cage. He put his nose in the narrow opening to try to figure out how many animals there were: there was the old lion they'd already admired, and maybe, at the far end of the room, a lioness. He stuck the gun in, aimed it at the lion, and pulled the trigger, but the trigger wouldn't budge. There had to be a safety on the gun somewhere; he flicked all the switches and levers

188 | ROBERTO SAVIANO

he could find, pulled the trigger so that the hammer snapped, but there was no gunfire.

"It's out of bullets, *strunzo!*" said Maraja.

Dentino broke in, yanking on Lollipop's arm: "*Jammo ja'*, get moving, you can do the safari ride at the zoo some other time."

They walked out the main gate with incredible nonchalance, all they had to do was wait for the private security patrol to go by, and then the regular patrol of the city police. Tucano texted them from outside to give them the all clear.

They deposited the bags full of weapons at the lair on Via dei Carbonari, where Drago' was waiting for them. His mother had given him permission to sleep away from home that night. He'd lied to her, saying that he was going to stay over at a classmate's from school. Drago' wanted to hear how it had all gone, but they were too tired to tell him anything. They simply said good night with a round of satisfied slaps on the back.

They all spent a sleepless, euphoric night. Each slept in his own bed, in a bedroom close to his parents' bed. They fell asleep like so many children on December 24, knowing that when they woke up they'd find presents to open under the tree. And that they'd wake up eager to tear the wrapping paper off that wonderful package containing weapons, their new lives, a chance to matter, a chance to grow. They fell asleep with the pleasurable discomfort of someone who knows that a great day is about to dawn.

TURK'S HEAD

They carried the weapons in their gym bags. The bags were bright green, and on them was printed POLISPORTIVA DELLA MADONNA DEL SALVATORE.

Maraja and Briato' had found them in the lockers, among the T-shirts and backpacks. They'd been there since the days when they'd stopped playing for the parish church soccer team. They were the most capacious bags they'd found, and the same duffel bags they'd once used to carry their suits and soccer shoes, they'd jammed full of machine guns and semiautomatic pistols.

Training in the countryside far from the city meant alerting the families out there, letting them know they were armed, that they were getting organized, that they'd received a shipment of real artillery. Too much noise: better not to; in the blink of an eye everyone would be wondering where the weapons had come from and what they planned to do with them. Better not to give away any advantages. Because as far as shooting went, they didn't really know how; they'd seen hundreds of tutorials on YouTube, and they'd killed hundreds of characters, but only on their PlayStations. They were strictly video-game killers.

Going out into the woods and shooting at trees and empty bottles was easy, but it meant wasting time and ammunition that could be better used to carve scars. Their training needed to leave a mark, there was no time to waste. They'd find targets in their own world, in the forest bristling with metal tree trunks and weedy cables. The roofs were teeming with targets: TV antennas, laundry hung out to dry. They just needed a nice comfortable apartment house. But even that wouldn't be enough. The noise of the shooting would force some carabinieri squad car to come nosing around. And a few police teams might swoop in to check them out, too.

But Maraja had had an idea: "A party, with fireworks, M-80s, ash cans, dragon-boom firecrackers, skyrockets, anything that makes noise. At that point, you can't hear any difference between their detonations and ours."

"A real live party, just like that? For no good reason?" asked Dentino.

They covered all of Forcella, Duchesca, and Foria and asked everywhere they stopped: "Who's got a birthday party coming up, or a wedding, or a first communion?"

Unleashed like dogs, they asked anyone, door to door, *basso* by *basso*, shop by shop. They asked mothers, sisters, aunts. Anyone who happened to hear of a party needed to tell them, because they had a nice gift to offer. That's right, a nice gift to offer. For everyone!

"Found it, Maraja: a lady right in the *vicolo*, where we can train . . ."

The apartment house that Briato' had identified was on Via Foria. It had a perfect shared rooftop terrace, spacious and surrounded on all sides by antennas that stood as thick as a troop of sentinels.

He had uttered the word *train*—in Italian *addestrarci*—so well and clearly that he almost seemed to be licking his chops to savor the taste of those four hard, almost professional syllables. *Ad-de-strar-ci.*

"The lady's called Signora Natalia," Briato' went on.

Her ninetieth birthday. A major party, a thousand euros of fireworks each. But that wouldn't be enough.

"We need more noise than that, Briato'. We need to find another party nearby, and there needs to be music, what we need is a band. *Quatte scieme cu 'e tamburi, doje trumbette, 'na tastiera.* Four idiots with drums, two trumpets, a keyboard."

Briato' made the circuit of the three restaurants in the surrounding neighborhood, and he found a party for a first communion, but it all still remained to be organized. The family didn't have a lot of money, and they were working out terms for the price. First communions are dress rehearsals for wedding receptions. From the outfits to the meals, hundreds of guests, and full-fledged financing: IOUs, shylocks. Money is no object.

"I want to talk to the proprietor," Briato' asked the first waiter he ran into.

"You can tell me."

"No, I have to talk to the proprietor."

"But why? Can't you just tell me?"

Before starting out on his rounds, Briato' had unzipped the bag and pulled out a pistol at random, just as a way to save time. He wanted to be sure there were no delays, he wanted the equivalent of a badge to make sure people paid attention to him. He was too much of a kid, too baby-faced, no marks, not even a scar that he'd gotten by accident, so he was forced to raise his voice, invariably. He pulled out the gun, unloaded though it was, and probably with the safety still on.

"*Allora 'o fra', 'a spaccimm'e chi t'è mmuorto,*" he started out, saying, "Okay, bro, fuck you and whoever raised you," and then went on, more calmly, "I'm going to say it politely: Are you going to let me talk to the proprietor, or am I going to have to split that fucking head of yours wide open?"

The owner of the restaurant was listening and he got down off the podium.

"*Ue' piscitiello, posa stu fierro che nuje appartenimmo . . . e te fai male,*" the owner called out. "Hey, kid, put down the gun, we're protected . . . and you're going to get yourself hurt."

"I don't give a fuck who's protecting you, I want to talk to the owner. Now is that really so hard?"

"That's me."

"Who's celebrating their first communion here?"

"*'Nu guaglione del vico.*" A kid from this street.

"Does his father have the money?"

"What money? He'd going to pay me for the meal on installments."

"All right, then, you need to take him this message, you need to tell him that we'll pay for the fireworks for the party, in the *vicolo* for three hours, we'll throw this event."

"I don't get it, what fireworks?"

"Fireworks, dumb-ass, ash cans, M-80s, bottle rockets. What do you call them? We'll give a fireworks show to the kid who's having his first communion, or do I have to tell you a third time? By the fourth time, I'm gonna get pissed off, though, let me warn you."

"Now I get it. But did you have to put on this whole production just to deliver this message?"

The proprietor conveyed the message. The *paranza* hired expert technicians and plenty of fireworks. A thousand euros apiece was the generous donation they made. Briato' had overseen it all.

And he wrote on WhatsApp in their shared chat:

Briato'
Guaglioni, the party in Foria is all taken care of. Get yourselves ready for the fireworks show.

The answers were virtually all the same.

Dentino
Uuà, that's huge.

Biscottino
For real, bro! That's great.

Lollipop
Uuààà!

Drone
Uuàà! I'm already there!

Pesce Moscio
Uààà! I can't wait!

Maraja
Nice work, bro! Saturday everyone's going
to the first communion.

The day arrived. They all parked their scooters in the atrium of the apartment house. No one asked them a thing. They went up onto the roof terrace, everyone was there. Dentino had dressed up special, Briato' was wearing a tracksuit, but he had a strange set of headphones on his head, the kind that construction workers wear when they're using a jackhammer. It was a silent procession, faces rapt in concentration, penitents ready for the sacrifice. In the distance, over all the roofs, a red sun was setting.

They unzipped the bags, and between the zippers emerged the black and silver metal of the weapons, gleaming insects full of life. One bag was full of ammunition, on each box was a length of yellow duct tape with the type of weapon it went with written in ink. Names that they knew very well, that they'd yearned for more powerfully than they'd ever lusted after any woman. They all crowded in, shoving and reaching for machine guns and revolvers as if they were discounted items on the stalls at the street market. Biscottino was rummaging furiously. "I want to shoot, I want to shoot!" Small as he was, he seemed to vanish into the arsenal.

"Slow down, *guagliu'*, take it easy . . ." said Maraja. "All right, the first to shoot is Biscottino because he's the youngest. And we always let the youngest and girls go first. What about you, Biscotti', *si' cchiù piccolo o si' 'na femmena?*" He asked if Biscottino was the youngest or if he was a girl.

"Fuck off," Biscottino replied. His insistence had seemed capricious and childish, and the others were happy to sidestep the first major embarrassment.

He grabbed a pistol, it was a Beretta. It looked like it had been used, and quite extensively. It was badly scratched the length of the barrel and the butt was worn away. Biscottino had learned all about pistols, anything you can learn from YouTube without ever having pulled a trigger. Because YouTube is always the teacher. The one who knows, the one who answers questions.

"All right, so the clip is right here." He grabbed the grip and pulled out the magazine, and saw that it was fully loaded. "This is the safety," and he flicked it off. "Then to chamber a round, you pull this slide back." And he tried to suit action to words, but he couldn't do it.

Until that moment, he'd seemed to know exactly what he was doing; this wasn't the first time he'd ever had a gun in his hands, but he'd never pulled a trigger. And he couldn't chamber a round on this one. He kept frantically trying to pull the slide, to chamber the round, but his hands kept slipping. He could feel the eyes of the whole *paranza* on him. Pesce Moscio grabbed the gun out of his hands, pulled back the slide, and a bullet popped out. "You see? There was already a round in the chamber." And with those words, he handed the Beretta back to him, without humiliation.

Biscottino aimed at the dish antenna and waited for the first fireworks to go off.

The first rocket went off, hurtling shrilly up into the air and ending with an umbrella of red stars in the sky overhead, but no one bothered to look up. Fireworks, the kind that make dogs howl and wake up sleeping children, can be seen from any balcony every night, and the ones that are used to warn and the ones that are there for celebrations are always and exclusively white, red, and green.

They all stared at Biscottino's arm; he narrowed his eyes and squeezed off the first shot. He held up well to the recoil, which went entirely into the air.

"*Ua'*, you didn't hit it . . . no good, my turn . . ." said Lollipop.

"No, wait: a clip for each, that's what we said."

"Are you serious? But who decided that?"

"He's right, that's what we decided," said Dentino.

Second shot, nothing. Third shot, nothing. All around them a succession of firecrackers, detonations, and fireworks were going off, and in the midst of all that mayhem, it sounded as if Biscottino was shooting with a silencer. He extended his arm, grabbed the butt of the pistol with both hands.

"Close one eye and aim. Go on, Biscottino, try harder," said Maraja.

Still nothing. But on the next shot after that, the fifth, just before the blast of an ash can, they heard a dull metallic noise. He'd hit the dish antenna. The *paranza* burst into applause. It was like a kids' soccer team celebrating their first goal. They leaped to their feet. They threw their arms around one another.

"Now it's my turn." Lollipop started digging in one of the duffel bags and grabbed an Uzi. "*Guagliu'*, this little machine gun scares me. *Miette, miette ncoppa a YouTube!*" Put this on YouTube, he crowed in dialect.

They grabbed their cell phones and, scattered all over the roof, held them up in the air trying to find bars.

"There's no damn coverage here . . ."

Drone intervened. These were his moments, when the hours he spent tapping away in the confines of his bedroom were no longer the easy target for mockery. He pulled his laptop out of his backpack and, logging into an unprotected Wi-Fi network, he set it down on the windowsill. The screen lit up their faces as the sky darkened. Drone took off his glasses and started typing. He brought up YouTube and typed in the names of the weapons.

Dentino imitated the actions of the guy in the video. Slow, skillful, formal gestures. Too many words, though, and too many explanations for a weapon that seemed fake, for a gun that even women could handle. There were plenty of videos of blond young women showing plenty of cleavage.

"Go on, *guagliu'*, and you tell me, between the machine gun and this chick, what do you like better? Are you looking at the machine gun or the chick?" asked Tucano.

"I really don't give a flying fuck about the chick when I've got the machine gun in my hands," said Dentino.

Some of them wanted to linger over those videos of gun-toting porn stars, others were starting to make fun of Dentino for choosing a gun for girls out of that whole arsenal. Still, he didn't care: he wasn't going to come off looking like a fool, with that submachine gun it was impossible to miss the target.

"What the fuck is this guy saying?"

The man in the video was speaking Spanish with a thick Mexican accent, but what he was saying was of no importance, those tutorials don't require language. Arms, body, weapon: that's all you need to teach a Mexican, an American, a Russian, or an Italian how to shoot.

Dentino positioned the submachine gun level with his nose, as shown in the video, and let loose a burst that almost sliced the dish antenna off clean. The gunfire from the Uzi resonated with flat reports and, in spite of the fireworks, echoed loudly.

It was an easy victory. There was a burst of applause from the rest of the *paranza*. And just then, the lights on the terrace and the streetlamps below switched on. It was nighttime now.

Pesce Moscio stuck his head into the duffel bags and rummaged, discarding the Berettas and the machine guns, until he finally found what he'd been looking for. A revolver.

"Look at this, *guagliu'*. It's a little cannon, a Smith and Wesson 686, they show one in *Breaking Bad*, too cool!"

He hit a bull's-eye on a spotlight illuminating the terrace with his first shot, leaving their figures a little more shrouded in darkness. Silhouettes of young kids on the rooftops, illuminated by the intermittent explosion of fireworks.

"That was easy. Try aiming at the antenna, the one that's behind the satellite dishes," said Maraja.

The bullet completely overshot the antenna and lodged in the wall, leaving a gaping hole.

"*Uaaa'*, you didn't even see it!" said Biscottino.

Pesce Moscio fired four more times; he was having a hard time withstanding the recoil, as if he were trying to keep his grip on the reins of a horse he was riding bareback. The pistol not only recoiled, it moved chaotically in his hand.

"*Adda murì mammà*, Dentino, look at this hole I made!"

Dentino walked over, Lollipop ran his finger around the inside and shards of rubble tumbled out.

"You recognize this hole? It's like your mother's pussy—*come 'a puchiacca 'e mammeta*."

"Shut up, you bastard . . . piece-of-shit purse snatcher."

Dentino let fly with a resounding smack to Lollipop's cheek, and in turn he put up both fists as if preparing to fight. He threw a right, but Dentino grabbed him by the wrist and they both fell to the terrace floor. "Hey, hey," everyone started shouting. Those two needed to stop, and immediately. They'd gone to all this trouble to find two parties and a band, they'd spent a small fortune on fireworks, and now they had to waste precious time separating these two assholes. A super-high white fountain firework burst up from below. A spectacular detonation that lit up the terrace and the whole *paranza*.

The two of them rolling on the terrace looked up, rapt for a moment, staring at the faces lit by the glare, like the dead by candlelight. Then darkness returned. Order had been restored.

They went back to the gym bags and then, finally, the time came for the AK-47s—the Kalashnikovs.

They picked up the Kalashnikovs, handing them around like sacred instruments, caressing them. "*Guagliu'*, allow me to introduce his majesty, the Kalash," said Maraja, wrapping his arms around it.

All of them wanted to touch it, all of them wanted to try shooting it, but there were only three: Nicolas took one, Dentino another, and Briato' took the third.

"*Guagliu'*, this thing is straight out of *Call of Duty*," said Briato' as he covered his ears with the absurd earmuffs.

They loaded while Drone held the computer high in the air as if he were carrying a pizza on a tray, to let it get a better online connection, and show everyone the video of *Lord of War* he'd selected. First they watched Nicolas Cage shoot, and then Rambo.

They were ready: ready, set, and they were off. Nicolas and Dentino let loose with bursts of bullets, while Briato' had his weapon set to single fire, so it emitted just a series of flat cracks. The targets they were having difficulty hitting till then had suddenly all been centered. They literally pruned the antennas lining the roof and tore to pieces the dish antennas that hung there, like ears dangling from a strip of cartilage. "*Ua'*, 'o Kalash," Dentino shouted. And all around them the branches fell from their pruning, so thick that in many cases they had to retreat, take shelter.

They laughed in gasping hiccoughs. They turned their backs to the roofs, in a movement out of a military procession that, random though it was, looked as if it had been perfectly synchronized. And they looked up from their toys all at the same instant, taking in an overweight cat busily rubbing against a sheet that no one had bothered to take down. Three bursts of gunfire that seemed like a single sweeping gust of power. The cat exploded as if it had been detonated from within. The fur tore off clean, as if skinned alive, and stuck to the sheet, which had miraculously remained pinned to the line. The cranium, however, vanished. Pulverized, or perhaps it had bounced away and now lay in the middle of the street. All the rest of it, a compact, steaming, reddish mass, occupied a corner of the terrace. *Munnezza*. Garbage

They were in a state of ecstasy and they didn't even notice that someone was calling them from down in the *vicolo*.

"'O Marajaaaaaa, 'o Dentìììì."

It was Dumbo, a friend of Dentino's, and Nicolas's brother, Christian. In spite of the fact that there was a sharp age difference between the two, they spent lots of time together. And they were also taking judo lessons together. Christian had an orange belt, while Dumbo was still stuck at yellow belt. Dumbo liked to take Christian places on his scooter, buy him a drink or an ice cream. But he especially liked talking with him because he didn't have to think too hard: he was a guy who was basically a little *abbonatiello*, Dumbo, none too swift on the uptake.

"'O Maraja, 'o Dentìììì," they called them again.

Then, without a response or permission, they came upstairs.

"*Guagliu'*, we brought a selfie stick . . ."

Nicolas was annoyed. He didn't want his brother taking part in the life of the *paranza*.

"Dumbo, where did you get my brother?"

"For real, he was wandering around like a lunatic trying to find you. I ran into him and told him that I knew where you were, on an apartment house roof, but why?"

"Nothing, just curious."

Nicolas was still constructing his *paranza*, it wasn't a finished product yet. They still didn't command respect, they still didn't know how to shoot, it wasn't time yet for Christian to be sticking his nose in his business. He was worried his younger brother might start boasting, shooting his mouth off. And for now it was better if no one knew anything. He needed to be the one who decided what to tell Christian, and therefore control what he could know and tell others. So far that had worked.

Dentino never hid anything from Dumbo. Ever. Which meant he

knew that they were shooting. But Nicolas didn't like it. Only the *paranza* was supposed to know the *paranza*'s business. If they did something, it was them and no one other than them. The people who were supposed to be on that rooftop terrace were there, and the people who weren't supposed to be there weren't. Period. These were the rules.

He thought about that while they offered to let Dumbo shoot and he turned down the offer: "No, no, these aren't things that concern me."

But Christian started rummaging in one of the two bags and grabbed a rifle. A second later and Nicolas was all over him. He was lifted off the ground and entrusted to Dumbo, who was now going to take him away, just as he had brought him—him and the selfie stick. Christian knew his brother well; when he had that look on his face there was nothing to be done. And so, without complaints or whining, he swiftly trotted after Dumbo and headed down the stairs, dragging the selfie stick with them as they went.

The rifle that Christian had pulled out was an old Mauser, a Kar98k, and Nicolas recognized it immediately: "Fuck . . . a Karabiner. My brother knows his guns."

Who could say what war this unbeatable German rifle had seen use in: in the 1940s it was the finest precision weapon around, but now it looked like an old piece of junk. It must have come from Eastern Europe, there was a Serbian decal on the butt.

"But what the hell is it?" asked Biscottino. "St. Joseph's staff?"

Maraja, though, loved that rifle. He gazed upon it raptly and ran his finger along the firing mechanism.

"What the fuck do you know about guns, this rifle is totally awesome. We need to know how to use these weapons, too," he said, addressing the *paranza* with the tone of an ill-intentioned trainer.

He lifted his finger to his nose to get a whiff of the good aroma of gun oil, then he looked around; the fireworks in the *vicolo* below were starting to die out, there wasn't much time left. If they weren't covered up by the detonations of the fireworks, they wouldn't be able to keep firing, even though, really, with all the noise of the night, their gunshots probably wouldn't scare anyone. Maybe someone might be alarmed, but still, seriously, no one would ever dream of making anonymous phone calls to alert the police or the carabinieri. Pesce Moscio, though, who'd been keeping his eyes on the time on his cell phone, was prompt in saying: "Maraja, we need to get moving. The fireworks are about to end."

"Don't worry" was Nicolas's response, while with his head tipped back he continued searching for a target and a good vantage point where he could set himself up with his rifle. The terrace they were standing on was very close to the terrace of the apartment house next door. These apartment buildings that shiver from top to bottom when you slam the front door just stand there, like aging giants: they've stood through earthquakes, bombing raids. Old *palazzi* from the years of the Viceroyalty, moldy with decay, constantly the vehicle for the same life-force, where the kids come in and go out with the same identical faces for centuries on end. Amid thousands of monarchist *lazzari*, bourgeois, and aristocrats, who had climbed and descended these same staircases and crowded these same atriums before them.

At a certain point, Nicolas had a vision: there was a vase he could see in the apartment house across the way. Not on the rooftop terrace, but on a fifth-floor balcony. A typical vase from the Amalfi coast, the mustachioed head of a Turk, with a large proud succulent plant atop it. An ideal target. A target for a sniper.

He needed a vantage point to shoot from, and Nicolas identified a small exterior broom closet, built in violation of code, originally just a sink that had since become, with a little cement and plywood, a small room on the terrace. He climbed onto the roof with just one hand, the other hand occupied with holding tight the heavy German Mauser rifle. Everyone watched him in silence and no one dared to help him. He positioned himself on the small square roof, then aimed the rifle at the Turk's head on the balcony: the first shot went wide. The detonation was muffled and the recoil was very powerful, but Nicolas managed to control it successfully. He posed like a genuine sniper.

"*Ua', guagliu',*" said Nicolas, "Chris Kyle, I'm Chris Kyle!"

The unanimous response was: "*Ua',* seriously though, Maraja, you really are the American Sniper."

Loading a ramshackle old Mauser like that was no simple matter, but Nicolas liked doing it and the *paranza* enjoyed watching his sequence of careful, precise gestures. They'd seen the same sliding rotating bolt in all the movies that featured a sniper, and so they remained transfixed, listening to the sounds of metal and wood. Clack . . . clack . . . He fired a second shot. No effect. He wanted to make sure the third shot went home at all costs. That ceramic head seemed to him like a gift from heaven, positioned there just so he could show off how good he would be at shooting anyone in the head, just like a real warrior. He squeezed his left eye even more tightly shut and let go with the third shot: there was a tremendous noise, the twang of metal, and an explosion of glass and bones. All together. A tremendous fracas.

This time Maraja was unable to handle the recoil. He'd huddled so tightly over the butt of the rifle; like all green riflemen he believed that it was enough to brace the butt in order to control the entire weapon, and all his muscles and concentration were focused there. Instead, the rifle, like a wild animal, lunged at him: the barrel smacked him in the face, his nose started to bleed, and his cheekbone split open, scratched deeply by the bolt. And since the shot he fired was making him fall over, to keep from toppling he jammed his feet down harder on the little patch of roof, which suddenly collapsed beneath him. Maraja fell and was swallowed up by the little broom closet. He landed on mops, brooms, laundry detergent, heaps of rusted TV antennas, tool chests, and pigeon spikes. The fall made everyone burst out laughing, an automatic instinctive reaction, but one that only lasted a second or two. The last bullet he'd fired had ricocheted off the balcony railing and had hit the plate-glass window dead center, pulverizing it. An old man came out onto the balcony in fright, followed closely by his wife, who glimpsed the heads of the kids on the rooftop of the apartment house across the way.

"What the fuck are you doing? Who are you kids, anyway?"

With great promptness of reflexes, Briato' grabbed Biscottino under his arms, the way you pick up a child when you bend over to hoist him onto your shoulders. He lifted him into the air, set him down on the apartment house cornice, and said: "Signo', forgive us. It was this little boy, he threw an M-80, now we'll swing by and pay."

"What are you talking about, you'll swing by and pay? Now I'm calling the cops. Who do you belong to? Who the fuck are you? *Figli 'e sfaccimma*." He finished by calling them sons of filth.

Briato' tried to keep the two old people out on the balcony as long as possible, while Nicolas and the others stowed all the weapons and boxes of ammunition back in the gym bags. They moved chaotically, like mice when a human foot steps into a room where the light has just been turned on. Seeing them, no one would have thought of the soldiers of a *paranza*. What they seemed like actually was a bunch of kids intent on taking to their heels, keeping their heads down to avoid being seen by their mother's friends, after breaking a window with a recklessly kicked soccer ball. And yet, earlier that same evening, they'd practiced shooting military-grade weaponry and they'd done it with all the curiosity and naïveté of children. Weapons are always thought of as tools to be handled by adults, but the younger the hand that works the hammer, the ammunition clip, the barrel, the more efficient the rifle, the machine gun, the pistol, and even the hand grenade. A weapon is efficient when it becomes an extension of the human body. Not an instrument of defense, but a finger, an arm, a cock, an ear. Weapons are made for young people, for children. It's a truth that applies at any latitude around the world.

Briato' did everything he could think of to keep the old people occupied. He dreamed up stories: "But no, we're guests here, we belong to the signora who lives on the second floor."

"And what's her name?"

"Signora Natalia, she just turned ninety. We threw a party for her."

"And what the fuck do I care about that? Call your parents, go on. You've shattered my whole picture window."

Briato' was trying to slow them down, to delay them, though he had absolutely no intention of paying for the window. The *paranza* had already spent too much money on the fireworks. They had money, sure, and plenty of it, considering that they were just kids, but even a penny spent on someone else instead of themselves was money wasted.

While Briato' was detaining them on the balcony and the *paranza* was gathering up the shells scattered across the terrace, filled with fear that someone might show up to confiscate their weapons, there was just a single thought in Maraja's head: to make up for the ridiculous showing he'd made by hurting himself with the rifle's recoil. He could have been proud, if the injury had been received in a firefight or from the explosion of a rifle, anything that was out of his control. Instead, he'd hurt himself because he hadn't known how to manage his weapon. Like a greenhorn, a rank beginner.

As soon as the old man put on his glasses to dial the three digits of the Italian emergency number, 113, on his cell phone, Briato' called out: "No, no, you don't have to call the cops, we'll come over right now and bring you the money." And with those words, they all shot away down the stairs.

They galloped down to the motor scooters they'd hidden in the atrium. On the street, they found all the stacks of burned cardboard remnants of the fireworks. Meanwhile, the party was still under way. There were also all the guests from the first communion and all the children and grand-children of Signora Natalia. Briato' was recognized: "Young man, young man, hold on a second. Let us thank you."

They'd heard that it was Briato' who'd paid, so generously underwriting this great spectacle. They wanted to thank him, in spite of the fact that they understood the underlying motive, though not the military motive—they couldn't even begin to imagine that—but they had figured out that this was a group of the System that wanted to win their benevolence. Thanking them was the right thing to do.

At first, Briato' tried to avoid the process, but then he realized he had no alternative: old people were insisting, and so in the end he let them hug him and kiss him. He did his best to remain as discreet and under-stated as possible, and just kept saying: "It's really nothing, I didn't do a thing, it's all okay, it was a pleasure for me."

People thought it was a gesture of benevolence on the part of a new group that was emerging into the limelight, and they wanted to give their blessings to that group. But he had two different, simultaneous fears. One fear devoured the other. Too much attention, attracting attention in a *vicolo* where he was not in charge, was a fear that paled in comparison with the fear of pissing off Nicolas, because it had been his idea to sponsor the fireworks show. In spite of it all, though, he was pleased, pleased that anyone recognized him for anything. And so he tried to get his motor scooter started, pretending that the spark plug had gone bad, but the truth was that he wasn't really pushing down hard enough with his thumb on the starter button.

Then a gesture from the *paranza* forced him to speed things up.

"*Jamm' bello*, Briato' . . ."

Everyone was following Nicolas, though they had no idea where, they tried to catch up with him, riding their scooters next to his and asking why he didn't clean the wound that was bleeding on his face. Most of all, they were afraid that the decision to travel around town with those weapons in the duffel bags might not be a safe one. And it certainly wasn't a safe decision: still, though, it made them feel they were ready for a war. Any war you cared to name.

TRAINING

The road surface was uneven, potholes everywhere: they sprout in the dozens after every rainstorm, like mushrooms. Once they'd passed Garibaldi Station and turned into Via Ferraris, the *paranza* was forced to slow down.

Nicolas was going to see a young Eritrean woman who lived in Gianturco. She was the sister of the woman who helped his mother keep house. Her name was Aza, she was a little over thirty, but she looked fifty, easily. She lived in the apartment of a woman with Alzheimer's as a caregiver. In that part of town, even the Ukrainian women wouldn't come anymore.

Nicolas had a hunch that this could be the perfect hiding place for the *paranza's* arsenal. But he said nothing to the others. This wasn't the moment. Everyone else followed his Beverly. Some of them had asked him, along the way, what they were going to be doing there. But once their first few questions went unanswered, they'd realized this wasn't the time for it, that they needed to follow and say nothing. When they pulled up in front of the apartment house, Nicolas parked his scooter and, when the others circled around him, revving and slamming on their brakes, unsure whether to stop or continue, he said: "This is our new arsenal," and he pointed to the front door.

"Who is it, though?" asked Pesce Moscio. Nicolas shot him a glare so seething with rage that Pesce Moscio sensed that if he held his gaze, he'd be tempting fate.

Dentino hopped off the bike behind him and stepped between the two of them, putting an end to the matter. "I don't care who it is. All I need to know is that 'o Maraja considers this a safe house: if he thinks it's safe, then we think it's safe, too."

Pesce Moscio nodded, and so did the rest of them.

The building was one of those nondescript, sixties-era structures that blended into the larger cityscape. The street was lined with so many scooters that the five of the *paranza* were hardly noticeable. That's why Maraja had made up his mind to hide their weapons here: they could show up at any hour of the day or night without ever being noticed, and what's more, he'd promised Aza that with them around, the Gypsies were bound to steer clear. It wasn't true; the inhabitants of the Roma camp didn't even know who these brash young kids were, bold enough to promise protection in a quarter that already had a boss.

Nicolas and Dentino rang the buzzer and went up to the sixth floor.

Aza was waiting for them at the door. When she saw Nicolas, she grew alarmed: "Hey, what did you do to your face?"

"Oh, it's nothing."

They walked into a completely dark apartment, redolent of the smells of berbere spices and mothballs.

"È *permesso?*" called Nicolas, the ritual call of politeness when you enter a home. "Can we come in?"

"Keep your voice down, the signora is sleeping . . ."

He didn't detect in that apartment the odor that he was expecting, the distinctive smell of an old person's home; even though he was moving too quickly to focus on details, he still needed to understand. The aroma of Eritrean food did suggest a less-than-reassuring thought: by now, Aza was running the signora's home as if it were her own, the old woman might be about to die, which meant that the place would soon fill up with family members, it would be occupied by the staff of the funeral parlor.

"And how is the signora?"

"God willing, she's doing well," Aza replied.

"Sure, but what does the doctor have to say about it? Is she still healthy, will she go on living?"

"That's up to God Almighty . . ."

"Let's leave God Almighty out of it, what does the doctor have to say?"

"He says that her body is healthy, but her mind is pretty much gone."

"Fine, good to hear. So the signora will go on living for another hundred years."

Aza, who had already received instructions from Nicolas, pointed to a high nook. Ever since the disease had devoured her brain, decades ago, the old woman had never looked there or put a hand to it. They got out a stepladder and shoved the bags in the back of the nook, covering them with shepherds from a manger scene, wrapped in heavy cloth, followed by Christmas ornaments and boxes of pictures.

"Don't break anything," said Aza.

"Even if I break it, it strikes me that the signora isn't going to be using any of this stuff . . ."

"Just don't you break anything."

Before climbing down, he grabbed three pistols from one of the gym bags and a sack of bullets from the other.

"Don't do these things in front of me, I don't want to know anything . . ." she murmured, her eyes downcast.

"And in fact you know nothing, Aza. Now, when we need to come by, I'll tell you that we're bringing groceries for the signora and you tell us what time to come. We'll show up, get what we need, and leave. If anyone I send causes you any kind of trouble, you've got my number and you just text me, telling me what kind of problems they've caused you. Agreed?"

Aza tied back her drab curls with a scrunchie and went into the kitchen without a word. Nicolas repeated the question—"Agreed?!"—this time in a more peremptory tone of voice. She ran water over a kitchen towel and, still without speaking, walked up to him and ran it over his face. Nicolas yanked his head away in annoyance; he'd forgotten his wound, the cut cheekbone and the bloody nose. Aza stood there staring him in the eye, with the stained rag in her hand. He touched his nose, looked at his fingers, then let her clean him off.

"Every time we come, you'll be given a present," he promised, but she seemed to pay no attention.

She pulled open the cabinet door under the kitchen sink and got out a bottle of alcohol. "I'll put on some of this. It needs to be disinfected." She was very familiar with wounds, an expertise she'd gathered at home in Eritrea, and which she'd capitalized on here, caring for the wounds and sores of old people. Nicolas didn't expect it; for that matter, he didn't expect the comment: "Your nose isn't broken, it's just a little dinged up."

He ventured a thank-you, but it seemed like too little somehow. And so he added a more heartfelt, more Neapolitan "*Grazie assai.*"

Aza shot him a smile that lit up her careworn face.

Nicolas stuck two pistols behind his back and gave one to Dentino. Then he said farewell to Aza, but only after giving her a hundred euros, which she tucked quickly into the pocket of her jeans before going back to the sink, where she rinsed the blood-reddened kitchen towel.

While they were hurrying downstairs, taking the steps three at a time, Dentino asked: "*Ma ch'amma fà, mo'?*" What are we going to do now?

Those pistols had been taken to be used immediately. In that rapidity, Dentino had recognized an order.

"Denti', you don't learn to shoot by aiming at dish antennas and walls."

Dentino's intuition hadn't been wrong. "Maraja, you say the word and we'll do what you tell us."

At the bottom of the stairs, Nicolas stood in Briato' and Dentino's way and repeated what he'd just said. He slowly and clearly uttered each word, staring at them as if they'd violated some fundamental stricture: "You don't get respect by shooting at dish antennas and walls, right?"

The kids knew what he was driving at. Nicolas wanted to shoot. And he wanted to shoot at living beings. But on their own, they didn't dare come to that conclusion. They wanted to listen to him stringing those words into a sentence. Putting it as clear as day.

Nicolas went on: "We need to do a piece of work or two, and we need to do it now."

"All right. *Adda murì mammà*, I'm in," said Dentino.

Instinctively, Briato' tried to argue: "Let's learn to use the guns better. The more we know, the better we can put the bullets where we want them."

"Briato', if you wanted to get training, you could have become a policeman. If you want to be in the *paranza*, you need to be born knowing what to do."

Briato' said nothing, afraid of winding up like Agostino.

"*Adda murì mammà*, I'm in, too. *Facimm' 'e piezze.*" Let's do these pieces of work.

Nicolas walked away from the two others and said, over his shoulder: "We'll meet directly in the piazza, in a couple of hours." He made an appointment where they always met, in Piazza Bellini. "See you there."

The motor scooters took off. The *paranza* was excited, they wanted to know what Dentino, Briato', and Maraja had said to one another, but they were willing to just twist the throttle and head for the piazza.

Nicolas, who'd been ignoring his cell phone until that moment, noticed that it was bursting with messages from Letizia.

Leti
My love, where are you?
My love, aren't you reading your messages?
Nicolas, where the fuck are you?
Nicolas, I'm starting to get worried.
Nicolas!!!????

                        Nicolas
                        Here I am, sweets, I was with the bros.

Leti
With the bros? For six hours?
But don't you ever look at your cell phone?
Don't say another word, I don't want to hear it,
you can just go fuck yourself.

Letizia was sitting on the saddle of Cecilia's scooter, a Kymco People 50. Her friend had covered the bike with stickers because she was ashamed of it. But Letizia didn't feel an ounce of shame, because when she was beside Nicolas, she always felt like a queen. There were times when she felt like telling him to go to hell, and she did, but it didn't mean a thing, it was nothing more than a lover's game. What counted was the reflected light that many mistook for power.

Letizia's Kymco was parked right there, at the foot of the statue of Vincenzo Bellini, surrounded by dozens of other motor scooters dotting the crowd of young people talking, drinking beer and cocktails, and smoking joints and cigarettes. Nicolas never rode his Beverly all the way here, he always parked it on Via Costantinopoli, and then he'd walk the rest of the way to the piazza. That wasn't the horse to ride in on before an audience.

He tipped his head in Letizia's direction, signifying: "Get off and come over here."

She pretended she hadn't noticed the gesture, hadn't received the order, and so Nicolas was forced to walk over to her.

He came closer to her. His aching nose brushed against Letizia's, and she didn't even have time to say, "My love, what have you done to yourself?" before Nicolas had kissed her hard, a lengthy kiss. Then, hooking two fingers around her chin, he pushed her away spitefully.

"Leti', *adda murì mammà*, don't you ever dream of telling me to go fuck myself. You got that?" And he turned and left without another word.

Now it was up to her to follow him. He expected it, she knew it, and so did everyone around them. And that's the way it went. It started with his brisk step, and her chasing after him. Then it was the other way around, with her turning her back on him as she sulked, and him pursuing her, with blandishments, and so it went, in a continuous alternation of fronts and backs, voices raised, fingers pointed, hands clasped, kisses stolen. All the while wearing down the basalt pavement of the city's historic center, wandering along the narrow *vicoli*, with "You shut up" or "Don't you dare" glossed by "My love, look me in the eyes, have I ever lied to you?"

The whole *paranza*, in the meantime, had assembled on Piazza Bellini.

While Nicolas was making peace with Letizia, Dentino and Briato' were doing their best to upholster their anxiety with convulsive tokes on the joints the *paranza* was passing around. Who would be their first target? How would it go? Who'd be the first to come off looking like a fool? Biscottino broke the tension: "But what's become of 'o Maraja?" And Lollipop went on: "Denti', Briato', *marcat' 'a peste*? What the hell happened, what did Nicolas do, did he give someone else our arsenal?" Lollipop hadn't even finished the sentence before Briato' slapped him good and hard, a smack his own mother wouldn't have dared. Along with the smack on the terrace, this was the second one he'd received that day. "'*O, scie*', hey, stupid, don't you dare to utter that word again in a public piazza."

Lollipop rummaged through his pockets, a standard overture before yanking out his switchblade. Dentino immediately drilled in on Briato', grabbing at his T-shirt, coming close to ripping it. "What the fuck do you think you're doing, you?!" he whispered harshly in his ear.

Lollipop, who had already pulled out *his* switchblade and flicked out the blade, found himself face-to-face with Pesce Moscio, forming a human barrier. "Oh, what's this? Now we have brothers stabbing each other?"

On the other side of the fray, Dentino said in an imperative tone to Briato': "Go apologize to him. This situation needs to get fixed here and now."

At that point, Briato' summoned up a smile: "Oh, Lollipo', sorry. *Ramm' 'a mano, jamme*. Let's shake hands, come on. Still, you were a little off, you know. The *paranza*'s business is strictly for the *paranza*. Not for half this piazza. *Controlla 'a vocca, 'o fra'*." Keep a lid on your mouth, bro.

Lollipop shook hands with him, gripping a little too tight: "It's all good, Briato'. But don't you ever think of putting your hands in my face again. Never again. But anyway, you were right. I need to zip my lips: *m'aggi' 'a stà zitto*."

Flames that flared up and died down in the space of an instant. But the tension persisted, it gusted over the *paranza* and spun everyone's emotions into little whirlwinds.

Dentino and Briato' no longer knew how to dampen the tension. Dentino could feel the pistol barrel, he'd shoved it into his crotch and it was scratching his ball sack. He liked it. He felt as if he were wearing a suit of armor, as if he were more than himself. There was a small group sitting next to them, and in exchange for the joints that the *paranza* was passing around, they offered slugs of rum and pear juice. Dentino and

Briato' were ripped on alcohol and hash. The piazza was starting to empty out. A few members of the *paranza* were answering their phones, replying to their parents' questions with lies: "Ma, don't worry, really, Mamma. No, I'm not out in the streets, I'm at Nicolas's house, I'll be home later."

The university students who recognized Pesce Moscio because they regularly bought hash from him in Forcella came over asking if he had any to sell them. He had little or nothing on him at the time, a couple of sticks of hash that he let go at fifteen euros apiece, instead of ten. "What an asshole I was not to come out with my underwear jammed full," and turning to Lollipop he said: "I ought to carry a kilo of hash everywhere I go, *perché cu 'a faccia mia m' 'o llevo tutto int'a mez'ora.*" The last bit slid into thick dialect, as he boasted that with the face he had on him, he'd sling the whole key in half an hour.

"Take care or that face of yours will become familiar to the carabinieri, too. And then that face of yours will wind up behind bars in Poggioreale Prison."

"Me? Lollipo', they know my face in Poggi Poggi, believe me."

Now the piazza was empty. "*Guagliu'*, I'm out of here," said Pesce Moscio, who could no longer turn a deaf ear to the phone calls from his father, and so everyone in the *paranza* slowly made their way home.

It was three thirty by now and there'd been no sign of Nicolas. And so Dentino and Briato' went looking for him at the lair. The quarter was still teeming with noise. As soon as they were inside the apartment they started searching. At last they found a little baggie.

"We'll get two good lines out of this, no problem."

Two lines of yellow coke, *pisciazza*. They rolled up the bar receipt and made a short straw. Pisciazza was actually one of the best varieties, but its color always stirred mistrust. The nostril sucked up all the powder, like a vacuum cleaner: "It seems strange, doesn't it, to snort *'a pisciazza*," said Dentino. "But instead it's good, it's excellent. But why is it yellow like that?"

"Practically speaking, because it's all base paste."

"Base paste?"

"Yeah, without all of the processes that come later."

"What processes?"

"Oh, well. I'm going to have to give Heisenberg a call so he can swing by and give you a free lesson."

They were still laughing when they heard someone fooling around with the door. Nicolas appeared with a smile that cut right across his face: "You're snorting all the *pisciazza*, aren't you, you bastards?"

"Exactly. But what the fuck have you been up to till now!" Briato' welcomed him.

"Did you leave a little for me?"

"Sure enough, bro."

"We need to do a piece of work."

"But it's four in the morning. What piece of work do you want to do?"

"We'll need to wait."

"Right, let's wait, that's better."

"At five in the morning we'll go out and polish off a couple of pieces of work."

"Namely what and who?"

"The pocket coffees."

"The pocket coffees?"

"That's right, *guagliu'*, the pocket coffees . . . the blacks. We'll pick off a couple of blacks while they're waiting to catch a bus to go to work. We'll swing past and take them down."

"*Ua'*, nice," said Dentino.

"Just like that?" asked Briato'. "I mean, without even having an idea of who they are, we just swing by one fine morning and shoot a random pocket coffee in the head?"

"That's right, and we can be sure that way that they're not under anyone's protection. Nobody gives a fuck about them anyway. Who's even going to investigate to find out who killed some black?"

"So is it just going to be us three, or should we call the whole *paranza*?"

"No, no. The whole *paranza* needs to be present. But the three of us are going to have the only guns."

"But those other guys are at home sleeping now."

"Who gives a damn, we'll swing by and call them, and they'll get up."

"Why don't we just do it ourselves . . . and no one else."

"No. They need to see. They need to learn."

Briato' smiled. "But didn't you say that in the *paranza* we are all already born knowing what to do?"

"Start up the PlayStation, eh," Nicolas ordered without answering the question. While Briato' was switching on the PlayStation he added: "Boot up *Call of Duty*. Let's play Mission One. The one where we're in Africa. *Così mi riscaldo a sparà ncopp' 'e nire.*" That last line was about getting warmed up for shooting blacks.

Dentino sent WhatsApp messages out to everyone in the *paranza*. "*Guagliu'*, tomorrow morning," he wrote, "early morning errand for the game we need to play." No one replied.

There it is, the opening screen of the game. "The Future Is Black" is what's written. But the future belongs to those who remember to reload their Kalashnikovs before anyone else. If you get too close to the guys dressed in tank tops, you'll find yourself with your guts spilling out of a machete wound, and if there's one of these blacks, then that must mean something. Second rule: stay under cover. A boulder, a tank. Actually, all you need is the trunk of a double-parked car. And in reality, you're not going to have the air support to call in if things go to hell. Third rule, the most important one. Run. Always.

They started playing. The machine gun kept firing as hard as it could. The game seemed to be set in Angola. The main character was fighting with the regular army, he had a camo uniform and a red beret, the objective was to shoot against irregular troops, guerrilla fighters, in horrible tattered guinea-tees with submachine guns slung around their necks. Nicolas kept shooting manically. He took gunfire but just kept going. At a dead run. Constantly.

At five thirty that morning they hurried over to the homes of the other members of the *paranza*. They rang Lollipop's buzzer, and his father's voice answered: "Hello, who is this?"

"Excuse me, Signor Esposito, it's Nicolas. Is Lollipop there?"

"For real are you coming around at this time of the morning? Vincenzo is sleeping, and then he has to go to school."

"It's just that we have a field trip this morning."

"Vincenzo!" Lollipop's father yelled. He woke him up and the first thing Lollipop thought was that someone was there to take him down to police headquarters.

"Papà, what's happened?"

"Nicolas is here, he says you have to go on a field trip, but your mother didn't tell me anything about that."

"Oh, right, I forgot." Lollipop grabbed the intercom receiver while his mother rushed over barefoot waving her hands: "Field trip, but where?"

"I'll be right down, Nicolas, I'm on my way." From the balcony Lollipop's father was squinting, trying to peer through the darkness, but all he could see was a bunch of heads milling around below. The kids in the street were doubled over with laughter.

"Are you sure you're going on a field trip? Tere'," he said to his wife, "call the school."

Lollipop was already in the bathroom, ready to head out the door, certain that it would be hours before they realized there was no field trip, before there was even anyone at school to answer the phone.

It went the same for Drago', Pesce Moscio, Drone, and the others. They went to get them at home, one by one. And eventually the *paranza* became a genuine *paranza*, a long line of scooters and yawning kids. The only one who wasn't allowed out of the house was Biscottino.

He lived in a *basso* facing Loreto Mare, the hospital. The whole *paranza* showed up at his house, with their swarm of motor scooters. They knocked at the door. His mother answered, clearly on edge. She knew they wanted Eduardo.

"No, Eduardo isn't going anywhere, and especially not with people like you, you're all no-good *gente 'e sfaccimma*," calling them pieces of filth.

As if the woman hadn't spoken and wasn't standing right in front of him, Nicolas took advantage of the open door and said: "Biscottino, come on out, *ja'*."

His mother stood face-to-face with him in all her massive abundance, hair unkempt over her face, eyes bulging: "*Ue', muccusiello*," she said, addressing him as the snotnose she took him for, "first things first, my son's name is Eduardo Cirillo. Second thing, don't you ever dream again of telling my son what he has to do when I'm standing here. *O pienze che mi fai tremmà 'a sottana?*" Her last outburst in dialect was a rhetorical question: she asked him if he thought he made her skirts tremble, and as she asked it she violently shook the hem of the nightgown she was wearing.

Biscottino didn't come out, in fact he probably never even got out of bed. His mother was scarier to him than Nicolas, scarier than the loyalty he owed the *paranza*. But Nicolas didn't give up: "If your husband were here, I'd talk to him, but you shouldn't get involved in this, ma'am. Eduardo needs to come with us, he has a commitment."

"Commitment, just what would this commitment be?" asked the mother. "And then I'll call straight over to your father, and we'll see. Don't bring my husband's name into this, because you don't even know who you're talking about."

Biscottino's father had been killed during an armed robbery in Sardinia. Actually, he was just driving the car, he hadn't done the robbery, all he'd done was work as the driver of one of the gang's two cars. And when he died he left a wife and three children. He worked for a janitorial services company at the Loreto Mare Hospital, which is where he'd met these coworkers of his, a gang that robbed armored cars in Sardinia. He was killed on his first job. The robbery had gone well, though, out of the members of the robbery crew, two had survived, and they had delivered to the widow a bag with fifty thousand euros, out of the million-euro take. And that was that. Biscottino knew all about it, and this story had been scratching at his gut for as long as he could remember. His father's coworkers were on the run, and every time he heard reports of their activities, he was sorely tempted to head out on their trail himself. Biscottino's mother had sworn an oath, as is so often the case with widows, to give her children a different future, not to let them be the kind of fool that their father had turned out to be.

To Nicolas, on the other hand, Biscottino's father, killed by the cops, fallen in the course of an armed robbery, was a martyr, a member of his personal pantheon of heroes who'd gone to get money for themselves— as he liked to say—instead of waiting for someone else to give them some.

"Edua', when *mammeta*—your mama—unties you from your bed,

give me a call and we'll come get you," he ended the conversation, and the whole swarm of the *paranza* buzzed off to where it was heading.

In the yellowish dawn, down semideserted streets, under sleeping windows and clothes and sheets left out to dry in the night air, the scooters, one behind the other, croaked in falsetto as if they were a procession of altar boys lined up for Mass, spitting out verdicts of undersized engines. To see them from overhead, you might think they were cheerful, as they went the wrong way up every one-way street they found between Corso Novara and Piazza Garibaldi.

They arrived at the bus stop behind the Central Station, a slalom through and around Ukrainians trying to find their bus for Kiev, and Turks and Moroccans, hunting for the bus to Stuttgart. At the far end, between the parking areas and the bus shelters, there were four immigrants; two of them were small and looked Indian—one slight, the other a little bulkier. Then there was a third with ebony skin, and the fourth might have been a Moroccan. They were wearing work clothing. The two Indians were certainly heading out into the countryside, they wore boots filthy with dried mud; the other two probably to construction sites, because their T-shirts and trousers were spattered with mortar and paint.

The *paranza* came roaring up, a swarm of motor scooters, but none of the men thought they were in any danger, since they had nothing in their pockets to rob. Nicolas gave the signal: "Go on, Denti', go, hit him in the legs." Dentino pulled the 9mm out from behind his back, where he had it pressed securely against his tailbone with the elastic waistband of his boxer shorts, quickly flicked off the safety, and fired three shots. Only one shot went home, and that was merely a flesh wound, it grazed the foot of the Indian. The man screamed only after feeling the impact. They had no idea why these people had it in for them, but they turned to run. On his scooter, Nicolas chased after the ebony-dark young man and fired. He, too, fired three shots, two that missed and one that lodged in his right shoulder. The young man dropped to the pavement. The other Indian lunged toward the station.

"*Ua'*, with just one hand I hit him," Nicolas was saying, as he drove the scooter with his left hand only.

Briato' accelerated and took off after the young wounded Indian who was trying to get away. He fired three shots. Four shots. Five shots. It was no good.

At that point Nicolas shouted: "You're just no good." The young Indian dodged to one side and managed to get into hiding someplace. Nicolas fired two shots at the running Moroccan and hit him in the face, taking off a section of his nose, clipped in full just as he was turning around to see who was chasing him.

"We took down three pocket coffees."

"We took them down? I don't seem to remember that we did any complete piece of work," Pesce Moscio said in a tense voice. Not being one of the chosen shooters was chapping his ass.

Pesce Moscio wanted to do the shooting himself and instead Nicolas only wanted to make up for the pathetic showing he thought he'd made on the terrace.

"They're wounded, they're still trying to get away."

The Moroccan with the ravaged nose had vanished, while the African with the lacerated shoulder was on the ground. "Go on," he said, handing him the pistol, taking care not to burn his hand on the barrel, which was still smoking hot. "Go on," extending the grip toward him, "*fa 'nu piezzo*, finish him off, shoot him in the head."

"What's the problem?" asked Pesce Moscio; then he yanked his scooter up onto its kickstand and went over to the young man, who lay there, repeating a simple and fruitless cry: "*Help, help me. I didn't do anything wrong.*"

"What are you saying?"

"He's saying he didn't do anything wrong," said Nicolas, without hesitation.

"No, he didn't do anything wrong, poor little pocket coffee," said Lollipop. "Still, we need a target, don't we?" He revved his motor scooter and leaned down close to his ear: "You're not to blame for anything, pocket coffee, you're just a target."

Pesce Moscio went over to him, but not so close that he could be sure his shots were hitting the target. He chambered a round. And from a few yards away, he fired two shots. He was convinced he'd hit dead center, but actually the pistol had kicked in his hand, and he'd only grazed him: the bullet had passed through the side of his throat. The young man lying on the ground was weeping and screaming. The roller shutters in the apartment house across the way were starting to open up.

"What is it, *guaglio*'? Weren't you able to finish your piece of work?"

In the meantime, he was out of bullets.

"I didn't want to wind up like John Travolta, taking a shit with his blood all over me."

The Indian who'd taken a bullet in his foot had managed to make his limping escape, and the young Moroccan man with his nose split in two had gotten away as well. The young African, with a bullet in his shoulder and his throat split open, lay writhing on the ground, in his death throes. On the square in front of the station a squad car appeared, proceeding in their direction from the front gates. The eyes of the SEAT Leon suddenly flicked on bright yellow and so did the whining curse of the sirens. It inched along like a worm. Someone had called the cops or, more likely, it was just patrolling among the departing immigrants, checking out the cafés opening early on Via Galileo Ferraris, and the already weary lights coming down from the apartments. The squad car had just chanced to venture up into the deserted piazza.

"Your mother can suck my dick," Nicolas shouted. "'A *bucchin' 'e mammeta*," and then, swearing, he led the charge: "*Adda murì mammà*, let's shoot these assholes."

They would never have done it, they were dangerously close to being caught, when Drone, who up until that moment had stood there watching, managed to stop the police car by unexpectedly drawing a pistol and emptying the entire magazine into the vehicle.

No one knew where he'd gotten the gun. He just started firing away, and his bullets hit the squad car's hood and windshield.

Briato' joined in the shooting, too, since he still had a few rounds in his pistol. One of the shots actually hit one of the two sirens on the squad car, not that he was even aiming at anything close. They managed to get away because at that point the police car slammed on its brakes instead of chasing them: not only because they'd seen smoke issuing from their engine, but because there were just too many *guaglioni*, and so they opted to call for reinforcements. At that point, the members of the *paranza* decided to go their separate ways.

"Let's split up, *guagliu'*, talk later."

They roared off, taking different routes, on the saddles of their scooters, with their fake license plates. They'd all already switched out the plates before getting caught in a police chase, but they'd done it only to avoid having to pay the insurance.

CHAMPAGNE

They had returned to their lair after deciding to take it easy for a few days: one or two had stayed home from school, faking fevers and queasy stomachs, others had taken the opposite tack and decided to go to school precisely to avoid arousing suspicion. But there were no suspicions to arouse. Though their faces had been glimpsed by two sleepy policemen at the end of the graveyard shift, no one had recorded them. Some of the guys were afraid they'd been caught on tape by a smartphone or a GoPro installed on a cop car's dashboard, but the police didn't even have enough money to put fuel in the tank, the last thing they'd think of paying for was a video camera. And yet the kids in the *paranza* felt the fear rise inside them.

After spending a week training on human targets, they met again in the apartment on Via dei Carbonari, as if nothing had happened. They went in without knocking, the whole *paranza* had the keys. They arrived one at a time, at different times. Some after school, others in the evening. It was all normal. It was all just as usual. Life had resumed in Forcella. Games of *FIFA*, where they'd bet cash or beers, and no one made any mention of what had happened, not even Nicolas. Only at the end of the

222 | ROBERTO SAVIANO

day did he go out and, after heading down to the bar, came back upstairs with a bottle of champagne.

"Moët et Chandon, *guagliu*'. I've had it with this nasty atmosphere. It was a great experience. What needs to be clear from here on is that we're going to train every week on an apartment house roof."

Upon which Drone said: "Yeah, but are we supposed to find a party with fireworks every week?" He'd been trying to work out a coast-to-coast by triangulating with his players, and now that he'd almost succeeded, Nicolas came out with this story.

"No party. We'll just shoot for a short time. Bang bang, a clip, or two at the very most. And we'll post lookouts downstairs. If someone shows up, the lookouts will give us the word and we take off across the roofs. But we have to make sure we pick apartment buildings you can get away from without having to go down the stairs. One apartment house after another. We're going to knock down every antenna in Naples."

"Nice, Maraja," said Pesce Moscio, who still had his eyes fixed on the screen, indifferent to the calluses produced on his thumbs by the joypad.

"And now let's drink a toast!"

Everyone stopped what they were doing to grab the first glasses they could lay hands on, and they were already raising them in the air when Dentino said: "You can't drink Moët et Chandon in paper cups. We've got to get some real glasses. There must be some around here somewhere."

They pulled open doors to cabinets and cupboards, and in the end they found champagne glasses, a legacy of the wedding dowry of who knows what family that had lived in that home—an apartment that had survived the bombings of World War II and the earthquake of the 1980s. Those stones had no fear.

"You know what I like about champagne?" Dentino asked. "The fact that once you pull the cork, you can't put it back in. That's just like us: no one can put a cork in us. We just need to let out all our foam." And he hurled the cork against the wall, which ricocheted, lost forever under a sofa.

"Right you are, 'o Dentino," Nicolas agreed. "Once our cork is pulled, no one can put it back in."

He filled all their glasses and then said: "*Guagliu*', first of all let's drink a toast to Drone, who got the cops off our necks."

All of the others took turns speaking eagerly to pay their compliments to Drone, while the glasses clinked and were drained: "Fantastic, Drone, bravo, Droncino, to your health, Drò!"

Then Maraja sat down, wiped the smile off his face, and said: "Dro', you saved us. But you also betrayed us." Drone started snickering but Nicolas wasn't laughing: "I'm not kidding, Anto'."

Antonio 'o Drone leaned closer to Nicolas: "Maraja, what are you talking about? You'd be in Poggioreale right now if it wasn't for me."

"First of all, who told you I didn't want to be in Poggioreale?"

"You're a complete jerk," said Drone.

"No, no, stop and listen to me: the *paranza* has to move all together. The boss makes the decisions and the *paranza* has to support them. Is that right or not?" Nicolas saw that all the others were nodding, and he waited to hear Drone's reply. Drone said: "E!" The letter *e*. But pronounced with all the imperative force of the verb, *è*, meaning "is." The most heartfelt utterance of a yes. The most affirmative of replies.

"You stole a pistol from the gym bags when we were up on the roof. True or false?" Now Nicolas had set down his glass of champagne and was staring grimly at Drone. He seemed to be waiting for an answer but not to care much what it was. He'd already made up his mind.

"True, but I did it for the good of the *paranza*."

"True, but my ass. How do I know that you didn't plan to use that pistol on all of us? Maybe you sold yourself off to another *paranza*." With a snarl, he slipped into dialect, suggesting who Drone might have sold himself off to. "*Te venniv a 'o Micione.*"

"Nico', what are you talking about? I have the key, I'm a member of the *paranza*. We're brothers. What are you saying?"

Dentino wanted to break in, but he remained silent. Drone held up the key to the door of the lair, the symbol of his membership. "The pistol defended the *paranza*."

"Sure, okay, but you used it to defend yourself, too: who gives a shit about the pistol. You're not trustworthy. This is a very serious infraction. There has to be a punishment."

Nicolas looked around at the rest of the *paranza*: there were some looking down, others evading his glance with their eyes on their cell phones. In the background the theme music of *FIFA* didn't seem to bother Nicolas, who continued: "No, *guagliu'*, look at me. We're going to have to figure out a punishment, all of us together."

Lollipop said: "Maraja, if you ask me, Drone just wanted to hold on to the pistol, that's all, he wanted to take a few selfies, that's all, right? He fucked up, but it's a good thing he did, otherwise they would have caught all the rest of us."

"Who says that's what would have happened," Nicolas replied. "Maybe we'd have been able to get away, maybe we'd have gotten off a couple of shots."

Briato': "Maraja, we didn't have any more ammunition . . ."

"Then they'd have caught us. And you think it's better to steal from your brothers? Is it better to let yourselves get screwed by Drone?"

And as is always the case with betrayals, the various sides naturally split up into accusers and defenders. It's an instinctive rule. What side you take is decided for you by the strength of your friendship with the accused or how you suppose you would have behaved in the same situation. By empathy or difference. By blood and by situation. In the case of the *paranza*, Drago' intervened; he knew Drone well because they went to school together at the Industrial Technical Institute: "Maraja, you have a point: Drone stole a pistol and didn't say a word to anyone, but when he did it, he didn't really think about it. He just wanted to enjoy having it to himself, but no way, he never would have used it. He was carrying it jammed down his shorts, and then he used it to defend all the rest of us. And that's all!"

Dentino, irritable and on edge, played the role of the prosecution: "Sure, but if everyone did like that, the arsenal would be completely empty by now. You can't do it where everyone just grabs what they want."

Drone tried to defend himself: "No, it's not like I was trying to steal. I just wanted to hold on to it for a while, I'd have put it back." He was standing in front of Nicolas, while the others, again instinctively, had gathered around in a circle. A tribunal.

"Eh, my ass, you'd have put it back. Guns need to be stored the way we all decided. So you can't do it. There needs to be a punishment, *ja'*, *bbasta*," said Pesce Moscio.

Briato' switched territory and went over to the side of the prosecution: "It's true we owe you our thanks for keeping us from getting arrested. But the fact remains that you stole a pistol, you still did something that can't be done."

Drago' threw his arms wide to get everyone's attention: "*Guagliu'*, I'm in agreement, too, that Drone needs to be punished. He fucked up, but he just wasn't thinking. He didn't want to hurt us. If you ask me, he just needs to apologize to everybody and we're done with it."

"Eh, but if we do that," Briato' pointed out, "then everybody can fuck up and just apologize."

When he finally finished drinking the third glass of champagne, which had softened him, Stavodicendo piped up, too: "Ask me," he said, "and I say there should be a punishment. But a light punishment, not a heavy one."

"No, if you ask me, we need a serious punishment, a heavy one," said Biscottino, "because otherwise just anyone can start stealing our gats." He'd kept out of the limelight the whole time, waiting for the right moment to speak his piece, and he'd pitched his voice to sound like a man, to make sure the others didn't think he was just spouting off again.

"But I'm not just anyone!" said Drone. "I'm a part of the *paranza*, I only took something that belonged to me, and I would have put it back."

Stavodicendo replied: "Yes, it's true, 'o Dro', but what the fuck would it have cost you to ask Nicolas, to ask all of us. That is, I was just saying that when you stop to think about it, you did something wrong, but not horribly wrong. There are things that are wrong, things that are horribly wrong, things that are slightly wrong, and things that are almost wrong. If you ask me, I was just saying, you did something slightly wrong or almost wrong . . . but you didn't go so far as to do something wrong or horribly wrong. That's what I was saying and that's what I think."

Drago' summarized the jury's point of view: "Listen, 'o Drone pulled a boneheaded move. Let's give him his punishment once and for all and be done with it." There was no more wiggle room for the defense.

"All right," Maraja decided.

"If you ask me," Dentino proposed, "since he stole with his hand, what we need to do now is cut off his hand."

Chuckling, they made fun of Drone: "*Ja'*, Dro', you'll wind up like 'o Mulatt', with your hand cut off!"

"No, even better," said Briato', "let's cut off his ears like in *Reservoir Dogs*, when they cut the ear off the policeman."

"Nice, that's just great! Let's cut off his ear," said Biscottino.

At first Drone was laughing along, but now he was starting to get annoyed. Dentino added, "But in *Reservoir Dogs* they set the policeman on fire. We need to burn Drone, while we're at it," and they all broke out laughing. "No, no, I think what we need to do," put in Stavodicendo, "is just like in *Goodfellas!*"

"Yeah, that's too great. We'll give Drone the same treatment that Billy Batts gets when Henry and Jimmy pound him bloody: *facimmo accussì!*" Let's do *that*, they crowed in excitement.

The atmosphere was relaxing. Nicolas had left his seat as judge, and now he was imitating Joe Pesci, while Drago' responded as Ray Liotta. "You're a funny guy."

"How the fuck am I funny? What the fuck is so funny about me?" And they went on with the rest of the dialogue from *Goodfellas*, which was something they did constantly, each time trading off Joe Pesci's role. Drone, as if lost in thought, or pretending to be, got up and headed for the door: "All right. Once you've made up your minds what you're going to do to me, let me know."

Maraja turned serious, like the face of a mime when they play at running their hand up and down over their face, first with a smile, and then, once the hand swipes down over the face, with a dead-serious expression. "Where are you going, Drone? First the punishment, and only then can you go home to *mammà*."

"Take it from me," Lollipop joked, "the best punishment would be to get Rocco Siffredi to come over and fuck him in the ass." There was an explosion of laughter.

"Yeah, yeah, that's a good idea," said Maraja. "That's exactly what I want to suggest to you. You have a sister, don't you?"

Drone had his hand on the door handle, ready to leave, still convinced he was in the middle of a skit. But that word—*sister*—fired point-blank like that, made him whirl around: "What about it?" he asked.

"What do you mean, what about it? Do you remember that movie *The Professor*? Do you remember when that one *guaglione* says, 'If you ask me, the professor was a little bit of a faggot'?"

"So, what about it?"

"Hold on. Let me explain. Do you remember?"

"Yeah."

"And do you remember what the professor asks?"

"What does he ask?"

"Eh, he asks, 'That girl who comes to see you is your sister, isn't she?' Now your punishment is you have to bring me your sister. That's exactly what you have to do. But you're not just going to have to bring her to me, because you didn't just insult me by stealing that pistol. You're going to have to bring her to the whole *paranza*."

"What are you saying, Maraja? Are you joking around?"

A silence fell over the guys in the *paranza* that was the calm before the decision.

"So now you bring us your sister, and she'll have to give a *chionzo*— a blow job—to everyone, to all the dicks in the *paranza*."

Drone took off like a rocket, racing past Nicolas, and the whole *paranza* stepped aside to let him pass. No one stopped him because no one had guessed at his real objective: the pilfered pistol that he had left on the windowsill in the bedroom of the lair. He grabbed the Beretta, yanked the slide to chamber a round, and aimed it right at Maraja's face.

"What the fuck are you doing?!" shouted Drago'.

Maraja looked at him with narrowed eyes: "Go on, nice work, just shoot. You all see this, *guagliu*'? Anyone who steals from the *paranza*, this is what they want to do. He wanted to screw us. It makes sense, it makes sense that you wanted to screw me, Dro'. Now let's see, come on, pull the trigger and then someone can put it on your YouTube channel."

Drone indulged in the thought of really pulling the trigger, putting an end to this stalemate and spattering blood all over the shocked faces of the *paranza*. Spatter that whole crowd of faces that were being held in gelatin by their state of shock. There wasn't another film plot to wind up this scene, or if there was, it didn't occur to him, because when he thought about it, there was no *paranza* in his head, he just thought about his sister, Annalisa, who was a whole different matter. He was gripping the Beretta tight, too tight not to think of it as a luxury, and that luxury had to come to an end. He lowered the pistol and sat down. The room was shrouded in total silence. *"Mo' quello che devi fare,"* Maraja went on pitilessly in dialect, *"è convincere soreta a venì ccà e ce lo deve succhià a tutti!"* Now what you've got to do is convince your sister to come here and suck us all off.

"Even me?" Biscottino's voice asked from the far end of the room.

"Sure, if you can get it up, even you."

"I can get it up, I can get it up," Biscottino replied.

"All right," Briato' shouted.

"This thing . . . I wasn't expecting it. We're going to have a bukkake," Dentino commented. That exotic word produced just one image in the minds of the *paranza*: a circle of men ejaculating on a kneeling woman. Their entire education had taken place on PornHub, and they'd been watching bukkake for as long as they could remember, dreaming of it as an unattainable chimera. Tucano was super-excited now, and he adjusted the elastic strap on his underwear to relieve the pressure. Drago' wanted to help Drone, so what he said was: "I'm not going to let her suck me off. We can decide, right, Maraja? Or do I absolutely have to stick my dick in her mouth? I've known her for a long time, Annalisa, I couldn't do it."

"Do whatever you want. After all, this is a punishment that *he* has to take."

"I like this thing," said Pesce Moscio. "It means that all of us will have to learn not to fuck up."

"No, but I've already learned that lesson," Maraja pointed out. "I don't need to be taught, I already know who we are. Otherwise we're just a group of fools." Nicolas had a vision of the *paranza* as a sampling of something that already existed. He liked the fact that, aside from Drago', none of them came from Camorra backgrounds. He liked the fact that he'd plucked them from people who would never have thought of belonging to a group. His friends, fated to belong to the *paranza*, weren't people he'd need to transform, they were only people he needed to single out and bring in. Drone took the pistol by the barrel and handed it to Maraja: "Go ahead and shoot me," he said. And then, looking around at all the others:

"Shoot me, go on, that would be better for me . . . it's better! Damn me that I bothered to save you all! Gang of assholes! *Banda 'e strunze!*"

"Don't worry," Nicolas replied. "If you don't make sure your sister comes here, then we'll shoot you. You're in the *paranza*—if you make a mistake, you die."

Drone had the taste of tears in his mouth, and like a real child he stormed out the door, slamming it behind him.

The next morning at school, he'd evaluated his options. He wondered if he could just quit the *paranza*, give back the keys to the lair, and vamoose. Or did he really have to give them his sister on a silver platter? How would he be able to convince her? And what if his sister agreed to do it? He might find that even more disgusting. What explanation could he give to his girlfriend if word got out? And what about his parents? He'd even tried to imagine himself talking to his folks when they came to visit him in prison; he'd envisioned them standing in front of his headstone in the boneyard. But it had never occurred to him that his father would say: "You made your sister give blow jobs!" That was something he simply couldn't imagine. And for the first time the romantic thought that assails so many teenagers, but that had never occurred to him before, appeared in the possibilities arrayed before him: suicide. It was only a rapid passing thought, it grazed his mind, and Drone filed it away immediately in disgust. He also thought about some way of taking revenge: sure, he'd made a mistake, but not such a serious one as to justify this kind of humiliation.

In the afternoon he summoned Drago' to his house.

Drone was pacing back and forth in the few yards of space in his bedroom. He kept his eyes focused on the floor, as if in search of some option he hadn't yet considered, only every so often he looked up to make sure that his drones lined up on the shelves were still where they belonged.

"Drone," said Drago', stretched out on his friend's bed, "this is a symbolic punishment. This thing isn't against you, against your sister, or against us. It's a way of making it clear that nobody should ever steal a weapon."

"But what if I just don't do it? What if I just quit the *paranza*?"

"'O Dro', those guys will kill you, he'll shoot you. He'll target you, for sure."

"So much the better."

"Don't talk bullshit," said Drago'. He stretched and got up from the bed, went over to turn up the volume on the stereo, so that motherly ears couldn't hear them, and stood in front of the S.S.C. Napoli 2013–2014 poster. "In the end, this punishment is designed to make sure the *paranza* gets stronger, and so no one will pull any more fuckups with weapons."

Deep down, Drago' had accepted Maraja's way of thinking. Drone had no allies. After his pointless conversation with Drago', Drone started posting pictures of him and of Nicolas on Facebook, it was his way of increasing his protection, it was like taking out an insurance policy on his life. If anything happened to him, it would become that much easier to associate his fate with Nicolas, he thought, or maybe it would actually push the investigators away from his friends and toward his enemies. Still, somewhere inside he still fostered the abiding hope that if Nicolas saw them, he might be moved to compassion.

But the passing days only increased his anxiety. The hours were a continuous torment that kept him from acting. He couldn't get any sleep and he walked around the apartment like a soul suffering damnation. The words bounced off him when his family spoke to him. His mother was pointlessly alarmed, like all mothers who hope to figure out what's going on by asking questions: "What's happening to you? Antonio, what's happening to you?" As if in the throes of a fever, Drone was consumed by indecision. Food nauseated him, as did all odors. His sister and his mother, one evening after dinner, walked into his bedroom: "Anto', what on earth has happened? Have you had a fight with Marianna?"

"No, of course not. I haven't seen Marianna for six months. Nothing's happened." That was his only answer.

"No, impossible that nothing's happened, everywhere you go you look so sad. Something must have happened. You've stopped eating. Did it happen at school?" On she went with her naïve attempt to list the possible causes for his misery, almost as if once she ran down the list and hit the right item he'd open up like a slot machine with three cherries in a row.

The ding ding ding of bells. The rush of coins. And happier than ever before. But Drone was armor-plated against all disclosures like a teenage boy, and they were guessing at the heartaches and sorrows of a little boy. Inside him, though, were the sorrows of wartime. The idea of disappointing his father humiliated him even more than the idea of dragging his sister into it. Or, almost. His father admired the fact that he was a nerd, even if he wouldn't have used that word to describe him, but Drone did help him on the job, helped fix and maintain his computer and tablet. And the only phrase that hammered in Drone's head was "You made your sister give blow jobs."

"Let me sleep!" on the other hand, was the only answer that he gave his sister and mother pestering him for explanations. He'd get over it and come back to them. One night, though, he got an idea. On his cell phone he had a few videos of the *paranza*, which he transferred to his Mac. He decided to open a YouTube account, and made sure it couldn't be traced back to his own ID: he wanted to upload the video of them shooting. He knew they'd arrest them all, including him. You could see their faces clearly, he'd filmed them all. But would that save his sister from humiliation? He wasn't certain. His forefinger hovered over the SEND button, it looked like the pendulum of a clock. He was sweating, he felt ill. He shut the laptop. In his head, the words of Drago', "those guys will kill you," but when had they become "those guys"? They'd always been "us." And instead, now, to describe the *paranza* they used "those guys." Then— that meant—he'd already been kicked out of the *paranza*, and in that case, why comply with their punishment? If only he'd just kept the pistol in his backpack . . . He knew how to use it, he'd even managed to neutralize that squad car and the cops in it . . .

The next morning, he couldn't manage to get out of bed when his mother tried to wake him, his forehead was burning up: he had a fever. On his phone he saw that several members of the *paranza* had been looking for him, even Maraja had texted him several times. He didn't answer all morning. He heard the home phone ring and a minute later his sister answer: "Yes, hi, Nicolas!" Drone catapulted out of the bed and grabbed the receiver out of his sister's hand. "Don't you ever dare to call my sister again, you got that?" And he hung up. "But what's going on . . . ?" Annalisa guessed that the sorrow hanging over her brother had something to do with the circle he'd drifted into, a group of kids the family had just started to notice, but she'd understood and hadn't said a thing, in part because she wasn't really sorry to see that, now, because of that group, her brother counted for something instead of spending his life uploading videos and focusing for obsessive hours on GamePlayer. The light of the *paranza* could even lend her some reflected luster.

Drone went back to the haven of his room. She followed him: "*Mo*', *amm*' *'a parlà*," she told him. Now we have to talk, using the voice of when they were little, when she placed the burden of her role as an elder sister upon him. She pulled out everything, even too much, because she got him to say things he shouldn't have. He said those things pacing back and forth the way he had with Drago', only this time, instead of a brother lying on his bed, now there was his sister, who sat up as she listened, her hands joined together, fingers knitted, on her legs.

"I'm in the *paranza* of Forcella. It's me, Nicolas, Drago' . . ." And so he went on, until he'd told the whole story of the firearms training on the rooftops. He heard Annalisa saying over and over again how crazy they were: "*Vuje site pazze, voi site pazze*." He took the hands that Annalisa clasped together in his, then released them and told her: "Annali', if you talk, if you so much as whisper a word of this to Mammà, you're dead."

Those words echoed off the S.S.C. Napoli poster, the gigantic drawing of Rayman, the selfies stapled to a corkboard hanging on the wall, selfies with Drone's favorite YouTubers. And then those little model drones, scattered everywhere, that he was so fixated on. Those other words— *death, machine guns, bullets*—had nothing to do with that bedroom.

Then he gathered his courage. He drank some water and, without even bothering to look at his sister again, he told her what had happened, and described the punishment they wanted to inflict on him for the mess he'd gotten himself into. Annalisa leaped to her feet: "You make me sick! You and your friends. You make me so sick! Do you still have the gun? The gun you used to shoot at the policemen? Then use it to shoot yourself. You can all shoot yourselves, or else just you shoot yourself." And she stormed out of the room, red-faced. How could she have felt proud of him until just half an hour ago?

Drone was in a state of despair. His sister's words struck him as a premonition, he knew that's how it would end. And in a way, that's how he hoped it would end.

In the days that followed, as if she'd been infected by her brother, Annalisa, too, showed an aversion to food and sleep. She did a better job, however, of concealing her malaise from her parents. She thought of all the solutions imaginable, and in the end her ideas, even the most radical and reckless ones, eventually ran down the rails of action—which are always the same, if you were raised in a certain territory. She started mulling over the best way to take revenge. Who could strike back against the people who had imposed this order on her brother? Deep down, Nicolas had to know that he'd levied too heavy a punishment for the crime committed. If someone had stolen that pistol, then he needed to be killed, Annalisa mused. But if the same person who had stolen it had also saved them all from arrest, then it wasn't fair to subject him to a punishment like this one. Pure logic. The thing to do wasn't to find a solution within that perimeter, instead she needed to jump outside it, the way you'd jump outside a circle of fire. But the two siblings never thought for even an instant about the possibility of moving outside the box. Annalisa was convinced there had to be some strategy for sidestepping the extortion. Reporting her brother for having committed a crime, in her mind, didn't mean winning justice. Instead it meant forming an alliance with someone: you ally yourself with the *paranza*, against the *paranza*, or with another *paranza*. They had demanded something of her that filled her with disgust. Worse still, something that seemed deeply unjust to her. If Drone had killed someone else's brother, if he'd caused them all to be arrested, all right, in that case Annalisa might have considered such a punishment deserved.

She was thinking as if she, too, were in the *paranza*. Everyone was in the *paranza* without realizing it. The laws were the laws of the *paranza*.

Annalisa was pretty certain, at this point. Perhaps she could go to see Micione, or ask advice of some friend who was a policeman. Or else get down on her knees and service the *paranza*. A prospect that was even more humiliating and dolorous than the thought that her brother was a weakling, a *chiacchiello*. For a fleeting instant she wished that Drone were more like Nicolas 'o Maraja, that he was like White. Instead, he was just Drone, a nerd who had dreamed of redemption by joining a group. Her eyes welled up with tears. It was all a filthy mess. No matter where you turned your eyes. She couldn't confide in anyone, not even her closest girlfriend, because if she opened her mouth then there was a risk of others deciding for her. It would take so little, for someone to speak with a parent, with a carabiniere, or a family friend who happened to be a judge at some dinner party: and then she'd no longer be the mistress of her fate.

Annalisa stayed out as long as she possibly could and then, exhausted and with her thoughts torn and tattered, she decided to return home. At the entrance, she found her whole family assembled. On the garage someone had written *Mariuolo*—scoundrel—and a childish drawing of an erect penis. The metal roller shutter had been kicked repeatedly. They were going to have to replace it.

"Why would anyone have written such a thing?!" asked the father, turning to his son as if he knew something about it. In his head he was guessing the boy might have gotten up to his usual tricks with his computers, maybe he stole someone's password, or defrauded some online store that didn't have adequate systems of protection. And so he shouted at him.

"Well? What have you done, then?" In that case, the mother was standing up for her son's innocence, and before the next few days were up, Drone found himself facing another trial.

"Talk!" Whap! A smack from his mother. "Who is it that's hurting you?" she insisted.

"Mammà, what if it was meant for Papà instead of me?" Drone started insinuating the shadow of doubt.

His sister asked him questions, pretending she knew nothing: "But who was it? What happened?" she asked as they climbed the stairs.

And at that point their father had been persuaded by his son that the graffito might actually be about him. He'd made him think about his last construction projects, perhaps he'd been too quick to heap blame on his son, he knew that the boy was spending time with a group of kids he didn't like, but what about the construction sites where he worked? Could it have been them? Drone saw him making calls on his cell phone, asking around, and, in the face of his father's fear, he collapsed. He didn't have the temperament of the *camorrista* that he aspired to be. In the stairwell, while his mother and sister were taking the elevator, he told his father that he needed to talk to him: *"Papà, t'aggi' 'a parlà."* When they caught up with Annalisa, who had just arrived at the landing, she stepped out of the elevator and said: "Antò, I didn't tell you, I made up my mind: you're right, we need to do what Nicolas says."

Their father asked: "Why did you utter that boy's name?"

"Nothing . . . Nicolas . . ."

"And what does Nicolas want?"

Drone was motionless. Has she lost her mind? he thought. Does she want to talk about the bukkake in front of Papà?

"Nicolas said that we all need to start a website, and that I need to be part of it," Annalisa replied.

"A website? About? What a filthy pig of a man he is?" her father commented.

"No, no . . . He's right, a website where we write about some of the things that happen in the quarter. Maybe we'll even be able to sell a little advertising . . . These days, people want to read about the things that happen in the street where they live. Not the things that are happening in Rome, Milan, and Paris."

Drone started breathing again, but he wasn't sure his sister hadn't really lost her mind.

Annalisa had understood, in the blink of an eye, that Drone had collapsed, that her father was going to wind up in a sea of trouble by reporting the *paranza* to the police to make sure the punishment never took place. They might have to move away for a while and they'd never call him back to work on construction sites as an engineer again. It was better to just shut up and obey.

Drone ate dinner without another word, and then went into his sister's bedroom: "Annali', are you serious about this?"

"Well, yeah, I have to. There's nothing else left for us to do . . . or should we go in and shoot them?"

"I'm all for it! You want to shoot? I'm in."

"If you shoot them, the ones who pay would be Papà, Mamma, and even me."

Drone stood staring down at his feet; on the one hand he was relieved, on the other, disgusted. It revolted him that he had been so weak. In his head he reran the images that had tormented him for days: the pistol stolen in secrecy along with the bullets, the few hours that he'd slept with the gun, and when he'd pulled it out to start shooting at the police car.

Annalisa took the telephone, made the call. Then she said, in a flat voice: "Nicolas, this is Annalisa. Okay. Organize this piece of filth, and let's get this guilt off my brother."

Drone started shouting "No!" and kicking and punching, destroying his consoles, he swept all of his drones off the lower shelf with one hand, and not even the sound of splintering wings distracted him from his fury. His father and mother came running in. "What was that?"

Annalisa knew he needed to shield her parents from the truth: "No, it was nothing. We just found out that the *Mariuolo* was meant for him."

"So you see? All right, explain," the parents demanded.

"I'm too pissed off," Drone retorted.

"Yeah . . . his friends accused him of stealing some files . . . But it wasn't him, it was someone else."

"Oh, well, you can explain what happened, can't you?" asked their mother.

"What explanation? *Chistu ccà più frequenta sta munnezza, peggio è,*" the father replied. "The more this one hangs out with garbage, *munnezza*, the worse he gets. He'll become *munnezza* just like them, I've always said it."

That was the phrase that broke Drone: "*Si' tu 'a munnezza,*" he spat out. No, *you're* the garbage. His father was tempted to retort, "How dare you?": the phrase that attracts discord like a magnet. He said nothing, but he was deeply hurt. "*Si' tu 'a munnezza.* Always doing nothing but contriving to get more work. Always saying that your friends are better than mine. Always something we don't have."

"You never went without anything, you never had to do without."

"Who told you that?"

Annalisa and her mother watched the clash. With every phrase the voices grew louder, and so did the fear that their neighbors might hear.

"Shut up, the two of you, that's enough," broke in the mother.

Father and son froze in position. Nose to nose. They breathed on each other and neither one would step back. Annalisa grabbed her brother by the shoulders, and the mother grabbed her husband. They separated them: one of them holed up in his bedroom, now in shambles, the other behind a door that had become an impenetrable wall.

Annalisa prepared her backpack, came out of the bathroom, and said: "I'm ready."

"Why the backpack?" Drone asked in a dry voice.

"Because I have my things in it."

"What things?"

She said nothing. Drone had a bitter taste in his mouth, his breath was foul as if his tongue had been smeared with mud all night long, the slime that rose from and oozed back down into his esophagus. He hadn't been able to save anyone. He had no power to do anything, against or in favor, and yet he was convinced, as was everyone else, that being admitted into the *paranza* would mean becoming something more, more than himself. But instead now he had to remain inert, helpless.

"Cheer up!" Annalisa went on. Now she was the one encouraging him. He was annoyed, and at this point his biggest fear was that his sister might actually like such a thing. But Annalisa wanted nothing so much as to get out of this situation as soon as possible.

They went downstairs and got on the motor scooter. Drone was driving, she was sitting behind him. They showed up on Via dei Carbonari, where the entire *paranza* already was. They knocked at the door.

Nicolas answered: "'O Dro', don't you have the key? Why did you knock?"

Drone said nothing. He just walked in, he was no longer willing to use the key. He went over and sprawled out on the sofa.

"Ciao, Annali'." Dozens of "*ciaos*" echoed through the room, like a "*buongiorno*" in a high school classroom when the teacher comes in. They were all beside themselves with excitement, but actually very worried.

"All right," said Annalisa, "let's get moving, and be done with this song and dance as quick as we can."

"Ehh," said Maraja, "as quick as we can . . . take it easy, now." And he lifted one hand into the air, waving it as if conducting a symphony, indicating that he was the director of this scene.

"Well, what a responsible sister you are. Not a bit like your brother, Antonio."

"I've heard enough about that," Annalisa replied.

Drago' just couldn't resign himself and said: "Oh, Maraja, but do you really have to do this thing? *Ja'*, he understands that he fucked up. But what the hell does Annalisa have to do with it?"

"Drago'," Maraja replied, "shut your yap."

Drago' didn't appreciate that: "I'll talk whenever the fuck I please! All the more because this is my house."

"No, this house belongs to all of us. It's your house, too. Now it's the *paranza*'s house. And anyway, it's not as if just because you repeat something a hundred times, the first time it doesn't work and the hundredth time it does. It doesn't work one hundred times in a row."

"It strikes me as overdoing it. It's just Drone who fucked up."

"Not again?" Nicolas said. "You don't want to pull out your fish. Then keep it in your pants. Done. Nothing more to say."

"We're sick of you, Drago'!" said Dentino.

Drago' shot a glance at Annalisa as if to say that there was nothing more he could do. On her part there was no hint of gratitude for his effort: the disgust that she felt for the *paranza* was all-encompassing. She went into the bathroom and, in the course of a few minutes, came out again dressed like a porn star. The *paranza* had never laid eyes on such plenty, such sensuality. Or rather, they'd seen it on YouPorn, on the countless channels of PornHub, the source of their only sentimental education, grown up as they had with laptops as extensions of their arms. Annalisa had figured out that she needed to present herself as an online video porno heroine. It would make it all that much faster.

There they all were. All of them in the room seemed to be lined up and arranged for a group photo, the short ones in front, the others behind them, and at the center, the moon-calf face of Biscottino. The schoolmistress had arrived. The class stood to attention. For a few seconds, they all felt sized up, passed in review. Some of them sniffed, others adjusted their T-shirts, some stuck their hands in their pockets in search of who knows what. Seen this way, across the distance that had been created with Annalisa's entrance, they looked like what they really were, a bunch of little kids. For that same long, drawn-out instant each of them seemed to answer for himself, there was no more group, no *paranza*, no punishment. The schoolmistress had come in to ask each of them what they would be capable of. For that indeterminate moment, in which they returned to their own faces, they were pushed out over a sort of void where they were defenseless or, more likely, aghast, their shoelaces untied, their thoughts astray, their eyes uncertain whether to stay still or dart away in flight.

But then there was a click, and everything went back to where it was supposed to be. Annalisa, who could never have experienced that wave of disorientation, kneeled down in front of Nicolas.

When it seemed as if Annalisa was about to begin, Drone looked down at his feet, put the earbuds into his ears, and turned the music up to full volume so he wouldn't have to hear a sound. But Maraja stopped her then and there.

"Drone, 'o Drone!" shouted Nicolas, forcing him to take out the earbuds and look up at him. "So you see what happens when you fuck the *paranza*? Then the *paranza* fucks you and all your blood. Get up, Annali', go and get dressed."

"No-o-o, not really!" Pesce Moscio, excited as he was, couldn't hold back.

"*Uaaa'*," said Biscottino, "no-o-o."

Drone would have liked to give him a hug, as if the lesson imparted had dropped onto him with its full weight. Nicolas, from the majesty of his sixteen years, felt so old and wise that he would gladly have let his hands be kissed; he wished his jaws were swollen like Marlon Brando's, Don Vito Corleone's, but he had to settle for the disappointed gazes of the *paranza*, Annalisa's astonished expression, and Drone's motionless gratitude, incapable as he was of speaking or even just modifying the incredulous expression that had taken over his face. It had all been a staged event. And Nicolas adored staged events, he felt as if he were writing the screenplay of his power.

Annalisa stood face-to-face with Nicolas, she was roughly the same height as him. She looked at him as if he emanated some repugnant odor, then uttered slowly and clearly: "You're all filthy pigs, including my brother." She breathed deeply. "But now you have to leave him alone: the guilt is removed."

No one ventured to respond.

Annalisa walked over even closer to Nicolas. "The guilt is removed, right? Say it!"

"It's removed, it's removed . . . Drone is in the *paranza*."

"Quite the privilege . . ." said Annalisa and, turning her back on them, she went into the bathroom to get dressed again.

The kids, standing in a circle, kept their eyes glued to her ass until she vanished behind the bathroom door. Then one after the other they went out the front door. As they filed down the stairs, Nicolas, leading the line, clucked his tongue to get their attention: "Kebab?" he asked. And the others replied as one: "Kebab, kebab!"

Only Drone stayed behind, to wait for his sister and take her home.

PART THREE

TEMPEST

The secret to the fried seafood specialty known as frittura di paranza is knowing how to choose the smaller fish: none of them can be out of balance with all the others. If you get an anchovy bone caught between your teeth, then you picked one that was too big; if you can recognize the squid because you didn't pick out a small enough one, then it's no longer frittura di paranza: it's just a big grab bag of fish you happened to have available. The frittura di paranza deserves the name when everything you've used can wind up in your mouth and be chewed and swallowed without identifying it. The frittura di paranza is made with the fish no one wants; only when they're all put together does it find its true flavor. But you have to know how to bread them, rolling them in the finest-quality flour, and of course it's the frying that really gives the meal its final benediction. Attaining the exact flavor is the battle that you fight on the iron of the frying pan, on the drizzle of squeezed olive juice, the oil, the soul of the wheat, the flour, the extract of seawater, the fish. Victory is won when it's all in perfect equilibrium and the paranza has a single flavor in your mouth.

The paranza is over quickly, as it comes into existence it vanishes. Frienn'e magnanno, *frying and eating. It needs to be hot the way the sea is* hot when they fish it at night. When the nets are hauled on board, on the bottom are these tiny creatures mixed in with the larger mass of fish, under-sized sole, cod that have swum too little. The fish is sold off and there they remain, at the bottom of the crates, among the chunks of melting ice. Alone they're worthless, have no market price, but gathered up in a cuoppo di carta—a paper cone—and fried together, they become prized delicacies. They were nothing in the sea, they were nothing in the fishing nets, weight-less on the scales, but several on a plate, they become an exquisite treat. In the mouth, it's all chomped up together. Together at the sea bottom, together in the net, breaded together, dumped together into the seething oil, together under the tooth and on the palate—one alone, the taste of the paranza. But once on the plate, there is only the briefest of moments to eat: once it cools, the breading seperates from the fish. The meal becomes a corpse.

Fast you're born in the sea, fast fished out of it, fast you wind up scorched in the pan, fast you're ground between the teeth, fast is the pleasure.

LET'S GO TAKE CHARGE

T he first to mention it was Nicolas. He and the others were at the New Maharaja, waiting for the beginning of the new year. The year that would launch them into their future.

Drago' and Briato' were on the terrace, crushed on all sides by the crowd. They were doing what everyone else was doing, which meant they were reciting the countdown while looking out over the sea off Posillipo, with a magnum of champagne, thumbs ready to pop the cork. They weaved from side to side, held up by that human tide rejoicing at the year that was about to arrive. Their physical contact with the light fabrics of the girls' skimpy outfits, the scent of the aftershave that belonged to an age that was not yet theirs, the conversations overheard between individuals who seemed to hold the world in their fists . . . and one overwhelming drunken spree. On the terrace, the *paranza* kept losing track of one another and then linking back up, one second jumping up and down in unison, linked together by their arms around one another's waists, the next second talking in loud voices with people they'd never laid eyes on before. But they never really lost one another, in fact they sought one another out if only to exchange the smile that stood for the fact that everything was wonderful. And the year that followed would be even more wonderful.

Five, four, three . . .

Nicolas felt it even more than the others, but he hadn't set foot on the terrace. When the DJ had invited everyone to go outside, where they could look out over the sea, he'd hugged Letizia close and tight, and had stepped into the flood of people, but then he'd frozen to the spot as she was swept away. He'd stood there, facing the big plate-glass windows against which everyone seemed to be packed as if in an overcrowded aquarium, and then he'd started walking backward, retracing his steps to the private room that now belonged to them, that through his efforts Oscar now had to keep unfailingly free for the use of the *paranza*. He took a seat in a velvet armchair, he let himself slam down onto it, indifferent to the fact that the seat was wet with champagne, and remained there until the others came in, upbraiding him as an asshole because he'd missed this one woman who was higher than shit and who'd stripped naked so her husband had had to cover her with a tablecloth. All Nicolas said was: "They need to understand that no one's safe anymore. That the apartment buildings, the shops, the motor scooters, the bars, the churches—they're all something we allow them."

"What are you trying to say, Maraja?" asked Briato'. He was on his seventh flute of Polisy and was waving the hand not holding the glass to waft away the stench of sulfur from the fireworks that were going off outside.

"I'm saying that for real everything that exists in this neighborhood belongs to us."

"Like fuck it belongs to us! It's not like we've got the money to buy it all!"

"What's that got to do with anything! We don't have to buy everything. It belongs to us by right, it's our property, if we want we can burn it all down. They have to understand that they need to keep their eyes down and their mouths shut. They need to understand."

"But how are they supposed to understand that? Are we going to shoot everyone who doesn't want to take orders?" Dentino broke in. He'd left his jacket somewhere and was flashing a short-sleeved purple shirt that left the tattoo of a shark he'd recently had inked on his forearm in plain view.

"Exactly."

Exactly.

That one word had been enough, and then it had driven so many other words, and more and more and more. An avalanche. Looking back, would they ever remember that it had all started with a single word? That it had been that one word—uttered just as the celebrations all around them culminated in a paroxysm—that triggered it all? No, no one would ever be able to reconstruct that, nor would they even be interested in bothering to. Because there was no time to waste. There was no time to grow up.

The people grazing peacefully on Piazza Dante realized something was happening from the swelling noise, even before they heaved into view. They sensed curiosity and danger, and for an instant everyone walking or just sipping an espresso froze on the spot. Piazza Dante is entirely enclosed by the eighteenth-century hemicycle of the Foro Carolino, and since it was transformed into a pedestrian island, the elegant arms of Vanvitelli's two buildings have attained a new scope and expanse. And so, in that sort of oasis of urban beauty, the sense of the happening was all the more powerful, a happening that might resemble a reprisal, a surprise attack. They were preceded by a buzz and the first gunshots fired into the air, while they were still offstage. The buzzing grew and grew and grew in volume until they burst into the piazza, out of the gate of Port'Alba, as compact as a swarm of wasps, and started firing wildly in all directions. They swept down at top speed, and spat out into the light, like a platoon advancing at the charge. They zigzagged across the piazza, under the monument to Dante, gleefully aiming at it, too, but then focusing their fire on shop windows and the smaller windows of offices and apartments.

This marked the beginning of the season of the *stese*, a term in dialect that describes Camorra rampages. Terrorizing the public was the cheapest, fastest way of laying claim to any given territory. The era of power in the hands of those who had taken command of the territory alley by alley, *vicolo* by *vicolo*, alliance by alliance, man by man, was over. The approach now was to flatten them all. Men, women, children. Tourists, shopkeepers, longtime residents of the quarter. The *stesa* is democratic in that it makes anyone in range of the bullets duck for cover. And it's simple and not especially demanding to organize. All you need, in this case, too, is a single word.

Nicolas's *paranza* had gotten its start in the *periferia*, the outlying quarters of the city. From Ponticelli, from Gianturco. A message in a chat—"time for an excursion"—and the herd moved out on their Honda SH 300s, on their Piaggio BV 350 Beverlys. Their weapons, tucked under the seats or stuffed down their trousers, all kinds. Beretta parabellums, revolvers, Smith & Wesson 357s. Even Kalashnikovs and Beretta M12 submachine guns, combat weapons with magazines full to the last shot, because the fingertip would lift off the trigger only once the gun was out of ammunition. There was never a specific order. At a certain point they just all started firing, in all directions, completely at random. They never aimed at anything in particular, and while they used one hand to twist the throttle and steer their way around obstacles, the other hand fired. They riddled the triangular "yield" signs with bullets, they shot up the mini-dumpsters that spewed forth a black blood, the filth of garbage, and then another twist of the throttle to rev the engine and veer out into the center of the street, the better to aim at balconies and roofs, raising the aim, though never forgetting shops, canopies, buses, and streetcars. There was never time to look around, only lightning-quick darting eyes under the full-face helmets to make sure there were no police checkpoints or teams of Falchi, cops focusing on street crime. Not even time to look around and see if they'd shot anyone. Every gunshot brought with it only a mental image, which was reiterated with each detonation: a head ducking and then the entire body seeking the ground, where it could flatten and disappear. Behind an automobile, behind the parapet of a balcony, behind a patch of greenery let run to seed, ostensibly there to embellish a traffic circle. The terror that Nicolas and the others glimpsed on the faces of all the people was the terror that ought to allow them to seize command. The *stesa* lasts only a few seconds, like a raid by special forces, and then, once you're done with one quarter, you move on to another. The next day they'd read in the local news pages how it had really gone, if there had been any collateral damage, any casualties from the battle.

And then it was time for the historical city center. "Let's do Via Toledo," Lollipop had suggested. No sooner said than done. They needed to spread fear there, too. "We need to turn everybody yellow," he said. The color of fear, jaundice, and diarrhea. The descent down Via Toledo, on the stretch right after Piazza Dante, built up to a breathtaking acceleration. Only Nicolas, in the demented roar of that cavalcade, managed to keep his wits about him and so he noticed, he couldn't help but focus on a figure—right past Palazzo Doria d'Angri, among the people who were throwing themselves to the ground—a woman who instead remained upright and steady on her legs, in fact, came walking forward to the threshold of her shop, under the sign that read Blue Sky. His mother recognized him, recognized them, and made no other gesture than her habitual one, running her fingers like a comb through her black hair. They rode past her and her shop and then shot up the plate-glass window of a clothing store on the opposite side of the street, a little way downhill.

On Piazza della Carità they slalomed through the trees and the parked cars, and they did the same thing in Galleria Umberto I, to hear the echo of their gunfire. Then they turned around and headed all the way back to the Disney Store, where a few of them fired low. A Slav who was playing the accordion released the air from his bellows midway through a melancholy song, then moved off slowly toward the Via Toledo metro station. He collapsed on the pavement just as all the others were starting to get to their feet. In the meantime, the kids had already set off for the Spanish Quarter, losing themselves on the steep uphill streets, toward San Martino, as if the swarm were about to take flight and veer out over the city, to gauge the effect of all that artillery. They measured their results, as always, on the evening news, but that night they glimpsed on the screen their first corpse: they saw the man bent over his accordion, in a pool of blood. He was known on the street for a song he often played, a song that told the story of a young woman who had asked for the yellow quince of Istanbul to keep from dying, but her beloved had only arrived three years later, three years later, and the girl had already been taken elsewhere.

"No, that's my hit," said Pesce Moscio.

"I'm pretty sure you're wrong, he's mine," said Dentino.

"He's mine," said Nicolas, and the others all let him have it, with a mixture of uneasiness and respect.

Now that they'd completed the *stesa*, forcing people throughout the area to dive for cover, the time had come to collect tribute. It was too early to take over the drug-dealing markets, the so-called piazzas, they weren't big enough to take that step yet. They clearly remembered Copacabana's lesson. "One or the other, either shakedowns or else you control the piazzas and sell hash and coke." Well, they were ready to do some shakedowns. The quarter was now a reservation without a master; this was their time and they were ready to seize it.

Nicolas had identified the first shop, a Yamaha dealership on Via Marina. On his eighteenth birthday the *paranza* had chipped in to pay the fees on his driver's license and every brother—every *frato*—had contributed a hundred and fifty euros out of his own pocket. His father had given him a Kymco 150, two thousand euros' worth of motor scooter, straight from the factory. He'd taken his son down to the garage and, chest swelling with pride, pulled up the roller shutter. The black Kymco glittered and at the sight of the red bow on the front mudguard, Nicolas had barely been able to stifle a laugh. He'd thanked his father, who'd asked him if he didn't want to try it out right then, but Nicolas had told him maybe some other time. And he'd left him standing there, wondering what he'd said wrong.

He'd taken the Kymco the next day. The red bow was gone. He zipped over to the dealership and got the other guys along the way, explaining where they were heading.

When the office workers saw the slaloming snake of the *paranza* winding around the motor scooters on display in the parking area, they immediately assumed this was going to be an armed robbery. It would hardly be the first time. The *paranza* parked their bikes outside the plate-glass window and Nicolas went into the offices alone. He started shouting that he needed to speak to the manager—'*o direttore, 'o direttore*—that he had an offer he wouldn't be able to refuse. The customers inside the dealership made way for him, looking at him with expressions of mingled fear and abhorrence. Who was this kid? But once the kid had singled out the manager, a guy in his early forties with a spectacular part in his hair and a Dalí-style mustache, he started giving him a series of flat-handed blows to the chest—whap, whap, whap—until he'd backed him into his office, a clear glass cubicle. Nicolas took a seat in the director's chair, propped his legs up on the desk, and then waved a hand to show the man he was free to pick whichever chair he preferred among the ones normally set out for prospective customers. The manager, who was massaging his chest where Nicolas had hit it, tried to reply but was hushed immediately: *"Baffetti",* Nicolas addressed him, nicknaming him Whiskers, "calm down a little. We'll be providing you with our protection now."

"We don't need anyone's protection," the manager tried to say, but he couldn't stop rumpling his striped shirt. That dull ache just wouldn't go away.

"Bullshit. Everyone needs protection. Here, let's do this," said Nicolas. He swung his legs down from the desk, walked over to the manager, and reached out to the grab the man's hand, which in the meantime had fallen still. He crushed it in his own and started giving him punches in the same spot where he'd smacked him earlier.

"You see my crew out there? They're going to swing by every Friday."

Punch. Punch. Punch.

"But right now let's get started by transferring ownership on a few items."

Punch. Punch. Punch.

"My Kymco. It's brand-new. Not even a scratch on it. Can I trade it in for a T-Max?"

Punch. Punch. Punch.

"You can, you can," said the manager in a gasping, tiny voice. "But what should we do about the documentation?"

"My name's Nicolas Fiorillo. 'O Maraja. Is that enough?"

Then it was time to deal with the street vendors: "All of the street vendors working Corso Umberto have to pay us," Nicolas stated. "We'll stick a gat in these fucking negroes' mouths and tell them to give us ten, fifteen euros a day."

After that, they moved on to the shops and stores. They'd walk in, tell them that from that day on they were in charge, then set their fee. Pizzerias, slot machine parlors knew that every Thursday they could look forward to a visit from Drone and Lollipop, who were in charge of collecting. "Let's go in for the weekly therapy sessions," they'd write in their chats. Soon, though, they decided to subcontract the collections to a few poverty-stricken Moroccans in exchange for the handful of euros needed for room and board. All very simple, all very convenient, all you needed to do was avoid stepping outside your own realm of expertise. And if a delicatessen owner objected too forcefully, you just needed to pull out the gat—for a while, Nicolas used the Francotte, he enjoyed it, it filled his hand, that old pistol—and jam it down the man's throat until you could hear him retching and gagging. But there were damned few who tried to hold out, and in the end there were even a few who self-reported to the *paranza* if, when they lowered their metal shutters at closing time on Thursday, they still hadn't seen anybody.

Now the money was coming in, and how. With the exception of Drago', none of them had ever seen so much cash at one time. They thought about the skinny wallets their parents carried, even after laboring all day long, struggling to squeeze out a little more money with extra jobs and odd jobs, breaking their backs, and now they felt that they'd figured out the world much better than their parents ever had. They were wiser, more grown up. They were more like men than their own fathers were.

They met up at the lair and sat around the table, counting out the lettuce, small bills and big ones. While they were passing a joint and Tucano incessantly pulled the slide on his pistol—by now it was a constant background noise, he hardly even noticed he was doing it—Drone added up the numbers, kept a running account, and jotted it all down on his iPhone, and when he was done, they split up the money. Then they indulged in the regular game of *Assassin's Creed*, ordered the usual kebab, and, having devoured the last bite, all free now to do as they please, went out to spend their gains. In a group, or else with their girlfriends, and occasionally all alone. Gold Rolexes, the latest-model smartphones, snakeskin Gucci shoes and Valentino sneakers, they wore designer clothes from head to foot, right down to their underpants, rigorously Dolce & Gabbana, and then dozens and dozens of red roses delivered to their girlfriends' houses, Pomellato rings, oysters and caviar and rivers of Veuve Clicquot consumed on the sofas of the New Maharaja—though to some extent those slimy, stinky foods sort of grossed them out, and so they'd leave the club and go eat a *'nu cuoppo di paranza fritta*, good and proper, standing up or perched on their scooters. The minute the money came in, it went right back out again. The idea of setting some aside didn't even occur to them: making money right now was all they thought of, tomorrow didn't even exist. Satisfying their every whim, leaving aside any thoughts of need or necessity.

The *paranza* was growing. The revenues were growing and the respect they could glimpse in people's eyes was growing with them. "People are starting to avoid us, which means they want to be like us," Maraja liked to say. They were growing, too, even if they didn't have the time to notice the fact. Stavodicendo had stopped washing his face with quarts of Topexan Complex daily wash; the acne that had tortured his face finally seemed contented with the work it had done, and had given him as souvenirs an assortment of marks that lent him a world-weary look. Drago' and Pesce Moscio had fallen in love at least three different times, with three different girls, and every time, they swore, this was it, the love of their lives. You could see them bowed over their smartphones, typing in phrases they'd found on the Internet, on specialized sites, or else declarations of undying loyalty: she was the prettiest, the sun that lit up their lives, she was the one who'd go on loving them no matter what happened. Briato' had surrendered to Nicolas's continuous mockery; Nicolas accused him of combing his hair back like *'nu milanese*, and so he'd shaved his head. For a while he went around wearing a flat cap, and every time he showed up, there were new rounds of mockery. "Fuggedaboutit!" they'd greet him in chorus. In and of itself, it was hardly an insult for someone like him who'd turned *Donnie Brasco* into a mantra that he recited daily, but he finally got sick and tired of it, and one day he just tossed the flat cap into a dumpster. Dentino and Lollipop went to a gym together and they were both in great shape, even though Dentino had stopped growing, while Lollipop just kept getting taller and taller and seemed as if he was never going to stop. They'd also learned to walk with their chests thrust out and their arms held wide, as if their biceps were so massive that it kept them from holding them close to their bodies. Tucano's already broad shoulders had become wider, more powerful, and increasingly the wings tattooed on his back looked as if they were about to take flight. And Biscottino had bloomed. From one day to the next he'd sprouted up several inches, and with all his bike riding, his legs had become a pair of palpating levers. Drone had taken off his eyeglasses and replaced them with contact lenses, and he'd also gone on a diet, with no more kebabs or fried pizza. Nicolas, too, had changed, and not because he'd become a regular consumer of cocaine, which didn't seem to have the same effect on him that it had on the rest of the *paranza*. His was a controlled euphoria. When Drago' talked to him, he could detect a continuous rumination behind his eyes: he talked, he kidded around, he issued orders, he acted the fool with the others, but he never lowered his guard, he never broke away from a process of reasoning that was entirely his own, and to which no one else was ever invited. Sometimes those eyes reminded him a little of his father's, Nunzio Viceré's, eyes that he, Drago', had never had. But these thoughts of Drago's were flashes of lightning that vanished the instant they touched the ground.

What were they turning into? There wasn't even time to try to answer that question. They just needed to keep going.

"The sky is the limit," Nicolas would say.

MARKETS

You can't break the silence because there's no such thing as silence. Even on a glacier at an elevation of thirteen thousand feet: something's always going to be creaking. Even at the bottom of the sea: you'll always have the ka-thump of your heart to keep you company. Silence actually resembles a color. It has a thousand different shades, and someone who was born in a city like Naples, or Mumbai, or Kinshasa can sense them and detect the differences.

The *paranza* was in the lair. It was payday. The monthly salary due to each member—each *paranzino*—sat in a heap of banknotes that covered the low glass coffee table. First Briato' and then Tucano had tried to divvy it up into equal shares, but when they were done, the numbers never added up. There was always someone who claimed they were getting less than someone else.

"Briato'," said Biscottino, who had found himself with ten twenty-euro bills and was staring at the C-notes that were crumpled in Drone's hands, "weren't you studying accounting?"

"No," Pesce Moscio cut in, "he fucked one of the lady teachers there, but she flunked him anyway." An old story, probably a false one, but they never tired of retelling it, and by now Briato' just ignored them, especially now that he'd proved incapable of divvying up the take correctly.

Drago' grabbed everyone's cash back and tossed it onto the table the way you do when you're putting an end to a card game, and then he froze in place with a twenty-euro bill held up in midair. He looked like a poker player ready to lay down a winning ace.

"What is this fucking silence?"

They all looked up, to get a whiff of that exact silence. Nicolas was the first to leave the lair, followed by all the others. Biscottino tried pointing out that in the movies, he'd seen it one time, before an atomic bomb goes off, there's always that same silence, after which, BOOOOM, ashes, but they were already out on the street, all lined up to watch Forcella get ready to take a break. Certainly, the background noise never ceased, and in fact it was nothing but a nuance, a slight variation, but it was enough.

The traffic at the fork in the road that marked the quarter had come to a halt, an old moving van with a faded name on the side had stopped at an angle and the back door was wide open. From the windows of the surrounding buildings, from the sidewalks, from inside cars with the engine turned off came offers of help, though uttered without conviction, just to curry favor, because those responsible for the work had already been identified. The *paranza* of the Capelloni. They were shuttling back and forth between the truck and the front door of the apartment house, the one where the single road turns into two, the place of honor. Old furniture, dating back at least a couple of generations, extremely heavy but untouched by the passage of the years, as if it had been stored under plastic slipcovers for decades. Three Capelloni were sweating under the weight of a statue of the Madonna of Pompeii that stood at least six feet tall. Two others were carrying a St. Dominic and a St. Catherine of Siena by their feet, while a third carried a Madonna with a halo. They were huffing and puffing, sweating and swearing in the presence of all that holiness. Alongside, like a sheepherder, White was shouting at them, telling them what to do.

"If we knock over the Madonna, the Madonna will knock us over."

And then there were crystal chandeliers, a sofa upholstered in a thick,

Pompeiian red fabric adorned by golden outlines of leaves, chairs with towering backrests, practically a set of thrones, armchairs, cardboard cartons stacked high with porcelain dinner services. All the things you'd need to set up housekeeping in high style.

If Maraja's *paranza*, standing with their backs to the walls of the apartment building across the way, had bothered to look up from that show and stare at a window thirty feet up or so, they would have seen the new mistress of the house leaning out of it: Maddalena, aka La Culona. She was offended by her husband, Crescenzio, aka Roipnol, because she so badly wanted to go downstairs with him, take a stroll through the quarter, get acclimated, in other words. But her husband had been adamant, refusing to budge, and in that still bare-walled apartment he tried his best to explain to her that he couldn't go out with her, it wasn't safe, but she was welcome to go, no one was keeping her. He'd done his twenty years behind bars, a little more time shut in behind the door of that apartment wouldn't really make any difference to him. Crescenzio tried to calm his wife, but the echoing sounds in that empty space and that kid, Pisciazziello, who wouldn't stop asking "You like the way we painted it?" rendered his efforts pointless.

Thirty feet below, on the street, the Capelloni were vanishing into the atrium and then reemerging empty-handed, ready for another load. Only White was doing nothing, except smoking one joint after another and gesticulating like the conductor of a symphony orchestra.

Nicolas and his *paranzini* hadn't dared to take so much as a step. They just couldn't move, they stood there openmouthed, continuing to stare like little old men watching ditches being excavated for new pipes. That wasn't someone moving house, that was the arrival of a king with his court.

Biscottino was the first to speak: "Nico', who is it?"

The whole *paranza* turned to look at Nicolas, who took a step forward, to the edge of the sidewalk, and in a cold voice that made chills run down their spines, said: "You see, Biscotti', it's rewarding to carry heavy furniture."

"But for who?"

"*Sacc'i'*," he said—I know who it is—and then he took a few more steps to break away from the *paranza* and walk over to White, whisper something into his ear as the man lit himself another joint, raised it to his mouth, and with his other hand squeezed the samurai ponytail that he'd grown—a stump of greasy hair. The two of them walked off together and entered the back room. The usual customers were out on the street, spectators like the rest of them. White lay down on the pool table, one arm behind his head, propping it up. Nicolas instead stood there, braced on both legs, motionless, his fists clenched, arms pressed close to his body. He was sweating with rage, but he didn't want to mop his brow, didn't want to show any sign of weakness in front of White. In the three minutes it had taken them to reach the back room, White, without much beating around the bush, had told Nicolas that from that moment on, the quarter belonged to Crescenzio Roipnol. That had been the decision. So he and his *guagliuncelli* had better just fall into line.

None of them had ever laid eyes on Crescenzio Roipnol, but they all knew who he was and why he'd wound up behind bars at Poggioreale twenty years ago, when Don Feliciano and his men were far away, in Rome, Madrid, Los Angeles, convinced that they'd established a power that no one else could crack. Still, Don Feliciano's brother, Viceré, couldn't contain those who wanted to take over Forcella and take advantage of the power vacuum. Ernesto Boa—one of Mangiafuoco's men, from the Sanità quarter—had set up housekeeping in Forcella. In order to seize control. To subjugate it to Sanità. The Faellas had come to Viceré's aid, their boss Sabbatino Faella, Micione's father, had arrived. And his armed right-hand man had arrived as well: Crescenzio Ferrara Roipnol. It was he who eliminated Boa, and did it one Sunday, at Mass, in front of everyone, as a proclamation that Don Feliciano's power remained intact only thanks to Sabbatino Faella. The never-ending struggle between the monarchies of Forcella and Sanità had once again been frozen, ensuring that the heart of Naples remained divided between two sovereigns, as the families from outside the city had always insisted.

He was an old-school junkie, Crescenzio was, and the only reason he'd been able to survive in prison was his father-in-law, La Culona's dad, who managed to get him a steady supply of Rohypnol behind bars. The tablets helped to quiet his tremors, to keep him from losing his mind after the umpteenth bout of cold turkey, but on the downside they'd slowed his reflexes a little—sometimes he seemed to be in a narcotic trance. Not enough to be a major problem, though, seeing that he'd been named district underboss.

Nicolas looked at the smile spreading across White's face, his brown teeth jutting out. That asshole, he thought to himself, had no idea what a slave he was.

"So you like to take it in the ass?" Nicolas began.

White stretched out even more on the pool table, putting both hands behind his head, as if he were lying in a field basking in the sunshine.

"You like to take it in the ass?" Nicolas said again, but White kept ignoring him, maybe he hadn't even heard those words. Just like he didn't feel the ashes from the joint as they dropped onto his neck.

"So is that the way you like it, 'o White? With or without a gob of spit?"

White sat up with a jerk, in an off-kilter yoga position. He took a greedy drag on the joint, as if to suck a mouthful of courage from it. And maybe to lessen his shame.

"Lemme get this straight," said Maraja. "'O Micione fucks Copacabana in the ass. Then Copacabana fucks Roipnol in the ass. And Roipnol fucks you in the ass! Do I have that right?"

White undid his ponytail and his hair tumbled down in a messy clump. "We take turns," he said, and stretched out on the pool table again.

Nicolas was furious, he felt like murdering White right then and there, bare-handed; felt like grabbing him by the throat until he turned blue, actually; he'd have liked to climb up to the fifth floor of the apartment house where Roipnol was now living and kill him and his wife, take over Forcella, take for himself what Copacabana had let him get a whiff of. But this wasn't the time for that. He left the back room and strode briskly back to his *paranza*, which hadn't budged a foot from where he'd left them. The Capelloni were moving an antique chest that was never going to fit through the main ground-floor entrance. Nicolas took up his place among his men, as if he were the last piece in a jigsaw puzzle, the piece that finally composes the complete figure. Biscottino, without turning to look at his boss, asked again: "But who are they delivering the furniture for?"

"They're delivering the furniture for the person sent here to make sure we become ants for 'o Micione."

"Maraja," said Tucano, "what are you talking about? We need to go see Copacabana right away."

"Let's go tell him that we understood the message."

The sound of shuffling feet, hands jammed down into trouser pockets, sniffing. The *paranza* had lost its contemplative calm.

"What do you mean?" said Tucano.

"I mean that Copacabana fucked us. He took away our keys to Forcella."

"So what do we do now?"

"Now we revolt."

Nicolas had summoned them all for a meeting at the New Maharaja. That very evening. He'd had nine little settees brought into the private room for his *paranzini*, while for himself he'd selected a red velvet throne that Oscar generally used for eighteenth-birthday parties. He'd ensconced himself on that throne and waited for them there. He was wearing a dark gray pinstripe suit that he'd bought a few hours earlier, following the conversation with White. He'd picked up Letizia and they'd walked into the finest store in the city center. And then he'd bought a pair of studded Philipp Plein shoes and a broad-brimmed Armani hat. Taken together, the effect clashed terribly, but Nicolas didn't care. He liked the way the light at the New Maharaja glinted off those five-hundred-euro shoes. For the occasion, he also decided to get his beard trimmed. He wanted to be perfect.

He was drumming his fingers on the brass armrests as he watched his army guzzle Moët & Chandon. Drago' had asked him what they had to celebrate, seeing that now they were going to have to report up to Roipnol, but Nicolas hadn't so much as bothered to reply, simply pointing him to the trays of pastry and the flutes of champagne. From the club, a rhythm came pounding out at 120 b.p.m., probably some boring birthday party that would go on for a while. Good, thought Nicolas when they were all there, and he asked his men to take a seat in the armchairs. He had them all before him, his apostles. A hemicycle in which all eyes were obliged to focus exclusively upon him. He turned his gaze from right to left, and then again from left to right. Drago' must have gone to the barber's, because the tangled shadow that he wore on his face that morning had now been neatened into a perfectly stenciled stripe of whiskers. Briato' had chosen a navy-blue shirt, buttoned up to the throat, while Drone had opted for a snug-fitting T-shirt. He'd just started going to the gym and he was working hard on his pectorals. Pesce Moscio, too, was dressed to the nines, for once he'd abandoned his oversized trousers for a pair of North Sails trousers with a slightly low-slung waist, hemmed high to show off his loafers.

They're all beautiful, Nicolas mused, as he gazed first at Tucano, then at Lollipop, Stavodicendo, and finally Dentino. And that thought, which if he'd expressed it out loud would have triggered a stream of mockery for the rest of the evening, passed without shame. Even Biscottino was beautiful, with that face of a child that hadn't yet lost the rotundity of youth.

"What's there to celebrate? That we're supposed to report up to Roipnol now?" Drago' asked again. Now Nicolas would be forced to answer, and Maraja was tempted to reply that they might already know why they were there drinking a toast, since they'd shown up dressed to the nines, as if they'd already sensed that this wasn't a day of defeat.

"The *paranza* never submits to anyone," said Nicolas.

"I get that, Nico', but now this guy's here, and the reason he's here is because that's the way 'o Micione wants it."

"And we'll take over the markets. We'll take them all."

There was no need to learn the mechanism. Nor was any explanation required. They'd grown up on it. That system of "franchising" was as old as the world, it had always worked and it always would. The proprietors of the piazzas were faces that they could clearly identify among a thousand others, sole directors of the merchandise who had only one responsibility: to pay, every week, the established quota to the clan that controlled that district. Where did they procure their merchandise? Did they have just one supplier or more than one? Were they members of the clan? Questions that only someone who hadn't grown up there would even think of asking. A form of soulless capitalism, which allows the proper degree of detachment, so that business can proceed without problems. And then, if the proprietors skimmed a little off the top, the clan could tolerate that, it was just a productivity bonus. Isn't that the way all corporations operate?

Taking over the piazzas meant taking over the quarter, taking charge of the territory. Systematic taxation and the monthly kickback from street vendors don't give you roots. They give you money, but they don't really change the way things stand. Nicolas could see it all laid out in front of him. Marijuana, hashish, kobret, cocaine, heroin. They'd do it all in the proper sequence, the right move at the right time and at the exact right place. Nicolas knew that there were certain things you couldn't avoid, but you could speed them up, and most important, you could leave your imprint on them, or better still, the imprint of your *paranza*.

There was no laughter. There weren't even crossed legs or the sound of fabric being dragged across the upholstery of the armchairs. For the second time that day, the *paranza* had become petrified. This was the dream that had finally found the path of words. Everything they'd done till that day had been a feverish gallop toward the goal that Nicolas had finally worked up the nerve to call by its name. The piazzas—the drug markets.

Nicolas stood up and put the palm of his hand on Drago's hair.

"Drago'," he said, "you take Via Vicaria Vecchia." And he lifted his fingers all of a sudden, as if he'd just cast a spell.

Drago' got up from the chair and raised his hands, palms turned toward the ceiling, pumping his arms up and down, as if lifting an invisible weight. *Raise the roof.*

The others applauded, and there were even a few shrill whistles. "Go, Drago' . . ."

"Briato', you're in charge of Via delle Zite," Nicolas proclaimed, and laid his hands on his hair.

"Briato'," said Biscottino, "if you want to be in charge, though, you need to do some push-ups every morning . . ."

Briato' pretended to punch him in the nose, and then kneeled in front of Nicolas, bowing his head.

"Drone, my friend," Maraja continued, "for you we have Vico Sant'Agostino alla Zecca."

"Fuck," said Briato', who had gone back for another glass of champagne. "That way, now you can use your little drone machines for our own good."

"Briato', just get the hell out of here, go on."

"Lollipop, you get Piazza San Giorgio."

Progressively, as Nicolas assigned the piazzas for the various markets, the chairs emptied out, and each one who had received his own zone—his own piazza!—would exchange compliments with the one appointed before him, wrapping him in a hug, taking his face in his hands and staring deep into his eyes, like a couple of warriors about to take the field of battle.

Stavodicendo got Piazza Bellini and Pesce Moscio got one that was between Via Tribunali and Via San Biagio dei Librai. "Stavodice', you're moving up in the world!"

"Denti'," said Maraja, "what do you think about Piazza Principe Umberto?"

"What do I think about it, Maraja? *Amm' 'a scassà i ciessi!* We need to bust everyone else's chops."

Nicolas turned around and went to pour some champagne. "We're done, right? Let's take charge!"

"What about you, Maraja?" asked Dentino.

"I'll take the delivery service, the floating market."

Biscottino, who was sitting in the armchair in the middle of the room, had watched Nicolas walk past him at least four times. He felt like a benchwarming athlete being ignored by his coach. Biscottino's lower lip was starting to quaver, he'd stabbed his fingernails into the armrests, he was trying to focus his eyes on some random point to keep from meeting the rowdy laughter of his friends, who had just raised a toast to the *guagliuncello* who'd been left with nothing to eat.

Nicolas threw back his glass of champagne in a single gulp and then told Biscottino to stand up. Shamefully he approached his boss, who laid a hand on his shoulder.

"You shat your pants, didn't you? Are your undies still dry?"

More laughter and more clinking champagne glasses.

Then Nicolas gave Biscottino a gentle slap in the face and assigned him a market. A market all his own. A piazza.

A piazzetta. *'Na piazzulella.*

Now the party could really begin.

AMM' 'A SCASSÀ I CIESSI

There'd been a terrorist bombing. They were all standing around Drone's laptop looking at the screen, where footage of the explosion alternated with photographs of the bombers.

"Look at the fucking beards those guys are wearing," said Tucano.

"*Ua'*, they're almost like the ones we wear," said Pesce Moscio.

"These guys have got balls on them, *guagliu'*," said Nicolas.

"As far as I'm concerned, they're just a bunch of bastards. They'll kill anyone. They killed a kid," said Dentino.

"Did they kill a kid of yours?"

"No."

"Then what the fuck do you care?"

"But I could have been there!"

"Were you?" And then he waited long enough to get a no in response and concluded: "They've got balls on them."

"What the fuck are you saying, Nicolas? *Guagliu'*, 'o Maraja has lost his mind."

Nicolas sat down at the table, next to the computer. He took his position there and looked them all in the eye. "Think it through. Anyone willing and ready to die to get something has a pair of balls on them, and that's that. Even if what they want is fucked up, religion, Allah, whatever the fuck it is. Anyone willing to die to get something is a real man."

"I think they've got balls on them, no question," said Dentino. "But they're wrong about what they're doing. They want to attack women, they want to burn Jesus."

"Sure, but still, I have much respect for anyone willing to die—*pe' cchi se fa murì*. I also have respect for them because everyone's afraid of them. This means you've done it, *adda murì mammà*, you've done it so that everybody shits in their pants whenever they see you."

"You know what, 'o Maraja? I like the fact that this beard scares people," said Lollipop.

"It doesn't scare me," said Biscottino, who still didn't have a hint of whiskers. "After all, just because you have a beard doesn't mean you belong to ISIS."

"No, but I don't mind it," said Nicolas, and he immediately posted, "Allahu akbar."

A second later, underneath his post there stretched out a list of indignant comments.

"*Ua'*, Maraja, they're piling on against you," said Briato'.

"Let them scream, who the fuck cares."

"You know what I think, Maraja?" asked Tucano. "I don't respect the ones who got rich without taking risks, because if you have money but you don't know how to shoot, you don't know how to take what you want. Anyone who has money because they get a massive salary, or a pension, if you ask me, that person deserves to lose their money. That is, I like people who are rich because they took risks. But no kidding around, these guys are filthy pigs: take and shoot children? No. Then you're just a disgusting mess of a man."

Stavodicendo got up for another beer, shot a glance at the screen, which was showing footage of the explosion for the umpteenth time, and said: "Then again, the fact that they die? I disagree. It's something for cocksuckers."

"Yeah, right," said Drago'. "'O brother," he went on, speaking to Nicolas, "it's one thing for a guy, I don't know, to get killed because he's trying to keep control of a drug market, do an armed robbery, or ice a target. It's another thing if he really wants to die. I don't like that. That's for assholes."

"Then we'll just be a *paranza* of little bait fish," said Maraja, shaking his head angrily, "dangling from a fishing pole. Like it or lump it."

"Maraja, why are you complaining? We're becoming the kings of Naples and you know it."

"Pecché nun è accussi che se cagna!" Because that's not the way you change things!

"I don't want to change anything," said Tucano. "All I want is money."

"But that's the point," said Nicolas, and his dark eyes flickered with light. "That's exactly the point. We need to command, not just make money."

"Amm' 'a scassà i ciessi," commented Biscottino. We need to knock it out of the park.

"Pe cummannà la gente ti deve riconoscere, s'adda inchinà, adda capì che tu ci starai 'na vita." To command, people have to recognize you, bow to you, understand that you'll be there for the rest of their lives. "People have to fear us—they fear us, we don't fear them," Nicolas concluded, paraphrasing the pages from Machiavelli that he carried emblazoned in his memory.

"But they already shit their pants when they see us!" said Dentino.

"Dovremmo tené fora 'a porta file di gente che vò trasì int' 'a paranza," Nicolas responded, diving deep into dialect: We ought to have lines out the door of people eager to see the *paranza*. "And instead we've got nothing . . ."

"All the better!" exclaimed Pesce Moscio. "How do you know a spy wouldn't come in?"

"Spy or no spy," said Nicolas, shaking his head, "the *paranza* has always been thought of as something at the service of someone in particular, like the police say when they arrest whoever pulled the trigger: the *paranza* of what's-his-name or such-and-such . . ."

268 I ROBERTO SAVIANO

"The armed branch," said Drone.

"Yeah, but I don't want to be anybody's armed branch. We need to be more, we need to eat up the streets. So far, we've just been focusing on money; instead, we need to think about taking charge."

"What's that mean? What the fuck are we supposed to do, in your opinion?" Tucano asked in desperation. He was starting to take this line of argument personally.

The *paranza* didn't understand; it was circling a significance without being able to grasp it.

"If you've got money, you're in charge. Period," Dentino commented.

"But with what money? All the money we have is what a real boss earns in fifteen days and the builder Criviello pulls down in a weekend!" Nicolas got down off the table and went to crack open a beer. "*Adda murì mammà*, there's nothing we can do about it. You don't understand, you'll never understand a fucking thing."

"Anyway," said Lollipop, to get out of the conversation, which had seized up like a beat-up old motor scooter, "that's why I like having this beard"—and he stroked his well-groomed beard—"because it scares people, 'o Maraja."

"I'm not scared of a beard," said Drago', sprawled out on the sofa and rolling a joint. "The guys in Sanità all have long beards . . . but I don't wet my pants when I see them."

"We don't, but ordinary people do," Maraja replied.

"I don't like these fucking long beards," Drago' reiterated.

"I do, and a lot, and Nicolas likes them, and 'o Drone likes them, so why don't you grow one: we need a uniform . . ." Lollipop piled on.

"Nice idea, this thing with the uniform," said Maraja. "But, *guagliu*', if you ask me, Drago' can't grow much of a beard . . . he's still just a kid, like Biscottino."

"Suck on this fish, *strunzo*," Drago' retorted, "and after all, we've got our wings. That's our uniform, on our flesh, it's not the kind of thing some barber can get rid of."

Nicolas had stopped listening. The markets had been divvied up, that's true, and he'd assigned one to each of them, but actually taking them was quite another matter. No one, except for him, seemed to have focused yet on the fact that there was quite a difference between the two things—the expanse of the sea. But he also thought that seas were made to be crossed and that, if you're born a fucker, then there are no obstacles that can stand in your way. The sky's the limit.

Nicolas really did believe in his own abilities and in signs. A few days earlier, before Roipnol had settled down in Forcella like a bloodsucking tick, he'd seen Dumbo out and about on his Aprilia SportCity scooter, and behind him, arms around him, a woman in her early fifties. He hadn't recognized her right away, because they were traveling at a crazy rate of speed, zigzagging in and out of traffic. So he'd kept an eye on Dumbo, and he'd finally figured out who she was. La Zarina, as in the Tsarina, the widow of Don Cesare Acanfora, aka Negus, and therefore the queen of San Giovanni a Teduccio and the mother of the new king, Scignacane. Her real name was Natascia and her husband had been murdered by L'Arcangelo's men for having allied himself with the Faellas, even though he'd previously worked for years in alliance with the Grimaldis. After mourning Negus, La Zarina had set herself one goal: to become the sole supplier of heroin in Naples. Nothing less, nothing more. No shakedowns, no army, just a crew of men defending that business. And her son Scignacane had been brought up to accomplish that mission. Not a boss, a broker. Then Micione had managed to find other supply channels and the Acanfora clan's line of business was starting to dwindle.

Never had a nickname been more appropriate than Scignacane. He'd never really recovered from the magic mushrooms he'd taken at age sixteen and now, at twenty-one, whenever he used too many esses in a row in a sentence, he'd start drooling like a dog and moving jerkily, like a chimp caught off guard by a sudden noise. "You need to snort it, not jab it in your vein," he'd say when he was talking about heroin. Because jabbing it in your vein meant you got transformed into one of the zombies from *The Walking Dead*, and just the sight of you was enough to make people vomit.

Nicolas was connecting the dots. Dentino–Dumbo–La Zarina–Scignacane–heroin.

Dentino and Dumbo were like a pair of brothers, and from there to Scignacane would just be a short step. There was a whiff of respect hovering around Dumbo, despite the fact that he was small and too soft. He'd never fired a shot in his life and violence frightened him, but he'd been through Nisida Reform School, say no more. Dumbo would never be a member of the *paranza*, and he knew that, but when Nicolas asked him if he could take him to see Scignacane, he didn't blink an eye.

"Sure" was all he said. One more dot had just been connected.

Scignacane welcomed Nicolas the way you welcome a stranger. Mistrustfully. He was sprawled out on his bed in the apartment he kept for guests, in San Giovanni a Teduccio, stroking a contentedly purring Siamese cat. He was watching some reality show on TV. Nicolas had been ushered in after being searched from head to foot by Scignacane's men.

"Scignaca', we want your heroin," said Nicolas. No preambles, just a straight lunge to connect the last dot.

Scignacane looked at him as if a little kid had walked up and begged to be allowed to shoot the nice gun, too. "Okay, so let's just pretend you came over to say hi to me."

"'O Micione buys from other markets and you know that."

"Okay, so let's just pretend you came over to say hi to me," Scignacane repeated mechanically. In the same tone of voice, stretched out in the same position.

"*Devo parlare cu mammeta?*" asked Nicolas. Do I have talk to your mother? He'd said it in a low, low voice, to reinforce the threat.

"'*O capo famiglia songo io.*" Scignacane had swatted away the cat, turned off the TV, and gotten to his feet. All in the space of a second. "I'm the head of the family." What he had in front of him was no longer a child, it was an opportunity. Maybe a leap into the void, sure, but still better than winding up crushed underfoot by Micione, who'd started buying from the Syrians lately. "But you need to pay me directly for the heroin."

"I can give you thirty thousand."

"Fuck, that's the price I'm paying for it."

"Exactly, Scignaca' . . . the heroin that we ship? Everyone needs to want it. I set the price at thirty-five euros a gram . . . these days, they'll sell you ordinary shit at forty, and really good shit at fifty. We offer the very best shit at thirty-five. Three months, Scignaca', and there'll be nothing but your heroin anywhere in Naples. Yours and yours alone."

The prospect of covering the city with his merchandise convinced Scignacane and, even while he was accepting, Maraja already had his next move in mind. That step was the more complicated one, because straightforward lures wouldn't be enough, nor would spectacular phrases, or *paranza* fishing lamps, useful only for small fry. Now he was going to have to explain the whole strategy in detail. He went to get himself another beer, and amid the shouts of the brothers who had started playing a round of *Call of Duty,* he texted Aucelluzzo.

This time he had no difficulty setting up the meeting.

Nicolas had to choose among the drunk, the fisherman, and the tough guy—*'o guappo.* The ceramics of Capodimonte were there, in front of him. This was the price he'd have to pay to Professoressa Cicatello. He went over to the sales clerk in the shop in the Tribunali quarter and pointed uneasily to the display case crowded with bombonières and statuettes.

"Which one?" she asked.

"That one . . ." he said, extending his hand and pointing at random.

"Which one?" asked the clerk again, her eyes trying to follow Nicolas's vaguely wavering finger.

"That one!"

"This one?" she asked, grabbing one.

"Yeah, okay, whichever one you think is best . . ."

He put it into his backpack, fit the full-face helmet over his head, started up the T-Max, and took off.

Entering Conocal was harder than usual; by now they knew his face. In spite of the helmet, he was afraid he might be recognized by Micione's men. He was sure of his *paranza,* these days, good soldiers that they were, they didn't enter unauthorized territories. Nicolas drove along, glancing right and left. He was afraid of a gunshot, or else a narcotics cop pulling up on him without warning. Because of that full-face helmet, the risk was by no means an unlikely one. He pulled up where Aucelluzzo had told him to wait: outside the butcher shop owned by L'Arcangelo's cook. In the blink of an eye, Cicognone hopped on the back of the T-Max. Now Nicolas was shielded, he had the benediction to enter the district.

He parked in the underground garage of the ocher-yellow apartment house. It was no longer time to win an arsenal of weapons. The *paranza*'s dope markets needed to be supplied with grass, and a dozen or so yards overhead was the man who could do that for him.

L'Arcangelo was sitting on a modular chair that reminded Nicolas of the ones they use in America for death row executions. Running out of L'Arcangelo's arms were four tubes connected to a machine with a blinking screen and, up high, a flask with dialysis solution. In spite of the complexity of the gadget, the welter of tubes, the red blood flowing through them, the unsettling, unmistakable presence of the purification filter, the patient's forced immobility, there was no sign of tension, nor did the machine produce any sound other than the barely perceptible beeping of the monitors.

"Don Vitto', aren't you well?"

Before answering, L'Arcangelo waved his free hand at the male nurse to move away from the armchair.

"What are you talking about? I'm fine."

"Then how come you're stuck in this armchair?"

"Do you think they awarded me house arrest out of the goodness of their hearts? The doctor told them that my kidneys are clogged up, and getting that documentation cost me a small fortune. Which means I can stay here under house arrest. And it's never a bad idea to get your blood cleaned up. If you ask me, at my age, clean blood makes you live longer, right?"

"Of course it does . . ."

"Maraja," said L'Arcangelo, and he uttered the words that followed with a smile, "I know that you're making good use of the weapons I gave you. You're shooting in all directions." Nicolas nodded, clearly flattered.

L'Arcangelo went on: "But you're shooting badly." He paused to take a look at the device that was pumping blood. "All the weapons you use, you're using them without gloves. You're leaving spent shells all over the place. Can you really be so dumb? What the fuck? Do I have to teach you the most elementary rules? You really are just kids."

"But they'll never catch us," said Nicolas.

"Why did I put my trust in a child? Why?" he asked, looking at Cicognone, who'd appeared in the kitchen doorway.

"Okay, should I just leave, Don Vitto'?" asked Maraja.

L'Arcangelo went on, without even listening to him: "The first rule that makes a man a man is that he knows that things won't always go well; in fact, he knows that things might go well once and then go wrong a hundred times. Instead kids think that things will go right for them a hundred times and will never go wrong at all. Maraja, nowadays you need to think like a man, you can't think that they won't get you anymore. If they want to get you, you need to make them sweat blood, they need to work hard. Maraja, so far you've just fired at the sides of apartment buildings . . ."

"No, that's not true, I've killed a person."

"Eh, no, *non l'hai acciso tu* . . . You didn't kill him. Some stray bullet, fired at random by who knows which *strunzo* from your *paranza*."

Nicolas opened his eyes wide. It was as if L'Arcangelo not only had spies but was looking directly into their heads.

"I trained by shooting at negroes . . ."

"Good for you! So now you feel like a man? What's it take to shoot at negroes? I was wrong, I never should have given you a thing . . ."

"Don Vittorio, we're taking over the center of Naples . . . what the fuck are you talking about?"

"*Aggi'a parlà con mammeta*, Maraja. I'm going to have to talk to your mother. All these curse words, do you ever hear a *guappo* talk like that? Since you're not here talking to your father, curb your tongue. Or else get out of here right away."

"Excuse me . . . Or actually, no, excuse me nothing. I don't report to you, I'm doing you a favor." Then he raised his voice: "*Adda murì mammà,*

I'm in charge of more than you are, you have to admit it, Don Arca', today I'm bringing you the oxygen that 'o Micione is trying to choke off here."

Cicognone walked over. He could sense the air heating up and he didn't like it. Nicolas's tone of voice wasn't appropriate. L'Arcangelo reassured him with one hand.

"Give us your shit, the stuff you can't sell here. I can be your legs and your hands. I'll take over the markets, conquer the piazzas, one after the other . . . your shit is just rotting here. You can't afford to sell it at fire-sale prices, otherwise you'll look desperate, but no one will come all this way to buy it. Only junkies come, and you can't live off junkies."

L'Arcangelo continued to hold off Cicognone with that raised hand. Nicolas wasn't sure whether he should go on or stop. But by now he'd crossed the Rubicon, there was no turning back.

"A dying man, Don Vitto', even if he says that he feels fine, isn't about to come back to life."

Now L'Arcangelo was gripping the armrest with his left hand.

"You're taking over the markets, are you? Actually, 'o Micione has everything under control. He owns Forcella, the Spanish Quarter, Cavone, Santa Lucia, Central Station, Gianturco . . . should I go on?"

"Don Vittorio, if you give me your shit, I'll force it onto every market!"

"You're going to force it onto the markets? Then you're not 'o Maraja, now you've become the wizard Harry Potter? *Harry Potter 'o mago?* Or maybe you're just one of San Gennaro's cousins?"

"*Nisciuna magia, nisciuno miracolo. Noi amm' 'a fà come Google.*" No magic, no miracles. We need to do just like Google.

The boss squinted hard, trying to follow the line of reasoning.

"Don Vitto', why do you think everyone uses Google?"

"*Che ne saccio, boh, perché è bbuono . . . ?*" Don Vittorio had no idea: Because it's good? he ventured.

"Because it's good and because it's free."

Arcangelo shot a glance at Cicognone to see if he understood any of it, but he was just standing there with a furrowed brow.

"Your shit is rotting on the vine, and if we give it out to all the market bosses without markup, they'll take it."

"Maraja, are you trying to use my mouth to give blow jobs?"

"All right, so 'o Micione buys grass at five thousand a kilo and sells it at seven thousand. In the piazzas he sells it at nine euros a gram. We'll sell it all at five euros."

"Maraja, just stop talking, you've spouted enough bullshit . . ."

Nicolas went on, staring at him: "The piazzas don't need to stop selling what 'o Micione gives them. They just need to sell our shit, too. Your shit, Arcangelo, is good, it's prime . . . but the quality alone isn't enough."

What Nicolas was saying was starting to penetrate, and now Don Vittorio had lowered his hand and was starting to listen carefully, as was Cicognone.

"I know who I want to fuck, the same as you do."

"Okay, but what do we get out of it?"

"Nothing, Don Vitto', exactly like Google."

"Nothing," Vittorio Grimaldi repeated, uttering that word, which seemed like a sharp blade to him.

"Nothing. The shit you have only needs to cover expenses. First we become Google and then, when everyone comes looking to buy from us, that's when we screw them. And we set our own prices."

"They'll all think that the shit is no good. The market bosses will assume we're trying to poison them."

"No, they'll try it and they'll understand. You've got to give us cocaine, too, Don Vitto', not just grass and hash . . ."

"Grass and hash, too?"

"That's right, grass and hash, too. You need to sell it at forty euros."

"Well, fuck me sideways, you know that I buy it for fifty thousand euros a kilo?"

"And 'o Micione sells it at fifty-five euros to the market bosses, who turn it around at ninety euros a gram, and when it's good shit, not when it's cut with tooth powder . . ."

"That means we're really giving it away."

"As soon as they start coming to us, we'll raise the price nice and slow, and we'll get it up to ninety, to a hundred. And we'll start moving it ouside Naples, too."

"Ha, ha." L'Arcangelo laughed loud and long. "We'll take it to America."

"Why not, Don Vitto', I'm not stopping in this city."

Now Cicognone was standing behind L'Arcangelo, and a smile had appeared on the boss's face.

"You want to command, don't you?"

"I already command."

"Congratulations, young commandant. But did you know that no one can trust you?"

"Don't make me drink piss, Don Vitto', just to prove that you can trust me. I won't drink piss."

"What piss are you talking about? You shithead. I've never seen a boss who hasn't done a piece of work. Let me give you some advice, Maraja: the first person who bothers you, take and shoot him in the head. All alone, though."

Now it was Nicolas who was closely attending to every word out of Don Vittorio's mouth. He objected: "Hey, but if I'm alone, no one can see it."

"So much the better. People will hear about it, and they'll quake in their shoes. And remember, before you do a piece of work, never have anything to eat, because if you get shot in the gut, it'll go straight to gangrene. You need to wear latex gloves, a jumpsuit, and shoes. Then you have to throw it all away. Got it?"

Nicolas nodded his head in approval, and he was laughing.

"All right, then, let's celebrate. Cicogno', get the bubbly."

They drank a toast to their agreement with a bottle of Moët & Chandon. They clinked glasses but their thoughts were far away. Maraja was dreaming of conquering Naples, and L'Arcangelo was dreaming of escaping the cage and taking to his wings again.

Before leaving, Nicolas reached into his backpack and pulled out his acquisition: "Don Vitto', what do you say, will the Professoressa like it?"

In the palm of his hand, a little boy was carrying a garland of roses.

"Very nice, this little *muccusiello*, this snotnose, an excellent choice."

While he was already climbing down through the trapdoor, he heard Cicognone's voice: "'O Maraja?"

"Eh?"

"*Si' 'o ras.*" You're the ras, the boss.

From the floor below, Maraja pierced him with eyes that looked like a pair of black needles and said: "'*O ssaccio!*" I know it!

WALTER WHITE

Nothing was working. It happened sometimes that the kids couldn't even get close to whoever was running the market, the piazza. Lollipop was the one who had it worst of all. They dragged him into a *basso* with the excuse that in there they could have a better discussion of the marijuana that the *paranza* had to sell, and then they'd cold-cocked him, knocked him out with an elbow to the nose. He'd reawakened two hours later, tied to a chair in a windowless room. He didn't know if it was day or night, if he was still in Forcella or in some tumbledown farmhouse in the countryside. He tried to shout but his voice echoed against the walls and, when he struggled to calm down and pick up any sound that might allow him to understand where he'd wound up, all he heard was the sound of water running through pipes. The next day, they freed him and he discovered that he'd spent a whole night in the *basso* that he'd entered in the first place. "Get the fuck out of here, *guaglioncello*, and tell your boyfriends to do the same." The others had been threatened, some of them had looked down the barrel of a magnum, Briato' had been chased by three motor scooters, Biscottino had taken a kick to the ribs and two days later taking a deep breath still burned his lungs. They'd treated them like children who'd dreamed they were *camorristi*.

The men who'd been managing the markets ever since the days of Cutolo had simply laughed Nicolas and his men in the face. They got their shit directly from Micione, and they had Roipnol to protect them. They didn't even want to talk about the grass and the heroin that their *paranza* had to offer. What were all these new ideas? Who did they think they were? Dictating their own rules to men who'd been born before these little assholes' parents?

"Maraja, not a fucking thing is stirring here. Let's lay these mother-fuckers out." At the New Maharaja, at the lair, on their motor scooters, Nicolas heard the same demand repeated every time a market rejected their shit. And by now they had lots and lots of shit. Since that night at the private dining room, two weeks had passed and they still hadn't obtained anything. Nicolas had procured some extra-large Samsonites to put the money in, but they still lay empty on the bed in the lair. Going to the arse-nal, getting out ten Uzis, and mowing down those bastards who refused to pay was a thought that had occurred fleetingly to Nicolas quite often, but then he'd stifled the thought and made the *paranza* swear on their own blood that no one would react with gunfire. They couldn't afford open warfare. Not yet, anyway. They'd find themselves up against Roipnol, Mi-cione, and the Capelloni. All at once. No, he needed to act surgically, strike one to educate them all, just like that phrase he'd put on his Insta-gram page. And then there were those words of L'Arcangelo's: "I've never seen a commander who's never done a piece of work"—uttered to deride him, to humiliate him, like the first time in his apartment when he'd made him strip naked. It was true, he still hadn't laid someone out dead on the pavement, but what had annoyed him most was the tone. That man, a prisoner in his nine-hundred-square-foot apartment, had given ev-erything to him and to his *paranza*—weapons, drugs, trust, practically with-out batting an eye—but he'd never wearied of lashing him with his words every time he thought it necessary. The respect that Nicolas had required and received from his *paranza* now demanded a baptism of blood.

The one who deserved the lesson was the one who'd had the oldest subcontract. Taking him down, Nicolas was convinced, would be like de-leting a piece of history. Then his *paranza* would arrange to write an-other piece of history to take its place, with new rules, with new men. No more skimming off the top of the sales, everything they earned needed to go straight into their pockets.

Mellone was a creature of habit. He ran his market, his piazza, the way a diligent office clerk punches in and punches out, only he didn't sit at a desk for eight hours a day because he preferred to sit in a bar and chug mojitos, his only vice, the legacy of a short-lived season on the run at other latitudes. He'd instructed the bartender on how to make a perfect mojito—the original recipe, none of those "misguided" cocktails that kids downed nowadays—and when the clock struck five in the afternoon, he stood up, rolled up that day's copy of *Gazzetta dello Sport* and tucked it under his arm, and went home, to an apartment five hundred yards away. He walked at a steady pace, then he'd go downstairs to the underground garage to make sure the cats had gobbled up every last one of the meaty chunks that he put out every morning when he left for the bar, outside the roll-up metal door of his parking unit. A boring, vaguely pathetic life that followed the rutted grooves Mellone had carved out so many years before.

Nicolas knew this routine, everyone knew it. He knew how many ice cubes Mellone took in his mojito: five, all identical; which pages of *Gazzetta dello Sport* he liked to read first: the international championships; and which cats he was feeding at the moment: a couple of brown short-hairs, who'd escaped from who knows where.

He'd told the *paranza* that they could take that day off, treat it as a well-earned break, do whatever they felt like, as long as they stayed away from the piazzas for a while—he needed to teach someone a lesson. He needed peace and quiet to do his work. He'd gone on Amazon and ordered himself a cheap outfit, a *Breaking Bad* costume. Hazmat jumpsuit, gloves, gas mask, and even a fake beard, which he'd immediately thrown away. He'd asked Dentino to bring him a pair of steel-toed boots, which no one was wearing on the construction site anyway. He'd jammed all these items into his school backpack, and then he'd hidden behind one of the cement pillars lining the lane running along in front of the underground garages in Mellone's apartment house. It was a perfect location because no one, except for Mellone, would have ventured down there. His garage was the last one in the row. Nicolas took off his clothes and dressed up as Walter White. Calmly, with thorough precision, plucking away the wrinkles in the latex gloves so they clung tight to his skin, smooth as flesh. The yellow hazmat jumpsuit fit him perfectly and, even though it was little more than a Carnival costume, the fabric seemed very durable. This needed to be a straightforward execution, without complications, reliably rapid and leaving no traces, at least not on his body. He pulled the hood over his head, with the gas mask tilted up onto his forehead, ready to be pulled down when needed. The two cartridges on either side of the gas mask protruded from the top of his head like Mickey Mouse ears. He hunkered down, resting his back against the pillar, gun in hand. With all the weapons he had available to him, he'd still chosen the Francotte: that was the gun he wanted for his first time. There was always the danger it might jam, but somehow he knew it wouldn't. The serenity with which he'd donned his outfit was now dripping down his back, down his arms, in rivulets of sweat. He did his best to get control of his increasingly rapid respiration, but none of his efforts served the purpose, because with every deep breath he took, different parts of his body reminded him that something could go wrong. A patch of sweat was spreading over the bluish gloves. What if he lost his grip on the now-slippery Francotte and dropped it? The crotch of the jumpsuit, which at first had seemed to fit him comfortably, now pressed tight against his balls. What if it cramped him just as he was striding toward Mellone? His knees were trembling. Yes, they were definitely trembling. And if he tried to control them, his lungs quit working properly. He upbraided himself, accusing himself of wetting his pants: What if the others could see him dressed up like that, and with a beet-red face? What would happen then? No more *paranza*, but as many individual *paranzas* as there were now members of this one.

At 5:15 p.m. a heavy footstep on the ramp announced the arrival of Mellone. Perfectly punctual. Nicolas had reckoned that it would take him twenty-seven steps to reach the garage door. He counted twenty-five, pulled down the gas mask, and stepped out with his pistol leveled. His lenses fogged up for a second. Just a second, but then he was able to focus on his target, the bald pate of Mellone. Now Nicolas caught a glimpse of that enormous Adam's apple, bobbing up and down in surprise, and he wondered just what it would sound like to put a couple of bullets right through the middle of it.

When they found him sprawled on the cement in front of that garage, word would spread that Mellone had stopped talking, once and for all. That there was someone else doing the talking now. Mellone didn't even have the time to wonder what the hell that alien creature was before Nicolas had pulled the trigger twice, in rapid succession. He'd fired without thinking, focusing only on the pressure of his fingers. His legs were still trembling, but he'd made up his mind to ignore them. The bullets lodged exactly where he'd aimed them, and the terrifying echo of the detonation was followed by the bursting of the Adam's apple. Pufff. Puff. Like the sound of a tire springing a leak. Nicolas grabbed his backpack and hustled out of there without even checking to make sure the man was dead. But dead he certainly was, because the news spread to everywhere and everyone, without even needing to write it in a group chat.

"Maraja, everyone in the gym was talking only and exclusively about 'o Mellone's murder."

That was the piece of news that had flown through the city, passed along by word of mouth. The day after Mellone's execution, they'd arranged to meet at the New Maharaja and Lollipop had walked straight over to Nicolas. Maraja was dancing by himself, and that phrase, whispered into his ear, resonated in his head for a moment, with all the intensity of the two bullets lodged in o' Mellone's Adam's apple. Pufff. Puff.

"Nice!" he replied, and headed for the center of the dance floor, but Lollipop blocked his way.

"But they all talk about it the wrong way, as if Roipnol pulled it off. A punishment because he'd started doing business with us. They turned it around, the killing, and that's how they're making it look."

Maraja had frozen in place and that phrase, too, had echoed in his head, only now the sound that he heard was an unpleasant one. The sound of legs trembling. He hadn't managed to put his signature on that murder because the *paranza* that he'd founded still didn't know how to lodge a claim of responsibility for its ambushes. So now just anyone could lay claim to that murder. He felt inadequate, he felt like a child. Nothing of the sort had happened for some time now.

He dragged Lollipop into the private dining room, where Drago' and Dentino were already sitting. Maraja interrogated them with a glance and they confirmed that the news had reached them, too, in that form, and there was more. They had received messages from a bunch of people who were working with the *paranza*, and they were all scared silly. "We aren't all going to wind up like 'o Mellone, are we?" they wrote.

"Me! That was me!" he felt like telling them all. "I did that piece of work!" But he held back.

In no more than twenty-four hours Micione and Roipnol had succeeded in crushing Maraja's *guagliuncelli* with the weight of their history.

Maraja let himself flop heavily down onto the throne that he'd used to assign the markets to his boys. He'd told Oscar that he was going to keep it there, and that if he wanted, he was free to go buy another one for parties. He stuck a hand in his pocket and pulled out a very thin packet of aluminum foil. Pink cocaine. He snorted it, the whole package. He didn't wrinkle his nose, he didn't run his fingers over his nostrils. It was a painkiller.

TANKER TRUCK

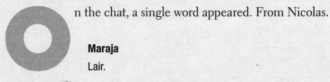n the chat, a single word appeared. From Nicolas.

Maraja
Lair.

It was a Saturday afternoon, the *paranza*'s free time. These were hours to spend curled up with their girls on a sofa while Mammà and Papà were doing the week's grocery shopping, hours to use pinning down the memories of the week that was ending. Drone had developed a Snapchat addiction. After giving them a brief lesson, he'd gotten the rest of the *paranzini* hooked too, and now they bombarded one another with blurry, jittery mini-videos in which there were just fleeting glimpses of lines of cocaine and snippets of panties, exhaust pipes and cartridges arrayed up on a table. A collage edited into rapid sequences that lasted only the seconds necessary to visualize and then, poof, vanished into the wind.

"Lair," Nicolas repeated two minutes later.

And all of them were in the apartment on Via dei Carbonari in no more than twenty minutes, because even when they were on their own fucking time, they could only stray a certain distance, they had to stay close enough to make it possible to bring the *paranza* together on a moment's notice.

Nicolas was waiting for them all, perched atop the television set, there was no way to crush that thing, even if Briato' had jumped up and down on it, and in the meantime he was texting back and forth with Letizia. He hadn't seen her in a week, and as usual she was pissed off. She'd made him promise to take her out for a cruise, just the two of them, and then maybe eat in a restaurant overlooking the water.

The *paranza* made its customary entrance, a tornado that filled up all the space available. Stavodicendo had grabbed Biscottino, pinning both his arms behind his back as he kneed him repeatedly in the ass, bumping him forward as Biscottino pretended to struggle, throwing his head back, hitting Stavodicendo with head jabs, but never much higher than the solar plexus. They both tumbled onto the sofa, quickly followed by all the others. The mountain of human flesh was something Biscottino had basically asked for, because as he was arriving at the lair he'd complained loudly that Nicolas's text had interrupted him just as he was about to get down to business with a terrifying hot piece of pussy he'd met on the Internet. None of the others had believed a word, and when he'd added that this girl was even attending university they'd all burst out laughing.

Nicolas immediately started talking as if he were addressing a well-behaved, orderly audience. And as he spoke, he commanded silence.

"*Amm' 'a fà i soldi*," he said. We need to make money. Drone was about to retort that that's what they were already doing: making money, and lots of it. Just with what they took in from the parking attendants at the San Paolo stadium, he'd already bought a two-thousand-euro Piaggio Typhoon.

"We'll go and get the money when we want it," Nicolas continued. He'd climbed down from the television set and sat on the glass coffee table, that way he could look all his *paranzini* in the eye and make it clear to them that money means protection, and protection means respect. Making money, and lots of it, is the way to conquer territory, and the time had come to pull off a major job.

"*Amm' 'a fà quintali di lattuga*. We need to make tons of lettuce. Only we're not just going to hand out C-notes to the others, on the outside,"

Nicolas said again, but without giving the others enough time to complete Lefty's observation, because he added: "We need to knock over a gas station."

The whole *paranza* was sitting on the sofa now, with Briato' and Lollipop at the two far ends, serving as bookends for all the others, who were packed into the middle.

It was Dentino, half-concealed by Stavodicendo, who was sitting on top of him, who broke the silence: "Who told you?"

"*Mammeta,*" Nicolas thundered. *Your mama.*

In other words, mind your own fucking business. Nicolas felt anxious, constantly in a hurry. There was never enough money. The others had a different conception of time, they were all lulled by the idea that things were spinning along nicely, in spite of the fact that there were still markets they hadn't taken over, but Nicolas had no time to waste. He was starting to think that he'd never have enough time. Even when he was playing soccer, he was always battling against time. He didn't know how to dribble, and he never even tried to send a teammate deep into the field, but he had adroit timing, he was one of those players that might have once been called an opportunist. He managed to be right where he needed to be, to punch a hole in the net. Simple and effective.

"We're going to rob the gas station attendant? Pistols in his face and he'll hand over all the money he's made in the day," said Drago'.

"That guy only takes credit cards," said Nicolas. "What we're going to take is the tanker truck, which means we'll take the truck and the fuel, both. There's forty thousand euros of fuel in that thing."

The *paranza* didn't understand. What were they going to do with all that gasoline? Fill up their motor scooters and their friend's scooters, too, for the next two years? Even Drago', who usually picked up on Nicolas's ideas on the fly, in full confirmation of the blue blood that flowed in his veins, seemed perplexed and had started scratching his head. No one breathed, there was just a rustling of asses in search of a patch of fabric on which to sit more comfortably.

"*Sacc'i' chi se la piglia,*" said Nicolas. I know who'll buy it.

Another rustling of asses on fabric, and a few sniffs here and there because it was clear that their boss was savoring the moment and that silence needed to be filled in with at least some sound.

"The Casalesi."

No more rustling or sniffing, no more lolling heads or elbows planted in one's neighbor's ribs. The *paranza* had fallen silent. Even the sounds from the street and the rest of the apartment house seemed to have vanished, as if that word, *Casalesi*, had deleted the presence of the entire city, inside and outside the room.

Casalesi was a word that, until that moment, none of them had ever heard uttered in front of the others. It was a single word that contained so many others, a word that took you around the world, a word that invoked men who had been elevated into the empyrean of the *paranza*. It made no sense even to refer to the Casalesi, because that would have meant alluding to ambitions impossible to satisfy. But now Nicolas had not only spoken the magic word, he'd even insinuated that they were about to do business with them. They wanted to ask him if he was pulling their leg, whether he'd ever even met them and how he'd obtained the contact, but they remained in complete silence because this was just too big of a thing, and Nicolas, who had in the meantime drawn closer, his knees practically touching Drone's, had started to explain.

The gas station stood along the state road that ran through Portici, Herculaneum, Torre del Greco, and continued south from there, all the way into Calabria, a road that cut each town in two and offered various escape routes. A Total gas station, exactly like so many others. The following Friday was when the new supply of gasoline would be delivered, and their job was to hijack the tanker truck and hide it in a garage not far away. At that point, they'd be contacted by two men from the Casalesi gang, who would pay them fifteen thousand euros. "Which will be ours to devour," Nicolas concluded.

With fifteen thousand euros, that would be a lot of devouring, and Nicolas already had a few ideas, but first he needed to designate which of his men were going to carry out the mission. He'd also thought about the fee attaching to the job. Two thousand euros apiece.

Pesce Moscio, Briato', and Stavodicendo freed themselves from the vise grip of the sofa and got to their feet. They wanted in. Nicolas said nothing, he didn't mention the two thousand euros—it was too late by now—and it was clear that those three were putting themselves forward to prove they had the balls, which isn't always a guarantee of success. In any case, the decision had been made, and Pesce Moscio, Briato', and Stavodicendo were going to hijack the tanker truck.

Before the fateful Friday they'd gone to scope out the route, just to make sure they didn't wind up driving down a blind alley with a forty-ton tanker truck. And they'd practiced on *GTA—Grand Theft Auto*. They'd equipped the bedroom in the lair with an Xbox One S and a 55-inch 4K television set. This was a mission that seemed to have been written specifically with them in mind, and it had become clear that driving a tanker truck at top speed down a highway was anything but a walk in the park. They kept crashing into things and catching fire, and even when things went well, they dropped the tanker trailer along the way. Stavodicendo started raising doubts about the feasibility of the operation, but Briato' silenced him immediately: "It's not like we're playing *GTA*, you know, this ain't Tierra Robada, this is Campania State Route Eighteen!"

All three of them pulled up at the gas station on Briato's scooter, and waited for the tanker truck to arrive on the opposite side of the road, their backs pressed against a low wall that marked the boundary between the asphalt and a field of wheat. They sat there, smoking one joint after another, talking nonstop, their veins flooded with the adrenaline that, luckily for them, the cannabis helped keep under control. Every time they heard the sound of a heavy truck braking, they stuck their heads up over the low wall to see if it was their target. When the white tanker truck with the Total logo on its side finally arrived, Stavodicendo was repeating for the fourth time a line from the movie *Il Camorrista* and almost failed to notice that Pesce Moscio had pulled a knife out of his pocket and had proceeded to punch two holes in his T-shirt. Then he did the same thing to his and Briato's T-shirts, and then they all pulled their T-shirts up over their heads. This was the quickest way to always have a ski mask on hand: two holes for the eyes in a T-shirt, and then you pull it up, uncovering your belly, your chest, and even a section of your back, but completely concealing your face. With these T-shirts perfectly adhering to their skulls, they looked like Spider-Men with torn suits. A quick glance to the right and to the left to check on the traffic they'd have to deal with and then, hands jammed down pants and guns now in hands, three MP-446 Viking 9mm pistols were now aimed at ten thousand gallons of gasoline. Pesce Moscio was the first one to reach the driver. He leaped up onto the running board and jammed the Viking under the man's nose.

"*Statte fermo. Te sparo 'mmocca.*" Hold still. I'll shoot you in the mouth.

Briato' took care of the gas station attendant, who had seen them coming with guns leveled and already had both hands in the air. He stuck the Viking into the back of his neck so hard that the attendant lost his balance and fell flat on the ground, both hands still raised.

"Hey, what are you doing?"

"Shut your fucking piehole, or it's over for you right now, right here, got that?" said Briato'.

"Get out," Pesce Moscio ordered the driver, but the man didn't seem frightened, quite the opposite. He hadn't taken his hands off the wheel, as if he were ready to drive away any minute now. All he said was: "*Appartenimmo, guagliu'.*" Literally, we belong. We're affiliated. "What the fuck do you think you're doing? They'll come and get you." All he said was what needs saying in these situations, in other words, that they were already protected by some family or some other person. They'd heard these words many times, from many others, the *paranzini* had.

"You belong?" asked Briato', who now had the Viking aimed directly at the gas station attendant's forehead. "Then that means you belong to somebody who ain't worth shit." While Briato' was teaching him his lesson, Stavodicendo had walked around the tanker truck, yanked open the door, and was now trying to drag the driver out by the arm. The driver was struggling, head-butting, and finally hauled off and gave a tremendous kick that caught Stavodicendo in the belly. The only reason he didn't tumble out backward onto the asphalt was at the last minute he caught hold of the handle; after that, he hurtled into the cockpit of the truck.

"Stavodice', what the fuck are you doing?" Pesce Moscio shouted at him. He kept the pistol trained on the driver, but he was petrified, a victim of the situation. Briato' stepped back toward the tanker truck, keeping the gas station attendant in his sights the whole time, and when he came even with the two others, caught up in a furious struggle, he fired a shot into the driver's shoulder.

"'A *bucchin' 'e mammeta!*" Pesce Moscio shouted. Your mother's a cocksucker! The driver's rolls of fat were bouncing up and down in time to the terror that Briato' had stirred in him with that shot. "What if you'd hit *me*?"

"Don't sweat it, everything's under control," Briato' replied. Stavodicendo, who would have had more of a right to be pissed off at Briato', seeing that he was the one who'd been in the truck, was dragging the driver down.

In the meantime, while they were fighting, the gas station attendant had got to his feet and went running off down the center of the road. Briato' took a couple of potshots at him, but the man was already gone. All three of them climbed into the truck, and Briato' slid behind the wheel. Getting the engine started and steering the tanker truck out onto the road was no problem, Briato' knew it very well from the online reading he'd done, on a few truck drivers' forums. He just hoped that the tanker was good and full, because otherwise the sloshing of the gasoline could all too easily make the truck swerve and fishtail and even go off the road. There were no sirens, so he opted for a cruising speed of twenty-five miles per hour. He could feel it, that roaring monster under his ass, and he had to be careful not to run over a compact car and do his best to attract as little attention as possible.

"*Ua*', it's too much fun driving this tanker truck!"

Nicolas had told them where they were supposed to take it. Just a short distance, a mile and a half, then turn right—a turn that Briato' slowed down to take at barely ten miles per hour, to keep from tipping over—and then another half a mile to a parking lot that looked pretty much abandoned. In the distance, close to the ramshackle enclosure wall, they'd find a two-bay garage—four simple walls of reinforced concrete and a slab of sheet metal for a roof—and there they were to park and wait for the Casalesi.

They climbed down from the tanker truck but stayed inside the garage, because those were their orders. The sun was setting and the sheet-metal roof was blasting a wave of heat down at the three of them that made the T-shirts with eyeholes cut in them cling to their chests. Later, when they told Nicolas the story, they couldn't say how long they'd had to wait in that blast furnace. Certainly, when they finally heard the roar of the motorcycle and hands banging on the metal strips of the garage doors, the light outside was a dot in the distance that backlit the silhouettes of the two Casalesi as they got off the bike. The *paranzini* didn't really know what to expect and their imagination had galloped away with them over the past few days, but still they were disappointed when they saw two unshaven, beer-bellied, short little men wearing stupid Hawaiian shirts and capri pants. They looked like they'd just disembarked from a discount cruise ship.

"Fuck, then, it really is true that you're kids! *Muccusielle siete*," said one of the two Casalesi, calling them a bunch of snotnoses.

Briato' and Pesce Moscio stared at them without speaking.

"What the fuck are you wearing?" asked Briato'. The adrenaline from the day was still pumping and his survival instincts had been somewhat dulled.

"You don't like?"

"*Nzu*," he replied, with a rising *n*, his tongue clicking between his two front teeth while his lips closed almost as if to give a kiss, and the sound came out of his nose more than his mouth.

"Strange, because your mother sees to my wardrobe," and he waved his hand in his partner's direction. "Give them these five thousand euros and then you get the hell out of here. Go on. *Jatevenne*."

"What did you say?" cried Pesce Moscio and Stavodicendo in unison.

"Why, doesn't that suit you, *moccusi*'? Already it's disgusting that I negotiated with 'o Maraja and he's not here, so just thank the Virgin Mary—*'a Maronna*—that we're giving you any money at all."

"Right here you've got forty thousand euros in gasoline," said Pesce Moscio. He needed to redeem himself and he didn't retreat when the Casalese stepped toward him.

"We're not giving you anything."

The other man, who'd remained silent till then, said: "Wait, do you know where we come from?"

"I know," he answered. "From Casal di Principe."

"Exactly. *A voi piccirilli ve magnammo e poi ve cacammo.*" We'll eat you small fry whole, and then we'll shit you out.

Briato' chambered a round in the pistol and said: "I couldn't give a fuck where you two come from. You just need to give us the money, the money, and that's that." And he pressed the Viking's barrel against the fuel tank on the trailer, the way he had with the gas station attendant's forehead. "If you don't set that cash down now, on the ground, I'll shoot into this fuel tank and we'll all go up in flames. You, us, and the whole garage."

"Put down the pistol, dummy. Come on, I'll give you eight thousand euros, you beggars."

"Fifteen thousand. And I'm giving you a hell of a bargain, *omm' 'e merda.* You piece of shit."

"*Nun 'e ttenimmo, nun 'e ttenimmo.*" We don't have it, the Casalese who had spoken first repeated as he backed away toward the motorbike.

"Hey, Hawaiian boy, look for the money, I bet you've got it," said Pesce Moscio.

"He said we don't have it. Take the eight thousand and try to avoid getting hurt."

Pesce Moscio pulled out his Viking, yanked back on the slide, and pulled the trigger. The noise was deafening, and Stavodicendo had the time to think that a tanker truck exploding, though, really ought to have been even louder. Then he realized that Pesce Moscio had aimed at one of the front tires. The two Casalesi had hurled themselves to the pavement with their hands over their heads, as if that was going to protect them in any way from ten thousand gallons of blazing gasoline. As soon as they realized that it had only been a warning shot, they got to their feet, brushed off their shirts, lifted the saddle of their motorbike, and pulled out the stack of cash they kept there.

"You see?" said Briato'. "All you needed to do was look, you had your ATM right there, under your seat, the whole time."

The fifteen thousand euros that Nicolas had taken off them, he had then proceeded to divide up into ten stacks after he'd handed five to the ship captain.

"We'll just set an all-in price, how's that sound? *Facciamo 'o forfait*," the captain had said. And *'o forfait* included the exclusive use of a boat normally meant for parties, weddings, and cruises around the Bay of Naples. The boat could carry almost two hundred people, and Nicolas wanted it all for just his *paranza* and their girlfriends. They'd set sail in two hours, just before sunset, and they'd sail around Ischia, swinging close by Capri and Sorrento. The agency wouldn't be able to take down the decorations from last night's wedding in time, but they'd throw in *aperitivi* and dinner, complete with two waiters. Nicolas said he'd take it, wedding decorations and all. In fact, so much the better, he thought to himself. He'd taken care of personally selecting the sound track for their cruise around the bay. Pop music, strictly in Italian. Tiziano Ferro. Eros Ramazzotti. Vasco Rossi. Laura Pausini. They were going to dance all night, clinging tight, and they'd remember it as the most wonderful evening of their lives.

The captain of the boat had decided that those youngsters were perfect specimens of the Neapolitan rich kids who jammed Instagram full of overblown images. Spoiled kids with more money than they knew how to spend. He soon changed his mind, when they showed up as a group. And he saw things clearly when, now out on the open water, at a gesture from the one who was clearly their leader, they all pulled out their pistols and started riddling the water with bullets. They were shooting at dolphins. Their girlfriends had tried to object: "*Sono così bellilli!*" They're so cute! they'd cried in dialect. But it was clear that they were proud of their boyfriends, who could afford to shoot at whomever they pleased, even those magnificent creatures. The captain had witnessed the whole scene from start to finish, and when he saw the dolphins, unharmed, knifing away through the water reddened only by the imminent sunset, he was uninterested in concealing his relief. "Captain," the tallest one asked him as he was jamming his gun back down his pants, "can you eat dolphin the way you eat tuna?"

On the main roofed deck, garlands and festoons of fake flowers were intertwined with satin ribbons. On the tables, there were still bunches of yellow and pink roses from the previous event. Pesce Moscio sat at one of the tables and performed the gesture of adjusting his tie, though he wore none, then he spread both hands out on the tablecloth and banged his right palm against the tabletop to draw the staff's attention. One of the waiters came over and filled his flute with champagne. Dentino and Biscottino, the only ones who hadn't brought a date, emulated him at the same table. Biscottino tried to act like quite the bon viveur, but after tossing back that glass of bubbly he squinted his eyes and then opened his mouth, smacking his lips.

The waiters asked if they could start serving dinner, and the three sitting at the table looked for Nicolas, who was leaning against the ship's railing, with Letizia at his side.

"Should we get started?" Pesce Moscio shouted in his direction.

"Let the party begin!" said Drago', both hands held up like a megaphone. And Nicolas gave his approval. There was then a general rush for the tables, one couple at each. But once they sat down, they felt lonely, isolated. That evening of all times, when they were all there together, on the salt water of the bay, in the dying light that made the distances incandescent and things closer to hand heartbreaking. They tried calling out to each other, from one table to another: "Hey, Mr. Stavodicendo, how's it going down there?"

"Ah, Dotto', Tuca', take it easy with all that *sciampagna!*" saying "champagne" as if it were written and pronounced like an Italian word. Then they all got up and moved to two tables next to each other. Pesce Moscio stuck a yellow rose behind his ear and declared that they were all ready for the dishes they'd ordered now. Let the meal begin. The waiter served the salmon.

"Try to behave like gentlemen," Nicolas advised them, poking his head into the dining room, "because now you really have become gentlemen," and then he went back out onto the deck with Letizia.

She snuggled close to him as they watched Mount Vesuvius shrink into the distance, veiled with evening mist. The whole city lit up in front of them. Just behind them, Ischia was entirely shrouded in the soft dark shape of Mount Epomeo.

Nicolas took Letizia by the hand and led her to the stern of the boat. He was walking behind her now, both arms around her, and she, leaning against the railing, slid into his arms, pressed against him not without a whiff of gentle lust: just enough that Nicolas was able to read a request into it. Nicolas increased the pressure because he felt sure that's what she wanted. "*Viene cu mme,*" he whispered into her ear—come with me—as the others shouted and sang along with the songs pouring out of the speakers.

They found a private room belowdecks, with a velvet sofa, and over it a porthole through which came the last light of day. Letizia sat down right on the edge of the sofa and Nicolas kissed her long and hard and ran his hands under her dress, in search of an easy point of access.

"Let's do it right this time," Letizia said, looking him in the eye. "With our clothes off."

Nicolas didn't know whether he should be worried about that "Let's do it right this time," about that sudden and unusual emergence from dialect into proper Italian, or about the simple but imperious request for nudity, because, for that matter, it's true that as long as they'd been doing it, they'd always made love half-dressed. Lots of other times Letizia had asked him if they could be alone, really alone, alone the whole night through, and it had never happened. This was the right opportunity. She pushed him away gently and unbuttoned his shirt.

"I want to look at you," she told him, and he unbuckled his belt, and as he was fiddling around with getting his pants off, he echoed the sentiment: "And I want to look at you." They lay down naked on the green velvet and explored each other with unaccustomed patience. Letizia caressed his sex and guided Nicolas's hand between her legs, and she had to apply determined pressure to make sure his hand stayed there and the fingers started moving. "Come to me," she said at last, and guided him into her. "Gently, gently, gently," she repeated, and he obeyed.

"You're my guy," Letizia whispered to him, and he especially liked the word she had chosen to use, *maschio*, which is related to both *macho* and *masculine*, not *uomo*, the more standard word for man: there are already too many *uomini*, but far too few *maschi*. As if he'd been summoned by some sweet and gentle inner ghost, he realized for the first time that she was a woman and that he was inside that woman, both of them mingled in the gentle light that was filling with stars inside the porthole.

When they came back out onto the deck, the ship had just passed the high rock cliffs of Sorrento and was steering for Naples. The kids were all at the bow.

"Let's drink to us," shouted Drago', "and to our city—*che è la cchiù bella d' 'o munno.*" The most beautiful city on earth.

They turned toward one of the two waiters, who was sitting, yawning, behind the glass, and went on: "*Oinè*, wake up! This the most beautiful city on earth, *capito*? And to hell with anyone who says anything bad about it!"

"*Sputtanatoli di merda*," said Drone with a vicious glare, accusing him of somehow deriding his beloved Naples. Meanwhile, the waiter got to his feet, trying to appeal to his colleague for help, as if to say: "What did we do wrong?"

"I'd never leave this place," said Nicolas, all gooey with his love for Letizia.

Drago' leaned over the railing and windmilled his right arm, as if he were about to throw a weight, a grenade, as far as he could, toward dry land.

"I see them, those tremendous fuckers, the ones who go to Rome, to Milan, the ones who look down on us, spit on us. I see them clearly, those 'Naples spitters,' those *sputtanapoli!*" he shouted. "And you know what I say to them? They have to die. All the *sputtanapli* have to die."

They all held their champagne flutes high and then tossed them into the waves. They danced until dawn, as the ship was pulling into port, and the *paranzini* and their girlfriends swore eternal faithfulness, in a collective exchange of wedding vows, in a ceremony of lifelong loyalty.

The days that followed were a long process of emerging from the coddled atmosphere they'd settled into on the cruise. This time each of them, in his own way, did his best to prolong as far as possible the honeymoon that had begun on the waters of the Bay of Naples.

Nicolas was heading over to Letizia's when the *paranza's* chat lit up on his phone. They were telling him to hurry over to Cardarelli Hospital, third floor, Pavilion A, with no more information than that. He texted Letizia to cancel their date. Then, immediately after that, another text: "I love you to the sun and the stars." And he reversed direction.

Waiting for him on the steps outside Cardarelli Hospital were Drago',

Dentino, and Lollipop. They were passing around an unlit joint, to get the smell in their noses and the taste on the tips of their tongues, indifferent to the glances of relatives and nurses. They had the look on their faces of someone who has something to say but doesn't know where to begin.

"What the fuck happened?" asked Nicolas, and beckoned for the joint. They threw their arms wide and pointed to an indeterminate point two floors higher up.

"They got injured. Briato' and Pesce Moscio," said Drago'.

Nicolas exploded; the sense of peace that the cruise instilled in him had already evaporated. He tossed the joint into the bushes lining the staircase and was tensing his legs to lash out at a lightpost with a kick when he got control of himself. His rage, too, had evaporated: what remained was Nicolas the opportunist, the one who managed to bring his adversaries over to his way of thinking, the soccer player who managed to catch the goalie off guard. He still hadn't set his foot back on the ground, and in that position he reminded Dentino of a heron, like the one he'd seen a few years ago while out with his class on a field trip to a WWF wild bird preserve.

Nicolas finally set his foot down on the step and said: "*Cuagliu'*, let's go visit the wounded men, and take them their presents." Uttering the word *wounded* made him feel that he was at war. And he liked it.

The presents were an old sexy calendar for Briato' and a jersey autographed by the team captain of S.S.C. Napoli for Pesce Moscio.

"*Guagliu'*, what happened?" Nicolas asked again, this time addressing his men who'd been wounded in battle.

"The Capelloni came into the back room," Briato' began. "We were making a bet, we had two scores we were sure of, when 'o White appears and starts staying: 'What the fuck are you doing?'"

"No, no," Pesce Moscio interrupted, "the exact words he said were: 'You've laid hands on Roipnol's gasoline.' We answered him: 'We didn't do a thing, *adda murì mammà*, what are you talking about?' At that point, Maraja, they pulled out these metal clubs, and I said to myself, okay, I'm a dead man already. Stavodicendo was hiding in the bathroom. Once he realized the way things were going to turn out, he exited through the window, piece of shit that he is—*che omm' 'e mmerda.*"

The Capelloni had taken Briato' and Pesce Moscio and broken their legs. Then they'd gone to Borgo Marinari and shattered the plate-glass windows of the restaurant where Stavodicendo's father worked.

Briato' tried to sit up straight, but he collapsed once again on his pillows. "They beat us bloody, I could feel the bones in my broken legs. And then they kept telling us to give 'em the money, give 'em the money, and they were going to town on us, really. I couldn't feel my legs anymore, but I couldn't feel my face, either, nothing. Then they put us in the car and dropped us off here at Cardarelli."

"In the car, I didn't understand a thing," said Pesce Moscio, "but 'o White kept saying that he was saving our lives, and that he knows us, and that Roipnol wanted to write our name on the ground, and that . . ."

Briato' interrupted him: "He kept saying the same thing over and over again, that he was saving our asses . . . and that now we had to start working for him if we were ever able to walk again."

"Yes, like fuck," Nicolas replied. He grabbed the calendar and leaned it against the wall. "Briato', what month do you like best? April has a nice pair of tits, right? Take a look at Lisella, you'll see how much better you feel right away."

"'O Maraja," said Briato', "when I get out of here, I'm going to be lame in one leg."

"When you get out of here, you'll only be stronger."

"Stronger, my ass."

"Then we'll get a bionic leg implanted surgically," said Drago'.

They joked around a little longer, they harassed a nurse, telling her that with the hands she had on her, they'd even let her insert a catheter, and once she'd left and they were all alone they looked at Maraja to find out what to do next.

"*Amm' 'a jettà 'n terra a Roipnol,*" and he turned the calendar to the month of June. Let's go lay out Roipnol.

They all burst out laughing as if it were just yet another joke.

"*Amm' 'a jettà 'n terra a Roipnol,*" Maraja said again. He'd leafed quickly through the calendar until he'd reached November, then he'd admired December for a while, and now he was leafing through the others.

Dentino laughed again and said: "But that guy never even goes outside."

"Maraja, 'o vò capì?" Pesce Moscio piled on, asking Maraja to understand the situation. He was trying to sit up, but his leg darted a stabbing pain every time he moved. "We're the only ones out on the street," he went on. "*Micione sta int' 'a gabbia a San Giovanni,*" he said, emphasizing the term *int' 'a gabbia,* stuck in a cage. "L'Arcangelo is stuck in a cage in Ponticelli, Copacabana is stuck in a cage in Poggioreale, and Roipnol is stuck in a cage in Forcella. We're out on the street. We just need to split it up among us."

"We need to catch him in a cage," said Maraja. He was starting to connect the dots, Maraja was. The fact that the Capelloni hadn't killed Briato' and Pesce Moscio meant that they'd been ordered not to. Micione was fighting for his territory, and three corpses from a single *paranza* would have caused too much uproar: he already had the police and the carabinieri hot on his trail, he couldn't afford to attract more attention from them with new bloodbaths. Micione was in no position to kill anyone, and he wouldn't be for a while now. Here was the opportunity, here was the space that no one else would ever dream of exploiting.

"Eh, impossible," said Drago'. "Roipnol's always assholes and elbows with Carlito's Way whenever he goes out. And plus, too, he never even goes out. La Culona doesn't go out much, either, and she always has a bodyguard when she does."

"Then we need to bribe Carlito's Way."

"No!" Lollipop interrupted him. "Carlito's Way won't betray. Roipnol pays him too much, and now that he's his butler, Carlito's Way is even acting like a boss all over Naples."

"He doesn't have to betray."

"You're high," said Dentino.

"Even when I'm high, I'm not high. I think straight."

"So, let's hear what the philosopher has to say."

"*Adda murì mammà,* I've got the key to open the door to Roipnol's apartment."

"For real?" asked Dentino. "Well, you're wrong about that, because it's a steel-reinforced door, and there's a forest of video cameras."

"But I have the real key," Nicolas went on. He'd slid his arms around Drago's and Dentino's shoulders, and he'd maneuvered them over to the two bedridden *paranzini*, with Lollipop closing the circle. Conspirators.

He asked in the tone of voice you use to ask a child a super-simple riddle: "Who's the brother of Carlito's Way?"

"Who is it?" said Briato'. "Pisciazziello?"

"And who's Pisciazziello best friends with?"

"Biscottino," Briato' answered again.

"Exactly," said Maraja. "Tomorrow morning I'm going to go grab Biscottino."

I'LL BE GOOD

Nicolas had everything clear in his mind, as if he'd found the precise equation. It was just a matter of convincing Biscottino, and in order to do that, he'd have to take him out and about, something the two of them had never done before. He made sure he was waiting right outside the school. Biscottino's mother took him to school every morning, because she wanted to make sure that he got there, safely, to class. She didn't trust her son's friends. Since she had to work, though, she couldn't get there to take him home. As soon as he saw the T-Max, Biscottino elbowed his way through his classmates crowding onto the stairs.

"Oh, Maraja! *Che staje facenno?*" What are you doing?

"Hop on, I'll take you home." Biscottino climbed on the back, proudly. The T-Max took off with a screech of rubber, and Biscottino let out a shout, while Nicolas laughed with gusto. After all, he was about to ask a lot of him, better to start out by giving him a treat. He chose the longest route. He drove slowly, stopping at traffic lights, easing into curves. He wanted to keep him on the powerful scooter because Biscottino was happy and it would make it easier to talk to him.

"Biscotti', everyone's saying that Mellone was rubbed out because he was with us."

"But wasn't he against us?"

"Exactly. But that bastard Roipnol—who's definitely with 'o White and the Capelloni—he's just now getting the dick that we slid into his ass out, and he's trying to turn it around and stick it up ours. That bastard! Now it's up to you to solve this thing."

With the word *you*, he revved up and took off, darted around a car, then another, bumped up onto the sidewalk to maneuver around a truck, and then slowed back down to the minimum speed he'd largely imposed on himself.

Biscottino's heart was pounding so powerfully that Nicolas could feel it through his back.

"Me? What do you mean?"

"Well, for instance, who is your best buddy?"

"Pisciazziello? . . . You mean Teletabbi?"

"Pisciazziello, exactly. And Pisciazziello's brother is Roipnol's bodyguard."

The T-Max screeched to a halt. Biscottino smacked his face against Maraja's shoulder blades, and before he could lodge a complaint, Nicolas had pulled over the median and was now riding along in the opposite direction.

"You need to go see Pisciazziello," he said, "and you need to tell him that after the murder of 'o Mellone, no one trusts me or our *paranza* anymore, and you can tell him that we wouldn't give you a market, a piazza, either. And you need to tell him that you want to work with him and that you can only talk about it with Roipnol himself. You need to get Pisciazziello to open the door for you. And then, the minute you're inside, you take out your gun and you shoot him."

He slammed his brakes on again, but this time Biscottino braced himself in advance with both hands. He wanted to shout, but in excitement. He felt like he was at an amusement park. Nicolas whipped the bike around in the opposite direction again, and now they were back in the lane they'd arrived in.

"But what does Pisciazziello know about anything? His brother's always outside the door, not him," Biscottino finally managed to get out, regaining a more comfortable posture, with his back straight, but Nicolas accelerated brusquely and zipped along down the center line of the road at 55 m.p.h. Traffic was getting tighter and the side mirrors of the cars were grazing the T-Max's handlebar.

"Carlito's Way goes around to collect money for Roipnol. That means he leaves him unguarded for a certain period." He fell silent and looked into the mirror. "You're shitting your pants at the idea of doing this piece of work, aren't you, Biscottino?! You can tell me, eh! There's no problem, we can find another solution."

"No, I'm not shitting my pants," Biscottino replied.

"What?"

"I'm not shitting my pants!"

"What? I didn't hear you!"

"I'M NOT SHITTING MY PANTS!!!"

Without slowing down, Nicolas pulled all the way over onto the right and continued along slowly, just as he'd started out, until he got Biscottino back home.

The equation had been solved.

Since the day they'd moved, Crescenzio Roipnol had never set foot outside their new home. His wife upbraided him for being a shut-in, and he had promised her he'd break that isolation. The truth was that Roipnol was too damned scared to go out. In fact, he was terrified, and he did his best to combat his terror with pills, but then he'd just started slurring his words more than usual, and that only pissed off Maddalena worse. A vicious circle, from within which, however, Crescenzio still managed to command the quarter, run the markets, and other solid resistance to Maraja's *paranza*. The hardest thing for Roipnol was managing to repress his urge to exterminate these kids. No murders, o' Micione had told him. Okay, Roipnol had replied, and he really couldn't say anything else. Roipnol's army was a scattered force. Loyal, powerful, but dispersed in all directions

because it was required to control and contain, two contrasting movements that at times like these could conflict and create unexpected fric-
tion. Even cracks and fissures.

What Biscottino saw—leaning against the same wall from which he
had just a short time before witnessed the transfer of the Madonna of
Pompeii—he might not necessarily call a crack, or even a fissure, but certainly a fuckup, a *strunzata*. How could it be that Roipnol, someone who
thought he was a king, could allow his page boy, Carlito's Way, to stay out
on his rounds for two hours, when he was just going down to pick up the
betting proceeds from the back room? Could someone who operated all
those markets and took credit for murders he'd had nothing to do with rely
on a chump like Pisciazziello to do his shopping and pay his bills? Perhaps,
Biscottino concluded with a thought that filled him with pride, Roipnol
deserved to die because he didn't know how to command his men.

When he arrived in Forcella the next day, he leaned the motor scooter
that Lollipop had let him borrow not far from the entrance to the Church
of Santa Maria Egiziaca, the one that opened out onto Corso Umberto.
He told himself church. He told himself saints. He told himself Madonna. He told himself Baby Jesus. He told himself why not. In there,
people help themselves, in there people make promises, in there people
seek confirmation, and with a shambling step he went in. It was a church
he knew, but only in a manner of speaking. Like everyone, he was accustomed to the gold, the sumptuousness of the images, and the profusion of
decorations: even to his friends from Scampia, Naples was the churches,
the apartment buildings, the gray and the ashy flames of the piperno stone,
all that beauty with no other purpose than to be beautiful. Beauty mixed
with holiness, superstition, and hope. And it was hope that drove Biscottino
into the church in search of saints, male and female, Madonnas, any interlocutor. He was overwhelmed by the images and colors, by the sweeping
gestures of fleshy arms, the sky blues carved out of the gold, the faces of
piety and martyrdom. He tried with the Madonna, or actually with the
Madonnas, but not a word came out of his mouth, he didn't know how
to put himself in touch with Her. "Madonna of the *Paranza* . . ." he said,

gazing at the sweet figure who perfumed the air from on high. He stopped, with nothing more to say. Or, rather, he postponed that prayer, as if he could only climb to those heights with patience, step by step. He searched for a saint, a recognizable saint, but to no effect. In the arms of Madonnas and saints, he saw the Christ Childs, the Baby Jesuses—those he could make out clearly. Without taking his eyes off the light that came pouring in through the cupola and the large windows along the aisles, he focused on a Christ Child, which actually sort of looked like him, though he'd never admit it to anyone. He straightened the collar of his T-shirt, adjusted the pistol stuck down his shorts, ran his hand over his head, and checked to make sure that the two little old ladies kneeling in their pews were paying him no attention. He let himself be inspired by the peace and quiet that magically settled him inside the church, as if it were a space protected from the outside world, even though that world could still be heard, its noise automobile traffic. "Jesus," he tried saying, and then repeated it: "Jesus." He remembered the gesture of prayer but couldn't seem to put his hands together, they wouldn't stay together, palm against palm, they just hung in the air. "Jesus, St. Cyrus, St. Dominic, St. Francis, let me go upstairs to see that asshole, and let the asshole come outside, let me tell him to go and let him go." In truth, he had a hard time envisioning the scene in these exact terms, Roipnol leaving, La Culona following him, but his prayer could only reach the boundaries of what was possible, and if he'd gone into the church for anything, it was to ensure that he could keep the Desert Eagle tucked away in his pants where it sat now, and that words might be enough. The word that can move the earth, when it wishes, when it can. That's why people pray, isn't it? Wasn't that why? And at that point another thought entered his mind. "Baby Jesus," he went on, "someday let me have a *paranza* all my own." He tried to add a promise since, he knew, if you ask for something, you have to give something in exchange. No words came to him, and so he ended his speech by repeating words that came to him in an ancient voice, a voice that was ancient even in him, even though he was a child. He said: "I'll be good." And that goodness presented itself to his eyes as a hero of the people, a Masaniello, someone with a sword, a superhero who took to the air from San Martino sopra Spaccanapoli and soared down over Sanità, swooping under the bridge. A bloody Christ, the rope that had lashed Him to the Column still hanging from His neck, seemed to look at him with understanding and pity. Luckily, He was confined in a glass display case. "I'll be good," he said again, and then left the church as quickly as he had entered it.

He knew he'd have no difficulty finding Pisciazziello in the general area, because La Culona thought of him as a sort of adopted son—her husband had been in prison too long, and now it was too late for her to have one of her own—and she liked having him around, just so she could play at having a family. And you trust your own son, don't you? Biscottino saw him just now, entering Roipnol's apartment house, and he ran to catch him. He explained that he wanted to work with that crew, playing the part that Nicolas had told him to play. And he did it very well, singsonging the words as he had in church. Pisciazziello must have mistaken that tone of voice for true desperation, because he just kept saying: "Why, of course . . ." Of course, he'd take him up, he'd even do it right now. He was heading there himself.

They galloped up the stairs and, in front of the armor-reinforced door, Pisciazziello looked up into the video camera.

"Signo', this is Biscottino, a friend of mine. He's shitting his pants now that Roipnol took down 'o Mellone. He says he's afraid that everyone who works with 'o Maraja's *paranza* are going to wind up the same way." Without realizing it, he'd used the same tone of voice that Biscottino had just used, and La Culona's metallic voice replied: "And right he is to be afraid. *Picciri'*, come on in."

Pisciazziello turned the handle and the door swung open. He took a step forward, but Biscottino grabbed him by the T-shirt and said, covering his mouth with one hand so the video camera couldn't read his lips: "*Tengo scuorno*—I'm ashamed—of doing it in front of you, I'd rather go in by myself." Pisciazziello stopped at the threshold. He seemed uncertain. What he was about to say would determine how that day went. If he'd insisted on going in with him, what would happen next? "Sweet Jesus . . ." Biscottino said to himself.

"Okay," Pisciazziello replied, "we'll see you round," and went downstairs.

Biscottino remained in the doorway for a few seconds, the time it required to feel certain Pisciazziello hadn't changed his mind, and then he entered the apartment, using the voices of Roipnol and his wife to guide him. He immediately recognized the furniture that he'd glimpsed from the street during the move-in and he could still smell fresh paint. La Culona was sitting comfortably on the Pompeiian red sofa, while Roipnol leaned over a dark hardwood desk. The half-closed shutters let a narrow shaft of light into the room and more light came from a standing lamp in the corner. In the interplay of shadows thus created, Roipnol's face seemed to be cut in two, day and night. That man with slumping shoulders and the facial features of an asp—tiny, close-set eyes, thin lips curved in a feral smile, shiny flesh—now practically resembled a Viking. He seemed neither surprised nor frightened, and for that matter La Culona had maintained her composure. Biscottino recited his phrase: "We're in charge now. You and La Culona need to clear out."

"Ah, that's news to me," said Roipnol, but speaking to his wife. Now the line of sight framed his ear, the back of his head, his freshly dyed hair. "You were still in your father's balls when I was defending your quarter by gutting 'o Boa. I was the one who kept our Mangiafuoco, from Sanità." Then he turned to look at Biscottino again. "Whoever sent you, you need to go back and tell them that Forcella is mine by right!"

"No one sent me," Biscottino replied. He'd taken a step forward, the slightest movement, to get better aim.

"*Muccusie',*" said Roipnol, calling him a little snotnose, and turning once again toward his wife, "how the hell do you dare?"

"You're going to get hurt, Roipnol." Another short step.

"Oh, oh, do you hear how this little *muschillo*"—the Neapolitan term for a child dope pusher—"roars. Do you think I'm afraid of a child like you?"

"It took me ten years to become a child, but it'll take me just a second to shoot you in the face."

The burst of flame from the Desert Eagle took a snapshot of the room. Roipnol openmouthed, both hands on his face as if he could do anything to protect it. La Culona, unexpectedly agile, throwing herself on her husband, she, too, laboring under the illusion that she could protect him. Then everything went back to shadow and light. Biscottino ran out of the living

308 | ROBERTO SAVIANO

room, and that's where he stopped, glued to the spot. He turned around
and went back, lifted the gun again, and took a bead on La Culona's ass
cheeks. Would the air leak out of those two beach balls? he wondered.
The bullet went straight into the right buttock, but no air came out. Disappointed, Biscottino finished off La Culona with a shot to the back of
the head.

He flew across the apartment and down the stairs with the headlong
speed of his ten years, ramming into door frames and railings, but he felt
nothing.

There it was, the front entrance, a few steps, ten feet, maybe. He could
already see the street, and then he couldn't anymore, because just then
Pisciazziello was coming back in with a *krapfen*—a doughnut—in his
hand.

The Desert Eagle was still hot, it was scorching Biscottino's skin, and
he thought for one insane second about pulling it out and eliminating this
witness, too.

"But what happened? Were those gunshots? What did you do?"

Biscottino's friend had stared at him, his face dusted with confectioner's
sugar. Biscottino kept running, tossing over his shoulder just *"Magnat' 'a
kraffa."* Eat your doughnut.

BROTHERS

The 'O Sole Mio beauty salon had a very limited website. A couple of photographs and a cell phone number. The girl who'd answered Lollipop's phone call had made him tell her twice that they were supposed to keep the beauty salon reserved until closing time—the whole place. *"Amm' 'a festeggià 'nu battesimo!"* He'd repeated that they were celebrating a baptism. The girl seemed more and more baffled: *"'Nu battesimo?* At a beauty salon? *Ma che stai pazziando?* Is this a prank?"

Lollipop had ended the call, and then he'd shown up ten minutes later, holding out two thousand euros to the girl, all in hundred-euro notes. Then he'd sent out the message over the chat:

Lollipop
Guagliù, this afternoon everyone comes to
celebrate Biscottì's baptism. Let's all go get a
suntan!

The message reached the *paranza* loud and clear:

Maraja
Uà, way too cool!!

Biscottino
Hai scassato i ciessi!!!

Stavodicendo
Wow, I'm going to get a full-body waxing!!

At three on the dot, when the shop was scheduled to reopen, the girl saw Tucano and Stavodicendo, first through the door, carrying in their crossed forearms the guest of honor. All three of them had their hair cut like Genny Savastano, and behind them appeared Nicolas with a red inflatable crown on his head that made him look really tall. Lollipop and Drone had popped it onto his head just outside the door. Right after him came Drago' and Dentino, covered with gold bracelets and necklaces that made them resemble nothing so much as the Madonna of Loreto, shouting: "Happy birthday, Biscotti', you're a big boy now!"

They all took a turn under the tanning lamps, then came a pedicure, a face wax, and a body wax, and finally they rolled a couple of joints in the relaxation room, all buddy-buddy. For Biscottino's baptism of fire, they'd brought a little baggie of pink cocaine they wanted the birthday boy, the guest of honor, to try. Nicolas pulled the baggie out of his bathrobe pocket and laid out a line on the teak bench, inviting Biscottino to enjoy the first dance: "We scratched the back of the Pink Panther, and look what a nice baggie of *sfuoglio* came out!" *Sfuoglio*: top-quality coke.

Biscottino took his first snort; to start with, he was handling it well, but before five minutes were up, he started jumping around, doing handstands and cartwheels all over the room, until the others couldn't take anymore of that activity and sent him off to take a nice long sensory shower.

While they were swinging in the hammocks, without a hair left on their bodies, except for Dentino, who'd insisted on keeping the hairs on his chest where a gold medallion swung on a chain, big enough to extend from nipple to nipple, Lollipop asked: "But why don't you take some of this money and fix your teeth, instead of wasting it all on these gold chains?"

"This way the girls like me better. I have a window in my mouth and they can see what I have inside me."

"We can all see the disgusting mess you have inside you clear as day," Lollipop retorted.

"What the fuck did you do to your teeth in the first place?" asked Drone.

It was a story Dentino never told. But since he'd started to be feared, to have a little money and a steady girlfriend, he didn't mind the defect anymore, it had become his distinguishing feature.

"I was playing basketball, right? And then I got in a fight with some asshole, and at a certain point he hit me in the face with the ball. Do you know how much a basketball weighs? It broke my two front teeth, one on top and one on the bottom."

"No, what the fuck, there's no way you were playing basketball! Who'd believe that! You're only a yard and change tall in the first place!"

"Oh, go fuck yourself," Dentino retorted. Then he turned around to look at Tucano, and he decided to ask a question he'd been wondering about for some time: "What about you, Tuca', why do they call you that?"

Tucano didn't look even a little like a toucan: his nose was small, his beard apostolic. It's just that one day, while he was riding on his scooter with Briato' behind him, an insect flew into his mouth. He started spitting, in the throes of retching, then he pulled over, jammed two fingers down his throat, trying to find the bug that kept fluttering and struggling against his palate and his tongue. Once he finally managed to get rid of the insect, he came out with this phrase: *"Ua'! M'era finito 'nu tucano in bocca!"* Wow, a toucan flew into my mouth.

Briato' had laughed till the tears streamed down his cheeks over that mispronounced *"tucano"* for *tafano*, or horsefly, and so the name Massimo Rea had been deleted from the collective consciousness of all those who knew him, and he had instead simply become Tucano.

"What about Briato', why do we call him that . . . ?"

Nicolas got out of the hammock and Lollipop said: "Silence, everyone, the king is about to speak."

Maraja, arranging the crown on his head, explained: "I was there. It was the last day of eighth grade and our science teacher asked everyone in the class to take turns saying what we wanted to be when we grew up. Everyone's reeling off lawyer, chef, soccer player, city commissioner . . . And all Briato' said was: 'Flavio Briatore.'"

Then Nicolas nodded his head and the others stood up. They went to join Biscottino in the sensory showers. He was lying belly down, under the jet of jasmine-scented water; every so often he'd open his mouth and take a drink. As soon as he saw them, he got up: "*Ué*, what the hell happened to you all?!" He kept touching his nose, as if he, too, had a horsefly up a nostril, and he looked at them in bewilderment.

They all got undressed together and suddenly found themselves naked, pressed up close. "Now let's measure ourselves," said Drone, waggling his big old dick and forcing all the others to look at it and look at the dicks of the other *paranzini*. They all automatically got in line, imitating Drone, dicks in hand and bellies outthrust. "Let's raise the flag!" and they all bent backward. "Break ranks!" Nicolas ordered, vanishing into the mist of steam emerging from the colorful shower stalls. Drago' grabbed Biscottino by the dick and dragged him around the room: "This'll make it get longer," he said, and the others all burst out laughing and then hurried into the showers, often in pairs, often moving from one shower stall to the next to try different colors or else to sample the sequence of aromas. Pesce Moscio concentrated and cut a fart, whereupon Drone pretended to die under a bright blue gush of beneficent waters.

"Do you like your party, Biscotti', are you having fun?" Nicolas asked him, and he pinched his cheek.

"Yeah, great . . . but where were you all?" he asked him.

"We were telling each other our stories, about how we got our names . . ."

Biscottino interrupted him: "Eh, in fact, I've always wondered why the fuck it is that Drone has such a great name. *Lo vulesse pure io accussì*— I wish I had one like that—because Biscottino really makes me puke!"

Drago', unrecognizable with his hair plastered down onto the top of his head by the spray jets, slapped Drone on the back: "Now this man earned his monicker. In all of Italy he's the only one who bought all thousand weekly inserts at two euros and ninety-nine cents from the series

Build Your Own Drone. Not only did he collect them all, he's the only one who ever managed to actually build the damned drone. And it even flew!"

"No, are you for real?" asked Biscottino, staring at Drone in amazement.

"*Ua'*, not even Dan Bilzerian has a drone!"

"What are you talking about, he has dozens. I'm one of his followers on Instagram."

"Me, too, and I've never seen a drone."

The masseuse, a girl Pesce Moscio would have liked, came in to tell them that 'O Sole Mio was closing, and that they needed to get dressed and go. The party was over. It would start up again a few hours later at the New Maharaja.

The city wears a crown on its head, a crown of buildings standing two, three, at the very most four stories tall, always waiting for an amnesty for their violations of the building code—settlements that have swollen until they've become towns. And all around them lies the countryside, a reminder of what the past must have been like for townships now attacked and suffocated by cement. It always surprised everyone, even those who weren't born there, that you need only take a couple of turns off the main road and you'd find yourself in the middle of farmland. And just a couple of miles in the opposite direction, Nicolas was bombarded by shafts of light as he bobbed his head to the beat of a song from the sixties, rearranged to a disco beat. Maraja was at the New Maharaja and he was pretending to enjoy himself at the graduation party for the son of the lawyer Caiazzo, legal talent for the Acanfora clan and the Strianos before they turned state's witnesses, as well as for the Faellas, soccer players, and VIPs of all sorts. The boy had majored in political science. His father had handled the drug-dealing case that had sent Alvaro behind bars. An hour earlier they'd finished their party for Biscottino. They'd surrounded him, locking their arms in a chain, and then taken turns dousing him with champagne. They'd drunk toasts to the piazzas, because now that Roipnol was dead those piazzas were going to belong to them. And then they'd drunk another toast to the health of Briato' and

Pesce Moscio, both wounded in combat. Last of all, they'd ejected the guest of honor, Biscottino, right out of the club: his present was waiting outside. His new scooter. But Counselor Caiazzo had brought a special gift for the whole *paranza*: the news of the conditional suspension of the guilty sentence from Maraja's old trial.

"Good work, Counselor," said Dentino.

"Moët e Chandon to celebrate," shouted Maraja, "two bottles . . . *amm' 'a festeggià!* We've got to party!"

"*Guagliu'*, it's a suspended sentence, it means that if you get sentenced again, they revoke the suspension, and you have to serve all those years."

They hoisted their glasses, crying: "Counselor, we're untouchable!"

Now Nicolas's head was elsewhere. He wouldn't be sitting down for more than two minutes at a time before he stood up, went into the private dining room, and then came back out, or he'd go and get an Acapulco— the lawyer's son had demanded that the party have a tropical theme— and then he'd go out and take a turn around the dance floor, put his arms around Letizia, exchange a few words with someone or other. But the whole time he kept one eye on his smartphone. The little numbers over the names in the chats kept clicking upward, but he was interested in only one name—a name that stayed at the bottom of his list. The DJ turned off the music and light filled the club; the time had come for Counselor Caiazzo to make a speech. The capillaries on his face were particularly prominent, and he'd unbuttoned his shirt almost all the way down to his belly button. Pathetic, thought Nicolas, but then when the lawyer called for silence and, a moment later, for a round of applause for his son, Maraja put down the Acapulco and clapped loudly, with conviction. Counselor Caiazzo had dragged a little white armchair to the foot of the canvas that depicted the Indian king, an armchair chosen at random out of the great abundance of chairs in the club—chairs that Oscar had made a great point of having reupholstered in a white fabric because, he said, this was a baptism. Caiazzo climbed up onto it and, as he tried to find a comfortable point of balance, started stepping on the cushion with his pair of suede Santonis.

"Thanks to you all," he said. "I see the faces of my friends, of my clients."

And someone behind Nicolas said: "Other faces, Counselor, can't be here, they're on an extended holiday . . ."

"Yes, I did my best, but we'll get them back here eventually! We'll get them back here, because I only represent innocent men."

Laughter.

"I'm so happy today to be celebrating the college degree of my son Filippo, now officially a graduate in Political Appliances."

Laughter.

"My daughter, Carlotta, has a degree in Letters and Postcards; and my eldest son, Gian Paolo, just didn't bother to get a degree, and now he runs a restaurant in Berlin. As you can see, they all decided to take their father as an object lesson: Don't turn out like me!"

More laughter. Nicolas was laughing, too, and in the meanwhile he brushed one hand over Letizia's ass while with the other, jammed in his pocket, he was waiting for his phone to vibrate.

"Anyway, Filippo, I have only the best wishes for you," the lawyer continued. "Enjoy this day and this party, a gift from Papà, and don't forget: You can always be unemployed tomorrow!"

A burst of laughter. The speech was over and the party could go on.

Letizia tried to drag Nicolas out onto the floor to dance because now the DJ had put on "Music Is the Power" and she couldn't keep her feet still. Nicolas was about to tell her that he really didn't feel like it that night, but Letizia was just so dreamy, wrapped tightly in that dress—and the way it left her whole back uncovered. Nicolas grabbed her from behind and gave her a lick on the back of the neck. She pretended to take offense and ran off, taking a few quick steps across the dance floor so her man would chase her, but just then Maraja's smartphone vibrated and this time it was the message he was expecting. A picture of a star-spangled sky and the words "The sky over my home is always the most beautiful sky on earth." Nicolas grabbed Letizia the same way he had before and, as she swayed her hips, rubbing up against him, he whispered in her ear: "If anyone asks about me, tell them that I'm in the private dining room. If they ask you in the private dining room, tell them I'm in the bathroom. If someone heads over to the bathroom, just say I'm out and about."

"But why, what are you getting up to?" asked Letizia, still dancing the whole time.

"Nothing, just a little errand. *'Nu servizio. Però hann' 'a sapé che sto ccà.* But it's important they think I'm still here. I'll explain later."

She watched him closely as he headed for the exit, in the alternating swaths of light and dark that made every motion isolated and unpredictable, confusing the bodies and making the faces overlap. And for an instant, as she danced with both arms high in the air, swinging her head from one side to the other, she thought she detected the flash of a stranger's glance upon her. Renatino, with his baby face, identical to the last time she'd seen him, around the time of the beshitting, and with a man's body in an army uniform. It was only an instant, then she lost sight of him, and on the opening notes of "Single Ladies" she ran to find Cecilia so they could imitate Beyoncé's choreography, any and all thoughts of Renatino forgotten.

Outside, a car was waiting for Nicolas. A navy-blue Fiat Punto, just like hundreds of others that you see go by on any street in any city. Behind the wheel was Scignacane, who without so much as a word of greeting let Nicolas get in on the passenger side. They took the Asse Mediano bypass. They drove out of the city. The song from before kept echoing in Nicolas's head. Only when he heard sheep bleating did he realize that he'd fetched up in another world. Scignacane parked the Punto on the side of the road and said: *"Jamm'a vedé sta pecora . . ."* Let's go take a look at this sheep.

They walked along, cutting across the fields. Scignacane navigated perfectly, checking to make sure he was setting his feet carefully by the light of the phone. Then, without warning, he came to a halt, so that Nicolas almost slammed into him. "Here he is, the sheep," said Scignacane.

He was sitting on a drystone wall that must once have served to mark off the land of a country home, now little more than a hovel, the walls half stoved in and with an improvised sheet-metal roof that downpours had folded in half. He was smoking calmly, and between one drag on his cigarette and the next, he was chatting with Drago', who sat next to him, checking his cell phone—that slightly crooked nose projected against the dark of the night every time he turned on the phone. In front of them, you could just make out a ditch, and they were amusing themselves by tossing in the rocks they'd piled up on the low wall. They looked like a couple of elementary school kids, Nicolas thought to himself.

It was the guy sitting next to Drago' who first noticed the presence of Nicolas and Scignacane. He turned his head and understood instantly. He turned back around to look for confirmation—if any were needed—in Drago's eyes, but Scignacane was already standing next to him, body against body.

"*Omm' 'e mmerda,*" he berated him. "Piece of shit, you ate at my house, behind my back."

"What are you talking about? I didn't do anything, anything at all, Scignaca'!"

Still sitting on the wall, he'd turned once again to confront Scignacane, who was now shouting into his face. Nicolas and Drago' were barring any escape route on either side. Behind him, only the ditch.

"Really? Nothing? Look at this," Scignacane went on, holding up a brightly glowing photo on his smartphone. "You recognize that? You recognize who this is?"

The guy tried to push his way through, shoving with his shoulders, but Nicolas and Drago' held him in place, gripping his arms and twisting them behind his back. Scignacane jammed his phone into the back pocket of his trousers and waved for the two of them to release him. The evening's weather had turned ugly and now the clouds were covering the moon, blocking even the faintest light from illuminating the scene. Even the sheep had stopped bleating. The only sound was the young men's breathing, and the even faster respiration of their prisoner. He no longer even tried to defend himself; this wasn't a situation that words could get him out of. Scignacane got a firm foothold on the uneven terrain and gave him a powerful shove that knocked him down into the ditch. He didn't wait for the guy to get back on his feet, he pulled out his pistol and fired at him, aiming the first bullet where he'd already decided it should go. In his face. But he only caught him in the cheekbone. An injury that disfigures and makes you scream in pain, but not a fatal gunshot. The guy in the ditch started apologizing, begging for mercy. He was spitting out words mixed with blood, blood that drained down his throat every time he tried to catch his breath. Only now did Nicolas notice that Scignacane was wearing latex gloves, and instinctively he wiped his palms against the fabric of his trousers.

Meanwhile, the guy in the ditch was shouting: "You shot me in the face! What the fuck is the matter with you!" But Scignacane wasn't done yet. In rapid succession, he fired, planting a bullet in his knee and another in his stomach. Nicolas couldn't help but think of Tim Roth in Harvey Keitel's arms, and just how long that agony could endure. How much blood is contained in a human body? He tried to reach back for a few glimmers of memory, but his thoughts were interrupted by Scignacane's last shot, which went straight into the guy's eye.

It took them an hour to fill the ditch back in, with shovels they'd found behind the hovel. The sheep had started bleating again.

Over the last few weeks, Dumbo and Christian had seen each other only a handful of times. And then nothing. Suddenly that friendship, which had entailed days at a time doing nothing, but doing it together, had evaporated. Christian hadn't dared to ask Nicolas anything: about the *paranza*, the hash, the weapons . . . everything came to him from Nicolas's lips, but it was Nicolas who decided when. It had always been that way between them, and anyway Christian knew that it wouldn't be long now before he'd get an invitation from his brother, an invitation to climb up onto another rooftop, with other weapons, to riddle other dish antennas full of holes.

Christian was lying on the bed, texting Dumbo, when Nicolas walked into the bedroom. His friend hadn't even read all those messages. The markers next to them continued to remain colorless. It was strange: Dumbo had never gone so long without checking his phone.

Nicolas had entered the bedroom the way he always did—shoving the door open with his shoulder, then kicking it shut behind him—and leaped into the air, landing on the bed. If they'd both extended their arms from each bed, they'd have been able to touch fingertips. Christian turned his head and saw the harsh profile of his brother's face pointing toward the ceiling. Then Nicolas closed his eyes and Christian followed suit. They lay there for a while, listening to each other breathe. It was the elder brother's prerogative to break that silence, and he did so by sliding his Air Jordans noisily off his feet, using his other foot each time. The shoes landed one atop the other. Christian opened his eyes, checked the color of the tabs on his smartphone one last time, and then clasped both hands behind his head. He was ready. He was listening.

"*Adda murì mammà! Scignacane mi ha scassato 'o cazzo,*" said Nicolas. I swear, Scignacane has fucking busted my balls but good. He'd uttered the obscenity *cazzo* as if exhaling excess air. He was getting something off his chest, and that oxygen projectile was mute testimony to the fact. Christian peeked over at his brother again. Nicolas was lying there motionless; only his lips were moving from time to time, in search of the right words. Christian turned back to stare at the ceiling, and he tried to focus on his own body. No, he didn't know to lie there like a dead man.

Christian knew the story of Scignacane very well. He knew it as a story come from afar, a war story, a rivalry, a match, a game he couldn't take part in, a battle in which his brother wore a helmet and a camo jumpsuit, and sometimes even carried a sword and wore a suit of armor. Christian had to stay there in the bedroom, maybe with his mother and father fighting within earshot, waiting for reports of what was happening at the barricades, on the borderline, in the citadel of *vicoli*. Everything had moved so quickly, lately. Nicolas's *paranza* had evolved and now it was dealing in heroin directly with the Acanforas of San Giovanni a Teduccio. With Scignacane. On more than one occasion, he'd wanted to ask the reason for that nickname, but he never had, maybe to keep from ruining the image that he'd constructed of the new king of San Giovanni. A sort of pokémon, half monkey and half dog, a capable runner, an unbeatable climber. And after all, the contact with Scignacane had come about through a piece of dumb luck, and thanks to none other than Dumbo. Dumbo had served a year in Nisida—and he hadn't talked, he hadn't given up anyone's name—and that's where he'd met him. This story, too, Christian had heard a million times, and every time that Dumbo himself told it to him—while he was giving him a ride on his Aprilia Sportcity or when they were stretched out, smoking a joint—he'd add another piece.

"He really is a piece of shit," Nicolas said again. And again Christian had turned to look at him lying on the bed in exactly the same position, but then he regretted doing it and turned quickly away: he didn't want his brother to catch him spying on him.

He's a piece of shit, Dumbo, too, had told Christian when he had asked him what this Scignacane was like. A piece of shit. Period. And Dumbo wouldn't say another word about him, which was strange for someone who liked to talk even when he shouldn't have, and maybe that's why Nicolas had chosen to keep him out of the *paranza*. In any case, Dumbo had wound up at the Nisida Reform School because, when he was thirteen years old, he'd helped his father loot a tile warehouse. Dentino and his father had taken part in the caper, too; they often worked on construction sites. But the two of them had managed to escape.

"Scignacane says that Dumbo fucked his mother, and that he's going around saying he did it, and that he even sent a picture of his dick to his mother's cell phone."

Christian didn't let his breath out, he didn't so much as move on the rumpled sheets, and this time he didn't even try to look over at Nicolas. This might be a trap. Perhaps right now Nicolas had turned his head and was waiting to meet his brother's glance, look him in the eyes—the same color, identical, the one physical trait they had in common—to learn the truth about Dumbo.

Dumbo told the same story. He said that La Zarina—Scignacane's mother—was crazy about him, and that he'd fucked that big old MILF, that's what he called her, *milfona*, more than once. "She's got a pair of tits on her that look like they were carved out of marble," he'd told Christian one day, right there in that bedroom. Then he'd made a gesture with his hands, making it clear that the ears that had earned him his nickname actually had nothing to do with being a faggot—*ricchione*, or big ears, Italian slang for gay men—as some people assumed.

Christian made an effort to interrupt the flow of thoughts and, without letting Nicolas see him doing it, took another look at his cell phone. Dumbo still hadn't read any of his messages . . .

". . . and then I went to visit Aza, at the arsenal. I don't want to go naked when I go to see Scignaca', *capisci?* If that guy finds out I'm in cahoots with the Grimaldis, he'll kill me. And then he kept calling me, where are you? *Fa' ampress'!, t'aggi' 'a parlà subito.*" Hurry up, I need to talk to you right away. Then Nicolas concluded: "*Capisci?*" You understand?

He understood, Christian did. And every time that his brother would tell him something and then end the phrase with "*capisci?*" a shiver ran through him. When Nicolas talked to other people, he only rarely conceded a "*capisci?*" and the others just had to run to keep up, but it was different with him. And he also understood that Scignacane was a real ballbuster, that in Nisida he'd hooked up with Dumbo for who knows what reason, considering that his friend Dumbo was one of those kids made of clay, the kind you can manipulate but only up to a certain point. Dumbo was a lot smarter than other people gave him credit for, Christian had realized that right away, and he also knew that the only reason he'd even gotten into trouble in the first place was his father, with that plan of his that sounded like a joke. One day he'd showed up at Dentino's father's house with an idea of how to screw the Romanians and the Macedonians who were undercutting their salaries and stealing their jobs—because the stroke he'd had might have messed up his leg and his arm, he used to say over and over, but his head worked fine, even better now, in fact. It was a simple plan, all they needed to do was get their boys, *i guaglioni*, and clear out the Vietri glass factory's warehouses and steal all the tiles, hold on to them for six months, and then start over. In other words, start their own market. Christian had only heard about the burglary from Dumbo, because deep down Dentino was ashamed of having gotten away and not being sent to Nisida.

The plan had sailed along smoothly until Dumbo's father got it into his head to pull down one of the heavy stacks of tiles from the metal shelving all by himself. He'd fallen down amid the dull crash of Vietri tiles shattering on the floor, pulling the whole shelf down on top of him. For a few minutes, they'd tried to get him out from under, but it was too heavy for their arms. So Dentino and his father had run away, cutting across the fields, while Dumbo had remained behind, tugging at his father, who was shouting at him to just cut and run.

Nicolas had loosened up now and was no longer talking in choppy, bitten-out phrases, but Christian continued to have a hard time focusing, and he couldn't understand why. Every word Nicolas spoke was important, you could learn from every phrase, so why did Christian seem to be incapable of listening with the rapt intensity that he'd always devoted to Nicolas's words in the past? There was something electric in Nicolas's immobility that didn't add up for him, something that also scared him a little and made him feel like writhing on the bed. But he had no intention whatsoever of getting up and leaving: even more than the evening he'd first brought the handgun home, at that moment, Nicolas, lying motionless atop the dark blue bedcover dotted with white clouds, seemed as invincible as any superhero. Christian took his hands out from under his head and wiped the sweat on his trousers. The mattress had become an anthill. His body itched all over, but he redoubled his efforts to lie there motionless and concentrated, like his brother.

"He had them search me, and he found my gat—'o fierro—on me right away. I wanted to bring Tucano with me; he might be crazy, but if there's action, he's always up for it. Scignacane insisted, I had to come alone, capisci? And then Tucano already wanted to kill everyone, just like Scarface. I get there and Scignacane is already on edge, but if you're setting a trap, trust me, you need to stay calm and keep your victim calm, that's when they screw you, when you're feeling calm. So they find the gat on me, and Scignacane starts getting pissed off, because nobody walks into Don Cesare Acanfora's house carrying a gat, and he says we're making money, so why would we think of shooting? And I tell him I have no idea of what might happen and what might not happen, all I know is that I feel better if I can shoot when I need to, capisci? And then he tells me, okay, whatever, and then he pulls out a cell phone that isn't his because it has all these little fake diamonds on the back, and in fact it belongs to La Zarina, and then he opens WhatsApp and shows me a chat between her and Antonello Petrella."

Antonello is Dumbo, Christian told himself, that's Dumbo. The itch at the back of his jaw, right under his ear, had become intolerable. He scratched himself in silence, driving his nails into the flesh in order to be as effective as possible, and out of the corner of his eye he glimpsed a movement. Nicolas had pulled his smartphone out of his trouser pocket, and now he was scrolling quickly down the screen with his thumb. A chat. An audio message.

"I recorded it all," said Nicolas, and then with the forefinger of his other hand, he pushed PLAY.

"So you see? You see?"

"Hold on, give me a second. No, that just can't be!"

"*E poi guarda ccà.* Take a look right here. He sent a picture of his dick, to my mamma."

"But *Mammeta*—your mamma—is going along with it."

"My mamma just didn't know what else to do."

"Are you saying *Mammeta* wanted to fuck Dumbo?"

"I don't know, *ho voglia 'e levà a miez'a essa e a isso.*" I just feel like killing them both.

"Do it, go find Dumbo and take him down."

That was his brother's voice, no doubt. It was Nicolas who had told him to "take him down." Christian knew it, it was his voice, for sure, and yet at the same time, it didn't seem like it. How could it have been his voice? He looked over at Nicolas, disoriented, but Nicolas was lying there, his eyes glued to his phone.

"No, we've got the Antimafia Squad on our backs because of the Taliban, and we've got the Americans after us, too. *Non putimmo fà un pezzo per strada così.*" We can't do a piece of work out in the streets just like that.

"Well, so what? Just don't do anything."

"Just don't do anything? Are you saying, that if someone offends *Mammeta*, you'd do nothing? . . . You've got Dentino in your *paranza*, he's Dumbo's best friend."

"Yeah, Dentino is practically Dumbo's brother. But Dumbo works for you, he's always around here."

"No, it's been a while since the last time I saw him. He didn't come in to get his monthly salary, he won't answer his phone. *Nun se fa vedé cchiù.*" I haven't seen him around. "And I can't order a full operation with my own soldiers *pe 'nu strunzill'accussì.*" For a little shit like him.

Without realizing it, Christian had closed his eyes; but he couldn't close his ears, and he somehow couldn't open his mouth. He wanted to say that Dumbo was one of them, just like Dentino. It was with Dumbo that he'd smoked his first joint, and Dumbo had let him drive his scooter down in the underground garage at his house. He wanted to say so, but he couldn't bring himself to interrupt the recording, it would have been like interrupting Nicolas: simply not possible. Also, the way his brother had started that whole line of reasoning hadn't given him permission to show any emotion, as if the words that were now filling the little bedroom had no value in and of themselves, as if they were simply another chapter in his education: all that counted was for him to listen and learn. And so he listened, he had to listen if he wanted to become like his brother, be up to his level, but still he kept his eyes shut and in his memory he hastened back to the funny faces that Dumbo would make to get him to laugh, to the time he'd taken him to the stadium to see Napoli play Fiorentina, and Dumbo had even let him drink his beer. He could almost taste it on his palate, while his ears continued to follow his brother's voice but also that other voice, both of them equally unreal.

"Someone needs to get him out into the countryside for me, out beyond San Giovanni. You can't tell him anything. Just that you're taking him somewhere, to a party. Get whoever you want. I'm not interested in the details. Then I'll show up, I'll ask him a couple of questions, and then I'll shoot him. Then it's done. È troppo 'nu scuorno, the shame is too much, this guy's going around telling everyone he's fucking my mamma. He sent her a dick pic, can you believe it?"

"But if you kill him like that, then no one will know you killed him. No one will understand the punishment."

"And no one is supposed to know. He just needs to stop breathing."

Maraja knew that every death has two faces. The killing and the lesson. Every death belongs half to the dead man and half to the living.

"What if I don't do it?"

"If you don't do it, then the business we're supposed to do together won't happen, either."

"But what does our business have to do with a dick pic sent to your mother?"

"'O Maraja, you really are just a kid. If someone disrespects *Mammeta* then they've disrespected you. If someone disrespects *Mammeta*, then you're never going to be able to wash that disrespect off your face. It means that they can do whatever they want to you. You're authorizing them to shit in your face."

"You understand, Christian?"

The recording was over. Nicolas put his smartphone back in his pocket, incapable of grasping his little brother's bewilderment. Christian nodded. Yes, I understand, is what his head conveyed as it bobbed up and down, but the rest of his body said the opposite. And a sort of scream was rising in his throat, but he didn't even know it was a scream. He could swim in the deep water, and he still didn't know how to swim. He wanted to shout out that Dumbo was a friend, a brother, a *frato*, and you can't just up and kill a *frato*. He wanted to ask Nicolas if it was right to kill a friend. He'd answered that question himself some time ago, but if Nicolas had agreed to it, then maybe he was right, couldn't that be? Maybe it *is* right to kill a friend who makes a mistake. What about Dentino? What did he know about all this? Christian had always been a little jealous of the friendship between Dumbo and Dentino. He'd never be able to compete, and that untimely thought made him blush in shame, and he turned his face to the wall, even if Nicolas wasn't looking at him. He pulled out his cell phone, and the tabs still hadn't changed color. He understood, sure enough, that Dumbo had been sentenced to death, and he also understood his brother's last phrase, his futile attempt to get Scignacane to think straight: Scignacane, who, like everyone Nicolas held in contempt, insisted on mixing blood and business, family and money. Nicolas hated people like him, he wanted to make sure that flesh and family had nothing to do with business. Money's one thing, your dick is another. Christian just wanted his older brother to tell him that he'd convinced Scignacane that what he was doing was bullshit; he just wanted Dumbo to text him back.

Nicolas changed position, lay on his side, and then dropped back, flat on his spine. He was about to start again, and for a second, Christian was tempted to do something, for instance, to get up and leave, say that he was going to the bathroom. He didn't have any exact words in mind, but his legs were ready to snap and lunge. He had the hands he now held stuck into his pockets; he didn't have words but he did already know what to tell him, namely that to him Dumbo was—*is*, he forced himself to think—more than a friend, another brother, who unlike Nicolas would allow his stories to be interrupted. And after that, he would also tell him that Dumbo had caused trouble for the *paranza* and so he knew that he had to be punished. Did he have to be punished? He had to be punished. He repeated the word *punished* and it ricocheted in all directions like a superball. Like the yellow superball that Papà had bought him at the stationery shop when he was still in elementary school. Punished. Dumbo. Enough is enough. But how long had all that silence been going on? Now I'll say something, thought Christian, but once again his voice failed him. And at that point, Nicolas started up again: "Scignacane started to threaten me: 'Oh, that's it. If my father, 'o Negus, were here, he'd have already killed you because you know him, because he's a buddy of yours. But I'm not him, *nun teng'e ppalle che teneva pàtemo*—I don't have the balls my daddy had—and so you might be bringing in good money, but if you won't do this thing for me, you can forget about my heroin, you can just go back to selling hash and coke and that's that. Actually, what's more, I'll even tell the Palmas in Giugliano that the heroin they thought they were getting on an exclusive basis, you're buying, too, *accussì non tengo manc' 'o bisogno 'e te frullà, te mettono lloro int' 'o frullatore.*' That way I won't have to put you in the blender, they'll do it for me. He'd made up his mind. And I asked him how we were supposed to get organized to do this thing. He told me he'd let me know. That we were going to have to throw this party."

He hadn't said "*capisci?*" and that was the signal for Christian that the conversation was over. They lay there in silence for a while, listening to the noises in the rest of the apartment house, the sound of flushing from the neighboring apartments, the voices of other families. Then Nicolas slid off the bed, picked up his shoes, and without another word shut the door behind him.

Three days later it was Dentino who texted Christian, he had to see him right away. He was worried about Dumbo. Nobody had seen him in days and now his parents were going out of their minds. They had even come over to Dentino's house, but all he'd been able to say was: "I can't find him, either. I don't know—*nun saccio*—what's become of him."

"The last time I saw him he turned and waved, they'd come to pick him up on a motor scooter," his mother had murmured, struggling to reconstruct events.

"Signora, you need to try to remember who it was that came to pick him up."

He'd started showing her a few photos on Facebook and then some videos with the *guaglioni* of the *paranza*, and now he was on Instagram. But the signora didn't recognize anyone. "I can feel it, something's happened to him . . ."

"Why no, why would you say such a thing?" Dentino had replied.

"Because Antonello has never been a boy who doesn't call home if he's staying out. Something must have happened to him. He'd surely have told you if he had to stay out for some reason, if something was happening, if he was so afraid that he had to go into hiding . . ."

"Into hiding from who?"

The mother had looked at him: "Wait, do you think I don't know what all you kids do?"

"Eh, what is it you think we do, Signo'?"

"I know that you work . . ."

Dentino didn't let her finish the sentence: "Sure, we work. And that's that."

Dumbo's father hadn't said a word, he just looked at the telephone, undecided as to whether he should call the police. "Don't call anyone, take my advice," Dentino had told them, adding: "I'll find Antonello for you. You know he's like a brother to me."

The parents hadn't replied and Dentino knew he only had a few hours' head start before they called the cops. He asked everyone he knew, and they all swore to him that they hadn't heard anything. Vanished. Dentino left Christian for last. That was his last best hope because, if he knew nothing, either, then there was nothing to be done for Dumbo.

Christian listened to this story in silence, too, and when Dentino was done, he said that he didn't know anything about it. He showed him the messages he'd continued to send him, texts that Dumbo would never read. So Dentino gave his small, motionless, slightly rigid body a hug, and promised Christian that he'd send him news soon. And for an instant, Christian found himself hoping that the news might be good.

In the days that followed, Dumbo's mother went to the police and reported him as a missing person. That very same evening the online news sites started talking about it. The phrase *lupara bianca* began to appear—a phrase used by newspapermen to indicate a murder where the body would never be found—though it meant nothing to the boys in the *paranza*. On the fourth day of searching, Dentino got a text from White: "They told me to look in 'o Bronx," the Bronx area of San Giovanni a Teduccio. The territory of the Acanfora clan.

Dentino tried to get more information out of him, but White wouldn't say anything more. Dentino went straight to 'o Bronx. He searched and searched. He was tempted to shout out his name, but nothing turned up. So he started going into bars: "*Guagliu'*, have you seen Dumbo?" and he showed pictures around on his cell phone. "No. Nothing. We don't know him. Who is he, anyway? From around here?"

Until La Koala, Dentino's girlfriend, wrote him on WhatsApp: "They told me that the last time anyone had seen Dumbitiello was in 'o Bronx, at La Vigna . . . where the old farmhouse used to be, where they graze sheep now." He knew exactly where she meant. He'd gone there a thousand times to chug vodka and smoke crack out of a glass pipe. He headed toward the tumbledown farmhouse. It was still daylight. He found nothing. He just hoped that maybe they'd tied Dumbo up, that they'd punished him by tying him to a tree. No such luck. As he walked along, his feet sank into the dirt. And he understood that someone had dug there recently. It had been four days and it hadn't rained once. *"Oh, Madonna mia. Madonna mia. No, no!"*

He started digging with his hands. He dug and dug. The dirt burrowed under his fingernails, it raised them up, it wound up in his mouth, it clung to his body because he was starting to sweat. A young girl asked him: "Hey, what are you finding? What are you doing?"

He turned around. "Do you have a shovel?"

She turned around and walked into this sort of ramshackle sheepfold, found a spade, and Dentino started to dig and dig, until he hit something. He stopped using the shovel, afraid he'd tear up the corpse, and went back to digging with his hands.

The face emerged. And then Dentino freed every ounce of his anguish: "No! No! Madonna!" A powerful bellowing.

They called the police immediately; they actually sent a helicopter, and the carabinieri pulled the body out of there. The parents arrived. Dentino's identity was determined and he was transported to police headquarters. They tried to question him there, but he just stared at the wall and gave monosyllabic answers to every question. He was in a state of shock. They released him the next morning. They could have indicted him, on his cell phone were the instructions that White had given him, and then La Koala's messages, too. He walked out of police headquarters and there was La Koala waiting for him. She gave him a long hug. He let her hold him close without moving a muscle, without responding to her caresses. His eyes were still. They climbed onto the scooter and Dentino said: "Let's go to the lair.

They went to Forcella and went to the apartment. La Koala stopped on the steps, respectful of the rule that no one could go in unless they belonged to the *paranza*. Most important of all, no woman had permission to go into the lair.

"Come upstairs," Dentino ordered her.

She simply obeyed the command. What she wanted was to see nothing, to be invisible. She knew that this would cause trouble, but she waited with him. Dentino wasn't moving, so she turned on the television, just to fill in the void. Dentino shrugged in annoyance and went to throw

330 I ROBERTO SAVIANO

himself down on the bed in the other part of the apartment. Then she heard a key turning in the lock and Tucano came in. When he saw La Koala he stiffened. "What the fuck are you doing here?"

Dentino came out of the room. "Someone killed Dumbo."

"Ah, and who did it?"

"Well, now, whoever did it is the one who did it, and what I need is to find out who it was. Because Dumbo wasn't a soldier, he didn't have anything to do with any of this. Now I want the whole *paranza* here." Dentino was a hand shorter than Tucano, but he was spitting all his rage right into his face, so Tucano pulled out his iPhone to summon all the others: "*Guagliù*, there's an urgent mini–soccer game to play this morning."

One by one they entered the lair, and the last one to enter was none other than Maraja. His eyes were puffy like someone who hadn't slept in days, and he kept scratching his whiskers.

Dentino attacked him immediately: "Maraja, now all the heroin that we're getting from Scignacane isn't finding buyers, it's still on our hands. If we go on buying it, if you guys go on selling it, then I'm leaving the *paranza* and I consider every one of you to be Scignacane's accomplices!"

"What the hell does Scignacane have to do with it?" asked Maraja.

"Dumbo worked for Scignacane's mamma, and she definitely has something to do with it. And don't try to act like you don't know, Nico', otherwise I'll have to assume you're covering for him. Dumbo wasn't a soldier, he wasn't affiliated."

"Just like us . . ." said Drago'. He was snickering, and as he spoke he was rolling a joint.

"Just like us, my ass," Dentino shouted, grabbing him by the T-shirt. Drago' twisted loose and drew his head back, ready to butt him. La Koala got between them, pushed them apart. "Don't act like little kids!"

"Drago', Dumbo never picked up a gat in his life. He never did anyone any harm, he was never a bastard!" Dentino shouted.

"'O Denti', did you bump your head? That guy moved all the heroin we ever sold . . . There must have been some mix-up, some fuckup . . . Someone tried to steal the shit . . ." Tucano ventured.

"Impossible. It had to have been an ambush, a trap they set for him!"

As he was saying it he was ashamed to realize that he was about to start crying. No one had ever cried between those walls before.

Drone was standing there, motionless; it seemed like some sort of vendetta to him. Before Dentino, he'd been the one who'd had to choke back tears welling up in his eyes, careful not to let even one spill over. Now Dentino was openly sobbing, and it was a shame—*uno scuorno*—for the whole *paranza*.

Drago' said: "Denti', we're here today, we're gone tomorrow. *T' 'o rriccuorde?* Don't you remember? Friend, enemy, life, death: it's all the same thing. We know that, and you know it, too. *Accussì è.* That's the way it is. It all happens in the blink of an eye. That's the way we live, no?"

"What the fuck do you know about how we live? *Pentito!* Turncoat!" That venomous word. The only word that could never be uttered.

Drago' yanked out his pistol and stuck it in Dentino's face. "I have more honor than you ever will, *omm' 'e mmerda*. You're here with the sister of a bastard, and who knows how many things of ours you've passed over to the *paranza* of the Capelloni, and you call me an *infame*? An informant, a turncoat? Get out of here, you and this slut, get out of here!"

Dentino said nothing, he wasn't packing, but his eyes focused on Nicolas. Him alone. The boss.

THE MESSAGE

Dentino had felt the belly growing day by day, even before she openly told him about it. He'd felt it, one embrace after another, as something that didn't used to be there, and now it was. Before it had been a tangle of arms, climbing atop each other for a quick hello, not just to make love. That's the way La Koala was. She grabbed you with her whole body. For some time now, though, Dentino had perceived a certain prudence in his girlfriend, as if she were afraid of being crushed by him, pressed by him. He hadn't asked her a thing, he'd let her be the one to tell him, Dentino had decided, and in the meantime he had let his imagination run free. What would they call him? His mother had always dreamed of a grandson—a granddaughter even more so—and she was also dreaming of a nice wedding, sparing no expense. Then another thought arrived, impetuous and irresistible, and every time he tried to push it away, it just kept coming at him. Getting rid of it.

La Koala had waited, she'd understood that he'd understood; he no longer touched her with the rough vigor of before—Dentino, too, had become careful. When they were alone, they now seemed like a couple of young sweethearts in the first throes of puppy love. And she, too, had started to use her imagination. She'd told herself she'd wait till the end of the first trimester—she grew rounder with every passing day, and some women in the quarter had already officially claimed there was a cake in the oven—whereupon she would inform Dentino that he was going to be a father. La Koala, too, wanted a little girl, and in secret she'd even bought a couple of pink onesies, in open defiance of Neapolitan superstition.

Then Dumbo had been killed, and her man had died a little bit, too. She wasn't able to speak to him because he was always out and about, busy with his own personal investigation to determine who had sentenced his friend to death. On the rare occasions when she was able to spend some time alone with him, Dentino never touched her anymore, he kept her at arm's length, and even refused to look her in the eye, because he didn't want her to glimpse the fact that he knew, that it was too late to keep that belly hidden from him, that by now everyone else knew, everyone but him. He didn't have any room for the life that La Koala was carrying within her. She tried to make him hers again, she caressed him and gentled him, but he'd lurch away from her and set off with a jerk on his hunt for the culprit. For the first time in their thing together, a chill had settled over them, paralyzing them, but the creature that La Koala had inside her continued to grow, demanding its future father.

Dentino hadn't eaten a bite in two days. He wasn't touching food, he wasn't drinking. And he wasn't sleeping. Forty-eight hours of a zombie existence. He went everywhere on foot, he'd decided that the motor scooter would keep him from fully gazing into the faces he encountered. And instead he wanted to look everyone in the face, because there he might be able to find a clue about his friend's murder. He'd also abandoned the *paranza*'s chat, and no one had tried to write to him privately to persuade him to rejoin. He was on his own now.

He went back to White, in the back room, but White insisted that he knew nothing, that someone had given him the message.

"And who gave you the message?" asked Dentino.

"The messenger," White replied. He'd grown another stump of hair, and he was slowly stroking it.

"And who is the messenger?"

"The messenger is this dick," he said, flashing him his middle finger.

He wasn't going to get any more information from White, even if he kicked him around the room. He was savoring the moment, White was, and now he was palpating both his stumps of hair. Dentino walked out, head low, thought of talking to La Koala, but she only knew what her brother told her, and then he didn't want to get her involved, he didn't want to taint her and the baby she carried inside her. He also mulled over the possibility of going to every piazza where drugs were sold, because they had surveillance cameras there, maybe they'd caught Dumbo aboard a motor scooter, maybe with someone else. The murderer. Then he tried to go see Copacabana, in prison, but he refused to accept his visit. He walked through the streets of San Giovanni a Teduccio for a whole day. Via Marina, Via Ponte dei Francesi, all the streets that run off Corso San Giovanni, Massimo Troisi Park. He strode along, head held high, brash and bold, as if out to invade a territory that didn't belong to him, because what he had in mind was to make sure he was noticed, maybe even beaten down if that was what it took. He covered miles the same way he'd conducted that investigation from the very beginning. All alone.

He wasn't really alone, though, because La Zarina was on the trail of Dumbo's murderer, too. She'd developed a real affection for that *guagliuncello*. He made her happy. He was always cheerful and he managed to infect her with that cheerfulness. And the rides they used to take on their motor scooters, from one side of the city to the other, how she missed them. They made her feel like a young girl again, and now for a stupid stunt, that damned picture of his cock, he'd paid dearly. La Zarina had tried to raise her voice and lecture her son. How dare he pry into her cell phone? But Scignacane could afford to stop being a son when he needed to, and he'd shunted the question aside with a shrug of the shoulders. Still La Zarina felt a debt of gratitude to Dumbo, with the lust for life that he'd transmitted to her, so strongly she could still feel it on her flesh. She started pumping her son's men for information, reminded them that Negus had created the empire that allowed them to live decently, and that they'd better not say anything to Scignacane about that conversation because she, La Zarina, could still hurt them, could still hurt them badly. And one after the other, they talked. They didn't know much about the operation itself, but by putting together the various pieces of the puzzle, La Zarina reconstructed the way things had gone. She wasn't interested in the details, the mechanics of the thing, she wanted the chain of command, so she could link up those responsible and undertake a vendetta. Who would die and at whose hand was also of no interest to her. Blood had to be washed out with blood, that was a rule as old as the world, and she knew how to start the cleansing process.

She did it all from her apartment, from her gilded cage complete with all the modern conveniences, a place only Dumbo had been able to tear her from. Dumbo had talked to her about the friend he'd done time for in Nisida Reform School, whom he'd protected from charges that would have sent him behind bars, too. That's the purest form of friendship, La Zarina had thought as she listened to that story, a friendship born of sacrifice. She'd ordered her men to get her Dentino's phone number. She thought about calling him, but it made her anxious. And so she wrote it all to him, she wrote that he was perfectly free not to believe her, and she ended the messages telling him that Dumbo's friendship had been precious to both of them, as precious as a majolica tile.

Dentino read the text dozens of times, and every time he did, his finger hovered over the DELETE button, but in the end all that rereading had dug a track, ever deeper. He was sitting in a subway car on Line 1. There were still three stops to Via Toledo. He deleted the text.

RED SEA

Mena was giving the last few stitches to the red dress she'd sewn herself in the shop, making use of a handsome length of crimson silk that one of her customers had given her as a gift. "Where am I going to go dressed like this?" she'd asked herself, but then she'd wrapped it around her in front of the mirror and imagined a simple line, without a collar but nicely snug at the waist, and she'd decided, "I'll go where I go, that's where I'll go," and she'd set about shaping the dress. Now, sitting at the table her husband had left set for her, the way he usually did when she came in late and he had to leave early, she put the fine finishing work on the tiny buttons that ran up the back: twelve little buttons, lustrous, an even fierier red. She'd had the buttonholes done for her—because that was quite an art, making button-holes, and there was old Sofia in Forcella, who served dressmakers and tailors in spite of her age and her incessant changing of spectacles—and she worked up from the bottom applying the buttons.

She saw Christian darting out of his bedroom.

"*Addó vai, a mammà?*" Where are you going, tell Mamma.

He replied something that sounded like "Nico' is expecting me," but she didn't hear him clearly. But where is Nicolas expecting him? She sat there, the needle pressed between thumb and forefinger, the red thread dangling. It happened frequently, but she never liked it when the younger one went out into the street with his brother. She set down needle and thread, placed the dress on the table, and leaned out the window that overlooked the walkways running along the front of the building and the street. Christian was down there. He wasn't moving. Maybe he was waiting for someone. As long as he's waiting, it's all right, she thought, and at the same time decided that she needed to try on this dress, make sure the way she'd put on the buttons wouldn't make it too tight. She thought to herself: That Sofia is blind, she's good but she's basically blind. She undressed with confident, quick movements and then, very cautiously, slid on the new dress, letting it glide down over her from above, both arms raised. She smoothed it over her hips, she felt her breasts take the room they deserved and spring into the shape they deserved: yes, now she'd be able to stitch on the little buttons that were missing. She turned with an automatic swivel toward the window. Christian was striding rapidly down the street, toward the Rettifilo, Corso Umberto I. "Where are you going?" she shouted. "A *fare 'nu servizio*," the boy replied, cupping both hands around his mouth before turning around again and loping off, as quick as a gazelle. To run an errand. '*Nu servizio*? Since when did Christian run errands, especially *servizi*? She knew the connotations of that word—what kind of thing was that for him to say? She dangled farther out the window until she saw her son disappear beyond the intersection. She went back to the dining room and looked for her cell phone. She could never find it when she needed it. She could never find it. She jabbed the needle into the spool of thread and felt with her hands under the dress she'd just taken off, under the mat, she rummaged through her purse, she looked in the bathroom, and there it was, on the sink. She dialed Nicolas's number, and he answered almost instantly: "What is it?"

"Why are you bringing your brother into these things? What does he have to do with it? Where are you?"

"Calm down, Mamma, what are you saying?"

"Christian was at home until two minutes ago. And now he's going to see you. Where? Tell me where."

Nicolas sat silent and went on listening, without listening, his mother's voice warning him, commanding him to send his brother back home.

He didn't want to, but he admitted: "I don't know anything."

It was Mena, at that point, who remained in silence. They exchanged silences like so many coded messages.

And then: "Get them to tell you. Get them to tell you where they're taking him. Get them to tell you right away." She knew that there's always a way to find out what's going on. She knew that this fair-haired son of hers could do whatever he wanted by now, and if he could do something, he needed to do it right away. "Get them to tell you."

And he replied: "Come downstairs, in the street. I'm on my way."

Mena left everything just as it was, didn't bother to lock the door behind her, galloped down the stairs with the red dress on, open in the back. It occurred to her only when she reached the downstairs entrance that she could have changed, but now she was there. She was there and she was peering down the street for the silhouette of Nicolas astride that goddamned bike of his. She searched for him right where she'd last seen Christian, but he arrived from the other direction, carrying the helmet he had for Letizia in one hand. Mena climbed onto the T-Max and held the helmet in her lap. She didn't even ask the question, she just waited for him to tell her where, where, where. "*Il cavaliere di Toledo*," Nicolas shouted as he accelerated. "The horseman of Via Toledo." A statue, a piece of modern art. "At the metro stop." It had only taken him two calls. One minute. Someone had told him. That's how he knew. But what did he know? What did he know? What was there to know? Under Mena's hair, which fluttered like a Jolly Roger out over the streets of the city, inside the forward-leaning, concentrated face of Nicolas there were swarms of questions and answers, there were certainties and superstitious dread. There was only one clear image that passed from him to her and back again, and they didn't know what to make of it: the modern statue that had been erected on Piazza Diaz, with this horse and horseman, this sort of off-kilter jockey, that who knows who had ever come up with.

Dentino, sitting in the metro car, was folded over, tucked in on himself, concealing the Beretta semiautomatic pistol dangling between his legs. It was as if he were clutching the weapon, caressing it, almost as if he were about to celebrate a rite. "Blood doesn't matter? Let's see about that. Let's see what happens if I touch your blood," he kept saying, repeating the same thought and each time leaning on the "Let's see," which continued to emerge like an oath pointing to action. On the screen of his cell phone was the text that he'd sent Christian: "Me and your brother are waiting for you at the monument on Piazza Diaz. You need to come do an errand for us. *Ci devi fare un servizio.*" And Christian had replied with a smiley face, the same emoticon multiplied by seven.

The next text was for Stavodicendo, checking to make sure that Nicolas hadn't left the lair to go home. Stavodicendo questioned him in return, inquisitively: "Where are you? What are you doing? What have you got in mind? Are you supposed to meet Nicolas?" And he wrote back that he didn't have anything in mind, that he just had an errand to take care of on Piazza Diaz. And Stavodicendo: "What kind of way is that to talk? What errand?" By then Dentino had simply stopped answering.

He reread it, feeling as if he were being watched by the people seated around him or gripping the handrails and poles. Were they looking at him because he was armed? Were they looking at him because he was on his way to kill a kid? Were they looking at him because he was who he was, a young man? He felt submerged in a world of grown-ups, or actually of old people, men and women destined to come to an end, a world where you couldn't even figure out why they weren't dead already. So many zombies. He knew he was alive, far more alive than all those other slaves. He reached down to touch the Beretta again; it made him feel strong, he knew that he was on his way to carry out a vendetta. Vengeance would be his. It was almost too late when he noticed that he was at the Via Toledo stop. He got out, let the people go past, the slaves, and flattened himself against the station wall before turning down the colorful corridor that ran to the escalators. Christian would ride down the escalator because that's what he had been told to do.

Christian was at the foot of the strange horse on Piazza Diaz. Nico' would come, Dentino was waiting for him down below, before the turnstiles, so he headed down. Dentino had asked him: he needed to go down into the metro station, had he ever been down there? No, he hadn't been. Then he should go, it was beautiful, a fantastic world. Christian had hopped onto the escalator and in fact, there it was, the fantastic world, sure enough! He rode down and above him there opened out an ever-narrower cone of light, light blue and green, a light blue, a green that slid down the walls, transmogrifying into pink, and it seemed like an aquarium, it seemed like pure magic. At school someone had told him that the Via Toledo metro station, so modern, so artistic, was one of the most beautiful on earth, but they'd never taken him to see it. Neither the school nor his family. Why is that? We have the most beautiful metro station on earth and we never go see it. Only ever to see the Castel dell'Ovo, only ever to the seafront embarcadero, only ever down to the sea, when the real sea was right here; in fact, this was better than the water sea, because here you had wave, grotto, volcano, and at the same time it became the sky, too. "This is something, Nico', you never told me about." The escalator kept descending and Christian rode along with his head tilted back, and the farther down he rode, the farther back he tilted it so he could remain inside that gush of light descending from on high, a silent gush, an ancient water, or maybe not, a light streaming down from space. He brought me here, to let me take this light blue trip, he thought. And when he found himself at the bottom of that exceedingly long escalator and he saw Dentino, he told him so, he said that that was a fantastic place, better than Posillipo, better than *The Lord of the Rings*. But Dentino didn't smile. He told him that now he needed to ride back up, because Nicolas would be expecting him at the *Cavaliere di Toledo*, the Horseman of Via Toledo. Dentino was there, and Christian wasn't surprised to see the *paranzino* with two broken teeth standing there rigidly, giving him orders. He didn't ask questions, he thought nothing, he just went "Wow" at the idea of going back up, and he hurried happily back onto the escalator to ride all the way back up, through the middle of that aquarium. Dentino let him ride up a way, and then followed him. It was an endless ascent, and for the second time, Christian lost himself in that green, that light blue, the light, until he emerged back into the disappointing light of day.

Nicolas and Mena saw him from the piazza. They saw him emerge from the tunnel of the escalator, and as he emerged they heard three gunshots, clear, confident, without an echo.

Dentino descended the same escalator, leaping several steps at a time to outpace the upward-rising machinery that would have dragged him back to the surface. Only when he got to the bottom did he stop to catch his breath, turning around to peer at the light up above, and, in the space emptied of people cleared out by the gunshots, he galloped to the platform to wait for the next train. There he realized that he was still holding the Beretta; he slipped it down his pants. And that image as well as all the previous images were already registered in the memory of the video cameras in the station: the one on the tracks that had recorded Dentino leaving the train and walking along in the crowd of other passengers, the one at the bottom of the escalator that had recorded Dentino waiting—and there he would have been seen clearly pulling out the Beretta and keeping it covered with his left hand—just as clearly as Christian would have been seen arriving, smiling, lit up by the adventure he'd just experienced as he descended through the cone of green light, only to ride back up, followed by Dentino, his arm finally extended, the first, the second, and the third gunshot, and then the gallop back down the escalator the wrong way.

Down in the metro and out on the piazza, people reacted instinctively as in a *stesa*: some of them threw themselves down on the ground, others turned and ran, a few froze to the spot, as if there were something to be understood.

Christian walked toward the monument with a gleaming smile that made him smaller, that absorbed him entirely, as if the show that he'd seen hadn't stopped filling his eyes. Then he had, perhaps, the vague sensation that he'd perceived something different inside himself, a seabird that had dived beak-first into his back and now was trying to emerge from his chest. But the sensation remained formless and his body slammed to the ground, as if he'd tripped, and on the ground it remained, arms sprawled wide, head bent to one side, eyes wide open.

Mena and Nicolas were still astride the motorbike. Mena got off first, all alone on the piazza, with her red dress open in the back. She walked slowly as if she were bearing a weight, as if fate were slowing her stride. She bent down over the child, touched him, moved her hands away with the palm held shut like a seashell over him, lowered them closer again, touched his forehead, caressed it, then took his head and placed it on her knees, closed his eyes, and let loose a rough sigh, saw the blood that was seeping out, and heard someone shout: "Call an ambulance!" No one dared to take a step. She was suffocating inside her head of hair. You couldn't see her anymore. And she couldn't see anyone else. Then she heard Nicolas shouting something, ordering the others, pointlessly, to stay clear. She heard him saying as if he were at the theater that that was his brother and that she was his mother. And maybe that's how it was, after all. But those standing around him couldn't help but notice how that young man with blond hair had twisted around, doing his best not to be seen, bent over, his helmet pressed against his stomach, how he started to moan, either seeking to weep or to repress his weeping. "God." He let the word escape his lips, and once he'd uttered that word, he started repeating it, "God God God," with no idea where to look except down at the ground. He was surprised to find himself retching, then it happened again, and he'd never felt as alone as in that moment, and so it was that he got rid of the helmet, letting it roll away from him, and he bent over his brother's body, with his mother. No one was coming out of the metro now. The circle of those who wanted to look grew larger, but under the *Cavaliere di Toledo* there were only Mena, Nicolas, and, by now invisible under the deep crimson of his mother, little Christian.

In the time that followed, Mena never shed a tear. She took care of her husband, who never stopped weeping, sitting on the bench in the hospital, on the chair at police headquarters, on the pew at church. Mena never exchanged a word with a soul, except to get through practical errands and respond to the investigations that, of course, the police were carrying out. From time to time, she gave Nicolas a sidelong glance. Left alone at home with her son and her husband, she finally took off the red dress and, once in a slip, she didn't put on anything else. She gazed at that dress with only two buttons on the back, smoothed it out on the table, grabbed it rudely, started ripping it apart, first along the stitching, then furiously rending the fabric wherever she happened to rip it, and it was only then that she dissolved into a scream, a rusty, metallic shout, that made even her husband stop crying. The television news reported in the days that followed on the "young boy murdered by the Camorra at the foot of William Kentridge's monument to the Horseman of Via Toledo."

The funeral was held five days later, in the quarter. Mena never stopped asking for flowers. She asked all the kids in the *paranza*. "I want flowers, you understand that?" and she'd glared at them angrily. "You know how to get them for me. I want the finest flowers in Naples. White flowers, lots and lots of white flowers. Roses, calla lilies, whatever is most expensive." She inspected the church and with a gesture dismissed the priest and the undertaker: "You aren't listening to me! I want flowers. I want so many flowers that you feel like fainting from the scent they put out." And so it was. And behind the hearse there walked so many people from the quarter and other people that no one had ever met before, who knows where all those people even came from, and she was glad they had come, Mena decided, *che qui nessuno adda scurdà questo piccolo mio, chesta criatura mia*. No one can ever forget my little boy, this child of mine.

Nicolas lagged behind his mother. He obeyed. He studied. He didn't miss a scene, a gesture. Like a real king, who knows who's there and who isn't and who shouldn't be. His men stayed close to him, and they expressed their mourning. They did it the way they knew how. They were lost in the midst of that mountain of white flowers that Christian's mother had insisted on.

There were Christian's classmates, a swarm of kids accompanied by their teachers, and there were also Nicolas's classmates and his teacher, Signor De Marino, pensive and speechless.

The casket, too, was white. A casket for a child. The *paranzini*'s girl-friends had all donned silk scarves because they knew what the tradition was and they understood they were to observe it.

Mena, dressed in black, her hair gathered back in a black lace shawl, locked arms with her husband, the gym teacher. She asked everyone to wait for the last trip to Poggioreale Cemetery and asked Nicolas to gather the *paranza* in the sacristy. "Your honor the priest will forgive us if, for two minutes, we take your place," she said, preventing the parish priest from following her and the *paranza* in full array, with Pesce Moscio and Briato', who stumped along, one on crutches, the other with an orthopedic cane.

Once they were together in the dim light of the sacristy, Mena seemed to fall rapt in meditation, but then she raised her face high, brushed aside the black veil, gazed at them one by one, and said: "I want vendetta," and then she corrected herself. "I want vengeance," and she went on: "You all can do it. You are the best." She took a breath. "Maybe you couldn't keep him from being killed, this son of mine, but fate is fate, and times change. Now it's time for the tempest. And I want you to be the tempest scourging this city."

Everyone in the *paranza* nodded their heads. All except Nicolas, who took his mother's arm and told her: "It's time to go." Outside the door to the sacristy, his father grabbed Nicolas by the shirt, he would gladly have lifted him off the ground if he could have, and he drilled into his eyes a gaze without shadows, then he began speaking, first in an undertone and then gradually louder and louder: "You're the one who killed him. It was you. It was you. You're a murderer. You're the one who killed him." Mena managed to free her son from his grip and threw her arms around her husband. "Not now. There's time for that," she said, and caressed him gently.

They all left the church, in the midst of the procession of white flowers, and waited outside for the hearse.

Aucelluzzo, dressed in black, walked over to Nicolas. He embraced him with a gentleness Nico' had never suspected he possessed: "Nico', my condolences. On my part, and from you-know-who."

Nicolas nodded his head without a word, his eyes never strayed from the white casket. He tried to step around him, he wanted to go to his mother, take her arm, but Aucelluzzo stopped him with a hand on his shoulder.

"Have you seen this?" he asked. "They're talking about you." He held out the newspaper. A front-page article drew a connection between the death of Christian, the death of Roipnol, and the new typhoon that was slamming down on the historic city center, and stated that it all had been triggered by a new *paranza*.

The coffin was shut up inside the hearse now, and Nicolas looked at the newspaper that Aucelluzzo was handing him. "*Guagliu'*," he said to his men, as they stood close to him, "they've given us a name: *simmo la paranza dei bambini*. We're the children's *paranza*."

Suddenly it started raining, raining hard, without thunder. The street blackened with open umbrellas as if all of Forcella and Tribunali had been waiting for that downpour as a form of liberation. Amid the tide of umbrellas, the hearse made its way forward, haltingly. Only the *paranza* were willingly drenched.

Death and water are always a promise. And they were ready to cross the Red Sea.

AUTHOR'S NOTE

One of the challenges of this novel is the use of dialect. The choice came naturally, but then the composition demanded work, cross-checking, patient listening.

I didn't want the "classic" Neapolitan dialect that is still what we find in the work of poets and authors writing in dialect, and in terms of transcription as well. At the same time, I wanted there to be a full awareness of that classical tradition. I therefore requested the help of Nicola De Blasi (professor of the history of the Italian language at the Federico II University of Naples) and Giovanni Turchetta (professor of contemporary Italian literature at the University of Milan), and I thank them both. Starting from that point, I sensed the malleability of that language; I felt that I could, here and there, force my way toward a living oral language, though reconstructed within the context of the written form. Where this deliberate manipulation moves away from the standard codes, it's because I've intervened as an author to shape, to filter, the acoustic reality of listening within the rendering of the dictation, an accomplice to the characters who were working with their "bastardized" dialect in my imagination.

TRANSLATOR'S NOTE

In translating *The Piranhas* into English, there were two particular stumbling blocks. One was the title, originally *La paranza dei bambini*, literally "The Children's Paranza." A *paranza* is a procession of fishing vessels; it is also a mob crew, or a loose association of young men. It is an exquisitely Neapolitan term, even when used in Italian. The title we chose in English was different, perhaps, but similar in meaning and heft.

The second stumbling block was dialect. Although Roberto Saviano addresses the issue of dialect in his Author's Note, he is writing in Italian and speaking to an Italian audience.

Neapolitan dialect is a great and literary language, with a tradition dating back before English. It is now, as the old saying goes, a language without an army. But there once was a Kingdom of Naples, and it had both army and navy in its six glorious centuries of history.

Neapolitan dialect is largely foreign even to most Italian readers of the book's original Italian version. That is why I have chosen to leave a certain amount of dialect in its unique and distinctive original form.

—ANTONY SHUGAAR

Antony Shugaar is a writer and translator. He is the author of *Coast to Coast* and *I Lie for a Living* and the coauthor, with Gianni Guadalupi, of *Discovering America* and *Latitude Zero*.